John Drake trained as a biochemist to post-doctorate research level before realizing he was no good at science. His working career was in the television department of ICI until 1999 when he became a fulltime writer. He is married with a son and two grandchildren.

PRAISE FOR JOHN DRAKE:

'Broad comedy, high drama, plenty of action, a pinch of sex . . . the genre has room for this cheerily debunking outsider' – *Daily Mail*

'Swashbuckling adventure on the high seas doesn't get much better than this. [. . .] John Drake writes beautifully, and you'll be torn between savoring the words and quickly flipping the pages. Any favorable comparison to Stevenson or Patrick O'Brian is totally justified.' – Nelson DeMille, #1 *New York Times* bestselling author

Also by John Drake

FLETCHER'S FORTUNE

JOHN DRAKE

ENDEAVOURINK

AN ENDEAVOUR INK PAPERBACK

First published by New English Library hardbacks
in 1992

This paperback edition published in 2017
by Endeavour Ink
Endeavour Ink is an imprint of Endeavour Press Ltd
Endeavour Press, 85-87 Borough High Street,
London, SE1 1NH

ISBN 978-1-911445-36-4

Typeset by Palimpsest Book Production Ltd, Falkirk, Stirlingshire

Printed and bound in Great Britain by
Clays Ltd, St Ives plc

www.endeavourpress.com

In fond memory of
David Burkhill Howarth

----------- DBH -----------

1946 – 2009

PATRIFAMILIAS AMATISSIMO
MAGISTRO DOCTISSIMO
INGENIOSISSIMO TECHNITAE
OPTIMO AMICO

Table of Contents

Introduction

In 2012 I bought at auction, a set of leather-bound volumes constituting the memoirs of the notorious Jacob Fletcher (1775–1875) together with the Fletcher Papers: several large boxes of letters, paper, prints, newspaper articles and memorabilia.

The memoirs were dictated by Fletcher to a clerk, Samuel Pettit, in the early 1870s causing huge embarrassment to Pettit because of the subject matter and coarse language used. But Pettit was terrified of Fletcher who regularly threatened to "gut and fillet" him if he did not take down every word, leaving Pettit to take his small revenge by adding footnotes to the volumes after Fletcher's death.

What follows is therefore Fletcher's own speech, interspersed with chapters of my own creation, based to the utmost of my ability on the evidence of the Fletcher Papers.

John Drake, Cheshire, 2013.

– 1775 –

Chapter 1

Such a tale of blood and vile perversion have I to set before you,
that I know hardly how to begin.

(From a letter of 14th November 1775 from
Erasmus Bolton, Surgeon, to Mr Richard Lucey,
Solicitor of Lonborough, Cheshire.)

*

Grayling shivered in his nightshirt as the wicked draught
shot up his spindly old legs. Grease from his candle
spattered over the bed as he tried to wake his master.

"Sir! Sir! Oh, dear sir!" he whined, as lightning blasted
out of the night to show the rain, blown horizontal
against the window. He jumped at the thunderclap and
an old man's tears of self-pity ran down his nose. But
at last Surgeon Bolton stirred in the bed and sat up.

Thick with sleep he blinked at the candle and cursed the cruel world that dragged him from cosy slumber.

"Godblessmysoul! Godblessmysoul!" he said. "Whatever is it?"

"Sir! Sir!" cried Grayling. "'Tis a mad man, God save us all! He's downstairs. He's all but broke in the door! Did you not hear him, sir?" Bolton saw his servant shaking in terror, and the spectacle stirred nasty thoughts in his own mind. *Could* it be an escaped lunatic? Could he be violent? In any case, he was already inside the house . . . Bolton sighed and threw back the covers.

"Never fear," he said, trying to be confident, "'tis a surgeon's duty to be summoned thus. I shall come at once."

Having dressed in haste, Bolton went downstairs in wig and black coat, with his box of instruments under his arm. In the parlour was a large man, spurred and booted, pacing like a tiger, with water running off his coat on to Bolton's best Indian rug. At sight of the surgeon he lunged forward and seized Bolton's arm.

"Mr Bolton!" he cried in a wild voice. "All hell and damnation is broke loose at the Hall! You must come at once!" Bolton recognised him. It was Stanley, Head Groom to Mr Coignwood of Coignwood Hall, and normally a sober and steady man. But Stanley dragged the surgeon ruthlessly out of the house and into the black night. Lightning split the sky, shadows leapt diabolically across Stanley's face, and Bolton shivered with more than cold as thunder rent the world to its roots.

"Up sir! Up!" said Stanley, hurling Bolton bodily into an open cart with a pair of terrified horses stamping and pulling to be off. He leapt to the box, cracked his whip and sped away at a pace that blew Bolton's hat and wig to the four winds, and left him hanging on to keep his seat. The horses were mad with the storm and Bolton cringed at such a gallop through the foul night, with stinging rain, sizzling lightning, and gouts of mud thrown up by the pounding hoofs. Coignwood Hall was only six miles down the Chester Road but by the time they arrived, Bolton was breathless, battered, soaked to the bone and freezing in every limb.

As they drew up at the front doors, servants ran out into the pouring rain to meet them, calling and shouting and clutching. The place was alive with mischief: blazing with light and figures scampering about in their night clothes. Hands pulled Bolton down and dragged him inside.

In the Great Hall, things were worse. On one side Bolton saw Mrs Maddox, the housekeeper, in screaming hysterics, with a pair of little servant girls clinging to her skirts and wailing along with her. On the other side was a group of fools with bowls of water and bloodstained bandages, making a dog's breakfast of ministering to a wounded man in an armchair. And all around, the household folk ran like chickens with a fox in the hen-house.

The Coignwood family themselves were nowhere to be seen.

"Thank God! Thank God!" cried a frantic voice. "The surgeon is come! 'Tis Mr Bolton!" A thin cheer rose up and Mrs Maddox paused to gulp for breath.

"Let me pass!" said Bolton, and forced his way through the press to the injured man. "Porter!" he said, recognising Mr Coignwood's butler. "Who did this to you?" All he got for an answer was groans, but examining the man he saw that Porter had been hit in the face and right forearm by a charge of small shot. He must have raised his arm instinctively to protect his eyes, and the arm, chin and forehead were spotted like a currant cake. The wounds bled freely but they didn't look dangerous. "Stand clear there!" said Bolton, taking charge. "Stanley! Get these people back. I must operate at once to remove the shot. And you there, Mrs Maddox! Fetch a fresh bowl of water at once!" Soon he was picking out the shot with a pair of forceps and this roused Porter.

"Mr Bolton!" he said in a feeble voice. "Sir! Spare your skills for one who needs them more than I . . . Poor Mr Alexander, sir, shot through the heart and bleeding his life out!"

"What?" said Bolton. Alexander Coignwood was Mr Coignwood's eldest son, "What happened man?" Porter dropped his voice still lower and beckoned Bolton to come close.

"A dreadful quarrel in the library . . . among the

family!" Sensing what might follow, Bolton looked furtively around and saw that everyone was listening with ears the size of donkeys' ears. Porter continued, "At first I ignored it as a good servant should, sir. But then there was a gunshot! So I had to go then, sir, didn't I? What else could I do?" He groaned and nearly fainted with the pain of his wounds.

"Go on man," said Bolton, and the mob of listeners edged closer.

"Sir," he said, "I'll never tell all that I saw . . . Torture couldn't draw it from me! But when I entered the library, my master whom I have faithfully served these twenty years . . . he abused me, sir, with filthy oaths! And then he ordered me out! And then . . . as I hesitated at the threshold, he raised a fowling piece and . . . and . . . he *shot* me!" From the look on Porter's face it was clear that even with his wounds to prove it, he still couldn't believe what had happened. But the listeners believed him all right and they nudged each other and whispered behind their hands. "Mr Bolton," says Porter, staring round-eyed at the Surgeon, "shall I die?"

"No," said Bolton. "The shot was nearly spent when it hit you. Mr Coignwood must have been at some distance from you . . . Now! Who else is with him? You must tell me." Porter frowned in concentration.

"The mistress, Mr Victor, and Mr Alexander . . . Oh, sir! Poor Mr Alexander is a-dying even this moment as we delay! Will you not go to him?"

"Yes!" said Bolton, making a swift judgement. "Your wounds are superficial." He snatched up his instruments and made to be off, but Porter spoke again.

"Be careful sir!" he said, biting his lips in anxiety.

"Why?" said Bolton.

"The master has his pistols sir . . ."

"What?" said Bolton, incredulously. "He'd never shoot *me* . . . would he?"

"My master is not himself sir," says Porter, "but will you not go to him, sir, you who has treated him for the gout these five years? You who are his doctor? Will you not go in and save poor Mr Alexander?"

There came a silence. All present had closed in to listen to Porter's tale. Bolton saw a circle of faces who'd clearly fastened upon him as the saviour of the hour — they were nodding in approval of Porter's words. Thoughts raced through his mind. The pistols would be the pair of Wogdons, with hair-triggers and made to Coignwood's particular fit. With those he could blow the pips out of a playing card at twenty paces . . . If he'd shot Porter, his own butler, what chance was there for Bolton? And a charge of shot was one thing but a pistol ball was another. The length of the library would not save him from that.

Yet Bolton had his reputation to consider. Twenty pairs of eyes were on him, with tongues to report his actions to the world. His position in society was imperilled. What would Lonborough think of a surgeon who was a coward? And of course, he told himself, he feared for the innocent lives of Mrs Coignwood and her sons. Finally, it was the thought of Mrs Coignwood being in danger that decided him.

With a sigh, he gathered up his courage and his instruments and proceeded to the library with a train of servants in his wake. Candles burned everywhere and the rain and thunder beat against the house. An evil hour indeed, but not as evil as the actual moment when Bolton reached the library doors. He was quite alone; the servants had kept back out of harm's way, even the stalwart Stanley. He could hear raised voices within, and as he reached out for the door handle he suddenly had the most awful feeling that he would faint, like a student seeing his first operation, and so make a complete ass of himself.

But he was spared that, and he tried the door handle. In his heart, he prayed it would be locked, but it gave easily and he looked inside. Two ladies knelt by the body of a groaning lad in a dark-blue coat and bloodstained shirt. The huge bulk of Coignwood, florid and sweating, was leaning on his stick with a long pistol in his hand. He glared at Bolton.

"Get away!" he said in a fury, and Bolton felt the most appalling fear as Coignwood stretched out his arm, and levelled the weapon at his heart. Bolton saw nothing in all the world but the dreadful black dot of the pistol's mouth. But the practice of surgery doesn't breed weaklings and though his knees were knocking, he stood his ground.

"Now, now, Mr Coignwood," he said, as best he could, "how are you today?" These were the words with which he'd always greeted Coignwood as a patient, and false though they were that night, they penetrated. Down came the pistol and Coignwood's fury collapsed into sorrow.

"See what they've done to me!" he said, indicating the others. "Not a penny shall they have of mine. I am resolved!"

"You bastard whoreson!" shrieked Mrs Coignwood, and leapt to her feet with obscene filth tumbling from her lips. Bolton was staggered. Like every other man in the county he was captivated by Mrs Sarah Coignwood, and had been since the first instant he met her. She was the stuff of fantasy: the men dreamed of her and the women died of envy. She was the queen of local society. She set the rules and lesser mortals followed as best they could . . . But there she stood with hair loose and no more clothes on her than a thin silk robe! As she screamed and stamped, it swirled open and her naked flesh gleamed in the candle light. Shocked though he was, Bolton's eyes bulged.

What with this and his close delivery from death, Bolton thought that his capacity to be shocked was now exhausted. But he was wrong, for another wonder came up as if he'd trodden on a garden rake and been smacked between the eyes by the handle. The young man in the uniform coat of a Naval officer, was Master Alexander Coignwood. But the lady kneeling at his side, in a fine gown, powdered and painted, and with white arms that any girl would envy, was not a lady at all, but his brother Victor! This young gentleman clung to Alexander like Juliet to Romeo. Mr Coignwood saw Bolton's jaw drop.

"Aye!" he said, in his grief and bitterness. "My son! My Alexander: a filthy sodomite! How can it be? A son of mine? All the expense to raise him as a gentleman and how does he repay me? Playing 'bedroom backgammon' with his own brother! Tonight I caught 'em at it, here in this very room where any servant could see. And that *woman*," he waved the pistol at his wife, "she joins 'em in their sport to glut her filthy appetites with her own sons!" He turned to the surgeon in agony. "Jesus Christ!" he groaned. "Can you believe that, Bolton? Her own children?" Then his face twisted, as rage mastered all else. "By God," he cried, "I swear I'll murder them all with my own hand!"

"Hypocrite!" screamed Mrs Coignwood and gathered her sons to her arms. She kissed each one full on the lips and turned again to her husband. "Hypocrite! I know you! And I shall never forgive!" Then she spat at him like an animal.

Coignwood raged at her and slapped his thigh in anger. But he'd forgotten the pistol, which barked into life, scorching a line down his stocking and blowing a hole through his shoe. Bolton saw his chance at once, and rushed forward, yelling for the groom at the top of his voice.

"Stanley!" he cried, as the big man entered. "Get Mr Victor away this instant and lock him up where none shall find him! And throw your coat over his head. Nobody must see him as he is!" Stanley obeyed at once but Bolton saw the eyes peering into the room and knew that thing was hopeless. The whole of Lonborough would have the tale within days unless the servants could be made to hold their tongues. But that was Coignwood's problem and Bolton had a busy couple of hours ahead of him.

There were two patients to deal with and Bolton was only too pleased to have the work to occupy his mind. He went to Alexander first, and found the lad's wound was not mortal. It occurred to Bolton that, given the elder Coignwood's skill with the pistol, this might be no lucky escape, however murderous the threats that had been uttered. In fact Alexander had been drilled neatly through the flesh of his armpit. Bolton noted the ball's entry point in the pectoralis major and its exit through the teres major. No nerves or vessels were torn, nor bones broken. The injury was modest and a full recovery could be expected. Bolton cleaned the wounds, extracting material from Alexander's coat and shirt, and bound him up.

The lad himself was stoic in the extreme, staring steadily into Bolton's eyes even while the latter was probing the wound. Mrs Coignwood too had calmed down and knelt at Bolton's side, chaste as a nun, while he worked. She thanked him for his help and begged him in her silky voice to keep quiet about the night's events. Busy as he was, her close proximity and that voice in his ear prickled the hairs on the back of his neck.

Mr Coignwood's injury was more serious, and Bolton had to amputate the big toe of his right foot. As he was very drunk Coignwood bore it well. In any case, he had something in his mind which left no room for anything else. He revealed this to Bolton as soon as his wife and sons were out of earshot.

"Bolton," he groaned. "Send for a damned lawyer. Send for Lucey, damn 'im. You'll do that won't you?"

"Of course," said Bolton, stitching away.

"Not a penny shall they have of mine, Bolton, damn 'em all three!"

When all was finished and the last of the blood wiped up, Bolton kindly tried to comfort his patient with the thought that now, at least, he would be spared the pain of the gout. But Coignwood fell into a rage again and called for his pistols. Under the great stress of the moment Bolton had forgotten that Coignwood's gout afflicted the big toe of the other foot.

– 1793 –

Chapter 2

God only knows why I've ended up where I am. I never wanted to be a sailor and I've done everything imaginable to escape the Navy, including murder and mutiny. I just wanted to be left alone to make a fortune in trade. And I'd have done it, too, given the chance. Instead of that, the Navy took me and as far as I knew it at the time, they only got me because of dog-fighting. Dog-fighting and a cross-bred monster by the name of King Bonzo.

King George caught me in 1793 when I was eighteen and an apprentice clerk at Pendennis's Counting House in Polmouth. Polmouth was one of the biggest seaports in Cornwall in those days and I was king of the castle in my little world; a fine strapping fellow who everyone liked (or so I thought). I'd bought King Bonzo the previous year though he wasn't entirely mine. I was just a partner in the ownership of him, with my friends

Enoch Bradley and David Ibbotson. Enoch, David I and I were bosom friends in those days, being the three eldest apprentices at Pendennis's. But it was me that bargained for Bonzo, because I could do that better than the others. We got the dog from a gypsy tinker and the sly rogue wanted ten guineas — salt of the earth, gypsies, provided you keep upwind of 'em and remember they're all liars — so I beat the gyppo down to two guineas, which was still an awful lot. But I'd made some money from one or two enterprises of my own, and the others put in what they had, and I let 'em pay me off for the balance, on reasonable terms (they were my friends, after all). In any case, the dog was worth every penny.

Personally, I never saw Bonzo as anything other than an investment. But Enoch loved him dearly and was fearfully proud of him. In so far as Bonzo ever recognised such a thing, you'd have called Enoch his "master" even though he was never more than half in control of him. This was because Bonzo was unhinged in his mind and had but two moods: docile and murdering maniac, and it was hard to tell when the one would switch to the other. But Enoch tried to win his love in three ways. First, he took care it was always him that took Bonzo his food. Second, he never went near him without a heavy cudgel to brain him with if necessary. And third, he never, never, *never*, turned his back on him. If once he'd done that, Bonzo would've had the leg off him, bless his doggy heart.

He kept Bonzo chained up in an old barrel, laid on its side, behind Mrs Wheeler's house where we lived with the other Pendennis apprentices. But nobody went near him other than Enoch and I'll tell you why. One Sunday, shortly after we'd bought the dog, we were looking at him from a window over Mrs Wheeler's yard. He was corpse-white and nearly hairless, with a mastiff's chest, a crocodile's head and thick bandy legs. By George but that dog was ugly!

"Not what you'd call handsome is he?" says I.

"No," says Enoch. "But he don't have to be. He weren't bought for that."

"Wait a bit!" says David. "What's the old mog doing?" And we all looked at next door's tattered cat that they kept half-starved and that used to cross our yard on his way home. The cat had smelt some scraps of food that Bonzo had left lying in front of the barrel. Bonzo seemed to be asleep and the cat's hunger was overcoming his fear. As the three of us watched, hardly breathing for what should happen, poor puss crept flat and silent across the cobbles till he came within reach of the prize. For a moment he hesitated with lashing tail as he gathered his strength, then . . .,

Crunch! Bonzo snapped him up so fast you hardly saw him move, and the cat snuffed out like a light. The three of us jumped as if we'd been bit, and gaped as Bonzo bolted down the cat's remains: meat, fur, tripes and bones.

There was no end of fun to be had with Bonzo, and a fine game for young lads of a summer evening was for us to go swaggering round the lower harbour, arm-in-arm and Bonzo on a lead. We'd seek out the local bullies and see who could curse them best. One look at Bonzo usually kept them docile, but any sign of fight and we'd run him at them, and let him have a nip or two. He'd go raging mad at this while we laughed ourselves helpless at the victim running off with his breeches in rags. We never slipped his leash though, we'd sense enough for that.

Indeed, bully-baiting was excellent sport, but this wasn't why I'd put down coin of the realm for Bonzo. I was mainly interested in the money he could make by dog-fighting. I was born poor and an orphan, and was apprenticed to Pendennis's on the charity of the local parson (something that the Rev. Dr Woods never let me forget!), so it's always been my aim in life to make money.

Dog-fighting, of course, is fallen away these days and respectable people shudder at the thought of it, and if it comes to that, it isn't my idea of an evening's entertainment. I'd prefer a slap-up meal with music, wine and good company, and a juicy trollop to follow (you don't get mud on your boots for one thing). But when I was a lad, folk saw these things differently. Dog-fighting was common then, and those who didn't like it, didn't bother going to see it.

So it was Enoch that looked out for a fighting dog,

and it was Enoch that chose King Bonzo. But it was me that saw all the gambling that went on over the fights, and spotted an opportunity. Of course, I laid no wagers myself. All gamblers are fools. But dog-fights offered serious ways to make money and that's what mattered to me.

The fact was that the sport was so popular that provided your dog was a good 'un and known to be a winner, the landlords of certain premises would pay you to bring your dog to the fights. And King Bonzo was a winner who was bringing in a steady income. By January of 1793, he'd grown so famous that we could ask a guinea payment every time he stepped into the ring. That and free drink for our party, the whole evening. As you can imagine, it was me that made the arrangements and took the cash on behalf of my partners. Afterwards we would split the money fair and square. And it always *was* fair and square. I could easily have kept more than my due, but even then I could see the folly of that sort of greed and I cannot warn you youngsters too strongly against it. Greed leads to spite and revenge and is the enemy of trade. The world is full of opportunities for profit, if you're quick off the mark and you deal straight, while greed has spoiled more tasty little arrangements than all the laws and all the "Peelers" ever made.

However, the best place for dog-fights in those days was Mother Bailey's speak-easy shop. [A "speak-easy shop" was a low private tavern which defrauded the

Excise of its licence by pretending that no liquors were sold in the house because the host was entertaining his friends without charge, while they chose to make him presents of cash; the two activities supposedly being unconnected. Such places were the infamous resorts of the vulgar. S.P.] It was up in the hills behind Polmouth, about five miles outside the town. They had sport of all kinds there; from cock-fights, to bull-baiting. On Saturday nights it was full of sailors, gypsies, poachers, and those of the local gentry who fancied the entertainment.

In fact it was just the place to round off a boy's education, and accordingly was strictly forbidden to apprentices. Mr Pendennis believed that church twice a day on Sunday was all the entertainment we needed, and Mrs Wheeler was ordered to protect us from other temptations. As she was fat and old, she did her duty by simply locking us in at night. This worked for the younger boys, but my friends and I were beyond such restraints and we came and went at will, provided we were discreet enough to let Mrs Wheeler pretend she didn't know.

Which brings me to the night of Saturday, 9th February 1793. We were at war with the French by then, which I have always believed to be the natural state of affairs between us and our dear neighbour, just so long as I don't have to be involved. All our seaports were busy with the Royal Navy, and the Press was working up and down the coast. But that was no bother to three bold Pendennis apprentices as we set out that night, since being apprentices, we could not be pressed. That was the law.

So it was out of Mrs Wheeler's yard, spurning the little gate and leaping the low wall in our eagerness, with Bonzo tugging at the leash. Enoch had muzzled him to guard his good behaviour and we were heavily wrapped up against the cold. The night was black as the devil's boot, but once we got out of town and up into the hills beyond, we began to chatter and sing. It was Saturday night, and freedom from twelve hours a day, six days a week in the counting house.

It was over an hour to Mother Bailey's, climbing slowly all the way. But you could see it and hear it long before you got there. Lights burned in the windows and music came across the cold fields. The closer we came, the brighter and louder everything was and we began to meet others on the road. Some of them had dogs and Bonzo began to growl nastily. It looked like a lively night and soon we were crossing the threshold and into the din and the light.

That night, Mother Bailey's was fairly heaving with bodies and the noise had to be heard to be believed. As we shoved our way into the crowd, a wild blast of music rose up twanging and wailing to the double-beat of an Irish drummer with a two-headed drumstick. The tune was "Lillibulero", the pace was furious, and two ragged lines of dancers, men to one side and women to the other, formed up and swept to and fro with stamping feet and lifted knees. The women threw up their skirts and the men roared with delight. They weren't natural dancers, any of 'em, but that music would have made a line of turnips bounce in time and it had me stamping my feet without even knowing I was at it.

As regular visitors to the establishment, we were received like gentry. Bonzo was anyway. He tugged at his leash and snarled left and right while the clientele greeted him by name and damned themselves thoroughly if he wasn't just the boy! The bolder spirits clapped him on the back, which made him jump all the more and raised roars of appreciative laughter. One fool even tried to feed him gin through the bars of his muzzle, but it dribbled all over the floor. Bonzo didn't appreciate this and wagged his head from side to side with a blood-curdling moan and froth dripping from his bared teeth. I thought it was a good time to leave him with Enoch. I had formalities to complete in any case, so I shoved through the mob to find the musicians.

These were half a dozen fiddlers, pipers, trumpeters and drummers, blaring away in one corner, with a greasy hat on the floor in front. I grinned at their leader and threw a sixpence into the hat.

"God bless you sir!" says he, not missing a note, and the others bobbed in my direction. Mine was the only silver in the hat, but the goodwill of the house was part of my purpose. The next transaction was the whole object of the evening. Mother Bailey herself was seated at a high table where she could survey the proceedings in comfort. Her bully-boys stood around her, from where they could be down into the room at the first twitch of a trouble-maker to put him out through the door with a boot up his breech.

She was no sight for the squeamish: over sixty, tankard in one hand, pipe in the other, in a filthy old sack-back gown; the fashion of twenty years earlier. The stays beneath hoisted her blubber up under her chin and the whole edifice quivered as she moved. And over all was spread white face-paint and black patches to cover the remains of her complexion.

As I caught her eye she slammed down her pot, opened wide her arms and let out a squawk, like a chicken delivering a red-hot egg.

"Here he is, boys! Here's my lovely! Come an' give us a kiss!" With Mother Bailey, there was nothing for it but face your front, step up, and plant one full on the lips. It was like kissing a sow's udders. But business is business, and after she'd pinched my cheek, asked if Bonzo was fighting fit, and I'd made myself join in the general laughter at the grand old joke of her groping a hand up my leg, I got a golden guinea out of the strong-box. "It's more 'n the dog's worth," says she, "but when I look at your brown eyes an' all the curls, I can't deny you nothing!"

Duty done, I went off to find my friends, who were squeezed into the hottest, tightest part of the room, in front of a line of barrels and jugs. Here, with a rail to keep the public back, half a dozen girls were busy drawing off strong beer, rough cider and cheap spirits as fast as the guests could pour it down their throats. The girls were part of the entertainment, being young and pretty, in a well-used sort of way. They had on loose, flopping shifts with wide-open necks. What with that and the total lack of cover beneath, when they leaned over to tap the barrels, the view was down to their waists and over the wobbling foothills between.

I gulped at the sight and my mates were licking their lips and muttering to each other. Then David said something to Enoch and the latter, gathering up his courage, lunged forward to grab what seemed to be on offer. But all he got was a vicious jab from the girl's knee, so neatly done that she never spilled a drop of drink as she did it. They were used to customers' tricks at Mother Bailey's and everyone howled with laughter except Enoch. The girl leered at him over her shoulder and poked her tongue out.

"Plenty of time for that later, my duck . . . if you've got the money!" says she. We thumped Enoch on the shoulder as everybody laughed again and he winced and sweated, bent double with pain. His eyes never left the girl, but for the moment he was warned off and settled down to get drunk instead. I'll say this for Mother Bailey's – there was enough drink to paralyse every living thing within the walls, and they didn't stint in serving it out.

And in those days, folk didn't deny themselves their pleasures for good manners as they do today. So at that end of the room, it was *all* hogs at the trough. Except for me, that is. I like drink, but I will not be drunk.

That night, however, we'd not been at it long before the musicians stopped playing and there came a roar of voices and a surge of movement towards the door. The evening proper was about to begin and we joined the flow outside. The cold made everyone gasp and thick steam curled up from the hot bodies. Out in the back yard we shoved our way to a ring of posts with planks lashed between them, to make a thing like an enormous tub, thirty feet across and four feet deep. The posts carried flaming torches, so all was brightly lit. The mob crushed against the planks, drunk and happy, and cursed the beaters-out, inside the ring, who slashed with horse-whips at anyone leaning in too far. The tarts shrieked, the gentlemen roared, and the bet-takers called the odds. Arms, sticks, hats and cudgels waved in the air.

Mother Bailey had another dais out by the ring, where she could see the fun without being squashed by the common herd. I was privileged to stand beside her, though my mates were not and Bonzo had to be chained up in a barn so he shouldn't run raving mad at the sight of blood . . . Not yet, anyway.

Then the beaters came out and the first two owners were tipping their dogs into the ring. They were fighting mad and leapt straight at each other, to the great delight of the crowd. Stones flew from their paws and they met with a heavy thump and locked jaws, rolling over and over. Dust, fur and blood sprayed in all directions as they fought like maniacs. It was a total combat of abandoned rage and could not last long. One of them caught the other under the jaws, ground home his teeth and jerked his head savagely to tear out a wound. Blood pumped steadily and the victim staggered. The owners jumped in to separate their dogs with clubs and the victor was paraded round. The loser was heaved out of the ring and dragged off to die, or to survive, whichever he could do best.

That was enough for me. I'd done my duty, I'd kept Mother Bailey sweet, and the money was in my pocket. After that I could leave the fun to them as suited it, so I sloped off back inside and sat down with a pot of beer to watch a couple of hardened sots trying to drink themselves to death out of the brandy barrel. With all Mother Bailey's girls outside, they had a clear run at it and were happy as saints in paradise.

To judge from the noise, it was a good night's sport with a dozen or more fights. They all sounded much like the one I'd seen, except for one pair who wouldn't fight and were howled off the premises together with their miserable owners. According to Enoch, Bonzo made short work of his opponent, sending him for cat's meat in double-quick time.

By midnight, we were back on the Polmouth road,

well pleased with a thundering good time, spent in the best possible company. We rolled along, laughing and bawling out songs at the tops of our voices. But just outside the town, the fun stopped. We rounded a bend and came face to face with something very unpleasant. About twenty yards ahead, our road ran across the river Pol by the old stone bridge that had been there since Queen Elizabeth's time. That night, there was a dark clump of humanity blocking the bridge. By the light of their lanterns we could see the gleam of cutlasses and shiny uniform buttons. It was the press-gang.

There was nothing down the Polmouth road for miles other than Mother Bailey's, and it was obvious they were there to catch a harvest of men coming home from the dog-fights.

"Look lads," says Enoch. "'Tis the Press."

"No bother to us," says David. "They can't take apprentices." We considered that and peered at one another in the moonlight pretending we weren't afraid. But we'd all stopped in our tracks, and we were wondering what to do. I thought of Bonzo.

"Enoch! Slip his muzzle," says I.

"Why?" says he.

"Look sharp, they're coming," says I and Enoch bent down and fiddled with the straps.

As we dithered, the men advanced swiftly towards us, wallowing from side to side as sailors do.

"Yo-ho!" says one of them in a booming voice. "You

must come-along-a-me!" This sounded bad and my heart began to knock.

"But we're apprentices," says I.

"Well bugger me blind!" says the leader of the gang with a great laugh. "D'ye hear, mates? These is apprentices!" He loomed up in the darkness and thrust his beery face at me. "See here, cocky, I'm Bosun o' this gang and I don't give a chinaman's fart what you are. The Navy wants men and there's an end on it."

As he spoke, his mates encircled us and I found my arm firmly seized from behind.

"Now buck up, me lads," says the Bosun, "and think of old England!" He pointed dramatically out to sea, "Just over there's the Froggy army, the which is ten times bigger 'n ours. And it's only our fleet as stands between them and a-raping and a-burning from one end of England to the other . . . But the fleet needs men! So let's hear no more fuss, but cheer up and be proud, for 'tis a noble service you go to!"

He really meant it too. He clapped me on the shoulder and smiled. I saw Enoch and David looking nervously at him, and then at me, and then at each other. I supposed they were looking to me for leadership so I pondered deeply on the Bosun's patriotic appeal. My bowels quivered with strong emotions as I recalled all that I had ever heard about service in the Fleet: desperate battles on the heaving ocean, thundering cannons and flashing blades. I pondered a while more, then did what any sensible man would do in my position. I kicked the Bosun violently in the galloping tackle and smashed my fist into the nose of the man holding my arm.

"OOOOOFF!" gasps the Bosun.

"GRRRRR!" roars Bonzo.

"Run lads!" says I, and clouts another of the gang.

Pandemonium: the Bosun sank, two men grabbed me, Bonzo bit everything, the lanterns went out, and the whole company swayed to and fro, bellowing and punching each other's heads in the darkness. Then up rose the Bosun, (mighty man that he was) full of fight and roaring above the din.

"Where is he?" says he, foaming at the mouth. "Where is he?" I tried to dodge but he caught my collar. Up went his arm with a cudgel and I cringed before the blow . . . only to gasp in wonderment as he shrieked hideously and leapt high up in the air. Hanging to the cheeks of his arse was our faithful Bonzo, teeth well into the meat and grinding down to the bone.

Everything changed. The Bosun's peril gave focus to the gang's efforts and they crowded in to save him. First they seized Bonzo and tried to haul him off: the worst of all possible things to do, once he'd taken hold. It only made him grip all the harder, as the extra pitch of the Bosun's screams soon told them. Next they drew out their cutlasses and fell to jabbing at him. But this was no good since neither dog nor man would keep still so they could stab the right one. Finally, one of them got a pistol into Bonzo's ear and managed to blow out his brains without killing the Bosun into the bargain. And so died a Noble British Dog. But by George, he went like a good 'un!

Once they'd levered Bonzo's jaws out of the Bosun, it was time for the reckoning. David and Enoch had run when I told them, and were long gone. But I was trapped and had to take my medicine.

If Bonzo hadn't weakened him, I suppose the Bosun might have killed me. As it was he took out his anger until some of his men pulled him off and I was lucky to be left with all my teeth and with no bones broken. My memories of the rest of that night are dim and painful. I staggered along with the Bosun kicking me whenever he felt he should. I fell down and was dragged up several times, and I remember climbing some stairs and a heavy door slamming. Then I was trying to sleep on the floor of a black, stinking room crammed with bodies and there was someone who coughed and spat in my ear all night.

And that my boys, my jolly boys, was how it felt to join the King's Navy when I was young.

Chapter 3

The old hog's choked on his claret.
(From a letter of 1ˢᵗ February 1793 to Lady Sarah
Coignwood at Bath, from Alexander Coignwood
at Coignwood Hall.)

*

The dining-room at Coignwood Hall was extremely quiet.
Candles gleamed and the light twinkled on the lavishly
spread table. After a while Alexander Coignwood got up
and walked steadily down the table to stand behind his
father, the late Sir Henry Coignwood.

Mastering his revulsion, Alexander hauled at the head
and shoulders. It took all his strength to move the limp
mass but finally there came a fat squelch and the grey
face emerged from its last meal to flop up and over the

chair-back. It came to rest with its eyes aimed at the ceiling and its jaws wide apart. Gobbets of food slid down the cheeks and wine ran over the sagging chin. Alexander stuck his fingers into the massive neck and felt for a pulse. He put an ear to the mouth and listened.

"Is he . . . ?" whispered his brother Victor, cowering at the other end of the table.

"Yes!" said Alexander, relishing the pleasure of the word and all that it meant.

"Are you sure?" said Victor, not daring to move. Alexander sneered. "Still frightened of him, little brother?" he said, and taking an apple from the table he stuck it into his father's gaping mouth. He laughed. "Never fear! The old hog's choked on his claret. The dropsy's taken him off at last."

"Horrible!" said Victor, shuddering. "How he called and called for his medicine."

"Which you had every bit as much pleasure as I in *denying him*," said Alexander, "so don't play the innocent with me, 'cos it don't become you!" Victor sniggered, then frowned.

"The servants," he said. "D'you think they heard?"

"No," said Alexander. "He didn't make much noise. Just croaking, wasn't it . . ." he looked down and gave his father's nose a playful tweak, ". . . just croaking, weren't you, Papa?"

"Don't!" said Victor.

"Oh shut up!" said Alexander. "He's gone." Victor

grinned and leaned back in his chair, affecting a histrionic pose.

"Leaving our darling mother a widow, poor creature! And she so young and so beautiful . . . "

"And so sad!" Alexander added.

"Yes," said Victor. "Still, think how well she'll look in black."

"Indeed," said Alexander. "I only wonder which of us should have the pleasure of writing to her with the news?"

"Oh you're the one for letters, Alexander. But do make sure you give *all* the details. What a pity she's gone to Bath. She'll never forgive herself for missing this."

Suddenly Victor shot to his feet with shining eyes as a thought drove all else from his mind.

"The keys! The keys!" he said and the brothers instantly fell upon the body, tearing and pulling at the pockets. This unsettled the dead mass and it slid into the darkness beneath the table. But Alexander and Victor fell to their knees and heaved together to draw it out into the light, bumping the head on a chair-leg and dislodging the apple which fell out and rolled away. The search continued.

"Got 'em! Got 'em! Got 'em!" shouted Victor, waving a ring of keys.

"Shut up!" hissed Alexander, forcing a hand over Victor's mouth. "You'll tell the whole damned house!" He snatched the keys. "Come on now. And quietly." With a last lingering look at the shape on the polished floor, where it lay so very delightfully dead, they left the dining-room. Alexander softly closed the door and they headed for their father's study. Victor was chattering with excitement and would have run all the way, but Alexander grabbed him in the dark corridor and twisted his arm savagely to bring him to heel.

"Quiet!" he said. "We've waited long enough for this, and now we've got it, we don't want the servants to know, do we?" He gave Victor's arm another wrench to make the point. "Understand?" he said. Victor gasped.

"You bastard!" he said and tried to bite.

"You bitch!" said Alexander and jammed his brother against the wall to keep him still. "Listen you bloody little fool. We've got the keys! Don't you understand? We can find out everything. All about the *Brat* . . . " Victor stopped wriggling.

"Then let go."

"Will you behave?"

"Yes."

"Promise!"

"Yes!"

The brothers straightened up, smoothed the wrinkles from their coats and looked at each other. They smiled, then laughed.

"The Brat!" said Victor.

"Yes!" said Alexander and jingled the keys in the air. He bowed and offered Victor his arm. Victor smirked, laid his fingers lightly on Alexander's hand, and the two went off together, the one bold and manly in his Service coat and powdered hair, the other slim and glittering in his French *incroyable* rig, the uttermost peak of fashion.

Ten minutes later they were inside their father's private study: the forbidden study which they had never been allowed to enter. The door was safely locked behind them and drawers, cabinets and strong boxes gaped open all around. Mere coins and bank notes were ignored as the brothers hunted busily for bigger game. Victor searched the desk for secret hidy-holes and Alexander reviewed the army of figures marching down the pages of a big ledger in his father's own hand.

Alexander was not an excitable man. He kept a tight control on himself, letting the world see only what he wanted. But as he read, his hands shook and he could not stop the nervous little phrases that jumped from his lips.

". . . more than we dreamed!" he muttered. ". . . Pottery manufactory sells £22,000 a year to the London trade, let alone foreign exports . . . Coignwood Hall and estate valued at £150,000 . . . gold bullion in the bank!"

"What?" said Victor, engrossed in his task. Alexander shook his head.

"Why was he content with a baronetcy? He could've bought a peerage!" He turned to his brother. "Victor! It's the answer to everything: your debts, mine and mother's. We knew he was rich, but Holy Jesus! This may be the greatest fortune in England."

"Ah!" said Victor as his fingers found a hidden spring and a small drawer shot out of the side of the desk. He snatched a wad of papers from the drawer and Alexander dropped his ledger at once. Both knew what this could be, and for once they did not squabble. They spread the papers across the desk and read them together.

"Where's the Will?" said Victor anxiously.

"Here!" said Alexander snatching at a document and they read its every word, dot and comma.

"So," said Alexander. "It really tells us nothing we did not already know."

"Quite," said Victor. "We already know what matters. The old bastard made a new will in '75 leaving everything to the Brat. He told us so enough times, didn't he?" Alexander nodded and jabbed his finger at the letters laid out before them.

"Anyway," he said, "look at *these*. It's everything about the Brat. Here's a letter to the mother!"

"How grotesque," said Victor. "A love letter from our father to one of his own servant girls — 'My own little true love Mary, from whom never shall I be parted' — how touching! Who'd have thought the old hog had poetry in him? What do you suppose happened to little Mary?"

"Died in childbirth," said Alexander. "It says so here — a letter from the Reverend Dr Woods of Polmouth. It seems the Brat was sent into the good doctor's care to be safe from his stepmother and half-brothers! Now what do you think of that?"

"What?" said Victor, affecting horror. "Would we have offered harm to a baby?" He produced a handkerchief and applied it to the corners of his eyes. "I weep with the very contemplation of it!"

He laid a hand on his brother's arm and looked into his eyes. "Why," he said, "could you imagine slitting a baby's dear little throat?" He frowned as a thought occurred to him. "No," he said, "that would leave marks, wouldn't it? Better to drown it in a tub." He put his mind to the problem. "It would have to be dry afterwards, of course. So I'd take off its clothes first, and then . . . "

"Victor," said Alexander, interrupting the discourse. "Do you know you make me shudder sometimes?" Victor smiled and took Dr Woods's letter. He kissed it.

"No matter," he said, "the child is now the man. But at least we know where he is."

"Yes," said Alexander. "After all these years, we can do something about him. You must go straight to London for the lawyers, and I shall go to Cornwall. At last we know where he is and we know his name: Jacob Fletcher."

Chapter 4

In fact, that's how it felt like to be pressed into the Navy and I spent the night locked into one end of an upstairs room behind a heavy oaken grating which ran from wall to wall and floor to ceiling, dividing the place in two. In fits and starts I noticed what was around me. Beyond the grating (which I was jammed against), I could see the filthy wreck of a room with some tables and chairs, and the accumulated rubbish of long occupation by a body of men. What light there was came from a few candles flickering on the table where some of our guardians sat or slumped asleep, supposedly keeping watch. There were nearly as many on their side of the barrier as on ours and, like us, they were mainly asleep on the floor. But they had far more room and they had blankets and straw palliasses.

It was not a pleasant night. I was lumped in with dirty

humanity in bulk. In that cramped place there was just room for me to slump on the floor with my back to the wall, the grating for a pillow and a rum-sodden fisherman beside me. Like everyone else in that lock-up other than me, he was pole-axed with drink. And yet the place wasn't quiet. All night, it echoed to the coughing and moaning of men who were neither properly awake nor properly asleep. In my waking moments I worried what might happen to me and how this dreadful mistake should be put right. For I knew just where I was: this was the "Rondy", the press-gang rendezvous at the "Three Dutch Skippers", an old inn by the lower harbour in the worst part of Polmouth. It was right by the harbour stairs, convenient for the sea. Everyone knew where the Rondy was and sailormen never walked past it alone or at night. But the Press had never worried me as I was supposed to be exempt . . . so what was I doing here?

Finally I fastened on to that idea; that come morning, all would be explained and I should go free. In any case, David and Enoch would surely tell Mrs Wheeler, and she would tell them at Pendennis's and my certain rescue would follow. And so the night passed and the dawn came up as it always does. Slowly the light brightened through the two windows of the big room. From where I sat, I could just see out of one of the windows. I could see the little waves twinkling across the water. A pretty sight, but one that filled me with dismay on that occasion.

Then the fisherman began to stir and to elbow for

room. He smelt like dung and looked like death. Slowly the whole herd awoke and began to talk and complain. The talk was all of ships and floggings and the horrors of naval life. Even worse, the fisherman, he was the one who'd been coughing all night, began deliberately to scrape his bare knee against the rough brick of the wall. He didn't like what he was doing, and set his teeth against the pain of it. Soon he had an open wound that trickled blood down his leg.

"What are you doing?" I croaked, all dry and gummy from the night.

"Taint fair . . . Shan't go," says he. "Wife and litluns at home . . . Navy won't take a cripple."

"What?" says I, but he ignored me. Bit by bit, he scraped out a crater in his knee, and now and again he stirred in some dirt from the floor. He was manufacturing the appearance of a chronic ulcer so as to seem unfit to serve. I came over weak at the sight of it and turned my back. But I couldn't avoid the sound of his movements or his gasps of pain as he stubbornly kept at the work. In my innocence, I thought that this was a truly horrible example of what men would do to avoid the Navy.

About an hour after dawn, things began to happen. A door opened at the far end of the room and an Officer entered. He was about sixty, with several days of white stubble on his face. Both he and his uniform were shabby and drooping and he was fat and awkward and leaned on a stick. As he entered, the gangsmen rose and those wearing hats removed them. Hitching up their belts and scratching their backsides, they formed an untidy line and awaited his pleasure. He came up to the grating and peered into the pen with baggy eyes.

"I'm Lieutenant Spencer, by God!" he declared, "Lieutenant Spencer and you'll learn to know me." He turned to the Bosun and damned him up and down. "Is this your night's work, Mr Bosun? Is this what you call men? I could find better in a Pox-Doctor's shop!" To my great satisfaction, I saw that the Bosun was having trouble in standing and was still in considerable pain from Bonzo's attentions.

Meanwhile, Spencer paraded up and down, bawling out curses till his belly shook, and driving his stick through the bars to stir the prisoners. Behind his back, I could see his men nudging one another and grinning at him. For this was all for show. Lieutenant Spencer was not a real Sea Officer at all. Not any more. He was just an old worn-out Lieutenant in the Impress Service. Later I came to despise such as he but at that moment, he was a figure of real terror.

Suddenly he changed his tune as he recollected a duty.

"Urrumph!!" says he. "Now listen here, you bloody lubbers; by the grace of our Sovereign Lord, King George the Third . . . God bless him!" (and would you believe it, there was an answering murmur of "God bless him!" from the prisoners around me) "... every man of you has the chance to enter voluntarily. And all who do shall receive the volunteer's bounty. But I warn you; them as don't step forward, I shall take 'em as pressed men in any event!"

There followed a calling of names and an edging forward as some dozen of the prisoners came forward and had their names taken in a ledger. I kept my mouth shut, knowing that I'd be released as soon as I could speak to the Officer. So did the man with the scraped knee; he was bitter contemptuous of the "volunteers".

"Damned fools," says he. "All they'll get is their rights took away and their money stole by the pay clerks."

And then my moment came and I could have fainted with the relief of it. I saw blessed salvation bearing down upon me without even an effort on my part. The Bosun dragged himself across to Lieutenant Spencer, trailing one leg all the way, and said something in his ear, while pointing at me. This sent the Lieutenant's eyebrows up to his scalp. He came across to me directly.

"Now then, mister," says he. "Is that right, you're a 'prentice?"

"Yes sir," says I.

"And what might be your name?"

"Jacob Fletcher. I'm apprenticed to Pendennis's Counting House in Wharf Street."

"Jacob Fletcher," he said and smiled at me; a big beaming smile which I took to be an attempt to ingratiate himself with me.

"Smile away, my lad," I thought, "and much good may

it do you!" I was already rehearsing what I should say to the courtroom about the abusing of innocent apprentices and the cruel murder of our poor little dog. My employer, Mr Pendennis, was the Mayor of Polmouth and a magistrate. Only imagine what was in store for Lieutenant Spencer when he came before Mr Justice Pendennis!

Spencer frowned and bit his lip. Ponderous engines of thought were turning in his brain like ancient millstones (looking for the way out for himself, I didn't doubt). He lowered his voice to a whisper, and beckoned me close.

"Thing is, Mr Fletcher," says he all respectful, "if I was to let you out right now, then these here swabs," he indicated the other prisoners, "why, there'd be no holding 'em whatsoever, d'you see? There'd be men killed in there and I'd be held responsible. So just bide a while till we empties the cage and you can be on your way before the day's out."

I wasn't too pleased with this but I thought I'd keep my temper in check and save it for the magistrate. So that's what we agreed and I sank down in my corner and tried to be patient. After a few words with the Bosun, Spencer left the room and things went quiet. For a couple of hours, nothing happened except that, outside the Rondy, a crowd gathered and began to call out names. These were the wives and relatives of the men taken last night. Some of the prisoners called back as they recognised the voices. And then one of the wives appeared.

The door at the far end of the room opened and I saw money change hands as a respectable-looking woman entered and spoke in whispers to the Bosun. Silence fell as the prisoners strained to catch what was going on. The Bosun led her up to the barrier and one of the prisoners greeted her.

"I'm here, m'dear," says he, and the two of them just stared at one another like lost souls. She was a tiny creature; well-made and pretty and not much older than me. And she was pale as a ghost and trembling.

"Now Missus," says the Bosun, "just a few words, mind, and I'll be watching everything you do." And he hobbled off to join his mates, well-pleased with his bit of business. I thought she had come to bid farewell to her man but she brought out a small bundle of linen and offered it to him without another word.

"What you doing there, Missus?" yells the Bosun. "What's passing there?" She unwrapped the bundle and held it out for him to see. It was no more than pieces of old linen.

"It's handkerchiefs," says she.

"Very good, my girl! Don't you just play me no tricks, or I'll tan the bare behind off you!" The gang roared with laughter at this and added some coarse suggestions of their own. But the girl seemed not to notice and pushed the linen through the bars and stood still. There was something not right here, but I couldn't see what. The prisoner spoke again.

"Just like we always said. Now go on!" With that, he put out his right hand so that it rested on one of the bars of the grating, and closed his eyes. With the briefest of hesitation, she fumbled in a bag that she carried, raised her arm and brought something flashing down on her husband's fingers.

"Clump!" and a thumb and forefinger went spinning to the floor linked by a flap of skin.

A gasp of horror burst from all who saw this fearful act. The man glared his teeth in agony as his wife stepped back, with one hand to her mouth and an axe dangling from the limp fingers of the other hand. Then the room went mad. The gangsmen bellowed and stampeded forward in a herd to seize the girl. She offered no resistance but, in his fury, the Bosun struck the small defenceless creature a terrific blow with his fist and knocked her senseless. This released the emotions of the prisoners in an animal yell. They bayed for the Bosun's blood and the grating strained as they hurled themselves at it and lunged out their arms to get him. For his part, he stood there looking sick and wondering what to do.

The noise brought Lieutenant Spencer into the room. He went up and down, slashing with his stick, till he had knocked order back into his men. Then he questioned the Bosun, and sheer curiosity brought silence as the Spencer pitched into the Bosun.

"Let her in 'just for a minute' did you, you shithead bastard?" says the Lieutenant, in one of his politer sallies. "By God, Mister, I've a mind to put you in there along o' *them*!" He pointed to us, to roars of extreme approval, and the Bosun shrank six inches in height at the very least.

When Spencer ran out of curses, he turned to the rest of his men.

"Get that female out of my sight," says he, and noticing the thumb and forefinger where it lay in the dirt, added, "and heave that wreckage over the side!"

Two of the gangsmen raised up the girl and carried her out. Another, taking Spencer at his word, picked up the "wreckage" and threw it out of the nearest window. There came a moment's pause, then a screech from someone in the crowd outside, followed by a roar of outrage.

Spencer nearly burst with anger at this and a perfect stream of filth poured from his lips as he beat his stick over the head of the luckless gangsman.

"Christ almighty! You bloody lubber! Don't you know no better than that? Don't you know the mob? Take *that*, you bastard! My oath, if they storm this place, you're in our front rank, my bucko, so's they can do for you first of all of us!"

Finally, Spencer broke the stick, threw away the stump, and went over to the window to see how things lay outside. He took off his hat and tried not to be seen, but somebody saw him and a stone came whistling up, to dash out a pane of glass and rattle across the floor. Spencer jumped back, grey-faced. He clapped on his hat and looked at his men.

"Damnation!" says he. "Pistols, boys . . . " And an untidy scramble followed as coats, bags and odd corners were scoured to unearth the gang's firearms. Among this slovenly company there was no such thing as an arms chest and men stood here, there and everywhere, loading and priming.

Meanwhile the shouting had increased outside and missiles were pouring through the windows. Stones, cobbles and the occasional dead cat came bounding in and the windows were rapidly cleared of glass. We prisoners were like schoolboys on holiday. Protected by our grating we could enjoy the fun with impunity, and a great cheer went up every time one of the gangsmen caught a clout from a stone.

"Now then, boys," cries Spencer, over the din, "when I give the word, aim over their heads and don't kill none o' the buggers if you can help it!" With much reluctance, the gang crept across the floor on its hands and knees, and sheltered against the walls and under the windows.

"Present! . . . Aim! . . . Fire!" says Spencer. About half the gang actually rose to aim. The rest kept well down, and fired at the empty sky. A ragged volley clattered out, and powder-smoke filled the room. Poor effort though it was, it did the trick and the mob ran for it to screams of fear. Silence fell as their pattering feet faded in the distance.

Spencer brushed the dirt from his coat and looked about him.

"Now then," says he. "Time these lot was on board of the tender. We should just have time before the mob gathers again . . . Move yourselves!" This set the gang bustling. They were not a smart crew but they knew their work and set about it after their fashion. The prisoners began to moan. They realised what Spencer's words meant, which is more than I did. I had no idea what was meant by that little word "tender". But Spencer was speaking again.

"Where's this lubber with the clipped wing?" says he. "Rout him out, Mr Bosun, at the double!"

"Aye aye sir!" says the Bosun, hobbling forward. He found some keys and opened the grating door to let out the wounded man.

Outside the grating, the man looked about him in much unease. He was white with pain and unsteady on his feet. The linen scraps were bound round his hand and he hugged the bloodstained mass to his breast. Lieutenant Spencer considered him.

"Pah!" says he. "No damn use to the Service now, are you? Couldn't run up a hoist of signals like that . . . Get out of here, you half-man! Go on!" and he pointed to the door and turned his back in contempt. The man looked back once at the other prisoners and slowly walked out of the room, free from the press-gang for ever. The prisoners murmured.

"Good luck to you, mate!" says one of them, half in pity and half in admiration of his dreadful courage. [All who admire Britannia's Navy will be saddened to learn that this instance of wilful mutilation to avoid service is not unique. The *Times* newspaper of 3rd Nov. 1795 reports the case of one Samuel Carradine, taken by the Press, who was visited by his wife while in prison awaiting transfer into the Fleet. Carradine thrust his hand beneath the cell door so that his wife might strike off his thumb and forefinger with a mallet and chisel. By this terrible means Carradine secured his release. S.P.]

After that, things moved fast. The business in hand was to transfer the prisoners from the Rondy to the hold of the Impress Service brig *Bullfrog*, at anchor in the harbour. (This was the tender Spencer had referred to.) The gang had it down to a drill; they'd let out a handful of men at a time and rush 'em down the stairs and out to a launch at the harbour stairs. To my surprise, I was seized and hustled out with the very first batch. I tried to call out to Spencer, but the Bosun clouted me back-hand across the mouth and we all went thundering down the stairs and out across the cobbles in the thin February sunshine. The mob was gone but a few bystanders were about.

"Jesus help that poor boy," cries one old woman. "The Press have took him!"

"No!" I thought. "No . . . they can't have taken me . . . it's all arranged with the Lieutenant . . . "

But I was shoved down the harbour stairs, down the old stone steps with the green weed and the smell of the sea, and into the stern sheets of a big launch. They made me sit on a thwart and I grabbed the gunwale as the boat rocked with all the bodies pouring into it. There were about thirty men aboard: eight prisoners and more than twice that number of gangsmen, with the Bosun in charge. No chance at all to overpower them or escape.

Some of the gangsmen took the oars and pulled for the middle of the harbour and the Bosun stared at me with vicious amusement writ all over his face. He was obviously pleased at my plight and I suppose he thought I was being paid back for Bonzo's attentions to his person.

I stared back in disbelief at the Rondy with its big naval ensign flying from an upper window. Where was Lieutenant Spencer? What was happening? I felt my chance to escape was fading away. And I was absolutely correct. Once upon any waters deep enough to float a ship, we were in the absolute power of the Royal Navy; which power stretched the whole world around and acknowledged no laws other than its own. I was, to all intents and purposes, lost to the world of land-living folk.

Chapter 5

As the harbour stairs grew smaller behind me, I began to worry in deadly earnest. Was it possible I actually was going to be pressed? I couldn't believe it. I tried to reason with the gangsmen in the boat but they just ignored me, and worse, the other prisoners turned nasty.

"Why you so special?" says one of them. "Better 'n the rest of us, eh? You just shut it, or I'll punch yer head!" There was a growl of agreement. If they were caught, then why shouldn't I be? That was about their measure. So I kept quiet and tried to think. I had more brains than the whole boat load together, so why couldn't I think of a way out? I decided to wait until we got to the tender. Surely there would be officers there who I could talk to. And while I thought, the gangsmen shipped oars. I looked forward and saw the bulk of a ship: His Britannic Majesty's brig *Bullfrog*, of one hundred tons, and a dozen four-pounder pop-guns.

Now I'll have you know that I've led a most eventful life (in the teeth of my own inclinations, certainly, but I have). I've sunk ships and I've looted temples. I've seen Jappos slit their own bellies and I've seen the Indian rope trick complete with the climber disappearing at the top. In addition, I've had more than my share of wounds: I've been shot by Frenchmen, sabred by Poles, knifed by a Turkish tart and bayonetted by our very own Royal Marines. The scars are all over me. But my time aboard *Bullfrog* hurt worse than anything. It left wounds of the spirit and it left memories that still come to me in nightmares after all these years between.

The game started with my first sight of *Bullfrog*. She was making ready for sea. Men were in the rigging and others were hauling on lines to raise the sails. I felt a sharp ache of fear. Where were my employers? They should have come for me by now. Enoch and David must have told everyone that I was taken by the Press, so why hadn't Mr Pendennis descended in his wrath to annihilate the felons and secure my release?

With a bump, the launch ran alongside and we were helped up the side with kicks and cudgels. My first experience of entering a ship and the strangeness of it fell upon me. It smelt of tar and wet and timber . . . and something else. Something nasty that hung in the background. We were immediately driven towards the hold where the cargo was kept. The cargo was men. The accumulated product of the Polmouth press-gang's activities over the last few days. The main hatch-cover was off, and as I reached the coaming, I looked down and my stomach heaved as I caught the full, hot reek of putrid sweat.

Down below was a seething mass of naked limbs, running sores and eyes staring up in fear and malice. There must have been a hundred men down there, under conditions that would have disgraced an African slaver. I was choked at the smell, disgusted at the sight, and terrified by the thought that these were the men we relied on to keep the French off! The only way down was by a knotted rope made fast to a ring-bolt in the deck. I thought I would die rather than go down that rope and cast about for something to do. I fastened on one of the tender's crew standing by. He seemed to be in authority.

The man was powerfully built; less than my height but thickset with his belly hanging over his belt. Like all the tender's crew, his face was tanned brown and heavily lined. Little black eyes glared steadily out of the leathery face, alert and vicious. He looked about forty years old and was swinging a length of thick rope from his right hand. It was three feet long and knotted at the free end; my first sight of a "starter".

How in God's name should I try to influence this creature? The mind of an ant in the body of an ape. I gave him my best effort, trying hard to sound confident. Thanks to Dr Woods, I had the voice of a gentleman and this was the time to use it.

"Sir!" says I. "There has been a great mistake."

"Ugh?" says he.

"A mistake, sir! I should not be here and I certainly cannot go down there." I contemptuously dismissed the hold and its inhabitants. So far, so good. I had his attention and a silence fell as those around me took note. Expression flickered across the flat face as he calculated what I might be. Finally he jabbed at the stern with his thumb.

"Cap'n's yonder," says he. "You go tell he what 'tis, an' he say what's to do." I looked where he indicated and saw an officer complete with cocked hat and sword.

"Thank you, sir!" says I and turned to go, taking him at his word.

Before I had gone one step, something crashed across my shoulders with ghastly force. It hurt more than anything in all my life and I screamed aloud as the shock scorched into my very heart. And there he was, grinning merrily and swinging his piece of rope, poised for another blow.

"Right, my lovely," says he, "you got till I count *three* to get down there, or I'll have the soddin' ears off you with the next one!" He was thoroughly enjoying himself and, of all things, would most like me to hesitate so he could strike again.

Well, I never was a slow learner and went down that rope like a monkey. He called after me. "Hey! Boy!" says he, and I looked up to see him leaning over the hatchway. "I'm Dixon . . . you remember me, cos I'm going to remember *you*!" And he laughed. What a jolly fellow! What a sense of fun! Here, truly, was a man who enjoyed his work. Soon after that they crammed in the rest of the prisoners from ashore and dropped the hatch on us.

I'll pass over the horrors of *Bullfrog*'s hold; it was like the Rondy only worse. It was filthier, nastier and far more violent. You had to use your fists just to keep standing and not be trampled into the deck. Added to that came the agony of seasickness once *Bullfrog* left harbour and shoved her bows into the big waves of the open sea.

Once *Bullfrog* had fairly cleared the harbour and was rolling westward up the coast, she fell into her routine. This was a continuous process of bringing men up from the hold to be examined, to be fed and watered and "to blow the stink off 'em" as the crew so aptly put it. A few of the pressed men were even allowed to stay on deck. These were good seamen who looked docile and could be useful in working the ship. I was included in this number, though in my case I'd have been better off in the hold.

It turned out that my friend Mr Dixon, who was Bosun aboard *Bullfrog*, was responsible for the choice of men. He had me up and rated me ship's scavenger: the cleaner, scraper and lowest form of life in the ship. His reason for this was to let him play a little game upon me. This consisted in his setting me on a piece of work then creeping up behind me to deliver a sudden whack with his starter when I wasn't expecting it. An unexpected blow hurts worse than anything you've tensed yourself to receive and Mr Dixon exploited that to the full. Whack! . . . Across my back. Whack! . . . Across my shoulders. Whack! . . . Around my legs. And always, there was Dixon with a smile on his ugly face.

I naturally thought to complain to the officer in command: Lieutenant Salisbury. Surely it was not permitted to abuse men like this? But Dixon wouldn't let me near him and in any case, before I could say a word, I had the good fortune to see what kind of man the lieutenant was.

He was another prize beauty. He looked like money and was immaculately dressed, there on that floating cess-pit of a ship, from his gold-laced hat to his silver-buckled shoes. He was young, no more than twenty, tall and thin and had an unhealthy air about him.

In the afternoon of that first day at sea, Mr Salisbury was examining a batch of prisoners up from the hold. Dixon was at his elbow and I was swabbing away nearby and had the chance to watch. Half a dozen men were lined up in their rags, steaming in the cold air, as he considered them with a handkerchief to his nose. Then one man collapsed and sank to the deck. I recognised the fisherman who had been working on his knee in the Rondy (Norris Polperro his name was).

"Argh!" says he. "Please, your honour, but it's this old leg. Been sick for years. Doubt I'll be any use to the Service at all."

"Dear me," says the Lieutenant, quietly and bent over Polperro with his hands clasped behind his back. "Show me the wound, my good man, for I'm something of a doctor and might venture an opinion." Polperro stirred with hope and showed the "ulcer".

"Ah!" says the Lieutenant, "I'm pleased to tell you that I have just the thing for conditions such as yours."

"Oh?" says the fisherman.

"Yes," says the Lieutenant and straightened up. "Mr Dixon, apply the treatment," and Dixon lashed out with his rope's end. Polperro leapt to his feet with a yelp and Dixon cut him neatly across the buttocks as he tried to skip clear. That far it was funny and a ripple of laughter came from the other men, but Dixon kept it up beyond reason. A rain of heavy blows upon a man who could only hop about the deck and try to dodge the worst of it. The slightest show of resistance would bring death by hanging. In his own good time, Salisbury stopped it.

"Thank you, Mr Dixon," says he, quietly. "A miraculous cure, as I live and breathe."

He and Dixon leered at each other in a shared moment of happy, brutal satisfaction. Then he turned to the other men, "And are there any more cases for the surgeon?"

There were not, and seeing the Lieutenant and his Bosun at their pleasure, I knew there was no escape for me.

Indeed there was none. Try as I might to do the work that I was set, and keep a look-out for Dixon, he would still catch me. It was persecution without pity or reason. I was used to being cock of the walk: living in comfort, surrounded by friends, admired for my wit, and steadily making money. And here I was, being tortured by a murderous anthropoid with not one thousandth of my intelligence. How could it be? And it got worse. It got so bad that I'm not even sure how long I was aboard *Bullfrog*, the days and nights blurred into each other as I sank lower and lower.

Probably it all happened over three or four days. But before chloroform was invented, the surgeons used to tell their victims that the amputation would only take a minute or two. And I doubt that eased the mind very much.

In my case, during those few days, fear and hatred of Dixon were turning me from a rational man into a lunatic. He was breaking my mind more than my body. Remember — I was barely eighteen, I'd been taken away from everything that I knew, and I was cold, wet and seasick into the bargain. And if you *still* think I'm whining, why don't you get some friend (choosing one with a strong right arm) to hit you as hard as he can with a rope's end? Then get him to hit you on the same place two or three times more, and calculate how long *you* could stand it.

Finally, one morning just before light, I reached the crossroads of my life. I was crouched, soaking wet, in the very bows of the ship by the "seats of ease". These are the ship's privies; boxes with holes in the top for the men to sit on, perched on a grating under the bowsprit. The grating was narrow and triangular, with ropes to grasp to keep you from falling off, but it was open to the sea on either side.

Dixon had set me the nonsensical task of standing by to swab over the seats after each use. I had been there all night and was light-headed with fatigue and the waiting for Dixon to creep up on me. *Bullfrog* plunged along, the bows swayed up and down, and every fresh wave threw a shower of salt spray over me.

I was in a singular state of mind. I had got it into my head that one more blow from Dixon would split me to the bones and my insides would fall out. The poison mixture of anger and fear, cooking these several days in my mind, grew so hot that I could contain it no more and I rocked to and fro in my torment. The only way out was to roll forward and drop into the smooth green waves. At least it would cool the pain. I took a breath, tensed my muscles to push forward and . . . SNAP! Like the turning of a lock, my mind cleared. I saw the way out. The dreadful threat of suicide passed, and I became my own man again. Immediately I got to my feet and crept quietly back over the bow to the nearest gun. Then I returned to my place and took off one of my shoes. Nobody had seen me.

And there I stayed until Dixon arrived, which he did when the watch changed in the early light. I had my back firmly against the bow bulkhead so he couldn't come at me from behind. He grinned as I stood up to face him.

He wouldn't hit me while I could see him, which was the whole point of his game, so I swayed with the motion of the ship and held his eye. For a moment, the perfect crudity of his face was marred by a frown of puzzlement. Then the frown was obliterated in a crunching of bone as I hit him in the forehead with heart, soul, mind and strength . . . and a four-pound iron round-shot swung in the toe of a stocking.

It took him by surprise but he was fearfully strong and though he fell, he didn't go straight over the side. He managed to catch the edge of the grating and hung at the full stretch of his arms, totally vulnerable, looking up at me in amazement.

I could see his stupid, brutal face straining with effort as he tried to follow the unbelievable turn of events. But this was no time for gloating and I stamped on his fingers in a passion of rage to make him let go. Splash! And he vanished under the bows, to be scraped, pounded and drowned as the brig passed over him. Farewell, Mr Dixon. He never even cried out. I shuddered heavily and dropped the shot after him. Then I sat down and took off my shoe to put the stocking on again.

Afterwards, I waited for the inevitable discovery of my crime. But nothing happened for a while, and then there was a lot of bustle and shouting for Dixon, though none of this was aimed at me and eventually things got quiet again. Slowly the incredible thought grew in my mind that perhaps nobody had seen what I'd done. I gathered courage and peered back down the length of the brig. Nobody was paying me any heed. Nobody was looking at me. Nobody was interested in me. Nobody was advancing upon me to throw me in irons.

I've often wondered what Lieutenant Salisbury thought about Dixon's disappearance, and what he put in the log: "Lost overboard in a storm" very likely, even though the weather was fair and Dixon a seaman of vast experience. That would bring the least discredit upon himself. Less, for instance, than "murdered by an unknown member of the crew", even should such an idea have entered Mr Salisbury's head. Such an entry might make a young Lieutenant's superiors think that he hadn't got proper control of his ship. And that could blight a young career badly. In any case, that very day we reached our destination, Portsmouth, and I was taken out of *Bullfrog* and beyond Lieutenant Salisbury's reach.

Chapter 6

Has not this officer done his dooty by yoo?
(From an undated, unaddressed letter, in a semi-
literate hand believed to have been written by
Lieutenant John Spencer of the Impress Service.)

*

The Right Worshipful Mr Nathan James Pendennis, Esq,
Lord Mayor of Polmouth, Justice of the Peace, and
prosperous merchant, was an imposing figure. From his
respectable wig to his buckled shoes and the snuff-
coloured broadcloth encasing his substantial belly, he was
a man who normally inspired confidence and respect.

But today on a cold Monday morning, enthroned in
his great chair, behind his desk, with his senior clerks
waiting upon him, he inspired only terror in the two

miserable worms that cringed before him. For Enoch Bradley and David Ibbotson, one of the great reckonings of their lives was upon them.

"You sir!" roared Pendennis at Bradley. "How dare you drop your eyes in that dissembling manner? Face me sir! Face me when you speak, or you'll never be employed again! Not by me nor any other in the land. I'm not without influence, sir!" Knowing how true this was, the wretched Bradley forced himself to look the Gorgon in the eye.

Mr Pendennis's inquisition had already been under way for some time and had first been directed upon David Ibbotson. As the latter had now reached a state of pitiful incoherence, Bradley knew that his turn had come.

"Now sir!" said Pendennis. "For the moment, we shall leave aside your iniquitous insubordination in attending the place of ill-repute, to which you repaired on Saturday night." Bradley licked his lips and thanked merciful God for this deliverance, however temporary. He was so relieved that he near-as-damn-it passed water in his breeches. "Instead," thundered Pendennis, making the papers jump on his desk, "we shall discuss the whereabouts of your fellow apprentice, Mr Fletcher, whose absence this morning brought this whole matter to my attention."

Pendennis paused, his chain of thought disturbed, and added in a quite different voice, "Fletcher — a young man in whom I had noted considerable gifts. It saddens me to learn that Mr Fletcher was part of your abominable expedition." There was a moment's silence, broken only by Ibbotson's snivelling, as Mr Pendennis considered this cruel disillusionment. His attendant clerks looked stern and shook their heads in sympathy. "However," said Pendennis, "you will now tell me exactly why Fletcher did not return with you on Saturday night." He glared at Bradley, awaiting an answer.

"It was the press-gang, Mr Pendennis, sir," said Bradley. "They took Fletcher and they tried to . . . "

"What?" cried Pendennis, shooting to his feet. "The Press? Those enemies of trade, those sons of Beelzebub!" His jaws worked and his fists clenched in fury at the mention of the hated Impress Service. His business depended on watermen and bargees, every one of them lawful prey to the press-gang. He had heavy investments in merchant ships whose sailings might be interrupted by impressment. He had loans outstanding to fishermen whom the press-gang might remove from all ability to repay him. "You pair of worthless dolts!" he screamed. "WHY DID YOU NOT TELL ME THIS BEFORE?"

"Er . . . Er . . . " said Bradley, not daring to say that Mr Pendennis hadn't given them the chance. Not daring to protest that Mr Pendennis had focused on their doings at Mother Bailey's to the exclusion of anything else.

"Never mind!" said Pendennis. "Did you not tell them you are apprentices? Did you not mention my name?"

"Yes sir, no sir," said Bradley, accurately.

"What?" cried Pendennis, misunderstanding. "Do you bandy words with me, sir?"

"No sir," said Bradley, quivering.

"Did you not tell them that to take an apprentice is contrary to law?"

"Yes sir," said Bradley, "Fletcher told 'em, but they took him anyway, sir." Pendennis ground his teeth with rage and turned upon two nearby clerks who ran like rabbits to do his bidding.

"*You*! Fetch my lawyer! *You*! Fetch the constable . . . Take a Pendennis apprentice would they?"

Within the hour Mr Pendennis, at the head of a considerable procession, had arrived at the Rondy and was putting Lieutenant Spencer to the same torment that he'd inflicted on Bradley and Ibbotson. At least that's what he was trying to do, but Spencer was an altogether tougher old bird.

"For the last time, I demand that you release Jacob Fletcher!" insisted Pendennis.

"Fletcher-be-buggered!" sneered Spencer. "I tells *you* for the last time, we ain't got no soddin' Fletcher!" He grinned, showing a broken line of tobacco-stained teeth. "Search for him if you like, matey. We won't stop you, will we boys?" and his men joined in his mocking laughter.

"Dammit, sir, are you telling me that you've already sent him into the Fleet?" said Pendennis.

"I'm tellin' you nothin', mister!" said Spencer.

Pendennis was no fool and could see he was beaten for the moment. He drew himself up and looked down his nose at Spencer.

"Very well, sir," he said. "You may think yourself clever, but I have the law behind me and I shall pursue this matter ruthlessly." Pendennis advanced a step and glared fiercely at Spencer. "And as for you, sir, I shall remember you most particularly. You shall curse the day that you crossed me!" and he turned on his heel and stalked out with his followers in tow.

Spencer watched him go in dull fury. His contempt for Pendennis, and all the other Pendennis's in the land, was fully equal to their contempt for him.

"You bugger!" he said, bitterly. "You'd be the first to squawk if the Frog navy stopped your bloody trade, wouldn't you? You'd be first to call for us to man the Fleet — just so long as we takes the men from some- where else!"

His Bosun came hobbling up, still out of favour over the incident of the clipped wing.

"Told him proper you did, Mr Spencer, sir, and no mistake!"

He turned to the men, urging a display of loyalty. "Didn't he, lads?"

"Aye!" said the lads half-heartedly.

"Who asked you?" said Spencer. "Shut your trap!" But the Bosun pulled his hat off and knuckled his brow.

"Thing is, beggin' yer pardon, sir, we was wonderin' when we was goin' to get the money . . . "

"Never you mind no bloody money!" snapped Spencer. "If I was you, mister, I'd be more worried about gettin' my backside cauterised before it festers."

"Aye aye, sir!" said the Bosun, pressing dangerously on into the storm. "We was only wonderin'... " But Spencer's temper snapped and the Bosun had to jump to get out of range of his stick. Finally, when Spencer had exhausted himself with rage, he stomped off and sat down with a bottle of rum in the dingy hole that served him as a private room. The more he turned things over in his slow mind, the worse they seemed.

Spencer was no coward. He was a coarse and shabby old bully but he'd face any man that came at him with sword in hand. He'd do that all right, but facing the courts was another matter. It drained the manhood clear out of him. What chance was there for an old tarpaulin like him? Especially when he'd taken a man that shouldn't be took.

But none of this was supposed to have happened. The gentleman had promised that all would be made right. The gentleman said he'd square it with the law. The gentleman had *promised!* And Spencer was to get twenty guineas in gold for the work.

He fell back in his chair and took a pull of the bottle. He cursed his own laziness in not going out with the gang. But how could he do that with his bad leg that was ruined in the King's service? He couldn't dance after young apprentices, could he? So he'd brought that shithead Bosun into the plot; a guinea for the Bosun and half-a-guinea per man for the gang, to bring in a named man. A *named* man! He groaned as he saw the Bosun telling that to the court — proof positive of wrongdoing. They'd break an Officer for that. They'd turn him out of the Service to starve in the gutter. That's the least they'd do.

Spencer thought of the gentleman again. What was his game anyway? Why hadn't he done right by him? Spencer had done his duty, hadn't he? Hadn't he delivered up the goods? And here he was cast up dismasted on a lee shore! Well, if he must sink, then that fine bugger should sink with him. He'd make all plain in the courts if need be.

At this, a great light shone upon Lieutenant Spencer. He smiled as he saw the way out of all his troubles. He would *make* the swab do right! He would write him a letter. The lubber was staying at the Crown Inn and a letter could go by one of the gang. He'd tell him to call off the lawyers or be betrayed in court. Half sozzled in rum, he roused himself and got pen, paper and ink from the landlord. Mumbling the words and chuckling savagely, he hauled the pen clumsily across the page in his heavy fist.

Chapter 7

I was most of a day in Portsmouth before being taken off *Bullfrog* and the meaning of what I'd done began to weigh on me. The calculation had seemed an easy one: since I was already prepared to drown myself, I had no fear of any punishment the Navy might inflict. So why not be revenged on Dixon? But now I *wasn't* facing certain death, and I was troubled. Moral scruples were not a problem; what Dixon got from me was natural justice. The trouble was I couldn't really believe I'd got away with it. I was terrified that someone must have seen what I'd done and that soon I'd be dragged off to face a hanging.

There was more, too. My confidence had taken a heavy battering from what I'd suffered over the last few days. And I had actually killed a man; not a thing that training as a clerk exactly fits a lad for, as you'll appreciate. No, you can't expect just to walk away from all that with a merry smile. So I wasn't myself for quite a long time after, and a lot of what happened next passed me by like a dream. For instance, if I'd had the wit to do it, I could have talked myself out of the Navy even then. Pressing apprentices was merely illegal, but pressing a *gentleman* was unthinkable to any decent Officer. And I had the speech and manners of a gentleman. [A favourite claim of Fletcher's which those who knew him might dispute. S.P.] But I said nothing, and as *Bullfrog's* pressed men were unloaded I found myself in a boat, with others, towed by a launch from one of the warships. There were lines of great ships at anchor, and the cold water splashed over the gunwales. A heavy depression was on me, and I went like a sheep to the butcher's.

First they sent us aboard an old hulk fitted out as a slop-ship with tubs of hot water and soap. By then, not only were we filthy, but we were hopping with livestock as well. So they scrubbed us clean and baked our clothes in ovens to kill the fleas. And they shaved our heads for the lice, and slapped on tar for the ringworm of those who'd got it. Then they weighed us, measured us and took our names, and a surgeon came to weed out those so obviously crippled that even the Navy wouldn't have them. For this examination, we were lined up stark naked in the freezing cold, and the hulk's crew sneering at the wretched state of us, with our white skulls and running noses.

After that we were left alone for a while and I got my clothes back (minus all my money, naturally) and we got an issue of food and grog. I was some days on the slop-ship and I must say it was better than life on *Bullfrog*. They left you alone for one thing, provided you didn't try to escape. They had marines with muskets to shoot you if you did that.

Finally they broke us into groups for different ships. To my surprise, there was some haggling over me. A clerk said I was down for one ship and an elderly midshipman said I was for another. As far as I was concerned, I didn't care where I went, provided I could keep quiet and not be noticed. I was only waiting to be dragged off to the hangman at any minute. In the end, there was another trip round the harbour.

This time I was taken off in a smartly painted boat manned by eight muscular seamen dressed all alike: blue jackets over white shirts and trousers, with a black handkerchief knotted at the neck, and to finish, the round, black-glazed sailors' hats that look like flattened top hats. This was the cutter and crew out of H.M. Frigate *Phiandra*, and at the tiller, commanding eight prime tars and five pressed men, was Mr Midshipman Roston, twelve years old. I wondered at this child in charge of full-grown men, but in charge he was and squeaked out his orders with complete confidence.

"Give way!" says he sharply, and the tars threw their weight on the oars. They rowed beautifully and all together, with a sense of harmony about the thing. They were as different as could be from the press-gang or *Bullfrog*'s crew, and actually seemed to enjoy what they were doing. I studied them for a while, as the boat darted off into the mist that hung round the anchorage. But I was too full of my own troubles to pay much attention to them or anything else.

Eventually, I noticed a strange sound. A booming, rumbling noise like a heavy wagon going over a wooden bridge, but without the hoofbeats. To any seaman it was a sound to prickle the hairs on the back of his neck, because, somewhere nearby, a ship was running out its guns. Then we shot out of the mist and there was the ship, *Phiandra*, a thirty-two-gun frigate of 700 tons. Her port-lids were up and a line of round muzzles glared at us. I could even see the eyes of the gun-captains squinting at me over their sights, as they knelt to take their aim. If she'd been about to fire, then that would have been my last sight on earth. But here in Portsmouth, this could only be a drill and it was. The ship was anchored without her topmasts and men were hanging over the bow with brushes and paint pots busily at work.

From inside the ship came the coughing and gasping of exhausted men, until a volley of orders set them all moving again to haul the guns back in. Through the gun-ports, I saw gnarled fists, straining limbs and fierce brown faces running with sweat. It was a vision of the inferno; a totally alien world that I wanted no part of. Unfortunately, it wanted me.

An instant later we bumped alongside and Mr Roston was screeching at us to make lively. Marines with muskets and bayonets herded us on to the quarterdeck where a committee was waiting to receive us: the ship's family of specialists, from carpenter to cooper, waiting to see what the Press had brought. It was all very businesslike, with the Purser at a trestle-table with ledgers, pen and ink, to record what they got. He was a stringy old Scot with a shabby-genteel air and an old-fashioned wig like a clergyman's. McFee, his name was.

But what stood out was none of these things. It was the officer in charge that caught the eye. Mr Williams, the First Lieutenant. He was something special. A man in his mid thirties, only of average size, but intensely handsome, with fair skin, black hair and movements like a dancer or an athlete, beautiful to watch. He put heart into the pressed men instantly, laughing and joking and slapping us on the back, while always letting us know that no liberties were to be taken. He had the same magic that Nelson had.

"Step up there, first man!" says he, and my friend of the scraped knee shuffled forward with bowed shoulders.

"Name?" says the Purser.

"Norris Polperro, sir," says he, and instinctively gave that peculiar salute that identifies a sailor, knuckling his brow and stamping with the right foot.

"Aha!" cries the Lieutenant. "Here's a real seaman. Thank God there's one among us!" He said it with such enthusiasm that Norris swelled with pride, straightened his back like a guardsman, and the misery of capture dropped off him like an old coat. "And what ships have you served in, m'lad?"

"*Alcide*, '74, under Sir Andrew Douglas, and *Hebe*, frigate, under Cap'n Sir Alexander Hood . . . I was Cap'n of the maintop under Sir Alexander, sir . . . "

"And so you shall be again! Mr McFee . . . enter this man as Cap'n of the maintop!" Mr Williams turned to the rest of us. "And are there any more like this among you?"

The smile was dazzling, and those who were seamen crowded forward. Even I, nonsensically, was searching my memory for any traces of seafaring experience with which to please him. I had none, of course, but I had something else.

As my turn came, McFee peered at me thoughtfully. Even with my shaven skull I didn't look quite like the rest. He offered me the pen.

"Sign your name here," says he and I dashed off my name with a flourish . . . beneath a line of roughly scratched crosses.

"Aha!" says Mr McFee. "A scholar, as I thought." He looked up and beamed at me. "One for my department, Mr Williams, with your permission?" But the Lieutenant glanced at my signature, looked me over, and put a hand on my shoulder like a father.

"What?" says he. "A fine big lad like this? To be no more than a clerk? You'll be a seaman, won't you!" I saw the daggers flashing from McFee's eyes at this rebuff and tried to think what was best. Even then I knew all about pursers. It was the only aspect of the Navy I'd ever taken an interest in, and for good sound reasons. The Purser was master of every consumable aboard ship. His opportunities for legal and illegal profit were legendary. Why, the rum alone was worth a fortune in graft, not to mention the tobacco, candles and salt meat. And the Purser's clerks stood no watches. At night they slept snug in their hammocks while common seamen were turned out to lay aloft in a howling gale. If my wits hadn't been dulled there could have been no question as to which offer to accept.

But all I could think of was avoiding trouble, so I took the offer of the more powerful man — the Lieutenant.

"I'll be a seaman please, sir!" says I, and McFee sneered in fathomless contempt.

"Good fellow!" says Williams. "I'll rate you a landsman in the afterguard, in my division where I'll keep my eye on you. And I'll enter you into Sammy Bone's mess. Follow him and you'll not go far wrong. Off you go now."

"Yes, sir," says I, as a heavy hand seized my elbow and a bosun's mate propelled me across the quarterdeck and down the companionway to the maindeck, all at the run.

In the kindly way of seafaring folk, he lost no opportunity to begin my instruction into their little ways.

"Lissen, you bleedin' farmer!" he spat into my ear. "Say 'Aye aye sir' to a bleedin' officer! Or even your bleedin' mother won't know you again, you bleeder! D'you hear?" With the barest hesitation I managed, "Aye aye sir."

"Huh!" says he.

Then we were picking our way down the choreographed pandemonium of a working gundeck. It ran bow to stern, the length of the ship, but there was barely room for all the gear crammed in. A heaving machine of men, iron and timber, jam-packed with not a place to set foot that wasn't occupied with some piece of tackle or other.

My guardian stopped by a young officer who was bawling in anguish at one of the gun-crews. He was a short man with a big head and ungainly limbs. He had on a round hat, like a common seaman, and was leaping alive with energy. This was Mr Seymour, the Second Lieutenant and master of the ship's guns. He was intent upon one particular gun-captain, who was stood shifting uneasily behind the breech of his piece, with the firing lanyard dangling from his fist.

"No. No. *NO!*" cries the Lieutenant, stamping his foot in a passion and swinging at the man's head with his speaking-trumpet. "Handsomely, you cock-eyed lubber! Get away! Get away, rot you!" He elbowed the man aside and grabbed the lanyard. "Like this!" says he, crouching to sight down the barrel. "Then . . . handsomely!" He tugged the lanyard and the firelock gave a shower of sparks and a whoof of powder. "Do it wrong again and the next balls rammed down that barrel'll be *yours!*"

The man grinned uneasily and the Lieutenant turned to me and the bosun's mate.

"And what do you want, rot you?"

"New hand aboard, Mr Seymour, sir," says the bosun's mate, saluting. "Sent down to drill with his mates . . . Sammy Bone's gun, sir."

"Well? Well? Get on then! Number eight gun, down there." He pointed at a nearby gun, then something caught his eye and he broke off in a fury and dashed up the deck. "Enemy on the *quarter* I said! You're training on the *bow*, you mob of Frenchmen, God rot you!" He kicked one man violently up the backside and swiped another round the ears with his speaking-trumpet.

"Ah . . . " sighs the bosun's mate, nodding in utmost approval, "that's the boy to make them bleeders jump!" Then he took me to number eight gun. "Sammy?" says he. "This here's for your mess. Mr Williams's orders." He jerked his thumb at me.

A skinny little man turned to look at me. He was naked to the waist and shining with sweat and his eyes were bright and black on either side of a sharp, ferrety nose. His hair was snow white and he looked old. He glared at me.

"Well, don't just stop stood there!" says he in a strong

Yorkshireman's accent. "Take hold o' this bastard tackle and haul! We're two men short here, you . . . "

And out tumbled the most amazing stream of inventive abuse that the mind of man could conceive. Compared to Sammy Bone, Lieutenant Spencer of the Impress Service was but a choir boy playing with his first dirty word.

So I took hold and hauled. All my natural inclinations turn me away from physical exertion. There's no profit in it. But Nature has made me big and strong and that day I was glad of it. I hauled and hauled till everything ached and I sweated like the others. I was dazed in my mind and entirely happy to melt in with the rest and do as I was told.

Later on I was sent into the depths of the ship to be issued with slops from the damp mysteries of the Purser's store. McFee was there with his Steward, busy with lists and papers, and the pair of them ignored me for a sufficient time to impress their great importance upon me. The clerk was a little plump man by the name of Danny Smith, with a piggy round nose and lips like a woman's. He turned my stomach over, and I kept as far back from him as possible, but McFee seemed to like him well enough.

Finally McFee condescended to notice me.

"Well, Smith," says he, "here's a gentleman as considers himself too good for the Purser's department. What do you think of him?"

"Gallows-fodder I shouldn't wonder, Mr McFee," says the other, and they proceeded to make a spiteful dissection of my appearance, like the pair of old women that they were.

Mr Williams's insistence that I should be a seaman had made a fine enemy for me in the Purser, but I left his presence on that occasion, staggering under the pile of goods he'd given me. This included a complete uniform such as I'd seen the boat's crew wearing, also canvas to make a pair of hammocks (one for spare while the other was washing), a blanket, a straw mattress, a wooden platter, a spoon and a cheap horn mug. Of course, the cost of all this came out of my pay so nobody was being generous. And I later found that every single item had something wrong with it through careful selection by Mr McFee; the opening salvo in the private war that the two of us would fight.

Then I blundered off, up and down ladders, to find Sammy Bone's mess. A frigate is too small a thing to get lost in, but it was confusing enough, with its warren of bulkheads and forbidden places with marine sentries. The Purser's store was on the orlop: the lowest deck, actually *below* the water line. Above that was the lower deck, lit during the day by gratings set in the gundeck above, but otherwise completely enclosed. The gundeck (also called the maindeck) was open to the skies in the waist, but decked over by the quarterdeck at the stern and by the fo'c'sle at the bow. The whole ship was about 120 feet long and 30 feet wide at its greatest dimensions. And 250 men were crammed into that to live, work and fight.

I found the lower deck soon enough and found Sammy and his messmates waiting. There were five of them, sat on benches round a legless table fastened to the hull by a hinge. At the inboard end it hung by a rope. Another five or six like it hung on each side of the deck like wooden ghosts of the guns on the deck above. All the messes seemed to have been given time to receive their new men. No officers were present and there was conversation up and down the deck. It seemed a peaceful place.

Norris Polperro had also been sent to Sammy's mess and he was already there, sat at the table with the others as if he'd been there all his life. He was a seaman and they'd taken him in as one of their own. But I was different and they knew it. They stared up at me with frank suspicion in their hard, peasant faces. Like most sailors, they were illiterate, ignorant and superstitious. We had not a thing in common other than youth. They all looked my age or perhaps a little older.

That is except for Sammy Bone, who was different from the others in every way absolutely. He was the oldest man in the ship and his intellect was needle sharp. Given any reasonable start in life, who knows where he would have risen? As it was, he was captain of the mess and the others took their lead from him. He stared at me without expression.

"Now then," says he, "sit down and I'll read you the

rules. Put your dunnage there." I unloaded my bundle and looked at him as I sat. He was a tiny man, no more than five feet tall. I saw that I was being judged.

"First, you're only here because Mr Williams says so. He says you're a bit of a gentleman and we should be glad to have you, but we chooses our own messmates aboard this ship, and we heaves out them as we don't care for. So if you find you ain't welcome, you go and see Mr Williams again. Aside from that, we keeps this mess clean and we likes to make a show." He indicated a line of pegs set in the ship's side above the table. They supported a row of polished pots and pans. "You ain't no seaman, so I'll tell you what a mess means. We stick together: messmate before shipmate, shipmate before marine . . . marine before dog! Understand?"

After that, he showed me where to stow my gear (there was another row of pegs for that, with canvas "trugs" hanging from them, one for each man's goods). Then he fell silent and they all stared at me.

I had no idea how to strike the right chord with them. I was thick-headed and very tired. I can't remember what I said but I wasn't well received and I was set fair for a bad start with my new mates.

Most of them got up and wandered off, leaving me and Sammy at the mess table. I had nowhere else to go and he sat and watched me. Finally I thought that I might as well wear the clothes I'd been given. After *Bullfrog* and the slop-ship, my own clothes were thoroughly ruined.

Awkwardly, I pulled off the remains of my shirt and fumbled with the new one.

"What's this?" says Sammy Bone. He was staring at me for some reason that I couldn't make out. My mind was so dulled that I had actually forgotten Bosun Dixon and his starter. So when Sammy came round for a look at my back and shoulders I couldn't think what he was doing.

He cursed and grumbled a lot, and suddenly grew more friendly. He even lent me a canvas bag to put my goods into.

"Here's a trug for you, mate," says he. "Just you let me have it back when you can. And don't worry, there's no starting, hardly, in this ship and only those get flogged who stand in need of it."

I believe he meant it kindly but the mention of flogging did nothing to put my mind at ease. I wanted nothing more to do with the Navy's addiction to corporal punishment. Unfortunately, I was not able to avoid it.

Chapter 8

This foul deed has ignited the patriotism of our people!
(From a special edition of "The Polmouth Monitor",
Wednesday 13th February 1793.)

*

The Bosun cursed from the bottom of his soul as the cart jolted over the cobbles. Every bump was agony to the suppurating punctures in his buttocks. He'd served in the Indies and he'd seen what happened to men bitten by snakes, but even they hadn't suffered like this. By God they hadn't!

The cart lurched round the corner of Mill Lane and into St Luke's Square. They rattled past the Guildhall and the church and headed for the Town Hall. Across the square, on the Town Hall steps, was a great crowd of people. Instantly a pang of fright drove the pain away. The Bosun knew very well what the mob might do to a press-gangsman caught on his own.

"Avast there!" he cried and, snatching the reins from the driver, he pulled the horse to a stop. Outside the Town Hall, heads turned and fingers pointed. A chatter of voices arose.

"Gimme them ribbons!" said the carter. "I got my orders from Mr Pendennis!"

"Damn your orders," said the Bosun. "Them swabs'll have my guts for garters!"

"No they won't," said the carter, "not today. They'll not touch you . . . Look at 'em." The Bosun looked and let go the reins.

"See?" said the carter and cracked his whip. The cart set off again and the Bosun groaned in pain.

Sure enough, the crowd opened to let them through and nobody raised a finger against the Bosun. There were no jeers, no waving of fists, and nothing was thrown. If he'd not known it was impossible, the Bosun would have sworn they were friendly.

"God save the King!" yelled a voice.

"Aye!" they roared.

"God save our Navy!" cried another and there was a fierce yell of agreement. The Bosun's head swum in amazement. They were helping him down and thumping him on the back as he passed through the crowd!

Inside the Town Hall, officials stood around as if

waiting for something. They whispered to each other and looked at him with strange expressions on their faces. Then silence fell as Mr Nathan Pendennis bore down upon him with grave and ponderous bearing.

"Sir," said Pendennis, "inauspicious as our first meeting was, I extend the friendship and comfort of the city of Polmouth at this fell moment," and he held out his hand. Nervously, the Bosun took it.

"Aye aye, sir," he said. He didn't know what the hell was going on, but you couldn't go far wrong by saying that. Pendennis saw the Bosun's mystified face and frowned.

"Surely, sir, you are not unaware . . . ?" he said, and he glared at the carter standing behind the Bosun. "Has he not been told?" he said, and the carter twitched in sudden guilt.

"No sir, your honour, sir. I thought he knew."

"Hmm . . . " said Pendennis. He took the Bosun by the arm and led him towards a side room. Three men stood at the door, two civilians and an Army officer. He introduced them to the Bosun. "Colonel Morris from the garrison, Mr Richards the surgeon, and Mr Granby of the 'Monitor'. We have, of course, sent word to the Naval authorities at Portsmouth."

"Aye aye, sir," said the Bosun, embarrassed in this exalted company.

"Sir, you must summon your courage," said Pendennis. "Never in all my years as a magistrate have I seen such a thing. One hears of the like in London, but not here in Polmouth." Opening the door, he led the way forward and the Bosun gulped as he saw what they'd got in there. Laid on a table, toes up and arms by his sides, was Lieutenant John Spencer. His clothes were wet and one shoe was missing. He looked peaceful except that his throat had been cut from ear to ear by a long stroke from a sharp blade, slicing to the bone and all but separating head from body. The Bosun staggered and they found him a chair.

"Sir, I must ask you to make formal identification," Pendennis said.

"Aye aye sir," said the Bosun. "That's him: Lieutenant Spencer."

"Damn the French!" said Colonel Morris, stepping forward, and the Bosun blinked at him.

"It is the Colonel's view," explained Pendennis, "that this is the work of French agents smuggled ashore to work mischief."

"Aye aye, sir," said the Bosun.

"What else can it be?" said Morris. He was one of the "light infantry" school, deeply impressed by the American wars and what could be achieved by initiative. He and the surgeon had examined the victim carefully.

"See for yourself!" he said, pointing at the corpse. "These are not the wounds of honourable combat! They struck him a coward's blow from behind to stun him, then cut his throat as he lay helpless on his back. Who but damned Frenchmen would do that?"

"The body was found this morning, in the harbour," said Pendennis. "Presumably they hoped to hide it."

"They shall not escape!" said Granby of the "Monitor", "This foul deed has ignited the patriotism of our people!"

"Aye aye, sir," said the Bosun. He looked at his dead officer and sighed as he bade a last farewell to the guinea he'd been promised.

Chapter 9

I joined *Phiandra* on 17th February when she was busy
fitting out for a cruise. She had most of her crew aboard
but was still awaiting her captain and it was not until the
27th that she finally sailed from Portsmouth, so I had ten
days to get used to the ship and my messmates in the
easy conditions of riding at anchor in a harbour.

I had accepted my lot for the moment, and was
kept so busy with Lieutenant Williams driving us all
to make ready for sea, that I had little time for
pondering over my recent adventures. So I learned
some of my duties as a member of number eight
gun-crew and got to know my messmates as individuals. There were six of us: Sammy Bone, Thomas
Slade, Jem Turner, Norris Polperro, myself, and Johnny
Basford who came aboard the day after I did. Of the
six, Norris and I were pressed men and the others

volunteers. All were seasoned seamen except myself and Johnny.

He was a strange creature, with round, silly eyes and an India-rubber face. He had been a farm hand before he ran off to sea to escape from his employer, one Farmer Basford of whom he had lived in terror. As they say in the countryside, "he had some holes in his thatch". Quite a number of them in my opinion. He didn't know his age or where he was born, or his proper name:

"Name?" says Mr McFee, seated behind his table, when Johnny came before the receiving committee.

"Johnny . . . " says Johnny.

"Johnny *what?*" says the Purser.

"He-he-he . . . " says Johnny nervously.

"Hmm," says McFee, looking at what was before him. I suspect he had dealt with the likes of Johnny before. The Navy had to take what was offered in 1793.

"I see. Then where do you come from, my man?"

"Farmer Basford do let I sleep in the barn, please your honour . . . so please don't you tell he . . . "

"Yes, quite," says McFee, scribbling away. "John Basford. I have entered you as John *Basford*. Do you understand?"

"He-he-he . . . " says Johnny. He did understand and was hugely pleased. He had a proper name at last. He never did learn to hate McFee as much as the rest of us. He was happy as long as he was fed and watered and nobody was being actively cruel to him at that moment.

Johnny and I, then, were the only landsmen in the mess. Norris, of course, had served before and was a fisherman by trade, and Sammy, Jem and Thomas were real old tarpaulins with a rolling bandy-legged walk and a pigtail worn doubled up all the week and long on Sundays. In fact, I say "old" but, Sammy apart, my mates were young. Norris was perhaps thirty and the others were all in their early twenties (though it was hard to tell with Johnny). This was typical of lower-deck hands. What with accidents, tropical fevers, the rheumatism and ruptures from the unending heavy lifting, sailormen did not last long. Some even managed to get themselves killed by the enemy, but that never was the main risk: ten men died of disease or mishap for every one who fell in action.

Sammy was an exception. He said that since there was nothing more left of him than skin and bone, then there was nothing for a fever to fasten on to. He must have been well over fifty, for he'd served in the seven years war and sailed in the fleet that took Wolfe to Quebec, and he looked even older with his brown, wrinkled face and white hair.

Normally such a man as Sammy would have been a Petty Officer, a Bosun perhaps, for his vast experience. But Sammy was Sammy and there was nobody like him. His own behaviour balked any attempt to promote him higher than gun-captain, though at that he excelled like no other man on God's ocean. And he was different

from all the others in his quickness of mind. For let me
tell you, that nobody who hasn't lived with them as I
have, could ever believe the absolute stubborn ignorance
of our lower-deck seamen.

Now don't misunderstand me. They knew the sea and
ships all right. Put them on a twisting deck in a black
night with icy water coming aboard by the wagon-load,
and they'd instinctively run to the right rope among the
spider-work of the rigging, and once there they'd haul
it, splice it, belay it or whatever, in double-quick time.
But that was all they knew or wanted to know.

To begin with, I was the only member of our mess
who could properly read or write. Norris could make a
show of picking through the large print of a newspaper,
but you wouldn't have called him a scholar. The others
were as ignorant of letters as an African savage, indeed
they were ignorant of the whole world of mankind's
written knowledge. Instead they cherished superstitions
that were rooted like mountains and beyond the reach
of argument.

My mates believed in an astonishing pantheon of
wonders: ghosts, mermaids, the sea-serpent and the
kraken. Norris thought that rocks could move to take
out the bottom of a ship.

"How can a rock move?" I asked. "It's against the
laws of nature."

"They bloody moves 'cos I seen 'em move!" says
Norris, angrily. "I seen one move when we was driven

in off Hore Stone in '87, in my dad's boat. The bugger moved under the old boat and broke her open and that was the end of my dad and two uncles! My own father! Now d'you see?"

"Aye!" said all the others and I had the sense to hold my tongue. I had to live among these men and had no wish to be thought a fool.

They believed in these things and many more, and believed with the faith of a Spanish Jesuit, except that I cannot really believe they were actually Christians in the real sense of the word. They were pagans, like the Greeks and Romans, believing in dozens of little gods and demons. They gave respect to our Chaplain's sermons on Sunday because the Rev. Brown's god was clearly a powerful one, but *He* was not *God* to them.

But the best thing that I learned about them was their devotion to strong drink, and how this could be turned to my great advantage. Indeed, it was the very making of me as a seafarer. The ration of drink for seamen was either a gallon of beer, or a bottle of wine, or half a bottle of rum, per man, per day. It was the light of their lives and whatever else might fail, the Navy took damn good care that they got it *every* day, 'cos God help the Navy if they didn't! We got it in two "whacks", one at dinner time and one at tea time. The allowance was vastly too much for me, but the tars guzzled it down and begged for more.

"Give us half your grog now, mate, and you can have

all mine tomorrow," was about the long and short of it. Here, all unexpected, was an opportunity for trading. At first I made little arrangements with my messmates. In exchange for grog, Sammy embroidered *Phiandra* on my hatband, as required by Lieutenant Williams for smartness, and which I could not do, and Norris made me a pair of nettles to sling my hammock by. But this was only a start, and soon I had other messes in my debt and was dealing on a large scale. Within a few days I was converting my credit into tobacco, a commodity which would keep, and which served as currency on the lower deck.

This won the approval of my messmates. They loved it and thought I was no end of a clever fellow, which was as well for they were a vital part of my business. Without their help I'd never have been able to collect my debts from the hardened, leathery characters I was dealing with. Fortunately, it was wonderful how persuasive my mates could be when gathered around a tar who was reluctant to part with his baccy ration. So I shared my profits with them and together we enjoyed more of life's little comforts than any other mess in the ship.

You'll have noticed I used a very odd word just now: I said I *shared*. This was because in Sammy Bone's mess there was no question of anyone having more or less than anyone else. Sammy's attitude to this was simple. If he'd found six golden guineas he'd have thought — "Here's a piece of luck! One for me and one for each of the lads" — It wasn't that he'd have *considered* keeping the lot and then thought better of it, because the thought of keeping the lot would never have entered Sammy's mind. Now it ain't natural for me to give away what I've worked for, but I was lonely and I needed to be accepted. So as long as I was in Sammy's mess, I shared my profits with my mates (enough to keep them happy, anyway).

The result of all this was that my life took the most wonderful turn for the better. I had friends again and I had the respect of those around me. Sammy, in particular, took a great liking to me. The one person who didn't like me was the Purser, Mr McFee. He still seemed to be cherishing the slight I'd given by choosing to be a seaman, and was directing his malice at my messmates as well as at me. Anything issued by him to our mess was the worst available. My business activities enabled us to keep ahead by buying from the other messes, but it was galling and I couldn't see why he should have taken against me so strong.

"What d'you expect, you daft bugger?" says Sammy when I mentioned this. "McFee paid £400 to the Victualling Board to get the Purser's berth, and now here's you setting up in opposition! Any road, what d'you expect from a Purser?" My mates laughed at this, for all seamen hated the Purser like poison. He wasn't any sort of Sea Officer, but simply the ship's monopolist tradesman who supplied their needs and stole the best of everything for himself. Long experience had taught Sammy to expect no better.

But within a week of my joining *Phiandra*, McFee overdid it and even Sammy was annoyed. One dinner time, Norris came back from the galley with our boiled beef and biscuit in a pair of mess-kids. He was red-faced with anger.

"That Smith!" says he, dumping his load on our table. "That greasy, back-door usher! He was in the galley with the cook, close as God's curse to a whore's arse and whispering in his ear. He's done something with our dinner!"

We leaned over the mess-kids and Sammy opened the first. Inside was as fine a selection of dense, ancient ship's biscuit as could be imagined. Hand-picked every one, and flinty hard. Sammy took one on the flat of his left palm, and tried to break it by the usual method of hammering with the right elbow (nobody who valued his teeth tried to break a ship's biscuit by biting it).

"Sink me!" says he, looking at the invulnerable biscuit.

He opened the second mess-kid and his face twisted ugly in anger. "Right!" says he. "That's it now. Something's got to be done." We all peered in, and there floating on top of our meat, was a large, fresh rat, not five minutes dead, with its belly slit open and guts spilling out.

"Jacob!" says Sammy. "You buy us a proper dinner and Norris, heave this one over the side. It's that bastard McFee. Smith don't do nothing without he tells him."

We did as he said but had hardly sat down to our meal when McFee himself appeared. This was most unusual. When the hands were at dinner, with the Officers in the wardroom at the stern, McFee kept out of the way. He knew what the men thought of him and how little authority he had on his own. But here he came, along the deck with Smith waddling along behind. As they passed each mess, ribald remarks followed them like a wake. Meal time on the lower deck was never quiet, with two hundred seamen and thirty marines crammed into that narrow space, all shovelling and talking at once, but today the noise rose ever louder.

McFee ignored this and pressed on towards our mess. Sammy nudged me in the ribs. "He's come for a gloat. To see how we like boiled rat. Watch me lad and you'll learn something!"

Sammy was right. McFee slowed as he passed our table and he and Smith turned to us and sneered. This done, they continued towards the companionway leading to the gundeck above. I couldn't believe the petty spite of it. That two grown men should do this.

Then Sammy was on his feet and calling out.

"Mr McFee, sir! Mr McFee!" The tone was urgent and pleading and I was surprised to see Sammy bobbing up and down and knuckling his brow with every sign of respectful deference. McFee affected to ignore him but Sammy continued.

"Please sir, Mr McFee, sir, you're a Bible-read man sir, can I ask your opinion on a matter of Holy Scripture?"

Now that was clever. McFee considered himself pious and I'd seen him roaring out the hymns when the ship's company were mustered for church. That hooked him fair and square and he stopped at the foot of the companionway. Smith, taken unawares, blundered into him and every eye turned to Sammy Bone.

"Thing is, sir," says he, indicating the assembled hands with a sweep of the arm, "these here lads, being none of 'em scholars, is unable to read the blessed scriptures for themselves and would be obliged for your advice on a matter of religion . . . " McFee was deadly cautious, but so convincing was Sammy's earnest and open manner that he was held. Not only that but all around men were nodding as if disputes on scripture were the burning interests of the lower deck. The force of Sammy's personality held the whole crowd of us in spellbound silence.

"Well?" says McFee, squinting like a trapped weasel.

"Thing is, sir," says Sammy, "it seems as how Judas Iscariot, that damned heathen as betrayed our Lord, may he roast in hell . . . it seems as how he fathered a love-child." At this, McFee puffed up in all the superiority of his learning. He leered at Smith, who simpered like an old maid.

"What a remarkable piece of scholarship!" says he with withering scorn and growing more confident by the second.

"Aye, sir," says Sammy, positively radiating humble respect. "And knowing you to be a learned man, sir . . ." McFee nodded wisely and struck a condescending attitude. "We was wondering if you could tell us whether it was Judas himself, or was it his bastard . . . as was the Navy's first Purser?"

A moment's silence then the roar of laughter hit McFee like a three-decker's broadside. Men fell off their seats in convulsions and tears flowed down every face. They howled, bawled, cheered and thundered with their fists on the tables. All except Mr Smith, who by a mighty exercise of the toady's art, kept a straight face, and Sammy who sat down in quiet content.

I thought McFee would die of apoplexy. His face was white, his lips were black and froth spumed from the corners of his mouth. He stamped on his hat and shrieked about hangings, floggings and haulings under the keel. But not a man paid any heed for they were crowding in to thump Sammy's back and offer him their grog.

But common seamen do not humiliate warrant officers with impunity, not even Pursers, and Lieutenant Williams appeared with the other officers, to investigate what sounded to them like a riotous mutiny. The two Marine Lieutenants, Clerk and Howard, roused their men (laughing as they were, with all the rest) and sent them to support Mr Williams's authority.

McFee was so mad with anger that Smith had to lead him away, fussing and clucking like a hen with one chick.

The Purser was still raving on about death and mutilation as he went. Lieutenant Williams looked around, guessed what had happened and pointed at Sammy.

"That man!" says he yelling above the din. "Take him in charge!" And Sammy was taken off to be held in irons below. We laughed and cheered as he was taken but we didn't laugh next morning when Lieutenant Williams mustered the whole crew for his judgement on Sammy. We stood before the quarterdeck rail with the officers looking down on us backed by the marines drawn up with a glittering hedge of fixed bayonets. Sammy stood to one side, bare-headed, between the Bosun and his mates.

Lieutenant Williams stepped forward and raised a book, for all to see. It was his copy of the Articles of War. [This would be the George II, 1749 Articles of War: a list of thirty-six regulations forming the basis of Naval discipline, and consisting mainly of crimes and punishments. Some captains chose to read the whole list to their men each day, which practice can have done little to lift the spirits of the crew, since twenty of the regulations allowed the death penalty. S.P.]

"Article nineteen," says he, "deals with the uttering of seditious words. It says, 'if any person in, or belonging to, the Fleet shall utter any words of sedition or mutiny, he shall suffer Death or such other punishment as a Court Martial shall deem him to deserve.'" He paused to let this sink in. It meant quite simply that he could have Sammy Bone hanged if he felt so inclined. That was the price of Sammy's triumph over a ship's Officer. I looked at Sammy but could tell nothing from his expression. His life hung on Lieutenant Williams's next words.

After a dreadful silence prolonged to the last exquisite moment by Mr Williams, he spoke again.

"Mr Bone!" says he.

"Aye aye, sir," says Sammy.

"Mr Bone, you can either go forward for court martial, or take my punishment now. Which shall it be?" The reply was obvious.

"Your punishment, sir," says Sammy.

"So be it . . . Mr Bosun! Rig the gratings and give him three dozen."

Instantly the Bosun and his mates lashed a pair of heavy gratings to the larboard quarterdeck ladder, to form a sort of giant easel. Sammy's shirt was pulled off and he was secured to the upright grating, arms splayed out above his head. His back was thin and white and he looked very old.

A heavy dread settled on the ship as the savage ceremony took its course. Mr Shaw the Bosun produced his cat from a red baize bag and handed it to one of his mates. The Surgeon poked Sammy to see that he was fit, and all the colour drained from the faces of the young mids. The Surgeon nodded, Mr Williams nodded, and the two marine drummer boys beat a long roll.

Nathan Miller, bosun's mate, drew back his arm and laid on with all his might. Nine lengths of knotted log-line whistled through the air to land with a flat smack across Sammy's back. A grunt was driven from Sammy's lips by the force of the blow.

"One!" cries the Bosun, and Miller drew back his arm again . . . Smack! And red lines began to show on Sammy's back, flecked with drops of blood where the knots had bitten.

"Ahhh!" says someone in a sick faint and one of the drummers collapsed like a corpse and his drum boomed hollow on the deck. A moan arose from Johnny Basford standing near me and I saw that he was beside himself with horror, face in his hands and retching heavily. But the other drummer kept going and Miller delivered the whole sentence of thirty-six strokes. Before he was done Johnny had joined the drummer boy on the deck and I felt as if the sky was whizzing round me in circles. Sammy's back was raw meat and the deck was speckled red for ten feet all around.

But Sammy never cried out from first to last, and when they took him down, he stood up swaying slightly and blinked at Lieutenant Williams.

"Mr Bone," says the Lieutenant, "I do hope that I shall not have to flog you again this commission."

"No sir," says Sammy. "Won't be necessary again." Lieutenant Williams nodded in approval.

"Mr Bone," says he, "I congratulate you on your

accurate assessment of risk from first to last of this business."

"Aye aye, sir," says Sammy very carefully. Then the Surgeon took him off to attend to his back and we were dismissed. Later, Sammy was welcomed back in triumph to the lower deck, his credit raised still higher than it had been before. As for Mr McFee, he was incensed at the lightness of Sammy's punishment and even more so by Lieutenant Williams's remarks at the end of it, for he knew that the same offence against any other warrant officer would have seen Sammy at the end of a rope. In all truth nobody loved a Purser.

So he kept up his games with our food and other supplies. But aboard that ship, he was a figure of fun for ever after and even the Officers called him "Judas" behind his back. We all told Sammy how clever he'd been, but he didn't agree.

"Bah!" says he. "'Assessment of risk' be buggered! I thought it'd be a dozen. Or two at the most. Bleedin' officers; I think some of 'em *likes* to see a flogging."

Chapter 10

I have always thought it an error to place any reliance whatsoever in my little brother.
(From a letter of 24th February 1793, from Alexander Coignwood aboard *Phiandra* at Portsmouth, to Lady Sarah Coignwood at 14 Dulwich Square, London.)

*

Lady Sarah Coignwood was forty-seven years old. But nobody would have believed it. Her women friends would have said thirty-five and her men friends never considered the matter. When *they* thought about Lady Sarah, which they did frequently and with glazed eyes, their minds were on other things. Consequently she could have any man she wanted including His Royal Highness Prince George, heir to the throne of England.

She'd picked him out with the particular purpose of spiting his mistress-in-residence, Mrs Fitzherbert, since that lady had previously made it her business to remind London that Lady Sarah's husband was in trade, thus excluding Lady Sarah from the best society after years of working her way in. Consequently, reports of the fits and hysterics thrown by Mrs Fitzherbert when she learned that her beloved "Florizel" (her ridiculous name for him) was betraying her, came as a soothing balm to Lady Sarah's social check.

Also, at thirty-one the Prince was tall, handsome, and partial to older women. So for a while he'd been amusing in himself. But Lady Sarah found him spoilt and immature, with a pitifully simple range of physical desires. What's more he was growing fat and was morbidly sensitive about it. In fact he flew into a rage if anyone so much as mentioned fatness in his presence.

This proved useful, for when Lady Sarah tired of him she was able to get rid of him with a simple note. This was sent in response to a typically gushing invitation from the Prince which she read aloud to her friends before reading them her own reply. Nobody laughed when they *heard* what she had written but they could hardly contain themselves when they saw it. It read:

Lady Sarah regrets that she is unable to accept any further invitations from the Prince of whales.

Every salon in London had the pun within an hour and all the wits of the day kicked themselves for not thinking of it, and many later claimed it as their own.

So ended the brief liaison with Prince George. But Lady Sarah never missed him for an instant. Casting aside a used lover was not the least hindrance to her life's work of indulging her greedy appetites. The only real check to that was the infuriating problem of debt. Over the years, she'd spent a vast amount of money in the fashionable centres of London and Bath. But since she *had* no actual money, everything had been on credit. Until recently this had been easy, as everyone assumed that on Sir Henry's death, she would inherit. But the old monster had been burning in hell nearly a month now, and the tradesmen were stirring. They were still polite but were beginning to present long and enormous bills.

These bills were the main, though not the only cause, for the filthy black anger that hung over Lady Sarah today. She cursed at the thought of them and paced up and down her expensively furnished salon in her expensive new house in Dulwich Square. Usually, the salon was her special delight, but not today. She'd sent away the usual hangers-on and there was no comfort in an empty room and she couldn't bear it a moment longer. She rang for a servant.

Instantly there came a scampering of feet and the door opened. As Lady Sarah had expected, it was Betty the new girl, fresh from the country with plump round limbs. Now of course, there could be no question of Lady Sarah's keeping *ugly* servants and, conversely had the girl been any serious competition to Lady Sarah, she'd not have stayed one second in the house. But Betty was a happy little creature with a golden smile that men were stupid enough to find appealing. And she *was* only sixteen.

Betty dropped a pretty curtsey, and carefully delivered the phrase she'd been taught.

"What is my Lady's pleasure?" she asked.

Her answer came quickly. In rapid succession Lady Sarah found fault with her, berated her, threatened to turn her out on the streets, slapped her face thoroughly and sent her away in tears.

Immediately Lady Sarah felt better and found a mirror to admire herself in. She adjusted the cascade of little curls from the high Grecian coiffure, and smiled at her gown. War or no war, she was ahead of the town with the next Paris fashion and it suited her very well. Translucent muslin with bare arms and a half-exposed bosom might not be *comfortable* in February, but what was comfort compared with fashion?

Later, when her son Victor glided into the room, she was quite cheerful.

"Dear boy!" she said and kissed him. "Sit beside me and tell me everything." The dear boy fiddled with his cane with one hand and his fancy buttons with the other. He hadn't much to tell and all of it was bad.

"So," his mother said, when he'd finished. "You had no more success with the lawyers than I had."

"No," he said. "*In principle* the 1775 Will might be overturned since it denies us our rights as the natural heirs. And naming a bastard as the heir is an affront to decency which *might* bring our case more sympathy in the courts. But it would be a long hard fight and . . . " he paused.

"*And*," continued Lady Sarah, "none of them will take up the case without sight of ready money."

"No," he said. "Our debts are public knowledge."

"Well," she said, pausing deliberately to observe the effect of her words, "it is as well that I have another son to rely upon." At once, Victor's weak little face twisted with envy and malice.

"Damn him!" he said. "Alexander! You always did favour him over me."

"Not at all, my love," she said, kissing his hand and stroking his hair, "I love you *both* . . . sometimes one, and sometimes the other." Victor snatched his hand away and she laughed.

"Never mind, Victor," she said, "I received a letter today from your brother, my dear Alexander, aboard his ship *Phiandra* at Portsmouth. Wouldn't you like to read it?" She picked up the letter from a nearby table and waved it just out of his reach. She'd always played them off against each other and never tired of tormenting them, especially Victor who always rose so easily to the bait.

"Give it here!" he said.

"Ask properly," she said.

"*Please*," he begged, and she let him have it. He read the letter hungrily and when he put it down his eyes were round in wonderment.

"Merciful heavens!" he said. "The words are guarded but do they mean what I think they mean?" Lady Sarah sneered.

"Would you rather he put it in plain words for anyone to read?" she said.

"But this is . . . *murder*!" said Victor, dropping his voice. "He incited the Captain of the *Bullfrog* to murder the Brat, and he's actually killed this press-gang Lieutenant with his own hand! My God, we'll all hang!" He fell back in the divan, trembling and dabbing at his brow with a laced handkerchief.

Lady Sarah looked at him and frowned. With Victor it was always hard to tell whether he was truly in the grip of an emotion or simply enjoying the pretence of it. Probably even Victor didn't know. And for all this display of feebleness she knew that he could be inch for inch as ruthless as Alexander when he chose to be.

"What else could he do?" she said, finally. "How else can we get rid of the Brat? Do you think he'll give up his inheritance for the asking? Do you think we should simply have gone to him and proposed that we take the fortune while he grinds his life away in trade?" Victor smiled.

"That's better," said his mother. "Strong action was

needed and it's hardly Alexander's fault if one agent failed him and another had a loose tongue. Alexander did what was necessary. He's got the Brat into his power, into his own ship. And a ship is a dangerous place, especially in time of war: with luck a French cannonball may do the thing for us!"

She leaned across and began to kiss his cheek, very gently, which she knew he liked. Victor sighed in contentment. She continued for a while and then, when Victor was nicely relaxed, she took the letter and made a play of reading it. She whispered softly to him.

"Have you seen how cleverly Alexander predicts your failure with the lawyers?"

Chapter 11

Sammy was tough as an old boot and recovered fast. Perhaps his long survival as a seaman was explained by unusual powers of recuperation. Either that or it was the fresh food we got in harbour that helped him. The one who suffered most from Sammy's flogging was Johnny Basford. He had a deep horror of flogging and went moping around for several days, whining and mumbling about his Pa and the dreadful beltings he'd received as a child. Usually, even if you asked him, he knew nothing about any parents he might have had, so it was a singular thing for the memories to be hauled out of his mind.

But soon enough, Johnny and all the rest of us had no time for moping, for on the 24th the Captain came aboard and preparations for sea were driven to a new and furious pace. We got the warning early that day when

John Drake

a new Lieutenant came out from the shore. He was a
grey, dowdy little man in early middle age. He puffed
with effort as he clambered over the side. Norris and I
were told to haul his sea-chest aboard from the boat that
had brought him out, so we saw him present himself to
Lieutenant Williams.

"Lieutenant Haslam come aboard, sir. I'm to be third.
Beg to report that Captain Bollington is arrived in
Portsmouth and resolved to sleep aboard tonight . . . "

"Damnation!" says Lieutenant Williams, and a look
of annoyance crossed his face. He was pondering on a
thousand things not yet ready. "Wouldn't you think he'd
give a fellow more time?" says he, and over the next few
hours he drove the crew into a pandemonium of effort,
scouring and polishing to make the ship fit for the imminent arrival of the almighty one.

When the great moment came, the entire ship's
company was mustered in its best clothes, gleaming and
scrubbed, with the ship in a glittering state of cleanliness
and a stairway with whitened ropes and shining brass
stanchions, rigged on the shoreward side so that the
Captain should not have to scramble aboard like a mortal.

"Boats putting out from shore, Mr Williams!" cries
the masthead and those with telescopes raised them as
one, like marines giving a volley. Then we stood in silence
and waited. Sammy had told me all about captains and
I knew what thoughts were in his mind.

"They can break you with their slightest whim. Some

won't have smoking and some won't let women aboard. And some flogs for spitting, or cussing, or just for being the slowest man at drill — same for the officers too — I've known a captain torment a young gentleman unmerciful 'cos the lad's father did him a bad turn years ago." And so we wondered what was coming until there came a bumping of boats alongside and THE MAN came up the ladder to a long squeal of Bosun's pipes from Mr Shaw and his mates. Every living thing in the ship solemnly raised its hat and Captain Bollington swept off his own in respect of the one thing present that was more important than himself: the ship.

He was a splendid sight, from the gold of his epaulettes to the gold of his shoe buckles. His uniform was beautiful and his linen snowy white. He was in his forties with a dark-tanned face, grey hair and blue eyes that darted six ways at once with intense interest as he ran the rule over his new command.

"Welcome aboard, sir!" says Lieutenant Williams, bowing politely, but the dignity of the moment was spoiled by the arrival on board of the Captain's suite of followers and place-men. In rough order of precedence, these were Mr Golding the Sailing Master, Mr Midshipman Percival-Clive, the Captain's clerk, his cook, his servant, and his band of musicians. These were half a dozen Sicilian dagos, waving their arms and gabbling (being foreigners and in the Captain's personal service, they were excused flogging and fighting).

When Lieutenant Williams had been introduced to
those worthy of that honour, the Captain came to the
quarterdeck rail and glared intently at the crew, drawn
up in the splendid uniformity of our *Phiandra* togs, on
the splendid neatness of the gleaming gundeck.

"Hmm!" says he, and nodded. "Well enough, Mr
Williams. You appear to know your business well
enough." Then he read us his commission from their
Lordships of the Admiralty (which ceremony made him
legally our master) and launched into a passionate speech
that reminded me of what the press-gang Bosun had
said on the night I was took. He damned the French
comprehensively for the bloody-handed, bloody-minded,
garlic-breathing, greasy, atheistical, regicidal revolution-
aries that they were — God's own truth, every word of
it: couldn't have put it better myself — then he thumped
the rail and waved his fist and roared that *Phiandra* shall
become the finest gunnery ship in the Navy, and may
God and all His angels just help the man who stands in
his way! And he declared that his sole ambition was to
smash, burn or sink everything French.

At a well-prepared sign from Mr Williams, we gave
him three cheers for this. Then, if you please, with us
in our Sunday best, he had the guns run out for drill
and with Mr Seymour at his elbow, came round personally to see how each crew performed. All of which most
wonderfully delighted the crew. There was intense relief
that Captain Bollington had no dangerous views on such

vital matters as spitting, cussing, baccy or women, and if he had a screw loose about gunnery, then nobody minded. He certainly was obsessed with guns. Between his arrival on board and the 27th when we set sail, tons of extra powder and shot were crammed aboard, paid for out of Captain Bollington's own pocket for the live-firing practice that he set so much store by. He even brought aboard a pair of long bronze guns for use as bow chasers. These were his own property, bored out for special accuracy at Bolton's ironworks in Soho, who also provided a quantity of special round-shot to go with them, smoother and rounder than regulation shot.

The actual moment of getting under way on the 27th was impressive. *Phiandra's* crew was still learning, but with a core of experienced men and with over two hundred hands to the work, the whole great machine of whirring blocks, humming lines and huge grinding spars, shook out its sails and heeled to the wind in seconds. I'd seen merchantmen put out from Polmouth many times, but that had been a slow matter, with one sail at a time spread to the wind. It was nothing like the thundering cascade of canvas as a man-o-war lets go every sail at once. The transition from the naked hulk to the rushing ship under its cloud of sails was a sight to see. My only regret was that I was seeing it as a participant and not a spectator.

We were bound for St Helens in the lee of the Isle of Wight to join a convoy and the ship's company was kept busy for hours trimming all to rights before lines were coiled down and we were sent to dinner.

However, not many of us wanted to eat that day. We were at sea for the first time in weeks, and it was a cold February day, with the big grey waves leading the ship in a sickening dance. The mids and the ship's boys were already hanging over the side and even some of the seasoned tars were looking green about the gills. Of my mates, only Sammy Bone was completely happy.

"Feeling the motion, lads?" says he to our mess. When nobody replied he produced a leather pouch and set it on the table.

"Oh no!" groans Thomas Slade. "Not that . . . "

"Clap a hitch on your jawing tackle!" says Sammy nastily, and continued. "Now this, my lads, is 'the old matelot's cure for the *mal de mer*'." He undid the cord at the neck of the pouch and shook out the contents. "You ain't never seen this, have you, Jacob?" says he, smiling at me in a fatherly fashion. He picked up the object and dangled it before my nose. It was a leather thong, about a foot long, with a hideous gob of slimy gristle lashed to one end. My stomach turned merely from the look of it, and all my mates stared at me expectantly. "Now what you do is . . . you just swallow this . . . and when it's half way down, you haul it up again!"

I heaved from the uttermost depths of my stomach, over and over again, and Sammy nearly choked himself laughing. I suppose the joke is thousands of years old and the sailors of Athens told it to each other aboard their galleys, but it comes new to each fresh victim. The strange thing was that I felt better afterwards.

In a couple of weeks we'd joined the convoy and were under the command of Admiral of the Blue, Sir David Weston, flying his flag in the brand new ninety-gun second-rate, *Ponderous*. He had a dozen seventy-fours and an equal number of frigates to see the convoy safely out of range of French cruisers. There was even the chance that the French might try to intercept the convoy with a battle fleet, so there was every possibility of imminent action.

The convoy itself consisted of nearly a hundred merchantmen and they were stuffed with the produce of the northern manufactories and worth a fortune in prize money. Some were bound for Spain or Portugal and others for Gibraltar, but the centrepiece of the formation was a double row of big ships, some of them up to 1,200 tons that rolled proudly along with all the swagger of a line of battle. These were starting the long, two-year haul out to the East Indies and back. They were John Company's ships with the size and look of two-deckers and mounting something of a battery of guns. In reality they weren't half so impressive as they looked. They could fight Malay pirates and the like but not a real warship.

The Admiral's strategy was to keep his line-of-battle ships together, upwind of the convoy, in case of the appearance of a French fleet, and to encircle the whole great cluster with a cloud of nimble frigates which would be his eyes and ears and would see off the more likely threat of privateers. How well this worked I cannot say. The seventy-fours and the big Indiamen kept station well enough; but for the rest, as merchant masters will, they pleased themselves.

This meant a busy time for the frigates, with constant signals from the flagship to chase this ship or that back into line, and Captain Bollington bawling himself hoarse at skippers who could not or would not obey orders. When all else failed we showed our teeth and *made* them do as they were told, with our guns.

Thus the first roundshot I ever saw fired was aimed across the bows of another British ship, a Newcastle collier named *Mary Douglas*. To judge from the look on Captain Bollington's face, another five minutes' disobedience from that ship would have seen the next shot fired into its hull. There was little love lost between the Merchant and the Naval service.

This went on for days as the convoy lumbered out into the Bay of Biscay. My seasickness faded and, despite myself, I began to enjoy life. For Captain Bollington and the officers it was a terrible time of work, worry and bother but for the rest of us it was simply exciting: dashing up and down the slow lines of merchantmen, firing off guns and generally enjoying our speed and power. A grand life for a lad and no mistake.

As well as doing our duty as sheepdog, Captain Bollington found time for gun practice and we began to appreciate the true depth of his passion for gunnery. Live-firing with shotted guns took place every day, and although I had taken part in gun-drill before, the exercise was a wholly new matter when carried out at sea, when the great clumsy guns took on a life of their own and rolled with the plunging decks.

Phiandra's main battery consisted of eighteen-pounder guns, each weighing forty-eight hundredweight with the carriage, and measuring nine feet six in the barrel. They were all new guns picked by Captain Bollington for the longest-range accuracy that was to be had. With a six-pound charge of powder, the range of these guns at one degree of elevation was 600 yards to the first graze of the shot upon the water.

Naturally, the shot flew much further than this, hopping and skipping unpredictably across the waves without the least accuracy. As the elevation increased so did the range to the first graze, but so did the accuracy decrease. At maximum elevation, the range might have been a mile for all I know, but never in all my service did I see a ship's gun fired in such a nonsensical way: at maximum elevation there was no talk of accuracy, rather it was a matter of pure random chance as to where the shot might come down.

In any case, for practice and for real action, Mr Seymour always had our guns laid point blank. Contrary to what I thought, this does not mean "very close" but to level the gun at zero elevation so the shot would skim flatly across the water to its target. That way there was no need to judge distance. Within its point blank range, what a gun pointed at, got hit – in theory, at least. And for our eighteen pounders, that range was 300 yards.

The guns were arranged in two rows, one to larboard and one to starboard running the length of the gundeck. They were numbered in pairs from fore to aft and one full gun-crew of ten men had charge of a pair. Our crew, Sammy's crew, manned the eighth pair back from the bow, and normally we'd fight one or the other gun. In the event of our being engaged on both sides at once, then each gun would be served by half the crew. Lieutenant Seymour was in charge of the gundeck with Lieutenant Haslam as his second in command. He also had six midshipmen, each with three pairs of guns to look after. In the deafening din of action, any commands would be yelled at close range into the ears of the mids, who would then shriek them into the ears of the gun-captains.

For our mid, we were given one Cuthbert Percival-Clive, the tall gangling adolescent that had come aboard with the Captain. He was a slovenly creature with a dirty-minded look about him and quite indifferent to his duties. He hadn't the slightest aptitude for the Sea Service. We called him "Poxy Percy" or just Percy for short.

But the Captain cherished him and loved him and

smiled upon him like the summer sun. And this for the best of all reasons. A reason that utterly transcended all matters of mere talent, or skill, or attention to duty. The fact was that young Percy's father was Sir Reginald Percival-Clive, a parvenu with an enormous fortune in West India sugar. And better yet, Sir Reginald's wife was younger sister to Billy Pitt the Prime Minister and Lord Chatham, the First Sea Lord.

Captain Bollington had moved heaven and earth to get Cuthbert into his ship, via the good offices of his wife who was a bosom friend of Lady Percival-Clive. And now there were not enough hours in the day for the Captain to give sufficient expression to his delight in getting the dirty little nose-picker, since it meant endless privileges for the ship; choice of guns, the best of stores and lots more beside. For there wasn't a clerk, official or even an *Admiral* in the Service who'd dare to do less for the ship in which the Prime Minister's nephew was serving.

By contrast, our gunnery Lieutenant, Mr Seymour, was a first rate officer who provided the technical competence that Captain Bollington needed on the gundeck. Of all the things that I unwillingly learned aboard *Phiandra*, the one that was dinned in deepest was Mr Seymour's gun-drill. He raced each crew against all the rest and against the clock for speed. And he made each do the work of all the others in the team so we could take over from those mown down in action.

And above all, we were practised each day, every day, over and over again. I remember every name of our gun-crew, which was Sammy's mess and four others: two marines, Charlie Moore and Peter Godolphin, and two men from other messes, Obediah Brompton and Donald McDouglas. Obediah had the important post of Second Captain.

In addition, to fetch cartridges up from the magazine, we had a shrivelled child of uncertain age, by the name of "Nimmo". He was one of about twenty ship's boys that lived in dank corners of the vessel down below the water-line. *Phiandra's* boys were all street urchins that had been "saved" by the Marine Society, who caught them, cleaned them, fed them a bit, gave them the scrapings of an education and parcelled them off in batches to serve afloat. Captain Bollington approved of this scheme and took his ship's boys from no other source.

I suppose even the Navy was better than starving in the gutter, and there was always the chance of getting a berth aboard a merchantman where they could earn more money and the conditions were better. Nimmo thought so anyway.

"I'm 'oppin out o' this ol' tub first chance I get!" says Nimmo on one occasion.

"Oh yes?" says Sammy, winking at the rest of us. "And where would you go, lad?"

"I'm shippin aboard a Indiaman an' I gonna make my fortune out east!"

"Oh dear me!" says Sammy. "I shouldn't do that if I was you."

"Why not?" says Nimmo.

"Well, mate," says Sammy, "I can tell you this 'cos you're a messmate and almost a man . . . "

"Yeah?" says Nimmo, wide-eyed.

"Fact is mate, them Indiamen skippers, well, they uses their lads for unnatural purposes!"

"Garn!" says Nimmo, suspiciously.

"Oh yes!" says Sammy.

"Cor!" says the boy. And that was the least of the tales Sammy told him. But Nimmo was part of number eight crew and shared with all of us the formidable effort of muscle and skill that went into gun-drill.

Boom! The gun fires and heaves back like a mad black bull.

"Stop the vent!" cries Sammy, and takes up the slack of the trigger line as the gun's recoil is held by the thick rope of the breeching tackle. He coils the line on the cascabel as Obediah jams a leather-sheathed copper plug into the touch-hole. This stops smouldering fragments being forced out when the rammer goes down the bore. A spark landing on a loose cartridge would kill us all.

"Sponge!" cries Sammy, and Norris and Daniel step smartly inside the breeching tackle as Thomas snatches the sponge down from the overhead hooks and wets the sheepskin head with water from our bucket. Daniel grabs the sponge and Norris and he together throw their weight on the long sponge-staff to drive it down the barrel. They twist the head well into the breech end and haul it out.

Daniel raps the staff hard on the gun to shake off anything brought out and Thomas whisks away the sponge to hurl it back into its hooks and pulls down the rammer in readiness.

"Load cartridge!" cries Sammy, and Peter thrusts a cartridge at Norris. This is a tight-packed flannel cylinder of gunpowder, sewn up along one side and gathered tight at the top. Norris shoves the cylinder as far down the gun as his arm will reach, then he and Daniel lean hard on the rammer, driving the powder-charge to the end of the bore. Two sharp blows seat it firmly in the breech.

"Shoot your gun!" cries Sammy, and Peter brings a round-shot from the racks and heaves it to Norris with a wad from the overhead net. Norris grunts as he tips the eighteen pound iron ball down the bore with a clang. The wad goes on top then Norris and Daniel ram it home. Instantly the rammer flies from Daniel to Thomas to the hooks above. Obediah jerks out the vent plug and the gun is loaded.

"Run out!" cries Sammy, and seizes the breeching rope to take up the slack as the gun moves. The handspike-men lever under the rear wheels with their five-foot iron-bound levers while I throw my weight on the lines with the other tackle-men to heave the gun's snout through the port — brutal heavy labour that leaves me gasping for breath with the sweat running off me in rivers.

"Well!" cries Sammy. "Prick the cartridge!" and Obediah thrusts a long spike down the touch-hole to check the cartridge is home and pierce it.

"Well!" says he.

"Prime!" says Sammy, and Obediah half-cocks the gun lock and opens the pan. He takes a goose-quill priming tube and shoves it down the hole. He grabs the powder horn from its hook and primes the lock. In all the racing speed of the drill, this must be done with absolute care; fortune permits not even one mistake with loose powder. He snaps down the lock-pan.

"Well!" he cries.

"Point!" says Sammy and again we take up tackles and handspikes to slew the gun bodily left and right to his command. There is no elevating as the gun is already levelled and Sammy cries, "Make ready!" as he cocks the lock and darts back to the full extent of the trigger line and we all stand clear. He leans on his right knee with the left leg clear of the recoil and takes his final aim over the sights.

"Fire!" says he and pulls the line. Boom! The gun roars again.

And all that, my lovely lads, was done a damn sight faster than you just took to read it. *Phiandra* was not a fast-firing ship as some were in the King's Navy, for Mr Seymour's emphasis was always on steady aimed fire, but if need be we could deliver three broadsides in five minutes.

At first, when I learned gun-drill, I was good for nothing but hauling on lines (and it's that that put all the muscles on me). But later, Sammy took an interest in me, beyond the need that we should all know everyone else's parts, to train me up as a gun-captain like himself.

And gun-drill, ruthlessly practised in the King's ships, hour after hour, day after day, is precisely what did for the bloody French and their maniac Emperor and his precious New World Order. Because as long as we could beat their navy, then their army couldn't invade England. And if they couldn't invade England, then they could invade whomsoever else they pleased, and much good may it do 'em . . . but our side would win in the end. And so we did, too!

What amazes me is that Boney never spotted where he was going wrong. After all, he *was* an artilleryman by training and you'd think a gunner would've worked it out, wouldn't you?

Chapter 12

Apart from turning *Phiandra*'s guns into something formi-
dably deadly, Mr Seymour's drills had two other effects
that were more interesting to me. The first was to confirm
Sammy Bone as the best gun-captain in the ship. It soon
got to the point that when we practised for accuracy by
shooting at a cask dropped over the side, Sammy wasn't
allowed to point our gun until all the other crews had
fired and missed. Then Mr Seymour would wave him
forward with a grin, and Sammy would blow the cask to
splinters.

"It's easy, lads," he'd say. "We points her as close as
we can, then the ship's motion does the rest. All I do is
fire as the gun comes on target." He meant it, too. He
never understood the complexity of the calculations that
he made so easily and unthinkingly in his head.

The other thing was more personal and I first noticed

it one Sunday as we were lined up by divisions for church. Captain Bollington always took this as the occasion to come through the ranks of us, to stare each man in the face and get a feel of what mood his crew was in. We were supposed to stand to attention for this, like marines, and I found that I could no longer do it properly. If I held my arms straight, they wouldn't rest flat, down the sides of my body. Rather, they stuck out at an angle with my clenched fists well clear of my hips. This was due to several weeks' heavy labour and wolfing down all the food that I wanted. I'd always been big, but now I was strong into the bargain. My arms bulged with hard muscles and I found I could do tricks like a circus strongman. I could shove our gun about unaided, I could juggle eighteen-pound round-shot, and I could carry Norris and Johann about, each under one arm, with Sammy riding on my shoulders.

I thought this was all pointless fun until I discovered that I no longer needed my mates when I went round the lower deck to collect my debts. The other tars seemed only too willing to pay up and I noticed how small and puny some of them now seemed. To my amazement, physical strength had a business value! This happy period of our cruise with the convoy was the best time I spent aboard *Phiandra*. I was at peace with myself, I'd got friends again and I was making money. I should have known it couldn't last, and it didn't.

What with the disorderly behaviour of the merchant ships and a couple of days of mist and bad weather, a morning came when, instead of being in a powerful fleet with a neat convoy, we found ourselves alone with three small merchantmen and all our comrades over the western horizon. And worse, we soon had company of another sort. Two smudges of sail appeared far away on our port quarter, bearing up from the south-east. Long before we on the gundeck could see them, the look-outs had identified them as French.

Leaning out through number eight gun-port, eventually I could see them myself. Each had a huge spread of canvas over a small hull, and was thrashing along at a tremendous rate, with white water boiling under the bow — the very incarnation of speed. Twinkling from the maintop was the blue-white-red of the French Republic. The first time I'd ever seen it.

"What are they, Sammy?" says I.

"Privateers!" says he at once. His eyesight was marvellous and his knowledge of ships profound. "The Frog navy has sloops and frigates for its cruisers like we do, but these is luggers. I'd say no more than a hundred tons apiece, with four-pounders, maybe sixes, on the gundeck and a big crew for boarding. They ain't no threat to *us* but they'll try and get round us and snap up one of them." He jabbed his thumb at our merchantmen.

Sammy was dead right. And for several hours the two Frenchmen played catch-as-catch-can with our ship. They worked as a team and their game was for one to try to draw us off so the other could take the prize.

To stop this, Captain Bollington repeated the Admiral's strategy in miniature; keeping to windward of the three sheep so we could fall on the wolves should they press home a real attack. And, for once, the danger was so immediate that the three merchantmen huddled together like children in fear of the bogeyman. This went on for hours as one after the other, the two luggers would swoop in as close as they dared, to tempt us to set off in chase. It was a waste of their time really for there wasn't the slightest chance of Captain Bollington's falling for this. And while we couldn't have tackled both at the same time, should they attack separate ships, it would be pointless since we could easily outsail the prizes and recapture them. Their only hope was that some freak of accident or weather would give them the advantage. Equally, they must take care to keep too far off for us to do harm to them. It was a dangerous game for them, played just outside the range of our gunfire, which they had judged to a nicety.

But though their effort might be futile, their seamanship won cries of admiration from our crew. It was a wonderful thing to see them come bounding across the waves as if bent on collision, then go about in a roar of canvas, their top-men nimble as monkeys in the rigging, to bear away on the opposite tack. Much has been said about the poor seamanship of the Republican French Navy and it's mostly true. The professional officers who'd run King Louis' Navy had all been murdered or exiled. But there was not a damn thing that any Englishman could have taught the crews of those two vessels. And I say it who hates the French like poison. I suppose they had volunteer crews and were at sea often enough to learn their trade.

Finally, they tried a new tactic. At wildly long range, one of them had the cheek to run out his guns and give us his piddling, pop-gun broadside.

At first their shot fell nowhere near us. We didn't see so much as a splash. But their fire was steady and regular with each gun sounding separately across the waves as it fired in turn.

"Hmm!" says Sammy with interest. "That's not like the Frogs. Looks like they've got their best man pointing each gun. Wonder how good he is . . . " Not everyone took this so calmly, especially when there came a horrifying SHOOOSH! of shot streaking between our masts, no more than ten feet over our heads.

I felt a sudden shock of fear, as if I'd been hit, and an audible gasp rose from our gun-crews.

"Why don't we give it to them buggers?" says a voice, to a growl of agreement.

"Silence!" cries Lieutenant Seymour. "I'll fire when I know I can hit something! They're just burning powder." But they were burning it for our special benefit and it made the crew uneasy. It was the first time we'd been under fire and, after all, there was always the chance of a lucky hit. Midshipman Percival-Clive seemed particularly to hold this view. He leaned out of our port, gulping at the puffs of smoke bursting from the lugger's guns, and bit his lip and chewed his nails.

"Can they hit us?" says he. "Is there a chance, is there a chance?" He muttered and moaned and spread anxiety like the plague from gun to gun. Mr Seymour should have shut him up, but he didn't. All his attention was given to judging the range to the Frenchman. I could see that Sammy was bursting to say something but recent experience had made him wary. Then Johnny Basford, in all innocence, copied Percival-Clive.

"Here, Sammy," says he, "can them Froggies hit we? Is there a chance?" Sammy beamed at him and answered in a voice loud enough to be heard from end to end of the deck.

"Is there a chance?" says he, "Johnny lad, they've got about as much chance of hitting us from there . . . as *you* have of ramming half a pound of butter up a cockatoo's arse with a red-hot needle!"

There came a roar of laughter at this, more than the joke deserved perhaps, which pricked the tension and made us feel better.

Mr Seymour had the sense to see the value of it and laughed with the rest. Then he looked at Sammy, and once again across to the Frenchman, and leaped up the companionway to the quarterdeck. He touched his hat to Captain Bollington and said a few words. The Captain nodded and Mr Seymour called down from the quarter-deck rail.

"Number eight crew! Run out the larboard bow-chaser! Lively now!"

"Aye aye, sir!" says Sammy, in great delight. "Come on, lads!" and he led the rush to the long bronze guns on either side of the bowsprit. Being slow-firing they were not run out as a matter of routine when we went to quarters, but left under their tarred-canvas jackets to protect them from the spray. Each gun-crew was practised with them but Sammy was their master.

"Train to larboard, Mr Bone!" says Lieutenant Seymour, but the order was superfluous. We had already cast off the gun's tackles and were hauling it through ninety degrees to secure it to the empty gun-port waiting in the quarterdeck bulwark. The gun was a beautiful thing, over twelve feet from muzzle to cascabel, gleaming golden bronze with leaping dolphins cast in metal above the trunnions. It was an Italian piece, nearly a hundred years old, with the gun-founder's name inscribed at the breech: *Albertus Ambrosius me fecit*, it said.

Through the bulwark gun-port the bronze gun glared at the lugger now about half a mile away on our beam. To give urgency to our actions, the lugger fired again.

John Drake

White smoke with a stab of orange, followed by a flat "thud" and the howling shot, then . . . CRASH! By luck or judgement she found us, and splinters flew from our hull.

"Move! Move! Move!" cries Sammy, as we strained to make ready the gun. "Nimmo! Get me a full charge from the magazine . . . Run!" The boy raced away, his leather cartridge box bouncing on its strap, as Sammy and Obediah screwed the gun's firelock in place by the touch-hole. The boy was back in seconds, and we loaded and primed in record time. All was ready and we had only to aim and fire.

Captain Bollington, Mr Williams and a crowd of others had joined Mr Seymour to watch the fun and every eye was on Sammy. Most men would have quailed at this but Sammy loved it. Careful fire at long range with a good gun was meat and drink to him.

Beside Sammy, Lieutenant Seymour hopped from one foot to the other in his excitement. Both were small men, but Sammy was thin as a stick where the Lieutenant was short legged and heavy. And Sammy was neat in his dress where the other was untidy to the point of comedy. At that moment he was bobbing his head from side to side, judging distances and looking at the gun and itching to do the thing himself. Captain Bollington guessed his mood.

"Will you not lay the gun, Mr Seymour?" says the Captain. The Lieutenant sighed and straightened up.

"With respect, sir, I'll leave it to Bone," says he. "Now then, Mr Bone, let's see if you can't knock a spar off that ship."

Then they all stood clear of the recoil and Sammy took command. He gave the gun two degrees of elevation, and trained it to his satisfaction. Meanwhile, thud! The lugger fired again, the shot going God knows where as she pressed closer under bulging sails, still keeping safely out of range of our main-deck guns.

Sammy took his sight, tightened the trigger-line . . . an instant of intense concentration . . . and . . . BOOM! The gun plunged back and we fell upon it like demons. Sponge-powder-RAM! Shot-wad-RAM! Heave-heave-heave! To run her out and point. Calmly Sammy took aim and fired, and our second shot shrieked across the water. Again we leapt to our drill, but in the middle of it came a great roar of cheering and all those about us were thundering Sammy on the back with expressions of enraptured joy.

He'd done it. And with only two shots. The lugger was dragging the wreckage of her foremast across her port bow, destroying the skilful balance of wind, sail and hull that had sent her flying across the waves. I could see her crew running like ants in panic to get her clear again.

But Captain Bollington was yelling orders at the top of his voice as he ran back to the quarterdeck followed by Lieutenant Williams. And in an instant we were securing the bow-chaser as *Phiandra* came through wind on to the larboard tack to fall upon our victim. By the time we were back at our main-deck gun, *Phiandra* was bearing down on the lugger with every sail set and the wind on her quarter, her best point of sailing, and she thrashed onward like a racing stallion. Every line sang and we leaned through the gun-ports cheering madly in the thrill of the brief chase.

The lugger had no chance of escape. She was barely making way. We were alongside of her in minutes, with topsails backed to take the way off our ship. Her consort sensibly ran downwind and left her to her fate. There was nothing they could have done. The pair of them together was no match for us with their pip-squeak guns.

With no more than ten yards between us and the Frenchman, our crew stood laughing and joking and slapping each other on the back. We were already guessing at the value of our fine prize and wondering how much we'd each get for her. Some of us were even calling out to the Frenchies, friendly as could be. After all, we'd won, hadn't we? We could afford to be jolly.

None the less, on both sides, every gun was primed and loaded, and far too close to miss. In fact we were so close that we could see faces staring and hear them chattering French at one another. They couldn't hope to fight but they hadn't hauled down their flag yet and they were cram-full of armed men.

Captain Bollington called across in French, which he spoke fluently. I presume he was calling on them to surrender, but there was only silence, and their flag stayed at the maintop. He called out again, but in the middle of it some infernal bloody maniac on their side yelled a command and their guns roared out in a deafening bank of flame and fire. Splinters flew, a burning wad whooshed over my head and, in the corner of my eye, I saw number seven's powder monkey smashed into a pile of steaming meat.

"Bastards!" yelled Lieutenant Seymour, "FIRE!" And *Phiandra* shook to the recoil of the larboard battery and four carronades. The carnage on the decks of the lugger was indescribable. That one broadside was all they got off and their vessel was reduced in minutes to a collection of wallowing wreckage stained and running with the produce of the slaughterhouse.

God knows what the Frenchies thought they were doing in firing on us. Perhaps they thought the surprise would even up the disparity of force. As it was they maddened our gun-crews and we did not cease firing until Captain Bollington and the Lieutenants pulled each gun-captain physically from his work.

Pierced through and through, the lugger went down in minutes; one of the few ships I ever saw sunk by gunfire in all my years at sea. Of all the men she had aboard, we managed to save about fifty. Some were killed by our fire or dragged below with their ship, but many drowned miserably, gulping and throttling within reach of our ship. We threw them lines and hauled them aboard as fast as we could, but there were so many of them and the water was cold and, like our own tars, hardly any of them could swim. They might have been enemies but it was a dreadful thing to see.

And then we had them to feed and to guard for the next few days until we caught up with the convoy and could pass them into the charge of one of the seventy-fours that had more room for prisoners than we did.

But a few of the prisoners stayed aboard for a while under the care of our Surgeon, Mr Jones. He was a good surgeon, unlike many that went to sea, and if he hadn't been a Wesleyan Methodist, who'd made a nuisance of himself with his Bible-thumping, he'd doubtless have carved out a good practice ashore. As it was, we had him and had given him little chance to exercise his skills so far.

Thus when the Frog prisoners came aboard, he and his mates were waiting to pounce on those that were wounded and whisk 'em down to the orlop where the knives and saws were laid out ready. And a merry time they had of it, too. There was nowhere you could go to get away from their patients' screams. But Mr Jones surprised everyone and managed to save three men who were so badly wounded as to be despaired of when they entered the ship. It wasn't until some time after we'd rejoined the convoy that these three finally appeared on deck.

They were dressed all neat and clean in *Phiandra* rig and heavily swathed in bandages. They blinked in the sunlight as Mr Jones brought them aft to show them off to the Captain. In all fairness, he'd done a fine job of stitching them together and I suppose he wanted his pat on the back. Also, the word had gone round that the Frogs had something to say of their own, and most of the ship's company gathered round to see what this was. What happened next showed a side of Captain Bollington's character that I don't think would strike too many echoes today. But it was common enough in those days.

The Frogs were taken to the quarterdeck and were received by the Captain and his Lieutenants. A murmur of surprise went round as we saw that the Frogs saluted just the same way as we did, and the Captain said a few words of praise to Mr Jones. Then one of the Frogs stood forward and launched into a flowery speech in English. He covered all the expected ground about how grateful they were and then struck out on a new tack about how the three of them were Bretons, loyal to King Louis, and wanted no part of what those damned rascals of Paris were doing.

"So, Monsieur le Capitaine," says he, "we shall have no more revolution and we ask only that we shall be taken into your ship, to serve under that flag!" And he pointed dramatically at the big ensign flying from the jack-staff astern. There was a silence and we turned to see how Captain Bollington would respond. He said nothing for a while, but his face went white and he trembled like a boiling kettle.

"Monsieur," says he, "never in all my service have I received so disgraceful a proposition! Don't you realise that you'd serve against your own folk and your native land! Don't you remember your shipmates who fell in action against my ship, and now lie dead in the bosom of the sea? I pray God that your own mothers should never hear of this!" He choked with the strength of his emotions, caught a grip of himself and continued. "Mr Williams!" says he. "Get 'em out of my ship this instant! Take them to the Flagship and let the Admiral decide on them."

And that was that. Over the side they went in double-quick time. But if you ask me, he was a bit hard on them. You'll not be surprised to learn that I take no cognisance whatever of French politics, but even I knew that some of the Frogs were loyal to their dead king and wanted to overturn the revolution. In any case, as far as I was concerned, if the Frogs wanted to fight one another, then the very best of good luck to 'em! All I'd ask is the pleasure of handing 'em the muskets to do it with. But I kept this opinion to myself because Sammy and the others thought the Captain had done right. In fact he'd touched precisely the right chord with *Phiandra's* people and they loved him for it. That's the sort of daft thing that marks out a leader.

So much for my first action and my first sight of the French. I'd emerged unscathed and seen a ship sunk, but I soon found that there were far more deadly battles to be fought against enemies aboard our own ship.

Chapter 13

In soliciting your most urgent co-operation, I beg to repeat, sir, that Mr Fletcher's inheritance is of so enormous an extent that whosoever holds it becomes not merely rich, but one who wields power in the land.

(Letter of 25th February 1793 to Mr Nathan Pendennis from Lucey and Lucey, Solicitors.)

*

In the late afternoon of Monday 4th March, a post chaise turned off the Great North Road into Lonborough. It was spattered with the mud of a long journey, and the gentleman within was invisible through the grime on the windows and the wraps that smothered him. But the horses were fresh from the last change and they came on with fire and steam, at a rattling pace.

Yapping dogs chased behind, and the populace (being solid Staffordshiremen) cast a critical eye over the expensive rig and the postillion in his livery.

"Whoa!" cried the latter, and pulled to a stop beside a group of onlookers. "Thirty-nine Market Street!" he cried. "Lucey and Lucey — firm o' lawyers! Half a guinea for the man who leads me there!" Five minutes later he was hammering the door-knocker at number thirty-nine, to announce his passenger, before throwing open the door of the chaise and turning down the steps, to let him out.

Awkward in his thick travelling-clothes and stiff from cold hours of sitting, the heavy figure of Mr Nathan Pendennis descended in dignity to greet the two men he had come so far to meet and who stood before him amazed at his sudden arrival: Mr Richard Lucey and his son Edward, solicitors to the late Sir Henry Coignwood and executors of his Will.

"Mr Pendennis?" said the elder Lucey. "Can it be you, sir? Come from Polmouth?"

"Indeed sir," said Pendennis, pulling off his glove to shake the other's hand. "Three hundred miles in under four days! Never in my life have I made such a journey: three nights at three different inns and thirty-one changes of horses — I counted 'em! Such fearful cost!" He shook his head in sorrow then set his jaw to the business in hand. "But considering the content of your letter of the 25th, Mr Lucey, I deemed it justified." He paused and looked around him.

"Quite so," said Lucey, recognising Pendennis's reluctance to say more in public. The two men exchanged glances and understanding passed between them.

"And you, sir, will be Mr Edward Lucey?" said Pendennis to the younger man.

"Sir!" said Edward Lucey.

"Now get you inside, Mr Pendennis," said Mr Richard Lucey. "'Tis bitter cold and there's a good fire inside." Pendennis looked uncertainly at the chaise and its driver. "Never fear!" said Lucey. "My people shall see to your machine and your man, and you shall lodge with myself and my son. I'll not hear of anything else." Gratefully, Pendennis allowed himself to be led to Mr Lucey's private office and sat before the fire. Refreshment was produced and life began to flow back into the toes that he'd not heard from for two days.

Pendennis sighed in comfort and considered the Luceys. He liked what he saw. The son was a man in his twenties with a serious and intelligent manner. A very proper young man, of whom Mr Pendennis approved. The father was better yet: a prosperous man in his fifties, like Mr Pendennis himself, with dark clothes and just such a wig as Mr Pendennis wore. True, he was thin and grey where Pendennis was robust and ruddy but, all in all, Pendennis felt that Mr Richard Lucey presented a most admirable and dignified appearance.

Simultaneously, Mr Richard Lucey was weighing up Mr Pendennis, and reaching similar conclusions. The result was that the two men achieved an instant rapport, which was all the more complete because the business that had brought them together was, for both of them, one of those rare occasions in life where obligation precisely coincides with inclination. For his part, Nathan Pendennis had caught the authentic sniff of vast wealth and felt it his duty to become the saviour and friend of its owner. And if he might poke the Navy in the eye at the same time, then so much the better! As for Richard Lucey, he knew exactly how things had stood between his friend Henry Coignwood and Lady Sarah, and was determined to deny her any benefit from the fortune.

So Pendennis and the Luceys talked and talked. Each party produced documents for the other to inspect, and Pendennis's eyes came out on stalks at the sight of Sir Henry Coignwood's Will of 1775, lodged for safe-keeping these eighteen years in the Luceys' office. Works of reference were consulted from the Luceys' bookshelves and candles were lit as the light faded. Finally, when agreement had been reached regarding action, a bottle of port was brought in to seal the matter.

"Gentlemen," said Richard Lucey, "I propose the health of Mr Jacob Fletcher!"

"Aye, sir!" said Pendennis. "And may not a second be wasted in our bringing him to his fortune!" They drained their glasses and passed the bottle round.

"Mr Pendennis," said Edward Lucey, "might I ask how much of these matters you were aware of before we wrote to you?" Pendennis frowned and considered his reply carefully.

"More than I thought, sir," he said, "for what I knew had a greater meaning than I believed. Mr Fletcher was apprenticed to me by the Reverend Dr Woods, a local clergyman now deceased, who was my friend for twenty years. I always thought him to be Fletcher's benefactor, but now I learn he was *paid* by Fletcher's father to raise up the child!" Pendennis shook his head and stared into the fire.

"Dr Woods many times hinted that Fletcher was more than he seemed," he said, "and I always thought him to mean that the boy was the illegitimate offspring of some noble house."

"Not so far wrong, sir," said Edward Lucey.

"But what of the stepmother and half-brothers?" said Pendennis. "Lady Sarah and her sons?"

"Degenerates, sir!" said Richard Lucey. "Such things go on at Coignwood Hall that I may not name. For decency's sake I shall say no more."

"Oh?" said Pendennis, expectantly, for in his experience any man who said that, would soon do precisely the opposite. Sure enough, after a brief pause, the words burst from Lucey's lips.

"The woman is a witch," he said. "Our grandfathers would have burned her. She has the face of an angel and the soul of a viper. I tell you, sir, it shall be my life's work to place the Coignwood fortune out of her grasp!"

He fortified himself with another glass of port and continued. "I'd give the money to the devil himself to keep it from her! She leads a secret life of perverse desires that none could imagine and few would believe."

"Indeed?" said Pendennis, his interest whetted more keenly still. He wondered how to ask for a more precise description of these desires, without appearing to have perverse interests himself. But Edward Lucey changed the subject before Pendennis could find the words.

"It was Victor and Alexander who broke open Sir Henry's desk at Coignwood Hall," he said. "They removed most of its contents before we got there and it was only by luck that we found a letter they'd missed. And that gave us your name, Mr Pendennis, and that of Dr Woods, for we never knew of either of you. We knew that Jacob Fletcher existed, but nothing else."

"Gentlemen," said Pendennis, "this is a deep business. Sir Henry was apparently most secretive where Fletcher was concerned, and took care that no one person had the whole story. We can only guess at his reasons, but in whatever case, we three must bring the young man to his inheritance as Sir Henry wished!" He looked at Mr Edward Lucey, "So, sir!" he said, "tomorrow you and I leave for London, to fight the Admiralty face to face, to liberate Fletcher from their clutches!"

"While I shall remain here," said Mr Richard Lucey, "to prove the Will as quickly as possible, and to guard against any moves that *the woman* and her sons may make."

With a bottle of port comfortably inside them, and the warm firelight on their faces, the three friends smiled and shook hands. They were civilised men, men of substance, men used to working the Law to their advantage. They were entirely confident of success.

Unfortunately, and in reality, they did not know what game it was that they were starting to play, nor how very deadly was that game, nor how utterly they were outclassed by the opposition.

Chapter 14

Once back with the convoy, we found ourselves the heroes of the hour. We'd sunk a French warship, after all, even if it had been a little one, and our officers had a grand time with boats hoisted out so they could visit their friends aboard other ships and relive every detail of our brief engagement over their claret. And Sammy Bone's fame spread throughout the Fleet.

So the Fleet rolled steadily south and west; we passed beyond range of cruisers from the French Atlantic ports, the weather grew warm and the merchantmen learned to keep station. Thus the Admiral grew easier in his mind and no longer sent us racing hither and thither with streams of signals. This gave Captain Bollington all the more time for gun-drill and for a new set of drills designed to practise us in the use of small-arms.

I always enjoyed pistol-drill, as it involved the great

fun of letting fly with a sixteen-bore Sea-Service pistol. Incidentally, a lot of nonsense is talked these days about how the old firelock pistol was hopelessly clumsy compared with a modern revolver and not one tenth as accurate. For the benefit of armchair experts I would point out that the usual range for pistol work in a naval boarding action was an arm's length. So what a Sea-Service pistol could, or could not, do in the way of accurate shooting, didn't matter. But what did matter was its proven ability to drop a man dead in his tracks with one shot before he could split your skull with a cutlass.

By some aberration of command, my first experience of pistol-drill took place under Mr Midshipman Wilkins: thirteen years old, five feet tall on his tip-toes and weighing in at six and a half stone. This officer did not have quite the same control over the men that some of his elders did.

I was sent forward with some others, including Johnny Basford, and found Mr Wilkins standing with his hands behind him in charge of an open box of pistols and trying to look as if he was privy to weighty matters of command that we knew not of.

"Take a weapon each, you men, and look lively!" says he and there came an eager scramble of hands into the box. Immediately we did what every fool does who gets his hands on a pistol for the first time.

"Bang!" says I, levelling at Johnny Basford and pulling the trigger.

"Bang-bang-bang!" says Johnny, jamming his pistol into my ribs and laughing merrily.

"Stop it! Stop it!" screams the Mid. "Don't you never, never, NEVER do that again, none of you! How d'you know they wasn't loaded, eh?" He was so angry that we all felt ashamed and he had our complete attention for a while, and he issued us each with a flint and showed us how to screw it into the jaws of the hammer with a bit of leather to seat it nicely home. But it didn't last long. I saw one mighty-handed dolt, who'd not the least understanding of what he was doing, hauling on the hammer with teeth clenched and sweat starting on his brow, till metal parted with a brittle snap.

"'ere!" says he stupidly. "It come orf! Must be a bad 'un," Mr Wilkins rushed forward and snatched it off him.

"Gimme that, you dunghead!" says he. "I'm responsible for these to Mr Williams. You be silent or I'll pass on your name to him!" The tar shuffled about, mumbling that it weren't fair and why couldn't he have another one, as the lesson continued. Mr Wilkins held up a greased-paper cylinder the size of a man's little finger.

"Now . . . how do we load with cartridge?" says he. A rhetorical question he should never have asked. We'd all seen the marines do that and half a dozen voices replied at once. "Silence!" says he, and picked on Johnny Basford who was shouting louder than most.

"You there! If you're so clever, show us how it's done."

"Aye aye, sir!" says Johnny. "First you bites his head off, and then you primes him . . . " He tore open the cartridge with his teeth, in the approved manner, keeping the bullet in his mouth. "Mumble, mumble, mumble," says he, pouring powder neatly into the open lock-pan. He snapped it shut, up-ended the barrel and poured in the rest of the powder. An admiring silence fell over the class. Perhaps there was more to our Johnny than we had thought.

Then we all staggered as the ship took an unusually large wave. I blundered into Johnny and he fell over. I helped him up and thumped him on the back in encouragement.

"Go on, Johnny!" says I.

"Now then," says Mr Wilkins, "get on with it: the ball! The ball! Spit it down the barrel!" Johnny stood moon faced and miserable, not moving. "What's the matter?" says the Mid.

"Please sir," says Johnny, "I can't . . . I swallowed the bugger." The subsequent laughter brought Lieutenant Williams to see what was going on. That ended the fun and there was no more pistol-drill under Midshipman Wilkins.

Lieutenant Williams was a crack shot with his own pair of duellers, which had rifled barrels and were built for accurate shooting. He used to amuse the men by blowing holes through ship's biscuits held up by volunteers, at the length of the quarterdeck. He never missed and he never had any shortage of eager, grinning volunteers.

But his real love was the sword, and he always had charge of cutlass-drill. Aboard *Phiandra* this was known as "cudgelling" since we practised with wooden staves about three feet long and an inch and a half thick. They had basket-work guards to protect the hand and were similar in size and weight to a Naval cutlass, with the advantage that should you hit your opponent, you didn't kill him.

I never liked cudgelling. It was entirely antipathetic to my inclinations, and the fact that I proved to be good at it makes not the slightest difference.

Mr Williams would demonstrate the various strokes and we would copy him, stamping up and down the deck, cutting into empty air. So far, so good. I had no objection to this. But then he would match us in pairs, to fight in a square chalked on the deck. The bouts were fiercely fought and only ended with a dropped cudgel, or a man driven out of the square, or a broken head — and that meant actual *blood* visible on the scalp. We were supposed to disdain mere bruises, God help us. Consequently, only those who were good at cudgelling had any liking for it. None the less, as with every other damn thing aboard ship, we had to pitch in with a will, like it or not, since Lieutenant Williams thought cudgelling was just the thing to bring out the aggressive instincts of the crew.

And so it jolly well is, me buckos, *for the common crew.* It's mother's milk to them, but I beg to differ where I'm concerned. Getting clouted over the skull with an oaken staff ain't my idea of fun.

Williams himself was a brilliant swordsman: fast, agile and clever and, without doubt, the best in the ship. He was in his very element at cudgelling; coat thrown off and sleeves rolled up, he would be in among us, slapping men on the shoulder, laughing and cheering with us and always praising the courage of the losers so they shouldn't feel bad. He was a natural born leader and men would give their utmost for him just for the enjoyment of pleasing him. It even worked on me a bit, just as long as he was actually there urging me on.

For unfortunately he picked on me at once. Being so big, it is hardly surprising that I was noticed, but he paid special attention to me and even developed in me a certain skill at the thing. I was so strong that any blow I struck came down with great force, and I'm fairly quick for my size. I'm no swordsman and wouldn't claim to be, but I suppose, in a heavy sort of fashion, I make a dangerous opponent.

So, you will ask, if I was so good, then why didn't I like cudgelling? The answer was a thug by the name of Billy Mason. He and his messmates were a prize collection of horse-thieves and pickpockets who were only in the Navy because some Judge or other had offered them the choice of that or the hangman. All ships have their bad eggs, and all of *Phiandra*'s were to be found in Billy Mason's mess.

And Billy was the acknowledged "cock of the ship", which is to say we knew he could knock down any other man of us that he chose. So we treated him with careful respect. Also, after Lieutenant Williams, Mason was the best at cudgelling too, and when I showed promise and began to knock heads, the Lieutenant insisted that I should be matched mainly against Mason.

"To the line now, Fletcher!" he would say with a beaming smile. "And our champion . . . " Billy Mason was an ugly beast with a battered face and short grizzled hair. He was muscle from head to toe and had the total confidence of a professional fighter. He was about forty, with a lifetime of victories behind him, and was the sort who would batter any man that stood in his way, old or young, fit or cripple, without thought of mercy. According to Sammy, he'd been an instructor at Mendoza's Academy in London, teaching boxing and cudgelling until he damaged too many of the clients. [Fletcher's memory must be at fault here. Mason could never have been employed at Mendoza's Academy since this was not opened until 1795, the year that Mendoza lost the boxing championship of England, to "Gentleman" Jackson. Possibly Mason worked at Brougham's Academy in the Haymarket, which ran from 1747-89. S.P.]

But Williams thought the world of him for his skill. Mason's style was very much the same as the Lieutenant's, with economy of movement and everything depending on the suppleness of the wrist. I got the measure of him the first time I was stood up against him.

"Come on, sonny!" says he in his nasal, Londoner's accent. And he beckoned with his free hand and dangled his cudgel to give the impression of being open to a blow.

"Go on, Fletcher!" says Lieutenant Williams, heartily. "No room for shirkers on this ship!"

"Go on, Fletcher!" yelled my mates, and there was a roar from all the others. They didn't like Mason, not one little bit, and they were itching to see him beaten. It quite put heart into me, all those men cheering me on. So I advanced, as I'd been taught, and took a swipe at him. It would have stunned a gorilla had it landed, but Mason leered at me and side-stepped. Then, whizz-clunk! And he rapped the side of my head.

"Come on, boy!" says he, and struck with the precision of a cobra: wrist, elbow, knee, always choosing bone, where it hurt like the devil, and never wasting force. That way it went on ever so much longer. He could have beaten me in seconds if he'd wanted, just by laying on hard. But he didn't, because he enjoyed the game too much. So his mates cheered and the rest groaned and I was made a fool of. I couldn't land a blow on him; he was just too good for me. And he could hit me wherever and whenever he chose. Finally, he deliberately struck just at the precise spot in the joint of my elbow, to paralyse the limb down to the very tips of the fingers. It was agonising and my cudgel clattered useless to the deck.

"Well done, Mason! Well done, Fletcher!" cries Mr Williams. "And now shake hands like the good fellows you are . . . give 'em both a cheer, you others!"

I had to face Mason regularly after that. Williams obviously thought it was fairer for me to take on Mason than to fight men who I could easily beat. And it gave Mason some exercise since I did at least put up more resistance than anyone else. Anyone except Lieutenant Williams, that is. On rare occasions he would step into the chalk square himself and demonstrate that even our Billy had a master.

But even then he never exerted himself to the full. He would fence just long enough to test his own skill and then end the bout with some joke that set everyone laughing, even Mason.

It was bad enough for me to face Mason twice weekly at cudgelling, but for some reason the swine really took against me and I found myself up against him in deadly earnest with every chance of being permanently crippled in the encounter. I only wish I could have avoided it but I was in up to the neck before I knew it. The game started with a fight in the galley at supper time. Fights in the galley were common aboard ship, for as well as the food that the ship's cook had worked his wicked will upon, we were allowed to prepare dishes of our own.

And this meant dozens of us packed into a narrow, sweltering space, with tempers getting short. Each mess had its own pot for this purpose and for a small consideration to His Highness the Cook, we could put them on his stove to brew up something to our own taste. All the pots came from the Purser's stores and looked alike, so taking another mess's pot by mistake was one more source of quarrels. As I'd grown so big, the job of collecting our pot was usually left to me. I could wade through the crowd more easily and was now adept at elbowing my shipmates in the ear to clear my path. About two weeks after we first started cudgelling, I was in the galley to collect our pot and an India curry stew that we had made. I shoved happily through the press, cursing the cook like all the rest, and reached for our pot when a hand darted forward and seized our pot.

"What's this?" says I in a bold voice, for I could see who it was: a long, skinny person by the name of Barker, with a peculiar eye that twitched so you never knew which way he was looking.

He was taller than me but less than half my weight and heartily despised by most of the crew since he had the reputation of passing on tales to the Bosun.

He'd been turned out of three or four messes for this till he found company that could put up with him. I sneered but he stared back, bold as brass, and had the cheek to argue with me.

"It's our pot!" says he, sharply.

"Shove off!" says I, and pulled his hand away. I would have left it at that but he grabbed my wrist and struggled with me. He had no strength in his hand but he annoyed me with his persistence.

"Bloody bastard!" says he. "*Thief!*" And there came a silence as men moved back. Cursing was nothing on the lower deck, but to call a man a thief was a deadly insult. A wave of anger swept over me, and without thinking I clouted him backhand and sent him spinning. There was no weight in him at all and he staggered back till he tripped and sat down with a crash on the deck. Everyone laughed, I felt no end of a clever fellow, and Barker got up.

"Laugh while you can, boy," says Barker, "I'm gonna tell Billy what you done."

"Billy be damned!" says I, and a loud cheer echoed round the galley. All the tars thumped me on the back and my head swelled up something amazing.

God Almighty, what a bloody fool I was! Barker had a nasty grin on his face but even then I couldn't see what was coming, and I went back to our mess like the King of the Cannibal Isles. Word of what I'd done went running up the lower deck before me, and gaining with the telling all the way. By the time I reached our mess, Sammy and the others had it pat.

"Here he comes!" says Sammy, beaming from ear to ear. "Told him proper, you did!" says Norris.

"He-he-he!" says Johnny Basford.

"Gave Mason his marchin' orders, did you?" says Sammy, and the first little shadow appeared on my blue horizon.

"No," says I, "it was Barker." The smile drained out of Sammy's face and he became deathly serious.

"Jacob, lad, you did say it to Mason, didn't you?"

"No, it was Barker."

"Christ!" says Sammy. "You've insulted Billy Mason before the whole ship. Don't you know that's one of his little games, pinching mess-pots? And he always uses Barker to do it. That's how he goes after them as he takes against."

"Sammy!" says Norris. "Here he comes!" We looked and saw a figure coming up the deck from the stern. He walked like a tiger, full of menace, and silence followed him like a wave. The whole deck heard every word that followed. He bore down upon us like doom and stopped at our table.

Close up he was even more frightening, if that were possible. His face was all bone. Heavy jaw, heavy brows, a shiny bald face with staring eyes.

"Sit!" says he, and the six of us sat down like dogs. Sammy did his best.

"Now then, Billy!" says he, merry as could be. "Let's you and I talk this over with a drop of rum. Norris, fetch the bottle!" Sammy reached out to take Mason's arm in a friendly gesture. Crack! Striking with fierce precision, Mason rapped his knuckles hard down on

Sammy's wrist. It was so sudden that Sammy, who'd taken thirty-six lashes in silence, yelped in pain. Mason sneered.

"Shut your face, you fucking old man. I ain't after you . . . it's him!" He jabbed a thick finger at me. "You, Fletcher! You gimme three things or I'll piss on you every time I see you. *One*, you give me my dinner, now!" He pointed at the pot of stew. I looked to Sammy for guidance and he nodded, every so slightly. I shoved the pot towards Mason. "Good!" says he. "And *two*, you say sorry you tried to take it off my mate." Again I looked to Sammy and he nodded.

"Sorry," says I, quietly.

"Loud!" says he. "Say it loud."

"Sorry!" says I.

"Now *three*, so everyone here knows who's the thief and who ain't, you bring me my dinner and you follow me back to my mess, walking behind me."

If I did that, it would mean shame and humiliation before the entire community that I had to live in. The whole lower deck was watching in intent silence. I looked at Sammy and he bowed his head. For once he had nothing to offer and the decision was mine alone.

"No," says I, "I've given you the dinner and I've said sorry. Isn't that enough?"

"It's all or none," says Mason.

"No," says I. I was afraid of him, but I was even more afraid of what he was asking.

"Good!" says he. "Then we'll meet tomorrow on the

fo'c'sle and I'll smash you good, Fletcher. My mate'll fix it with this one." He pointed to Sammy and grinned like a death's head. Then he picked up the stew-pot.

"You can keep this nigger's shit," says he, and up-ended the pot on to our mess table so it slopped out and ran everywhere. Then he stalked off and left us wrapped in shame for the way that one man had dominated the six of us.

"Come on, lads," says Sammy, "let's clear this away," and we set to, awkwardly like drunken men.

"Can't we go to Mr Williams?" says I, desperately. Sammy sneered.

"Bleedin' Officers! What do they care?" He nodded towards the stern. "They'll know all about it by now and be placing their bets and telling one another what a set of British bulldogs they've got on the lower deck. You'll just have to fight him, Jacob." Then he looked me over and a thought occurred to him. "Any road, why not? Look at the size of you, you great bugger, maybe you'll win!"

Sammy tried by every means to put heart into me, but my soul was like lead. I was very young, remember, and better men than I were afraid of Mason. Sammy himself had told me that soon after *Phiandra* was commissioned, a mad Irishman, strong as a bull, by the name of O'Meara had challenged Mason, who stamped him thoroughly into the deck, putting out one of his eyes and breaking all his fingers. O'Meara was discharged from the Service after that, and he'd never be the same man again.

Soon after Mason had gone, his chum Barker came swaggering up to our mess, sneering fit to turn milk sour at the range of a mile. He and Sammy fixed the time for my meeting with Mason. As usual the place would be the fo'c'sle, where any fights among the crew always took place, keeping as far as possible from the notice of the officers. This suited both officers and men, since the former could pretend they were unaware of what was happening and the latter could enjoy the spectacle in peace. And if this seems strange to modern tastes, I would point out that in my youth, any gentleman thought it his right to exchange pistol-fire with any other gentleman who had insulted him. So in leaving the crew to settle their differences, the officers were only extending the same courtesy to us.

In the intervening time I can only say that I was glad the Navy kept me too busy for really serious worrying and sent me to my hammock too tired to do other than sleep. None the less I was hoping that any impossible thing might happen so I didn't have to face Mason . . . please God let it be tomorrow and the thing all over . . . please let it be three weeks ago . . . or the minute before I pushed Barker, so I could let him take the damn mess-pot . . . But it did no good and the fell moment came when I was heading for the fo'c'sle with my mates and Sammy pouring words into my ear about how to hold my fists, and how to give a punch, and a dozen other things I paid no heed to. I felt sick and empty. My heart was galloping like a horse and my knees shook.

Most of the crew were gathered there with Bosun Shaw and Sergeant Arnold, of the Marines, to keep order. The betting in the ship had been furious, and these two had backed opposite sides. The Sergeant had his money on Mason, and the Bosun on me. In all truth the thing was as official as any other activity aboard ship. Everyone knew what was happening and the officers had laid their wagers like all the rest.

I saw Mason surrounded by his cronies, already stripped to the waist. His brown face and hands looked odd against his white body, but he was all hard muscle and looked terrifying. He was dancing about on the balls of his feet as the pugilists do, stabbing the air and weaving his head about.

"Fletcher!" says he, at the sight of me. "Come on, sonny!" And his mates laughed and cheered. Especially Barker. Then Sammy was pulling off my jacket and shirt and jabbering at me. I saw his face, anxious and serious, trying to give advice, but none of it penetrated the funk I was in, and soon the Bosun was bringing Mason and me to the "scratch" line chalked on the deck. The bout would end when either man could not stand and come up to scratch. There were no other rules.

"Go to it!" says the Bosun, and stepped out of the way. A sea of faces surrounded us. Men were on all sides and in the rigging, eager and gawping with delight. Dog-fights and the like are fun, but there's nothing so congenial to the human spirit as watching two men punch each other's faces flat when there's no limit to the damage they're allowed to inflict, and when neither of them is you yourself. I stood as Sammy had told me and raised my fists, but I felt like death on a cold Monday morning.

Mason danced in and jabbed his right fist at me. Instinctively I caught it on my left arm. He grinned and did the same again. I caught that one too. This wasn't so bad, after all. Perhaps I was better than I'd feared. Then he did it a third time and I moved to intercept the blow, just as he'd intended . . . WHIZZZZBANG! And something landed with sickening force on my nose. I never even saw the blow coming.

Blood sprayed out and the deck went spinning round. Mason was laughing, and his mates were laughing at the simple, fool's trick he'd played on me, and in he came again. He threw a blur of punches to catch my attention then kicked a spot on my knee that left my whole leg numb with pain, darted under my guard to seize me by the waist and threw me over his hip to land on my back. As I struggled up he kicked me hard in the kidneys and the pain of it sent me down again. Then he slid clear to let me rise and led me lumbering after him like a harpooned whale, so he could treat the company to an exhibition of his skill. Jab! Jab! Jab! On my wounded nose, relaxed and easy and effortless. Each blow was agony but my months at sea had made me tough and it was some while before I went down again. Or rather, this time, I felt that it was me that was upright and the deck that came up to meet me with a crash. I thought that was the end of it, but a bucket of cold seawater was emptied over me and my mates lifted me gasping and blowing to my feet. The shock of it cleared my head and I saw that Sammy Bone was slapping me about the face to wake me up. He was furious and I realised he was yelling at me.

"You've not even tried to hit the bugger! What are you, anyway? What sort of man are you? Put your head down and go for him! Look at the bloody size of you! And if you won't fight then don't bother coming back to our mess, 'cos you're not wanted!" He slapped me, ringing round the head. "Can you hear me?" he cried and glared into my eyes. I nodded. "Then go and hit him!" Sammy cried. "HIT HIM!"

He shoved me forward, and there was Mason smiling and just itching to carry on. Christ but I hated that man! He'd beaten me fair and square. But that wasn't enough; he wanted more, he wanted to do real harm. And there he stood, relishing the pleasure of it, the swine. The trouble was that, despite my enormous strength, I was afraid of him. And didn't he just know it! I'd not hit him 'cos I hoped that he'd leave me alone if I didn't make him angry. But he *wasn't* going to leave me alone. I could see that. So what was I going to do? It was another turning point in my life, as important as that moment in the bows of *Bullfrog*. Terror is dangerously close to rage and I could just as easily have dropped on either side of the divide.

But I thought of Sammy's words, and they set off something within me that I never knew was there. The fear vanished and a mad anger took its place. I rushed at Mason, swinging wildly. He was a devilish fine boxer and hit me heavily, once or twice. But I was berserk and couldn't be stopped, and he got the full weight of my sixteen stones. I battered through his defence by brute force and planted a good one under his ribs.

The shock ran up my arm and the air squeezed out of him like a bellows. His legs sagged and he swayed on his feet, gasping for breath with his eyes half-closed. He didn't know if it was Monday or Friday and was wide open to a blow. Instantly, I swung my right fist full into the middle of his face, with all my might. Smack! It sounded like a round-shot hitting a cow. Down he went and his head hit the deck with a wallop that the Captain must have heard in his cabin.

Triumph and delight — Bosun Shaw snapped his fingers in Sergeant Arnold's face, the tars cheered, and every effort of his mates could not rouse the unconscious Billy Mason. Sammy said afterwards that the only thing that had marred that wonderful moment was the fear that I might actually have killed the bastard.

Then I was paraded round the ship, large sums of

money changed hands all round and my messmates (who'd bet their grog on me) collected enough drink to float the ship.

Mason recovered soon enough and hated me like poison ever after. He didn't forget and he didn't forgive, and by no means was he done with me. But he knew now that he had a master at fist-fighting and he didn't come back for more. From time to time I would see him with his messmates, glaring at me and muttering as if he was waiting his chance. But that's all he did, and I wasn't frightened of him any more, for the fight had changed me. It altered the whole way I saw the world. I'd always felt superior to others by being clever. But now I felt physically confident as well, if you know what I mean. And more important still, the fight brought me my first promotion.

Chapter 15

What evil deed has been worked upon your son I do not know, but the boy is broken in spirit. And so I send him home to you, in the hope that a father's care may, in God's good time, set him right.

(Letter of 25th March 1793 to Mr Richard Lucey from Mr Nathan Pendennis at Clerk's Court, London.)

*

Nobody would have guessed from the splendour of Lord Dunn's London house, or the powdered wigs of his footmen, that the noble Lord was penniless. But he was, since his father (the ninth Earl) had devoted his life to claret, gambling, and the whores of Drury Lane, until his career was brought to an untimely end by the combined assaults of drink and the clap. The ancient title had then devolved upon the present Lord Dunn, who for the next twenty years worked like a plantation black to put things right. But today, despite his efforts, even the splendid house and the powdered wigs were still in pawn to the money-lenders.

Consequently, in his unending search for money, the tenth Earl was often forced to receive as social equals individuals who, in his father's time, would have come in by the tradesmen's door with their hats in their hands. But Lord Dunn was a skilful politician and nobody would have guessed from his pleasant conversation how much he disliked the self-important, puffed-up, provincial mayor who was sipping his sherry at this moment — not to mention the sanctimonious little grub of a lawyer that he'd brought with him like a pet monkey.

But the mayor and his monkey had been making trouble all over London these last weeks, rattling the cages of the Admiralty and getting themselves introduced to persons of influence. And so they had now come to Lord Dunn, one of whose remaining assets was the gift of half a dozen parliamentary seats. All this effort, it seemed, was being expended on behalf of some apprentice or other, who'd got himself pressed when he shouldn't have, and had now thought better of it.

Lord Dunn looked again at the letter of introduction that the mayor had brought with him. The signature was one he respected and the content urged him to give the matter his consideration. But he'd have done so in any case, for his information was that money was involved; very much money. The apprentice, one Fletcher, was rumoured to be heir to a fortune and therefore in a position to show his gratitude to those who helped him.

Lord Dunn cleared his throat and interrupted the mayor who was droning on about the iniquitous behaviour of the Admiralty in claiming to be unable to give up a man simply because he was in a ship away at sea!

"Gentlemen," said his Lordship with a smile, "I agree with everything you say!" Mayor and monkey raised their eyebrows. "It is indeed hard to secure justice for a wrongly pressed man," he said, "and I should be happy to do what I can to help you." He noted the expressions on their faces and smiled to himself as he saw that they knew what was coming next. They might be provincial but they weren't so green as they looked. He continued, "But to do all that I should wish to do on your behalf, I should have to incur considerable expense. So I regret that it would be impractical for me to serve your interests . . . without being advanced one thousand guineas in gold."

"My Lord," said Mr Nathan Pendennis, without blinking an eye, "we are deeply grateful for your gracious condescension, but regret that we can advance no more than two hundred guineas, and that not in cash, but only as a promissory note . . . "

Ten minutes later, Mr Pendennis and Mr Lucey were being shown out of Lord Dunn's house by a respectful servant. They turned right along the wide avenue, bustling with the carriages of the mighty and the fashionable, and made for their modest lodgings in Clerk's Court.

"Four hundred and fifty guineas on Fletcher's release and fifty in advance," said Pendennis. "I believe he'd have taken less but I want his active co-operation."

"You are a most skilful negotiator, Mr Pendennis," said Edward Lucey. Pendennis shrugged his shoulders.

"Thirty years' experience, Edward my boy," he said. "But now we must labour to keep his Lordship at work. He and all the others we've seen. If we don't keep them at it, they'll slack off! We must . . . " But he saw that he'd lost his companion's attention. Lucey was gaping at a richly dressed young lady driving a perch phaeton drawn by a magnificent pair of silky-black horses, while her gentleman escort lounged beside her. Smartly she cracked the whip and the phaeton sped forward to slip between a gap in the traffic ahead. Lucey was fascinated. She drove like a coachman, and young ladies didn't do that in Lonborough. He was still seeing the great city with fresh eyes.

Pendennis smiled. He was fond of young Lucey. His wife had delivered up a string of daughters to bless their union, and though they were his own flesh and blood, they were indubitably daughters and were not sons, and would never *be* sons. And Edward Lucey made him feel young again just to look at him. So he kept his thoughts to himself and left the lad to enjoy the sights.

Later as they entered Clerk's Court, he indulged young Edward still further.

"Mr Pendennis," said Lucey, nervously, "as we have achieved so much today, I wonder if I might spend an hour taking a turn about the town? I should much like to see more of it and we have been so busy . . . "

Such a request from one of Pendennis's apprentices, with all its implication of time wasted in idleness and pleasure, would have drawn a shrivelling blast from his lips, but that was different.

"Of course you may, Edward," said the great man benevolently. "Just ensure that you return by four o'clock. I believe Mrs Jervis has a fine joint of mutton for our dinner!"

"Thank you, sir," said Lucey, and went off without a care in the world to explore the wonders of the metropolis by himself. Pendennis smiled to see him go and knocked at the landlady's door. Neither he nor Edward Lucey noticed the lady and gentleman who'd been following them for some days, patiently awaiting this opportunity.

*

Pendennis did not worry at first when Edward Lucey was late for dinner. He kept asking Mrs Jervis to delay serving the meal until at length she told him that either it came to table now that minute — or it burned. So he ate a miserable meal alone. Knowing what a sensible lad

Edward was, he did not get angry at all, but a heavy feeling of dread fell upon him. He imagined every disaster that could blight a stranger in London, from falling in the Thames to being trampled under a team of dray horses. As darkness fell he worried more, and such was his agitation that he joined Mrs Jervis and her husband in their kitchen, for the comfort of their company.

Later, Pendennis and Mr Jervis roused the neighbours to search the streets in case Edward had lost his way. After some hours, having found nothing, all parties gave up and went home. Pendennis and Mr and Mrs Jervis then sat wringing their hands together until shortly after St Giles's clock struck two in the morning, when they heard a carriage stop at the entrance to Clerk's Court. Instantly its door slammed and the horses were whipped up to draw it rapidly away. Seconds later there came a faltering tap at the front door-knocker.

Pendennis and the Jervises raced to open the door and there, crouched on the doorstep, was a figure whom they hardly recognised: dishevelled and hanging his head like a man drowned in shame.

"Edward!" cried Pendennis. "What have you done? Where have you been?" In reply Lucey covered his face and wept. They drew him inside into the kitchen where the fire was still burning. Edward sat where he was put, swaying unsteadily in the chair and holding his head in his hands. The drink on his breath could be smelt from one end of the room to the other. Pendennis was embarrassed in the extreme. He could see the sidelong glances passing between Mr and Mrs Jervis. *They* thought it only too obvious where Edward had been and what he'd done!

"Madam," Pendennis said to Mrs Jervis, "I beg that you leave me to talk with the boy. I must get to the bottom of this, and he'll talk more freely to me alone."

"As you wish, sir," said Mrs Jervis, thinking how she'd worried half the night, and stalked off on her dignity, followed by her husband.

But Pendennis got not a word of explanation out of Edward Lucey. Whether he pleaded, argued or raged, all that Lucey would say was that he could no longer join in the work of liberating Jacob Fletcher and bringing him to his fortune. He said it with sobs and gulps until, as Pendennis was shaking him by the shoulders, he was hideously sick all over Pendennis's breeches and shoes.

Next day Lucey was extremely ill and unable to get out of bed until late in the evening. His shame was deeper still and he would not look Pendennis in the eye, but begged to be sent home to Lonborough. Pendennis was mystified. He knew the debaucheries that young men got into and he knew that they were usually ashamed afterwards. But this was excessive. Pendennis was sure that something more was involved, but Edward Lucey would not, or could not, say what.

Pendennis put up with this situation for two or three days, to give Edward the chance to get better. But he didn't. If anything he got worse, moping around and refusing absolutely to take any part in the enterprise that had brought them to London. Finally, and with real regret, Pendennis sat down to write a letter for Edward to take home to his father.

Chapter 16

The day after my fight with Mason, the Bosun came up to me with a proposal. He beamed from ear to ear, still relishing his successful wager with Sergeant Arnold, the two being great rivals.

"Now then, young Fletcher!" says he, poking me in the ribs, "How'd ye like to better yourself aboard this ship?"

"I'd like it very well, Mr Shaw!" says I.

"Well and good," says he. "I've the need for another mate in my department, to keep the crew sharp, and you might be the lad for the job."

I was. Indeed I was. And in more ways than he knew. I could hardly contain my delight. He, of course, saw only the superficial case: as Bosun, he was responsible for the smartness of the crew in all matters of seamanship. Which meant clouting their backsides to send them more speedily on their way; the genial duty of Bosuns since time began. And the more the men feared the Bosun the easier was the task. But Mr Shaw was getting fat, and the grey stubble on his chin told that he was not so young as he had been. So he looked to his mates for support and at present he had four, all chosen for ugliness and the size of their fists. I suspect he saw me as the flagship of his little fleet and he made my duties crystal clear.

"You must stick close to my elbow and pay attention to me. That way you shall learn your craft. But most partic'lar of all," says he, frowning in concentration, "should ever I point out one o' the hands, like *this* . . . and should I just wink at you like *this* . . . " and he did a little pantomime of actions to demonstrate, "Why, you just knock the bugger senseless!"

"Aye aye, Mr Bosun," says I, and he nodded in contentment, simple soul that he was.

And, of course, I could do what he wanted; there was no man on the ship that could stand up to me now. Which in its way is a fine and wonderful thing. Many's the time in my career that I've been grateful for Mother Nature's making me so almighty strong. But to my mind, a bear is strong, and so is an ape, but I see no particular merit in either beast because of it. I don't for instance think them better than a man, and I've never thought that *I* was better than other men just for my being so strong. No, to my mind I have far more important talents

— talents that were going to be *fully exercised* in the Bosun's department.

What I cared about was the fact that the Bosun was responsible for the ship's stores of rigging, blocks, cordage, cables, tar, paint, and her boats and all their fittings. All of which commodities were highly valuable on the open market.

Oh joy! Oh rapture! Only the Purser had a better opportunity for private dealings than the Bosun did. And here was I about to enter in upon this happy fraternity. The Bosun bought and sold for the ship, he was courted by tradesmen and was a trader in his own right, selling off materials "condemned as useless" to the King's Service. And best of all, while Mr Shaw was a good seaman and master of the horny-handed part of his work, one look at him told me that he was a mere clod where accounts and book-keeping were concerned. I saw a happy future for myself once I had secured his confidence and made myself invaluable in helping out with the important side of things.

And so pride goeth before a fall. Mr Shaw said he'd speak to Lieutenant Williams to confirm my rating as Bosun's mate, and I walked on air to find Sammy Bone and tell him of my good fortune. I blurted it all out, full of merriment, and he nodded and smiled a strange smile at me and pointed out one or two things I hadn't considered.

"Well done, lad," says he. "Of course I'm glad to see

you making your way . . . but you know it makes you a man apart, don't you?"

"What?" says I in surprise.

"Well," says he, "who is it swings the cat aboard a man o' war? Might make it hard for you to stay in the mess . . . " Then the full meaning of his words dawned upon me, and a great hollow ache opened in my breast. I'd never had a family of any sort (I certainly didn't count Dr Woods and his scraggy sister) and I realised how much my messmates meant to me. So what if one of my mates got himself a flogging . . . and *I* had to give it?

"Hold hard," says Sammy, seeing my expression. "I only said maybe. I'll talk to the lads and see what they think."

He did, and the verdict was that I should stay in the mess for the time being, rather than going in with the Bosun and his mates. This was a great relief since they were a coarse and stupid lot, but more important was the simple fact that my messmates wanted me to stay. So I was able to continue much as before. It had been a shock, though. Always before I'd never had to bother with anyone but myself, and suddenly here I was tied to five others! So I stayed in the mess, looked after my grog and baccy enterprises, and saw to it that my messmates dined off the best that the ship could provide. Also, I began to work my way into the Bosun's confidence.

This took a while but eventually I had the full picture.

As I had thought, his accounts were ludicrous: scraps of blotched paper, scrawled upon in a clumsy fist and jammed into an old ledger without the least semblance of order. His heart was in the right place, poor fellow, and he'd done his best: some paint here, a barrel of tar there, sold to friends in the merchant service. But he hadn't the least idea how to balance his accounts and only kept his head above water by payments to sweeten the clerks from the Navy Board who were supposed to audit his accounts. Fortunately I was able to show him the right path and within a couple of weeks of my promotion, we had a nice little nest-egg of stores laid aside, all duly entered in our books as lost or destroyed, and only awaiting the first opportunity to be sold off.

And I played fair with him. I could easily have deceived him and taken the lion's share, but it has always been a principle with me that business should benefit all parties.

"Blessed if I knows how you do it," says he, the first time he came to look at the splendid neatness of our new accounts, "but you're a wonder, you are, Fletcher. Blessed if I know how I ever did without you!" He nodded at me thoughtfully and rasped his thumb over his bristly chin. "You know what, my lad?" says he. "I reckon you'll go far in the Service." (This I solemnly enter on record as the first time that such a thing was ever said to me.)

And then this happy period of my time aboard *Phiandra* came to a close. In due time, the Admiral considered he was safely beyond the power of the French, and gave leave for his escorting warships to turn for home. The flagship and a couple of the frigates were bound for the Indies with the merchantmen, and the seventy-fours and most of the frigates were under orders to return to Portsmouth at the first opportunity. On April 15th they parted company from the convoy in an impressive display of fleet manoeuvring. I was seaman enough to appreciate it by then, and to understand the monstrous effort of human skill and muscle that set a dozen great ships, thousands of tons of oak and iron, moving together like dancers in a ballroom.

But *Phiandra* neither stayed with the convoy, nor turned for Portsmouth. Instead she reaped the benefit of being commanded by the man who'd got the First Sea Lord's nephew in his ship. Captain Bollington revealed a special commission from their Lordships, to cruise the French coast, at his discretion, to wreak havoc upon the enemy's trade.

This best of all possible duties meant that we were free to grab every French merchantman we could lay our hands on and send it home for an English Prize Court to buy from us. Naturally, the bulk of the prize money went to Captain Bollington and the officers, but every soul aboard would share in the loot and all hands were overjoyed at this wonderful, wonderful news. Thus did Captain Bollington become a licensed pirate, as did Nelson, Collingwood, and all the others in their time. So those of you who frown upon the selling-off of the king's tar and paint might like to bear in mind what it was that drove some of our noblest and best to engage the enemy.

But first we had to bid farewell to the flagship with all due ceremony. And for this we were all tricked out in our Sunday best, with yards manned and the ship spotless clean. As we came alongside the great three-decker the Admiral could be seen on the poop, gleaming in his gold lace, in the midst of his gleaming officers. Our band gave "God Save the King" and theirs replied with "Heart of Oak" (but not half so well as our Sicilians).

"Good day to you, *Phiandra*!" calls the Admiral.

"Good day to you, sir!" cries Captain Bollington. "Permission to leave the fleet, sir?"

"You may proceed about your duties, sir!" came the reply and we treated the fleet to a flashy display of seamanship as we bore away on our new course towards the far-distant French coast. We'd got very slick at our trade by then and the whole thing was done without a word said or command given. Two hundred men working as a united team. It almost made me proud.

We enjoyed fair winds for a couple of weeks and were no end of a jolly company as we ploughed steadily back towards fat prizes and wealth for all hands. It was common knowledge that our destination was the great bay of the river Aron, south of Bordeaux and just north of the French border with Spain. Captain Bollington had special knowledge of the area as he'd lived there as a child when his father was in the Diplomatic service.

The great anchorage of Passage D'Aron was a major centre of French merchant shipping, and Captain Bollington aimed to put his special knowledge to practical use in some sort of large-scale cutting-out expedition. Excitement aboard *Phiandra* was intense and the ship ran with rumours as to exactly what the Captain had planned.

In the event, we might have saved ourselves the trouble, for what our Captain had planned was as nothing compared with what the sea had planned. We were a couple of days sailing from France when the weather turned nasty. The sky went dark and the air got cold, and all hands were turned up to make ready for what was coming. Captain Bollington bawled and hollered, the topmen swung like monkeys, and there was a vast deal of hauling on lines for the rest of the crew. The object was to take in as much sail as possible, to remove completely the upper yards (t'gallants and royals) and to secure the rest with preventer slings and braces. Also, hand-lines were rigged all about the fo'c'sle, quarterdeck and gangways, to give us something to hold on to.

Hand-lines! What a jolly sight they are to see. Because what they mean is that very soon it's going to be so bloody rough and the decks are going to bounce so bloody high that even the saltiest old tar among you (stap his vitals and shiver his timbers) won't be able to stand still and break wind without hanging on for dear life. So if ever you're on a ship where they rig the hand-lines, then take my advice: go below, get the largest bucket you can find, and stand by to heave.

With a south-wester blowing us straight towards France, Captain Bollington chose to run with the storm rather than lie to.

"Mr Williams!" says he, shouting over the rising weather.

"Pick a pair of strong men to support the quarter-masters."

"Aye aye, sir!" says he and turned immediately to me.

"Fletcher! At the double now, stand by the quarter-masters and give aid to steady the wheel!"

So I took my place at the wheel, together with Nathan Miller, another of the Bosun's mates: a man near as big as myself.

Even landsmen know what a ship's wheel looks like, so I'll not describe it, except to say that *Phiandra's* wheel was double. That is, she had two wheels, one in front of the other, fixed at either end of the drum about which the steering tackles were wound. These were raw-hide ropes that ran down to the lower deck where they ran through pulley-blocks to act upon the "sweep", a twenty-foot beam, joined to the top of the rudder as a giant tiller. As we turned the wheel, the ropes pulled the sweep one way or the other to move the rudder. In normal use, two men steered the ship, standing one on either side of the foremost wheel. Each man had a compass in its binnacle before him so he could follow his course. This was an élite task and the chosen men, the quartermasters, were mature seamen of great experience.

On that day, Nathan Miller and I manned the aftermost wheel to provide extra strength. We had not been more than a few minutes at the wheel when the main storm hit us. It came with a blast of wind that set every man leaning against it and clutching his hat. Mine was whisked away and went spinning into the dark like a mad bird. Not three paces away, Captain Bollington was shouting something into Mr Williams's ear, his cupped hands nearly against the Lieutenant's head. But I heard nothing over the shrieking of the wind. Then a blinding torrent of rain came down like steel rods, bouncing knee-high off the deck and stinging like a Bosun's cane.

Phiandra lurched forward under the enormous power of the wind and the wheel shuddered like an animal. The four of us heaved mightily to hold her then, for all the effort of our struggle, we stared upward as a series of piercing reports . . . Crack! Crack! Crack! . . . came from aloft, sounding over the storm like musket shots. And there were the fore and main topsails, torn from their gaskets and streaming in tattered rags, ripped and shredded by the impact of the wind. And that was only the beginning. Even as we looked, the mizzen topsail went as well, with a crackling of rent canvas, torn from its lashings to join its fellows in ruin. But the reefed courses held and drove *Phiandra* onward to bury her bows in the sea. Spray crashed upward as she plunged onward and showered the length of her decks, so we never knew whether it was rain or sea that was drenching us.

And after the shock of the wind came a great wall of water. A train of waves of such immense size that the seven hundred tons of our ship were whisked up bodily, leaving an unholy coldness in the floor of every man's belly as she rose, then the very reverse as she dropped like a stone. This was my first real storm at sea and I could never have imagined the size of those waves. Some were fully the height of our topmasts, from their black troughs to their foaming crests. One minute we were high in the air, with a fine view of the torment all around, and the next we were sunk in a heaving valley of ocean with our line of sight ending mere yards away in a living wall of greeny-black water.

And all the time we struggled with the wheel to hold her before the wind. It was vital to take the great waves on our stern. Any one of them, should it take us broadside on, would take out her masts and roll her over like a barrel.

It went on for hours. The daylight went and the night came, lit by sheets of lightning. We were deafened by the wind, flogged by the spray and exhausted by the lurching, jerking wheel. One of the quartermasters suddenly dropped at the wheel and Lieutenant Williams instantly took his place. There was no chance to get the man below so Captain Bollington and Lieutenant Seymour lashed him to a carronade slide to keep him safe.

The struggle with the wheel was immense, and as many men as could joined us to hold the ship on course. The Captain and all three Lieutenants took their full part in this. And then a great wave came down over our stern, roaring like a thousand cannons, and broke full upon the quarterdeck. The blow came like a giant's hammer and buried us all in seething water. Instantly, the noise of the storm vanished in a green, swirling hiss as the waters closed over us. Lungs strained and eyes popped as the ocean tried to snatch us away. Then it was draining off, our heads were clear and we were coughing the salt water out of our throats. In that moment I saw a mad jumble of smashed gear — lockers, signal flags, shoes and the like — go slithering along in the flood. The compasses, binnacles, lamps and all were among the wreckage as it went over the side in the next roll of the ship.

Beneath our feet the waves beat in the stern windows and made a clean sweep down the gundeck, annihilating the Great cabin, the day cabin and the Master's cabin, together with the ship's chronometers and charts, as the flood drove all before it, as far as the fo'c'sle. On its way, it tore loose a gun and set it plunging murderously with every roll of the ship.

The ship staggered under the blow. But worse was to follow: the wind got up still stronger and drove the ship onward so she buried her bows in the waves ahead. With the huge pressure of the wind in her sails and the intolerable weight of water aboard, she didn't rise to the waves as she should, but crashed bodily through them. Her timbers groaned and shrieked in their every joint, and we said our prayers all the harder.

Then Captain Bollington was bawling something at Lieutenant Williams and the Lieutenant was nodding. He turned to me with a smile and shouted into my ear.

"Are you with me, Fletcher?" says he. (Holy Jesus, what a question! What did he expect me to say . . . "No"? or "Perhaps"? Or "Not just at the moment, thank you"?)

"Aye aye, sir!" says I, weakly. He beckoned me to follow and the Captain took my place at the wheel. Judging his moment as the vessel rolled, Mr Williams threw himself bodily at a hand-line and hauled himself along. I did my best to copy him but I hadn't his sea-legs or his agility. He looked back and smiled.

"Come on, Fletcher," said his lips, though the wind blew the sound away. He looked so confident and so much better at the thing than I could ever be, that I shook my head in admiration. He must have seen that, 'cos he laughed with all the gaiety of a child at his birthday party. And then, while I was hanging on with all my strength in imminent fear of being washed away, would you believe it but he actually let go the line with one hand and clapped me on the arm?

"Come on, Fletcher!" he cried. "We'll show 'em, you

and I!" He wasn't one bit afraid and was undoubtedly enjoying himself. I'd never seen such a display of reckless disregard for fear. But more was coming, for we'd the loose gun to deal with.

Chapter 17

On the main deck, we found the Bosun with a team of men at the pumps. Every hand who could be brought to the work was heaving away at the cranks to drive out the water that had come aboard. They were souls in torment: clenched teeth, closed eyes, straining like cart-horses. They had the same look of desperate agony on their faces that you see in runners as they flash through the last yards of a race, fighting to be first past the post. And well might they strain, for the life of every man-jack of us hung on their work. If they didn't clear the ship of the tons of water now sloshing neck-deep in the holds, and if they didn't do it fast, then she'd never rise to the waves again and the wind would just drive her under. That's if the ship's fabric didn't come apart first, under the impact of her collisions with the waves.

Lieutenant Williams said something to the Bosun and

Mr Shaw pointed forward. There was Lieutenant Haslam and a couple of men with ropes trying to catch the loose gun. Haslam was clumsy and was having trouble saving himself, let along stop the gun. Mr Williams grinned at me and beckoned again. He was struggling with the nettings on the weather rail. He hauled us out a hammock apiece: a sausage of canvas, as long as a man and pulled into a hard cylinder by marline hitches.

"Under the wheels, Fletcher," says he. "Catch it when it's still and jam these under the trucks." I nodded.

Imagine the most dangerous game in the world: boxing on a tightrope over a chasm, or a blindfolded pipe-smoking competition in a powder magazine. Think along those lines and you'll get some idea of what it was like to trap a broken-loose eighteen pounder on the deck of a man o' war in a gale of wind.

Everything moves in every direction. Everything is wet and slippery. Everything is underfoot: ring-bolts, tackles and gear just waiting their chance to trip you up and lay you out for the lumbering gun to roll upon. Everything is in league with the gun, and the gun itself is an elemental force: too heavy to be stopped once it's under way. Your only chance is that the gun is too slow to gather speed and you are nimble, except that on that occasion, my fingers were too cold to feel and my shoulders ached with hours at the wheel. Particularly the right shoulder.

"At my command now!" cries Lieutenant Williams,

and Mr Haslam gratefully gave way. "Steady, steady, steady," says Williams, agile as a panther and always closer to danger than any of us. Suddenly, the gun ground up against the mainmast and we leapt forward but I stumbled on something, my knees and elbows smashed into the deck and I felt the quivering of the planks as the gun rumbled back towards me with the next roll of the ship. But someone was hauling me clear; there was a wild scream as a man's leg went under the grinding wheels, and the monster crashed into another gun, jamming its long nose into the tackles. And that was the end of its fun. Lieutenant Williams leapt in and jammed his hammock under its rear wheels.

Once stopped, it was relatively easy to lash the loose gun to its brother. It meant a double strain on the lashings holding the tame gun, but that was only one of the smaller threats facing the ship at that moment. So Lieutenant Haslam did what he could for the man the gun had crushed and Lieutenant Williams and I dragged ourselves back to the quarterdeck where I relieved the Captain at the wheel. The Lieutenant studied the ship's motion.

"I believe she's easier, sir," says he.

"Indeed she is," says the Captain, "and the wind's dropping too." It was a steady blow now. Fiercely strong but it didn't come in gusts as before and there was no doubt that *Phiandra* was riding the waves as her builders had intended. We were saved for the moment. At least we thought we were.

For soon the dawn came and the morning light showed us the most terrible thing a sailor can see. We discovered we'd been blown along at a tremendous rate and were far, far closer to France than our officers had thought. They'd thought we were still in open sea, with room to manoeuvre. But we weren't. France had reached out its arms in the night to catch us, and a long black line of cliffs was in plain sight from the quarterdeck. They were all around us in a great bay and as the daylight strengthened we could see the white waves pounding the rocks at the foot of the cliffs. I looked at the other seamen manning the wheel and saw the dread in their eyes.

You who've grown up in an age of iron-built steamers cannot imagine the horror of that moment. Nowadays, should a ship find herself embayed on a lee shore, she'll go full ahead on her engines, and a turn of the wheel'll send her forging out to sea with her funnels puffing merrily (and her Captain taking sherry with the passengers most like). She can go straight into the eye of the wind if she wants.

Well, you couldn't do that under sail. Captain Bollington instantly put down the helm and tried to sail her out close hauled. But it was no good. She'd never clear the northernmost headland of the bay and the Captain, Lieutenant Williams and Mr Golding, the Sailing Master, were in urgent conference, hunched against the wind and spray, shouting to be heard.

"I says we must wear ship," says Mr Golding. "If we

tries to tack her in these waves, her weather bow'll go under. She'll never come through the wind and we'll be thrown all aback and cast ashore."

"No!" says Lieutenant Williams. "It won't do. We haven't the sea room. A cable's length of leeward and we're lost. We must tack!"

"I agree with you both," says the Captain. "We can't wear and I doubt we can tack. Summon all hands to make ready an anchor at the lee cathead and pass a spring from the aftermost gun-port. I shall attempt to tack and if that fails, I shall clubhaul."

Lieutenant Williams and Mr Golding hesitated a second and looked at each other.

"You'll *clubhaul*, sir?" says Golding, and you could see the fear on his face.

"Unless you have a better suggestion!" says the Captain, and Golding licked his lips.

"Aye aye, sir," says he, and the ship was thrown into furious activity in an instant. All hands were put to work, every man and boy from the cook to the Sicilian bandsmen, to work the desperate feat of seamanship that the Captain was going to attempt. After all, there was no point sparing anyone. If this wasn't done quite perfectly correctly, then we should all drown together.

So two hundred and fifty of us blundered about in the narrow confines of a creaking, rolling frigate, intent on a back-breaking task and in immediate fear for our lives. We brought up the great, awkward bulk of a cable and laid it out on deck. We secured it to the ring of our best bower anchor at the lee cathead and the Bosun and his mates stood ready to let go the anchor at an instant's notice. We led a hawser from the capstan out through the aftermost gunport on the lee side and forward, to be secured to the same anchor ring. And I was stood by number sixteen gun-port and given an axe to cut the hawser on command.

When all was ready Captain Bollington put down the helm and tried to bring her head through the wind. But the sea wouldn't have it. The headsails were laid flat aback, the ship staggered horribly and wind and water came roaring over the weather bow; not just spray but green seas rolled across the fo'c'sle.

"Let go!" cries the Captain, and the Bosun knocked out the clamp that held the anchor. The cable sprang up like a live thing and shot smoking over the side, with men leaping clear. One touch of a running cable will skin you to the bone or drag you down after the anchor. *Phiandra* swayed deeply as the anchor bit into the bottom and the cable pulled at her head, and her motion entirely changed as she fell downwind, swinging to her anchor. This was the moment when we lived or died.

The hawser was shorter than the cable and was supposed to perform the whole purpose of the manoeuvre, which was to drag *Phiandra's* lee quarter bodily round into the wind to leave the ship on her new tack, free to sail clear of the bay.

Number sixteen port where I was waiting with my axe, was under the quarterdeck, so I couldn't see what play of wind, cable and hawser were doing, but by God I could feel the ship moving under me! And I could see the anxious faces of those around me who knew what these movements meant far better than I did. Then the very fibres of the hawser squeaked and stretched as the colossal load came on. If it parted now we were lost. For a moment the ship hung at the bottom of the triangle of cable and hawser. Everything quivered like a bowstring.

Then, "Slip the cable!" cries the Captain, from the quarterdeck, and *Phiandra*'s bow jumped to leeward as the Bosun's team did their work and the pull of the anchor vanished. A second's delay then, "Cut!" cries the Captain.

"Cut!" says I and swung my axe. But my right shoulder was still aching and made me miss with the first swing. I wrenched the blade from the deck and tried again. Bump! The hawser was gone and *Phiandra* was heeling to the wind and coming round, round, round, as the yards were swung to fill the sails on the new tack.

Then we held our breath as she gathered way and raced for the open sea at such a speed that the slightest touch on the rocks would smash her to splinters. Finally she thrashed past the breakers with no more than yards to spare, and made her escape. I didn't know at the time what a desperate thing the Captain had done, nor what a magnificent feat of seamanship he'd performed. It was only in later years that it really sunk in, from the silence that fell over any audience of seamen when I told the tale. They all knew what clubhauling was, but none of 'em had seen it done.

After that, the gale blew for a few hours more and I had to take my place at the wheel again, but finally it subsided and we had more work to do in repairing our rigging and sorting out the shambles below. The stern windows were a gaping hole, spars were sprung and lines parted everywhere. And down in the hold, shattered water-butts slopped side by side in foul bilge water, with the ruined remains of biscuit, flour, raisins and salt meat.

One after another, the ship's specialists came before the Captain with their tale of woe. His face grew longer and longer with each one. Finally he could stand it no more. In his turn, Mr Morris, the carpenter, came to report. And Captain Bollington thoroughly lost his temper.

"Damn your blasted eyes!" says the Captain. "What do you mean 'unstepped'?" The carpenter turned his hat in his hands and sighed. He was half dead with lack of sleep. He explained again.

"She be *unstepped*, sir. The foremast, sir. I done what I could, sir, but she needs to come out for it to be done proper like. An' I can't do it afloat. What she needs is . . ."

"Damn you, you bloody lubber!" cries the Captain. "D'ye dare to tell me you can't make it good? Is that it?

God damn you for an idle, useless landsman! Damn me if I won't have the Warrant off you! Are you telling me she must go into dock for repairs?"

The carpenter dared not reply, but Mr Williams intervened.

"Begging your pardon, sir," says he. "But even if we could make shift with an unstepped mast, there's half our food and water spoilt."

"Yes, sir," says Lieutenant Seymour, "and the charts are gone and our . . . "

"Damn you both," says the Captain, in a rage, rounding on the two Lieutenants. He pointed accusingly at the wretched carpenter, "Do you take his part against *me*? Damn you all, I say! I am determined to fall upon the French with the utmost despatch, and you cowardly lubbers will have me put in to port for repairs! Do you not see that the instant we drop anchor in England, some rogue of an Admiral will take away my commission?"

"But sir," says Williams, "the foremast is unstepped . . ."

"Do you argue with me?" roars the Captain, and flung down his hat. "Dammit, you puppy, I'll break you for that. Damn! Damn! Damn!" And this formidable man, who'd just saved our lives with his seamanship, stamped his hat into the deck and turned his back in a sulk. He simply couldn't face the idea of returning to Portsmouth and running foul of some officer powerful enough to extinguish his independent command. For this could so easily happen. Frigates were useful and all admirals were short of them.

"Have it your own way," says he to the weather rail. "Take her in if you must." And he stood there for hours, ignoring us all, as Lieutenant Williams supervised the work of putting the ship to rights and feeding the crew. The Captain wouldn't even take part in setting course for home, but left that entirely to the Lieutenants and Mr Golding.

I was sent to join the Bosun again and helped drive the men to splicing and mending of the rigging. Everyone was still wet so I didn't notice for some time that the wet running down my right arm wasn't water, and that it had a connection with my aching shoulder. Finally, the Bosun noticed blood running off my fingers on to the deck and sent me below to find the Surgeon.

"Off! Off!" says Mr Jones. "Bare the wound! Let the dog see the rabbit." And he hauled off my jacket and shirt to find the source of the Nile that was streaming down my arm.

"Ouch!" says I, as he found what he was after.

"Tch! Tch!" says he. "And how did you do this, my man?"

"Don't know, sir," says I. "It must have happened during the storm. I was too busy to notice, I suppose."

"Yes," says he, "a common enough phenomenon in men who are excited or impassioned. Hmm . . . something sharp and narrow has pierced your shoulder . . . here!"

"Ouch!" says I, again, as he probed the wound and pondered on its cause.

"Some fragment of splintered timber, I should imagine, driven like a spear by the force of the tempest. As neat as if it were incised! Hmm . . . well, whatever, 'tis a clean wound and judging by the size and strength of you, I doubt it'll kill you." So saying, he put in a couple of stitches and bound me up tight to stop the bleeding. "Come and see me tomorrow, or at once if the bleeding does not stop."

But it did stop and the wound healed fast. I thought no more of it, especially as others were hurt far worse than me. The man whose leg had been smashed by the gun survived Mr Jones's amputation and then died from the gangrene a week later. And the quartermaster who'd collapsed at the wheel was drowned sitting upright, when the great wave came over our stern. Next day I saw him go over the side, sewn in his hammock with a round-shot at his feet. Our Chaplain read the funeral service and all hands stood to attention.

After that, once Captain Bollington had finished moping, and once he'd swallowed his disappointment, and once he'd accepted that *Phiandra really* was too storm-damaged for adventures against the French, and that she *really* could not be repaired at sea, he brightened up and had the wit to touch on precisely the thing to make all hands strive from the depths of their souls to get the ship safely to Portsmouth.

"Now lads," says he, to the assembled crew. "I am resolved to exert every influence at my command to ensure that on our return to Portsmouth every man shall be paid in full . . . "

"Three cheers for the Cap'n!" cries the Bosun who, thanks to me, had his own (business) reasons for seeking a quick return to harbour. The men cheered merrily. Given this Captain's powerful connections they felt they'd actually get some of their money.

"Furthermore," says the Captain, "as our stay in harbour may be prolonged, I see no reason why the wives should not be brought aboard."

This met with thunderous, spontaneous cheering that put the previous effort to shame. At first I was puzzled. But Sammy explained later, and when we reached Portsmouth after a couple of weeks of slow, painful sailing, I received the most intensive education that ever a young sailorman was given, on the subject of "wives".

Chapter 18

Another hand's breadth lower and I'd have run the blade into his lung. I know this is failure, but by such a narrow margin that I remain confident of eventual success.

(Letter of 25th April 1793 to Lady Sarah Coignwood from Alexander Coignwood aboard *Phiandra*.)

*

The Wardroom of His Majesty's Ship *Phiandra* was much like the Wardroom of any other frigate. It was at the stern on the lower deck. The main deck was above and the orlop was below. The marines berthed immediately for'ard, and the ocean berthed immediately aft. Over the heads of the occupants swivelled the great oaken sweep that controlled the rudder, drawn this way or that by the ship's wheel. Creaks and groans sounded eternally from the sweep's tackle, but nobody noticed. They didn't even hear it any more.

Down the centre of the Wardroom ran a long table with occasionally a battered chair drawn up to it, or more commonly somebody's sea-chest. Except when it was cleared for meals, this table was covered with the sort of clutter that gentlemen keep about them: old newspapers, books, swords, sextants, pistol cases, a flute, a hunting horn, a fishing rod and a tame rat in a cage. This was so despite the First Lieutenant's passion for smartness, because the Wardroom was the place where the ship's gentlemen lived, and even discipline had its limits.

After the Captain, the gentlemen of the wardroom were the elite of the ship's people. First came the three Sea Service Lieutenants and the two Marine Lieutenants, all holders of the King's Commission and therefore gentlemen by definition. Next came those Warrant Officers whom the Navy's ancient traditions treated as gentlemen: the Master, the Surgeon, the Chaplain, and the Purser (even he). Finally, there was Mr Webb, the Master's Mate. He was a first-rate navigator who stood watches like a Lieutenant. Everyone knew that as a ship's boy of fifteen, he had brought the sloop *Bouncer* back from the West Indies with all her officers dead of the Yellow Jack. Mr Webb had been voted a member of the Wardroom since he was thought fit for that honour, despite the lack of Commission or Warrant.

On Thursday 25th April, the day after Captain Bollington's spectacular feat of clubhauling *Phiandra* off a lee shore, Alexander Coignwood closed the door to one of the tiny cabins that ran in rows on either side of *Phiandra's* Wardroom table. It wasn't much in the way of privacy. The door was no more than canvas stretched over laths and the cabin walls were matchwood. Every word spoken in the Wardroom came plainly to him. Every movement in the other little hutches on either side, every smell even, makes itself known. But he didn't mind that. Even on a flagship the accommodation wasn't much better. And with the Great cabin swept away, Captain Bollington himself wasn't faring any better at the moment.

Alexander's clothes were soaking wet and he was exhausted beyond the imaginings of landsmen. He'd not slept for two and a half days, and for most of that time he'd been too busy even to think about rest. Most men would have dropped into the inviting cot just as they were. But not Alexander. With his last gasp of strength he removed his clothes, made an effort at drying himself on a canvas towel, pulled on a nightshirt and climbed into bed.

Even now, when the blessed opportunity had come, he did not instantly fall asleep. And it wasn't the cold or the uneasy movement of the ship that kept him awake. No, he had to compose his mind. There was something he had to think through to its end.

He remembered the moment when the sea came over *Phiandra's* stern and swamped the group of men clustered around the wheel. He felt the chill of the water as it covered him, and the shock as it took him off his feet. He felt his left hand clench as it gripped the hand-line, while his right hand groped for the hidden knife and jabbed it into the broad back in front of him.

Nobody saw. In the stress of the moment, Fletcher never even noticed. And he, Alexander, felt the satisfying thump of the blade sinking in and the tug as he instantly snatched it out. But he'd had to wait till he was actually under water before he could strike, or someone would have seen. So he was aiming blind. And worse, the water dragged at his arm. The result was that instead of a neat death-stroke into the kidney, he had delivered a mere stab into the shoulder.

Alexander sighed. Alone and tired, actual tears came to his eyes. It had been so close! Had the blade entered a hand's breadth lower, it would've run into the lung — a slow kill, but sufficient. It was galling to come so close and yet fail. But he didn't weep for long. He was used to self control. His whole life had been a struggle to contain a self that must not be seen by the world. The struggle had been so very hard that from time to time he'd lapsed and the consequences had been unpleasant. Duels and money had been needed to wash his reputation clean (and even so, a stench remained).

To maintain even this partial hold on his own nature,

Alexander Coignwood had to be as disciplined as a Prussian Grenadier. So first he calmed himself, then he resolved to succeed *next* time, then he planned the letter to his mother to report all this, then he pulled a blanket over his head and slept like a child.

Chapter 19

"Ah, would you, sir? . . . Take that! And that! And THAT! Conceived in lust you *were*, continue in it you shall *not*!" Whack, whack, whack, for the good of my soul. My gracious guardian and benefactor, the Rev. Dr Woods. I can't remember what sins of mine drew such beatings, or what I might have said or questions asked, probably in all innocence, but by George I remember the good Doctor laying into me with a riding crop till his arm tired. "Conceived in lust you were," was a favourite phrase of his, and he said it to me many times. As a child I knew it was shameful but not what it meant. Later, as I learned about life, I supposed that I must be a tart's whelp, laid at the church door and raised on the Doctor's charity. It was part of the reason for my overwhelming passion to make money and better myself in my own eyes. So thank you good Doctor for that.

But I give you this jolly insight into my early life not for the fun of it, but to explain an oddity of my character as it existed in May of 1793 when *Phiandra* crawled back into Portsmouth to await repairs. There I was, eighteen years old, in the pride of my youth and strength and stark terrified because I was about to be challenged to make good some boasting that I'd been indulging in, on a matter that I knew little about, and for which Sammy and my other mates had been smacking their lips all the way home. It lightened their load and speeded their every endeavour.

In the event, they had to wait a few days for what they wanted. First, Captain Bollington had business to attend to and needed to spend a couple of nights ashore. This included minor matters like reporting to the Naval and Port Authorities, and arranging repairs and fresh stores for the ship.

But it mainly involved the really important business of pulling strings mightily to preserve his precious independent command off the French coast. More important to the crew was the matter of pay. *Phiandra* had been in commission since February 24th when Captain Bollington joined her. But the ship had been receiving men for months before, and some of her people, including Sammy, Thomas and Jim, had been on Mr McFee's books since November of the previous year. Others of the crew were due the Volunteer's Bounty and none of us had received a penny piece so far, and all that was to be put right in a single lump sum.

Finally, on a Wednesday morning, a large iron strongbox came out in a launch under the care of two dapper little gentlemen from the Pay Office with their wigs and spectacles. With marines on guard, Mr McFee's table was rigged on the quarterdeck and the entire crew mustered to be paid. Thus did the enormous sum of nearly three thousand pounds in silver and gold pass into our ship. A joyous occasion indeed, complete with our Sicilians thrashing out merry music. But not a fraction of the joy that was to follow.

The sight of the Pay Office launch heading for the shore told all the world that *Phiandra*'s men had now been paid, and this gave the signal for a flotilla of small craft to head towards us, like actors awaiting their cue. There came a roar from the men and the ship rolled as they ran in a body to the shoreward side of the ship for a better view of what was coming.

"Mr Bosun!" cries Lieutenant Williams. "Muster the men aft!" And the whistling of Bosun's calls filled the air, summoning all hands to the quarterdeck ladders where we were summoned when Captain Bollington had something to say.

I found myself beside Sammy Bone and my messmates. Sammy grinned at me and nudged me in the ribs.

"Shan't be long now, lad!" says he, and in reply I gave a knowing wink and nudged him back, keeping up my act to the last.

"Silence on the lower deck!" bawls Mr Williams and

a hush fell on the company. The whole waist aft of the quarterdeck was packed with seamen looking eagerly up at Captain Bollington and the officers.

"Mr Williams!" says the Captain. "Would you be so kind as to cast an eye on those boats and give me your best opinion?"

He nodded at the flotilla. Lieutenant Williams raised his glass with a mock-serious flourish and examined the boats.

"'Tis the men's wives, sir, I do declare," says he.

"Very good, Mr Williams," says the Captain. "Then send the young gentlemen ashore with the Chaplain, and you may receive the wives aboard."

A howling and yelling of delight greeted this and I don't think that any ship's boat in all the history of seafaring was ever more swiftly swung out and lowered. Then the Chaplain was assisted over the side with all the chattering middies and their traps. The older ones, who had a good idea what was afoot, looked none too pleased but the youngsters were hopping from one foot to another in delight at the holiday. (The ship's boys, you will note, were left to witness everything that followed.)

Unobtrusively, Captain Bollington left the quarterdeck and retired below. An atmosphere of carnival gripped the ship with every man hanging over the rail and calling to the boats. There seemed little order in the ship and by now I was up on the quarterdeck by the mainmast shrouds. Sammy and I climbed up for a better view and the men roared with pleasure at the sight of the dozen boatloads of "wives" now closing fast.

As for me, a pit opened up in my bowels. For apart from one boat which was full of Hebrew pedlars, and apart from the boatmen at the oars, those boats were crammed with the flower of the whores of Portsmouth. *Phiandra* was about to be boarded by women. And I knew all about women because the Rev. Dr Woods had told me all about them. By George but he told me! He told me about women and SIN and SHAMEFUL DISEASES that were the ruin of fine young men (I've often wondered how he became such an expert on the matter). Then that fine Christian scholar would deliver another whacking and down we'd go on our knees to pray for my deliverance from the daughters of Jezebel. So I'd had some education from my guardian. Also, Polmouth was a seaport full of sailors, and one of God's laws is that where there are sailors there are women. So I'd seen them flouncing and ogling and trying to catch Jack Tar's eye. So, my jolly boys, it wasn't as if I didn't recognise a woman when I saw one.

What's more, it wasn't as if I wasn't *interested* in women. For when I grew older and started hopping out on Saturday nights to places like Mother Bailey's, I met women face to face. And some of them were delectable, and mighty great fun to be with. And besides, my pals told me all what they'd been up to. So I wasn't ignorant either. But thanks to Dr Woods, I'd never actually done anything myself, because too much of his teaching had taken root in my young mind. As the Jesuits say: "give me the child 'til he's seven, and I'll give you the man!"

So when Sammy and Norris and the others had explained what having the "wives" aboard really meant, I'd pretended to be as pleased as they were. I had to — by then I was such a fine fellow among the ship's company that I just couldn't bring myself to admit to my virgin innocence. That's what pride can do for a man. So I'd nudged and chuckled and joked with my mates, while wondering what I would actually do when the girls arrived.

And now they had. Nearly three hundred of them, and the fear pressed down on me. And they didn't come quietly. They screamed and laughed and giggled and waved and shouted and smoked and swore. They rocked the boats so the boatment cursed and the water splashed over the gunwales. Then they shrieked in fear and rocked all the harder. They were all the colours of the rainbow in their gaudy clothes and big, flowery hats.

Then one girl screeched out over all the rest.

"Yoo-hoo!" says she towards *Phiandra*. "Look at me!" And she struggled dangerously to her feet in the swaying boat, turned her back and lifted her skirts to wriggle her bare backside at us, all pink and round with plump thighs and white stockings bound up with red garters.

The men cheered wildly, the girls yelled all the louder, and the boatment pulled with a will. And then . . . and then . . . words fail me to describe the scene that followed. At once a dozen lines snaked down over the side and through the gun-ports to aid the vital work of bringing the girls aboard. In seconds they swarmed everywhere. Pandemonium broke loose and the Navy's savage discipline, backed by the bayonet and the cat, the discipline that could hang or flog at will . . . simply vanished.

I saw Mr Webb, Master's mate, struggle with one of the men for a girl who'd taken both their fancies. The seaman won, knocking down his officer and seizing the girl with a whoop of delight. Such an assault merited death (at least) under normal circumstances but on this occasion the Lieutenants wisely kept away. For one thing, there was a special boatload of choice young ladies from one of Portsmouth's more exclusive pushing-schools for their particular attention.

Soon there were more women than men aboard and an orgy of drink and lust was in full swing. Men too eager even to go below dropped their breeches and leapt aboard there on the very deck for all to see, all thrashing skirts and legs in the air. Then suddenly I ceased to be a mere spectator. The crowd parted and there was Sammy Bone, arm in arm with a couple of girls. One was a plump little bouncing blonde with huge breasts and a bottle of brandy. The other was black haired with dark skin like a gypsy, flouncing along in a brilliant-red dress. Sammy was beside himself with glee and had started well into the brandy.

"Here he is, girls!" says he. "Say hallo to Jacob! He's a whopper though, ain't he?"

"Ooo!" says blondie, in a high, amazed voice with pouting lips and round eyes. "Is he that big all over? Might have to charge double for him, girls!" And the three of them howled with laughter. But I was riven to the spot, my knees turned to jelly, and all the world was like a little blob of colour seen through the wrong end of a telescope. I heard Sammy speaking, but very faint and far away (which was odd because he was bellowing into my face at two inches range).

"This here's Polly Grimshaw," says he, introducing the gypsy. "She'll look after you." Then his leering, happy face was gone and the girl was staring up at me, twining her fingers through her long hair and affecting to smile coyly over her shoulder, while her tongue slid in and out like an amorous snake.

"Hallo, Jacob," says she in a rich Devon voice. "Ain't you a big boy then!"

"Guggle-guggle-guggle," says I, backing off. But she pressed herself against me, warm and soft, and her perfume swirled around my head. I had never experienced a woman's presence like this and it made me shiver in my terror.

"Let's see how big you really are!" says she and darted her hand into my breeches like a ferret after a rabbit. I gasped in horror and fled.

Using all my strength, I forced through the press,

closing my eyes to the things I saw, and fought my way down the quarterdeck ladder, across the main deck, down through the main hatchway and on to the lower deck. Here the going got easier, for precious few people had bothered to go below just yet. I pressed on further, down on to the orlop, to the dank, dark, stink of the hold, among the casks and ballast, below the water-line. There I came to rest in a dark corner up against one of the massive oaken knees that braced the deckhead to the hull. I slumped down with my back against the timber and my legs stretched out before me.

Slowly I got my breath back, listening to the riot going on above, and wondered what to do next.

But horror of horrors! What was this small, dark figure that crept towards me, giggling and panting from the chase. What was it that had followed me down to the darkness of the hold?

"'Allo Jacob," says she, in that chocolaty voice, "this is nice, ain't it? All quiet, like," and she crawled over my legs and settled herself down with her hands on my shoulders and her warm rump on my thighs and her eyes gleaming down at me no more than a foot from my face. She wriggled her hips and her bosom bounced under my nose, plump and luscious in her inadequate bodice with not a trace of stays underneath.

"Go away!" says I in a feeble squeak. "Go away, you . . . woman!" She laughed and tried to kiss me, but I pushed her away. She changed tack, running her fingers over my neck and chest and scratching my ears with the tips of her fingernails.

Every last hair in my body prickled at this treatment and I came over all peculiar. But still I pushed her off. "Here!" says she, not pleased. "What's this?"

"Go away!" says I. "I don't want you here!" This time she was annoyed.

"Oh? Like *that*, *is* it?" says she, hands on hips and shoulders high. "What are you, then? Are you one o' them as likes it better doing it up his mate's behind?" I gasped, shocked to my toenails at this hideous suggestion. Even Doctor Woods hadn't warned me about this one, but I knew what she meant.

"Certainly not, madam!" says I, right up on my dignity. "You just leave me alone . . . I . . . I'm a good boy, I am . . ." God knows from what depths of my childhood came these pathetic words, but much to my surprise they set Polly Grimshaw rocking with laughter.

"Oh my! Oh my! 'I'm a good boy'! Lord bless us all . . . " And strangely, the heaving and shaking of her body right there on my lap, and the sheer beauty of her as she laughed and her hair tumbled about, these things began to work an effect upon me and I stared at her in fascination as the fear and embarrassment died.

"'Ere," says she, at last, "you ain't never done this before, have you?"

"No," says I.

"Well . . . no matter, my duck," says she kindly, "that

don't matter at all. Not at all it don't. We all have to start sometime, don't we?" And she leaned forward and lifted my chin and kissed me.

If I live to be a thousand I shall never forget that moment. This time, such a thrill of pleasure ran through me as I would never have dreamed possible. Then bit by bit, and inch by inch, she wriggled and moved and unbuckled and unbuttoned, until nothing was between us and her skin lay hot against mine. Finally, and skilful as any helmsman, she guided me deep inside her, and I damn near unhorsed her with the frantic bucking of my first love-making.

And not more than ten minutes after, I had reloaded and run out again, and she was holding on hard and leaning back against my knees and laughing fit to bust as I drove at it again. And there wasn't one bit of embarrassment that time.

The following days passed in one great spree of drink and women, as I got my education rounded off as a seafaring man. And so it went on, while the money that had entered the ship passed through the temporary possession of the crew, to its predestined home with the ladies of the town and the Jew pedlars who came aboard with them, bringing all the cheap and flashy goods that sailors love to buy. I guess it took from the Wednesday to the following Sunday for *Phiandra* to be picked clean. To the seamen, money was a thing that came out of the blue and was there to be spent in a monstrous debauch.

By Sunday the merchants and most of the women had gone. All that was left were some cheap cranky watches from the Jews, some powerful memories, and a few cases for the surgeon's mercury. I say *most* of the women were gone, for some fifty or sixty stayed aboard of their own free will. Some really were the wives of men aboard ship and were making the best of this opportunity to visit their men. And some were girls who had taken a fancy to sweethearts who they were reluctant to leave just yet. To my sorrow, Polly Grimshaw was not one of these. In those few days I had fallen for her something powerful and I wanted to keep her for ever. I wanted her for her sparkling eyes and her rich black hair and the shudder that ran down my spine when she laughed.

"I'll come back and marry you, Poll," says I. "I'll look after you."

"Course you will, my duck," says she, not without sympathy, even though she'd heard those words a thousand times before. And then she was over the side and into a boat and the boatman shoving off. He set sail to catch a shoreward breeze and I climbed into the rigging for a last sight of her as she disappeared.

I wept bitterly. Not only had I lost my love but she had cleaned me out as thoroughly as the dullest, stupidest man in the ship. She had pierced my ingrained caution with money and carried off my pay and all my hard-earned profits from rum and baccy. *Me!* She had done this to me! Still, there was always the reserve of stores laid aside by me and the Bosun. I dried my tears and went off to find him. It was time to set about converting them into cash.

Fortunately we were soon thrown into the hands of the very people to expedite this piece of business. With the whores mostly out of the ship, Captain Bollington re-emerged, anxious to set the ship's repairs in motion. To the best of my knowledge he took no part in the orgy and let it run its course, as he had planned.

And soon there was a busy coming and going of dockyard officials, tradesmen and craftsmen of every description. Our damage below decks was made good, new stores were taken aboard and, finally, *Phiandra* was lashed alongside a sheer hulk rigged with huge spars to support the foremast while they restepped it securely against the keel.

Among all the tradesmen who came aboard, it was not hard for me to spot a likely customer and I impressed the Bosun still further by negotiating better terms for our stores than ever he'd dreamed possible. In fact it entirely shifted the balance of my relationship with him. He was so dazzled by the prospect of endless deals of this kind, that ever after, he was more like my employee than my officer though, of course, I remained respectful towards him. Common sense dictated that from a novice to a veteran Warrant Officer. It would have been so easy, and so stupid, to upset him and spoil everything. But I was always polite and as a result he did just precisely whatever I wanted. (I offer that as a lesson to you young-sters.)

The first fruit of this new situation was a wonderful opportunity to get back to that other, and better, life that I'd been torn away from. You'll note that I'd prospered somewhat aboard *Phiandra* and I'd found the means to make some money. But selling off ship's stores, although a good thing in its own right, was small beer compared with what I could achieve ashore. And there was a darker side. Lurking always in the back of my mind was the fear of what I'd done aboard *Bullfrog*. So the sooner I was out of the Navy's clutches the better. Then the world would be mine. I could change my name, and go where nobody knew me, and bury for ever the chance of being brought to account for Bosun Dixon. After all, I thought, there was no special value in the name of Jacob Fletcher.

Chapter 20

I now see that you were only too right in your denunciation of that woman. Should my wife learn what I have done, then the torments of hell will be mine.

(Letter of 1st April 1793 to Mr Richard Lucey from
Mr Nathan Pendennis at Clerk's Court, London.)

*

On Sunday 31st March, nearly a week after he had sent Edward Lucey home to his father in disgrace, Mr Nathan Pendennis attended divine service at St Giles's Church. Usually Pendennis took much pleasure in going to church. He paid keen attention to the sermon and enjoyed the music if there were any. But today he was distracted and could not settle.

The fact was that he missed young Lucey. The work

that Pendennis had so much enjoyed when there were two of them had become a burden for him alone. There was nobody to talk over the day's events with. There was no admiring audience to compliment him on his skill and energy. And despite Pendennis's efforts, the Admiralty still had not given up Jacob Fletcher. Pendennis had finally come to believe what the Admiralty Clerks kept telling him, namely that Fletcher was in a ship at sea and any further action must wait upon the return of that ship to port.

As he sat in his private pew (reserved for one shilling a week for his use alone), oblivious to the service and wondering what reliance might be placed on the promises of assistance that he had secured, he noticed that a lady was trying to catch his eye. He was struck by the piercing sweetness of her face and the elegance of her clothes. Obviously this was a lady of considerable consequence and impeccable respectability.

But he did not know the lady, and could imagine no reason why she should wish to make his acquaintance. He sighed — even as a young man Pendennis had never drawn the attention of fine ladies — and at first he thought he must be mistaken, so he looked about to see who it might be that she was really looking at.

But the lady persisted, and nobody else returned her glances, and Pendennis realised that she really was trying to catch *his* eye. Fat, middle-aged and entombed in marriage as he was, his heart beat a little faster. He risked a brief, courteous nod towards the lady to acknowledge her. She seemed satisfied with that and sat throughout the rest of the service in dignified attention to the Parson. Afterwards, as Pendennis left the church, he saw her waiting for him in the street. To his alarm, and yet delight, she approached, and with every dainty step his fascination grew. At a distance she appeared an unusually fine woman, but close to, she took his breath away.

His head whirled with emotions. He was no man for adventures. He was a serious man, a man of business. But within all true men (even Nathan Pendennis) there hides a tiny spark of hope where beautiful women are concerned. And that spark is not quenched by age, nor dignity, nor anything short of death. So poor Pendennis experienced afresh all the sensations of his youth, when first he fancied himself to be in love with his future wife. He saw that the lady was not young, but none the less she was such a woman as he'd never imagined. Such skin! Such eyes! Such mounds of lustrous black hair, such a delicacy of scent! And then she spoke.

"Sir," she said, with fluttering eyes and every delicate sign of embarrassment, "pray do not think ill of me for thus speaking to you without introduction, but my desperate situation permits of no other course. Are you not Mr Pendennis of Polmouth? For if you are he, then I cast myself upon your mercy."

The voice was like the rest. It caressed the ear and intoxicated the mind. The sound alone would have won his heart, let alone the power of the words themselves. Before even she'd explained what peril she was in, or how he might help her, Pendennis was wringing his brains to find any way that he might please her, to find any way to lift the despair from that angelic face — he was hooked, gaffed and landed.

"Madam," he said, "I am indeed Nathan Pendennis of Polmouth and I am entirely at your service, but how do you know me?"

"Sir," she said, "forgive me! For I have contrived to have you pointed out by one who knows you. I am here on purpose to meet you and I beg that you will grant me enough of your time to explain my predicament."

"Your servant, ma'am," he said, and looked at the bustle and clamour of the street. "But here?"

"I have a carriage," says she. "Will you come to my house?"

So Pendennis went with her. And before she'd gone two steps, the paving being rough, the lady accidentally stumbled and Pendennis was forced to draw her close to save her from a fall. Thus together they went up into a closed coach with a pair of matched horses and a liveried coachman on the box.

Once inside, Pendennis never noticed which way they went, for the lady began to sob gently and looked to him for support. All too soon, they arrived at a house in Dulwich Square, a new construction with five floors and a basement, all stuccoed in white and doubtless costing a fortune. A servant opened the door as they alighted, and the lady clung to Pendennis's arm. As they entered he could only gape at the magnificence of the furnishings and decorations all around.

"Welcome to my house, Mr Pendennis," she said, and Pendennis finally thought to ask a vital question.

"But who are you, ma'am?" he said. "What do you want of me?" She faced him with a sudden look of devilment in her eyes.

"I am Lady Sarah Coignwood," she said, and watched him closely.

Pendennis stopped in his tracks. It was like being snatched from a warm fireside and plunged into an icy pool. He drew himself up and spoke with all the dignity he could muster.

"Ma'am," he said, "I cannot remain here. We may soon be upon opposing sides in the courts. I support the Fletcher interest!" The shadow of a laugh passed across her face, then her manner changed like the turning of a page in a book.

"Sir," she said, looking into his eyes, "a cruel injustice is being worked upon me. Only you can save me and I beg that you hear me out. I appeal to your honour as a Christian gentleman."

Pendennis was only a man. He dithered for a second then followed where she led. They entered a room which was like her. It was furnished and dressed to her personal taste. To Pendennis, curtains were curtains and chairs were chairs, but even he could see that everything in that room was designed to please the senses. So in he went, as eager a fly as ever followed the spider into the web.

She sat him down on a sofa the size of a wagon, closed the doors and came to sit beside him. The worst of it was that every fibre of Pendennis's reason shrieked at him that he was doing wrong. He knew in his bones that he should get up and run while he could. But he hadn't the strength.

"Will you take wine, Mr Pendennis?" she said.

"No, ma'am," he said, "it is not my custom." But she pressed a brimming glass into his hand, and poured words into his ear. Afterwards he could never recall quite what she'd said, but at the time he experienced the delight of being told secrets that were only for intimate friends.

Several glasses of wine later, Pendennis was red faced and thick of speech. His lips were wet and he was no longer master of himself.

"You must believe me," she said, taking his hand and edging closer.

"Yes, yes," he said, shivering all over. Her words said one thing, but her every movement said something else.

"Bless you, sir," she said, and clasped his hand to her bosom and kissed it. She looked up at him and smiled like the houris in the Muslim paradise. Pendennis's last reserve crashed down like the walls of Jericho. He seized her and kissed her, passionately and longingly.

Even as he did it he feared a rebuff, but to his wonderment she welcomed his advances and responded in ways he'd never dreamed of. She twined her limbs around him and said such things in his ears and did such things to his body that he was engorged with lust. He tore at her garments and pressed his lips to her breasts, her belly, her thighs, and all the time the gleaming flesh writhed and the lovely face smiled and invited more.

Pendennis staggered to his feet, the better to throw off his clothes, hopped from one foot to the other, hurled his breeches over the sofa and pressed down upon her body to enter in. He gasped in pleasure as she seized him, to ease his path he thought, then choked in agony as ten sharpened fingernails drove viciously into the tenderest part of a man's entire body, shedding drops of blood on the sofa.

And so, with Pendennis's passion brought to an abrupt halt, Lady Sarah screamed loudly and sprung her trap. Without a second's delay, the doors burst open and in rushed half a dozen toughs led by a young gentleman in the most foppish clothes imaginable; he looked more like a parrot than a man.

"Mother!" he cried.

"Victor!" she cried. "Help me! Help me!"

"Villain!" he hissed, and pointed dramatically at Pendennis. "Seize that man!" and the whole pack fell upon their victim and dragged him, dazed and wondering, to his feet. Pendennis expected a beating but no blows were struck. Rather, they held him with his arms pinioned while Victor Coignwood attended to his mother.

He draped her in a robe to cover her nakedness, though she'd been standing in perfect composure with not a stitch on, even with all those men goggling at her. She seemed not to care, and stared steadily at Pendennis, in triumph. In horrible dismay, and in pain from his injury, Pendennis realised what a trick had been played on him. Swiftly, his feelings turned to anger.

"Damn you all!" he cried. "You shall all suffer for this!"

"And you shall *hang* for it," said Victor. "You shall be taken up on a charge of rape."

"What?" said Pendennis. "Rape? With this trollop? By Heaven, I see it all! You led me on of a purpose, you jade!"

"And how much leading was required, sir?" she asked. "Did I bind you and force you to my will? I think these good fellows will testify to your actions." Pendennis looked at the "good fellows" and saw a choice sweeping of the gutters of London.

"What, ma'am?" he said in contempt. "These scum? Brought in a penny a head I shouldn't wonder! And had they come in a second earlier they'd have found you with your whore's legs clasped about my neck, urging me to it!"

"Filthy beast!" said Victor, and struck Pendennis across the face.

"How dare you, sir!" roared Pendennis. "Don't you know I'm a magistrate and Lord Mayor of Polmouth? I'll have the law on you for this!"

"So you are a magistrate, are you?" said Lady Sarah.

"Indeed, I am ma'am!" he said.

"Then tell me this, Mr Magistrate. What chance of acquittal would you give to a man caught in the act of rape, by seven witnesses?" She paused to let Pendennis think that over, and as he stood there in his shirt, with his breeches on the other side of the room, the peril of his situation began to come home to him. Lady Sarah smiled and continued.

"And even if some miracle should bring about your acquittal," she said, "what would the good people of Polmouth think of their Lord Mayor were he to stand trial for rape? Think of it, Mr Pendennis. Your neighbours would read the details to one another from the newspapers, and you would be caricatured in every print shop in the land. Perhaps you have a wife? Perhaps you have children? What should they think of their Papa?"

Pendennis hung his head. She had him. No punishment that the law could exact could scourge him worse than this. He might well defeat her in the courts but he could never save his reputation.

"Damn you," he said, in a low voice.

"Ah!" she said, "I perceive a change of mood." She turned to her ruffians. "You may go," she said, "but wait outside." And they trooped out, grinning at one another.

"Now, Mr Pendennis," she said, "those fellows are mine to command. They will say what I tell them, or hold their tongues. And there is still a way for you to leave this house a free man." Hope surged in Pendennis's breast. He knew that some further dishonour must be involved, but he could not help himself. He only had to imagine for one moment what his wife would say and do should ever this story come out.

"Name it!" he said.

"It is simple," she said. "All that has happened here can be forgotten on certain conditions. You shall abandon all efforts on behalf of Mr Jacob Fletcher. You shall pester the Admiralty no more. You shall withdraw your support of my husband's Will of 1775. You shall persuade the Luceys to abandon all their actions in the matter and you shall tell me everything you know."

Pendennis ground his teeth and clenched his fists in anger. But he could see no way out. He looked at Lady Sarah and her son Victor, now reclining at their ease on the very sofa where he had been shamed. They smiled at him with fathomless contempt. Suddenly his jaw dropped as a mystery was no more.

"You devils!" he cried. "This is how you treated Edward Lucey!"

"How clever of you, Mr Pendennis!" said Lady Sarah. "You are quite correct, except that in Mr Lucey's case, I allowed things to run on a little longer, he being a surprisingly *gifted* young man — unlike your small and miserable self!" They laughed at him merrily and Pendennis shuddered with disgust.

But he was broken. Just like young Lucey, he was finished in this business. All that he could do for Fletcher now would be to write to Richard Lucey saying that he, Pendennis, must be excluded from all secrets and plans. For anything that he knew could be wrested from him by the Coignwoods. Richard Lucey must carry on alone. Pendennis took some comfort from the fact that at least Lucey would be warned. At least he would know precisely how dangerous their enemy could be. And in this estimate of the threat posed by the Coignwoods, as in every other aspect of his dealings with them, Pendennis was completely wrong.

Chapter 21

Phiandra was anchored so close to the shore that we could see all the busy life of the great seaport. With little to do and weeks of repairs ahead, the world ashore beckoned like the sirens that called to Ulysses. Some of the men, like Norris Polperro, had families they'd not seen for months and talked of nothing else than the hope of getting out of the ship. With the Captain spending so much time ashore at his politics, responsibility to prevent wholesale desertion fell on the first Lieutenant, Mr Williams, who took the usual precautions.

As a Bosun's mate, I had had a hand in this myself and took my turn at the oars, rowing a guard-boat full of marines slowly round the ship. Their orders were to shoot any man trying to run; and the faithful promise of a flogging for the whole boat should any one get past us.

And so I made my first move.

"Why can't just some of us go ashore?" says I to the Bosun. "Those of us who can be trusted . . . I wouldn't run, you know that, Mr Shaw, and I'd vouch for my messmates as well. If you were to put it to Mr Williams, as a Christian act, he might agree. It would give some of these poor devils some hope, you see."

It was an interesting moment. I was the goose that layed golden eggs and Mr Shaw had no wish to lose me. And he was wondering what game I was playing. He knew I was cleverer than him. He leaned his head on one side and scratched at the stubble on his chin.

"Why d'you want to go ashore then, eh?" says he. "And why d'you want to take them others?"

It was time to play my ace. I dropped my voice.

"Fact is, Mr Shaw, I want to have a word with some friends ashore. I think I could find us a customer for a cable."

A look of awe came over his face. *Phiandra* carried 100-fathom hemp cables of twelve-inch circumference and weighing a ton and a quarter apiece. He'd never dreamed of selling so massive and ponderous an item and the guineas twinkled in his mind. I could see that I'd got him but I continued without a pause. "But I need my mates along, d'you see, to make it look right. Mr Williams isn't going to let me off the ship on my own, now, is he?"

He smiled happily and went off to see Mr Williams

who, as I'd thought, proved receptive to an idea coming from so trusted a personage as the Bosun. Next morning, my messmates and I were paraded before Mr Williams on the quarterdeck. The news was all round the ship that Sammy Bone's mess were to be given shore leave and all the crew were there to witness the event. And they all approved. They all hoped it would be their turn next. Like the born leader he was, Mr Williams made the most of this. He singled me out at once.

"Fletcher!" says he, and looked me straight in the eyes. I felt uncomfortable. "I am resolved that should this experiment succeed then all the other messes shall have their chance. So give me your hand, and your promise to return in twenty-four hours. I look to you as a Warrant Officer, to see that all goes well." That was pitching it a bit high; I was only a Bosun's mate. But it was typical of the man to make that sort of gesture. I shook his hand and promised. And so did all the others: Sammy, Norris, Thomas, Jem, and happy, stupid Johnny Basford. Then we got three cheers from the crew as we went over the side to be rowed ashore.

Soon we were strolling along George Street in the thick of the press of people: porters, carters, servants, children, dogs, cats and gentlefolk – that was the life of Portsmouth. It was wonderful. Hawkers yelled, wheels rumbled, hoofs clattered and doors banged. It was like being drunk and we swaggered along merrily. But as we went past a grand house with big windows on the ground floor, Sammy pulled us to a halt.

"Avast, mates," says he. "There's us!" He pointed to one of the windows. With the bright sunlight of the street and the dark interior of the house, the panes of glass were reflecting like a mirror. Warships do not provide mirrors for the convenience of the hands, so this was a novelty. I saw the happy faces of my mates grinning at me out of the glass. And then I was brought up sharp. Among the figures was a broad, muscular man, dominating the group. He was a seaman from head to toe: tanned skin, rolling gait, *Phiandra* togs. Precisely the same sort of alien creature that had so frightened me when first I was taken aboard a man o' war . . . and it was me! It was the most amazing shock to see how I was changed.

My mates laughed and pointed at each other, and made faces at the glass, but Sammy saw what was going on in my mind.

"Aye lad! You're not what you was," says he. "What's the matter, don't you like it?" I said nothing because I didn't know what to say. And then we moved on and paraded round the town 'til we were fed up with looking, and we sought out a place to get drunk. In Portsmouth there were a thousand grog-shops and ale-houses catering for sailors, and I was happy to pay for my mates' drink out of my latest business profits, so by evening we were sat round a table in the public room of a dingy establishment called the "George and Dragon". It was full of seamen and reminded me of the "Three Dutch Skippers" in Polmouth, where I'd been pressed all those months ago.

I decided it was time to raise a sensitive matter. I still hadn't mentioned that I wasn't going back to the ship, and I had an uneasy feeling about the matter. The trouble was that my mates had all promised to go back. Personally I'd have promised anything to get my freedom, but I knew them well enough to know that they might see things differently, though God knows why. They were all skilled men, who'd do far better in the merchant service than ever they would in the Navy.

"Well, lads," says I, finally, "here's goodbye to the Navy as far as I'm concerned." I raised my tankard and drained it. They didn't understand at first and I had to make clear what I meant. They caught my drift soon enough and the looks on their faces told me that I'd guessed correctly. Every man of them intended to go back and, what's more, they expected me to go with them.

"We've got to go back!" says Sammy. "What about all the others? If any of us runs, there'll be no shore leave for anyone else. And some of 'em's got family in Portsmouth that they wants to go and see." They all stared at me, frowning. It was like the first time I joined the mess. I felt an outsider again.

"But I'm not a sailor," says I, desperately trying to make them understand, "I was an apprentice. I never wanted this." I turned to Norris for support. "What about you, Norris, you've got a family. Aren't you coming?"

"No," says he, with a surly look. "My brothers'll look to my wife and child'n, just as I'd look to their'n . . . I ain't gonna run!"

"Why not?" says I, astonished. "You were pressed just like me. And you tried to get out of it . . . you made that wound on your knee!"

"That's as maybe," says Norris. "'Tis the way of seamen to fight the Press. But 'tis the way of things for us to *be* pressed in time o' war. What about them buggerin' Frogs, eh? Who's to save old England from them if there ain't no Navy? And we are the Navy; we man the ships and fight the guns . . . Anyway, I promised."

Sammy and the others nodded in agreement. Aside from Johnny, who was an idiot and didn't matter, they'd all volunteered into the Navy so I wasn't surprised, but Norris's attitude was beyond me. A mixture of patriotism and a determination to keep his promise to Lieutenant Williams, particularly the latter, and I couldn't shift him, try as I might.

In fact I soon gave up. I knew how stubborn my mates could be and how useless it was to argue with them once their minds were set.

"Well, I'm going," says I. "I was never bred for a seaman and I've got a life ashore to follow."

"Aye, lad," says Sammy. "You've got all that money

to make, haven't you? I hope it keeps you warm of a night once you've got it. Never you mind about your promise."

That made me angry. What did I owe the Navy? Why should I honour a promise to a Service that had taken me against my will, and taken me illegally at that! I said as much to Sammy, lost my temper thoroughly, and walked out in a rage. It was dark outside and I blundered off, not caring where I was going.

But before I'd gone far, everything became most peculiar. Seconds after leaving the inn, I felt a sickening blow on the back of my head and the thump of the cobblestones into my face as I went down. But I wasn't quite unconscious and was aware of someone turning me over on to my back. A hand curled round my chin and pulled back my head, baring my throat . . . then there was a confused struggling of bodies and finally I was sitting up with my back to a wall with the world sizzling around me and Sammy Bone shouting at me.

"Jacob! Jacob!" says he, peering into my face. "Get him up lads, get him inside." And I was hauled to my feet and half-carried back into the "George and Dragon". I tried to walk but my feet wouldn't work. They sat me down at the same bench I'd just left and scraps of rag and some water appeared and Sammy was bandaging my head. I noticed Norris's hand was being bandaged as well, then I slipped forward on to the table and the world went away into blackness.

When I awoke, it was light and I was in the same room, which was even dirtier in the daylight. My mates gathered round grinning as I stirred, and they were joined by the landlord in his filthy apron.

"Right!" says this beauty. "Now he's awake you can all bugger off! I'll have no trouble in my house." But Sammy rounded on him and threatened bloody murder if he didn't leave us be and deliver up the breakfast we'd already paid for. The landlord went off muttering.

"We had to run through your pockets for the money, lad," says Sammy, "but we needed the cash or he'd have heaved us out last night, and you weren't fit for that." I nodded and my head ached horribly.

"What happened, Sammy?" says I. "Did something fall on me?" He wouldn't answer straight away, but sent Johnny Basford off to watch the door. Then Sammy and the rest of my mates sat round me in a ring of chairs, like conspirators.

"He's a good boy, is Johnny," says Sammy, "but the poor lad can't be relied on to hold his tongue. He don't understand, you see. But for the rest of us, Jacob, you should know by now you can trust us with anything." He had a strange look on his face and I couldn't see where he was driving.

"What's this, Sammy?" says I. "What's happening?"

"That's just what we was wondering, my lad!" says he.

"Aye!" says the rest.

"We've been talking half the night, Jacob, putting

together one or two bits and pieces, and we don't rightly know how to make sense of it." He settled back to tell the tale and I listened with growing amazement. "When you left here last night, you went out in such a state that Norris and I ran after you to bring you back. We thought that if you was determined to run then we couldn't stop you, but we couldn't part with a messmate without a kind word." Sudden guilt struck me.

"Sorry Sammy," says I, "I didn't mean to . . . "

"Stow it!" says Sammy. "It don't matter. Anyway, soon as we got outside we saw you going up the alley and a man running after you, quiet as a cat and moving fast."

"Jesus Christ! One second later and he'd have had you. He came straight up behind you and hit you on the head, and down you went. We jumped on him but Norris had to grab the knife or he'd have done you anyway." Norris grinned and held up a bandaged hand.

"Tryin' to cut your throat, he was," says Norris.

"Aye," says Sammy, "and he weren't no ordinary robber neither. When we laid hold of him, he didn't try and run like you'd expect. No! The bugger was fighting mad to get at you. He was firm fixed to kill you, Jacob! And another thing . . . show him, Norris."

Norris held out a small shiny object. A button with the Admiralty anchor embossed upon it.

"He had a mask on his face and a black cloak, to hide what he was," says Norris, "but I got hold o' this from the coat underneath." Norris shook his head. "We nearly had him, Jacob, but he was wriggling like a greasy pig and trying to stab us. And then when he saw it was no good, he ran off in the dark . . . but I got this."

I stared at the button in disbelief. It was from the uniform coat of a British Naval Officer.

"Aye," says Sammy, "and remember that jab in the back you got from a splintered spar? Well I wonder if it *was* a spar and not a knife? In that case it's an officer on our own ship that's after you, which is likely the case, 'cos why should he go after a strange matelot he's never seen before? But, then . . . why should an officer try and murder you? There's plenty of officers as takes against a man for no good reason, but they don't shove a knife in him, do they? Not when there's a thousand legal ways to get the poor sod. And there's more . . . Go on, Norris." Norris looked glum and needed some urging from Sammy but finally he came out with something truly dreadful.

"Jacob," says he, "I want you to know that in the reg'lar way o' things I'd have kept silent to the grave, d'you see?" He looked anxious, so I nodded and he continued.

"When we was on that tender, the *Bullfrog* . . . " At this, I guessed what was coming and went cold with horror. ". . . one morning, I was sent on deck with two others, Oakes and Pegg their names was, to help work the ship. And we was by the foremast and we saw the Bosun go after you . . . and we saw . . . we saw what

you done . . . " His voice faded and I blinked at them.
I was found out as a murderer. How would they react?

"Tell him all of it, Norris . . . go on!" says Sammy,
nudging him.

"Well, I thought, good riddance to him!" says Norris.
"I seen what he was doin' to you. And he'd already given
me the hell of a logging', and anyway, what sort of a
seaman is going to betray a shipmate, I ask you? So me
and the other two kept quiet and later on they was sent
into other ships. I dunno where they are now."

"And? And?" says Sammy.

"And, a couple o' days before that, I seen that
Lieutenant Salisbury, him as was in command o' the
Bullfrog, I seen him point you out to the Bosun, deliberate
like, and they was talkin' about you, an' I heard a little
bit. The Lieutenant said: 'He's the one: I have my reasons'.
That's what he said and the old Bosun, he started pickin'
on you right after that." Norris shuffled awkwardly as
he finished his story and looked to Sammy for approval.
Sammy nodded and Norris relaxed.

"And there's one more bit," says Sammy. "Seems we've
got an officer aboard who's not behaving like a gentleman
should, right? Well, that blondie I had when the girls was
in the ship, she said some of the girls was nervous of
coming out to *Phiandra* 'cos they'd heard one of our
officers is a wrong 'un. He likes doing funny things:
things the girls won't do, even in the line of business.
Now, Portsmouth tarts ain't particular, so God knows

what's behind that! But she didn't know who it was and I took no heed at the time. I'd other things on my mind."

He finished his tale and they all stared at me, expectantly.

"Well," says Sammy, "the way I see it, Jacob, some Officer's out to kill you privately. And in all my years I never heard the like where common seamen was concerned, but then we always knew you as a gentleman, from the way you talk. But if you're a gentleman, then what you doing here? Gentlemen don't get pressed! Now, we're your mates, come what may, d'you see? But it's time you was straight with us, my lad." He paused and looked at me hard. "So just what *are* you Jacob?"

I didn't know what to say. I certainly didn't know what was going on. The main thought in my mind was a great relief that my mates didn't think I was a murderer. And I was stupid enough to be flattered that they thought I was a gentleman. Well, I had the manner, didn't I?

So I told them all I knew. I talked and talked and it all came out. They got the whole story of my life and they listened quietly, with Sammy asking a question now and then. I stopped when the landlord came in with our breakfast and carried on when he went out, and I saw Johnny grinning at me from the doorway. It was near midday when I was done.

As I told the story things fell into place and I realised I'd been singled out from the first and someone had been pulling strings like a puppet master to get me into

Phiandra. Lieutenant Spencer of the Polmouth press-gang, Lieutenant Salisbury and Bosun Dixon of *Bullfrog*, and the Midshipman aboard the slop-ship that sent me to *Phiandra* must all have been involved. But who was pulling the strings?

"I reckon it's him in our ship," says Sammy. "It was all planned to get you close to him. And now he's come after you himself, ain't he? The others did their part but there weren't nothing personal in it. *This* one really hates you."

"But why, Sammy?" says I. "I've got no enemies."

"Dunno," says Sammy, "P'raps it's in the past. You don't know who your ma and pa was, do you? But never mind that. What worries me, is finding out who your little friend is!"

He pointed to the coat button on the table. "There's six of 'em aboard with them buttons on their coats: the Cap'n, the three Lieutenants, the Master and his mate. Which one is it?"

Chapter 22

You disgust me. I'm done with you at last. I've excused too much for your mother's sake and now I am sick at heart for what I have closed my eyes to.

(Letter of 10th June 1793 to Alexander Coignwood aboard *Phiandra* from Admiral Williams.)

*

Ivor, Lord Williams of Barbados, Knight of the Bath, Admiral of the White, sat in an armchair in the library of his London house and glared attentively at the creature standing before him. The Admiral was only sixty, but thanks to a hard life he was sickly and retired from the sea. Also, the concussion of heavy guns had left its effect on him and it seemed to him these days that people didn't speak out bold and clear the way they used to.

Indeed it was hard to tell what they were saying unless you paid close attention to their faces, particularly the lips. He'd also noticed that it helped if you cocked your head on one side and cupped a hand behind your ear. It was just as well that his eyes were still sharp.

Unfortunately, today, he was not at all pleased with the person that his eyes beheld. The fellow was a Sea Officer, a Lieutenant by the name of Salisbury, who'd come knocking at the door, claiming to be a friend of the Admiral's nephew. That, and his uniform, had persuaded the servants to let him in, and had obtained him this interview. But one look at the man persuaded the Admiral that he'd not get in a second time.

For although Lieutenant Salisbury's uniform was smart as paint, and although there wasn't a single grain of dirt anywhere upon him, there was a lank and greasy look about the man himself that turned the Admiral's stomach.

And neither did the Admiral like what the fellow was saying.

"So, my Lord," said Salisbury, stooping forward with an oily seriousness, "I had hoped that my close connection with your nephew might lead you to do something to get me employed."

"Employed?" snapped the Admiral. "What d'you mean, 'Employed'?"

"I had hoped that you might influence the Admiralty to give me command of a ship."

"But you've got a ship, haven't you? What about this *Bullfrog* you told me about?"

Salisbury smiled patiently and tried to explain an affair that caused him no little pain.

"I'm afraid, my Lord, that there was some trouble in the ship. The unexplained loss at sea of my Bosun, together with certain legal actions on behalf of an apprentice who had been illegally pressed, caused their Lordships of the Admiralty to take away my command."

"What?" said the Admiral. "Don't see why that should be! Men are lost at sea. That's the way of things. And men get pressed in time of war. Are you telling me that's the only reason they took your ship from you?" Salisbury looked shiftily round the room and confided in the Admiral.

"I am afraid, my Lord," he said, "that there are those at the Admiralty who dislike me personally, and seek only the chance to blight my career."

"Huh!" said the Admiral. "Now fancy that! But come to the point, man. What d'you expect from me? I'm damned if I see any reason to help you."

"Oh?" said Salisbury. "Are you entirely sure, my Lord? Have I not explained that I am a close friend of your nephew Alexander? Does that mean nothing to you?"

There was a brief silence. The Admiral frowned and certain thoughts, kept many years at the back of his mind, stirred like the awakening of a nest of spiders.

Suddenly the Admiral was afraid. He wanted no more of this conversation.

"I bid you good day, Mr Salisbury!" he said.

"No, my Lord," said the other, "that won't do!"

"Damn you, sir!" said the Admiral, and reached for the bell to summon the servants.

"My Lord," said Salisbury quickly, "your nephew is engaged in a plot to kidnap a man and, I think, to murder him. He forced me into this plot and I, too, am his victim. If I were to make public all that I know of your nephew, I could ruin him. And if you refuse to help me, I will do it." He paused for breath and looked at the Admiral, frozen with the bell in his hand. Salisbury knew that he had won a point. "So, my Lord," he sneered, "will you do nothing to help him? Do you care nothing for your family?"

With those words, Salisbury over-played his hand. The Admiral cared for his family more than Salisbury dreamed. He cared for Sarah, his adored younger sister, and he cared for her son Alexander. From her earliest childhood she had captivated the Admiral and she could do no wrong in his eyes. For her, he'd advanced the boy's career to the limit of his power. Even now, Alexander was at sea only because Harry Bollington owed the Admiral a favour and so had ignored the evil whispers that followed Alexander wherever he went.

But now, the Admiral's nose was being rubbed deep into things that he'd striven to keep it out of. He was a rough man who'd lived in a rough world, and this sort of plotting sickened him. But far more was he sickened by finally having to accept that Alexander, for all his courage and skill and seamanship, was rotten to the core. He knew that he must grasp the nettle and cast him off.

First, however, there was Mr Salisbury's threat. Admiral Williams rang the bell loudly. Heavy footsteps sounded and his butler entered the room. Now it was Salisbury's turn to be frozen in anticipation.

"Lieutenant Salisbury," said the Admiral, "I've heard what you say, and here is my reply. Should you breathe one word of your wicked lies around the town, then I shall use my uttermost influence and spend my last penny piece to see *you* ruined! I'll not rest till you starve naked in the gutter." That said, the Admiral turned to his butler. "Chapman! This gentleman is never to be admitted again to my house. Do you understand?"

"Yes, my Lord."

"And now, you will apply your boot to his backside as many times as are necessary to see him on his way."

"Yes, my Lord," said the butler, and reached for Lieutenant Salisbury's collar.

Chapter 23

I suppose I could still have got free of the Navy even then. But I was too curious. I didn't know what I really was, you see, and here was the possibility that somebody else *did!* At bottom I was ashamed of what I was. But a conspiracy of Sea Officers was trying to kill me, so I must be something more important than a whore's bastard, mustn't I? And there was the little matter of Sammy and Norris saving my life. After that, and in the teeth of my better judgement, I couldn't look Sammy in the eye and say I was going to run.

Anyway, I went back to *Phiandra*, and all the way out to the ship we talked about what was to be done. Sammy said that they should have to take turns guarding my back, and we made a thousand guesses as to who my secret enemy might be.

But it was all wasted effort, for we could none of us

imagine who it might be: the Captain? Mr Williams? Mr Seymour? Sammy said they were the finest officers he'd sailed under in thirty years. Or what about Mr Webb, the Master's mate? He was a Lieutenant in all but name and respected by everyone for his skill as a navigator. And in any case he was a small chap and couldn't have put up the fight that my attacker had. Similar considerations applied to Mr Haslam and Mr Golding, the Master. They were both of them too old and slow. And even if we did work it out, what could we do? Go to the Captain (assuming he wasn't the one) with our unproven suspicions? We'd be hanged for mutiny most like. In fact, there were so many ways for an officer to ruin a lower-deck hand that it could be dangerous even to let my enemy know I suspected him. So we went back to our duties quiet as mice and kept the thing to ourselves.

Everyone was pleased to see us, the other messes duly got their shore leave and Lieutenant Williams drove us and the dockyard people half mad with his eagerness to be at sea again. Fortunately, life on a King's ship doesn't encourage pondering and speculation, and I had plenty to keep me busy. For a start, I had to tell the Bosun why we were not, after all, about to sell a cable. But that was no problem. I've forgotten what tale I told him, but he swallowed it whole. He was so much under my spell by then that I swear he'd have believed me if I'd said all the dockyard tradesmen had suddenly grown honest and were refusing to buy the King's property.

Then, towards the end of June, a much-awaited letter from their Lordships of the Admiralty told Captain Bollington that all his mighty string-pulling had borne fruit. His piratical orders to raid the French coast were reaffirmed. And not only that, but he'd managed to increase the size of his expedition. We were to be accompanied by his nephew, Andrew Bollington, Lieutenant and Commander of the cutter *Ladybird*, which was ready for sea at Portsmouth.

Ladybird had the reputation of being an uncommonly fine little ship: a man o' war in miniature, with eight four-pounder swivels and a pair of carronade twelve-pounders. She was no more than sixty feet long and her crew was thirty men. But she was built for speed with a huge spread of fore-and-aft sail; one of the fastest ships in the Navy. The addition of this nimble vessel would be invaluable for scouting and for catching anything too fast for *Phiandra* to come up with.

With his beloved orders in his hand, Captain Bollington threw all his energies into getting the ship ready for sea. Within a week the work was complete and *Phiandra* set sail on 5th July with *Ladybird* following astern. After their fun with the "wives" and their shore leave, *Phiandra*'s crew were as happy a band of brothers as ever put to sea. That is, of course, with the exception of one unknown maniac pursuing a secret blood-feud, and me, the object of it.

Given fair winds we should reach the mouth of the

river Aron in a week at most and then Captain Bollington's game would begin in earnest. In the meanwhile, the ship's eternal cycle of drills went on with even more energy than before. Lieutenant Seymour had us at the great guns even as we were clearing Portsmouth harbour. And there I saw something that set me off on a game of my own and one infinitely more agreeable than the blood and carnage that was awaiting us on the French coast.

As a Bosun's mate, my station at general quarters was on the fo'c'sle where four carronade twenty-four-pounders and a file of marines came under the command of the Bosun. Mr Shaw was impressed with my time under Sammy Bone and rated me Captain of number one carronade. Number two crew was entirely made up of Irishmen, led by a merry, handsome fellow by the name of Matthew O'Flaherty. And O'Flaherty had a girl running cartridges for his gun. [Modern readers will be shocked at the suggestion of a woman's presence aboard a warship on active service, especially since Admiralty regulations specifically forbad this. But there is much evidence of their presence. The memoirs of Mr John Nicol, who served deep in the magazines of *Goliath* at the battle of the Nile, and thus could see none of the action, state "any information that we got was from the boys and women who carried the powder", and further "I was much indebted to the gunner's wife who gave me and her husband a drink of wine now and then". S.P.] She was small and pale, with jet-black hair and a serious, unsmiling face. For gun-drill she was dressed in seaman's rig, which suited her very well. In fact she washed all remaining thoughts of Polly Grimshaw clean out of my head. I mentioned this to Sammy later and he warned me off.

"Very well," says he. "You can look, but don't you touch! Her name's Kate Booth and she's O'Flaherty's girl. She took a fancy to him and stayed when all the other girls was turned off."

"Well," says I, with a hungry look in my eyes, "we shall have to see about that!"

"No!" says Sammy firmly. "Men fight over drink and they fight over money, but that's nothing to how they fight over women!" He saw the confident grin on my face and shook his head. "Now listen to what I'm telling you, Jacob," and he spelt it out to me, jabbing his forefinger into me for emphasis. "If it's over women it don't matter how big you are. You'd get it in the back one dark night and that'd be that! You've already got one mad bugger trying to knife you; d'you want *two*?"

"Oh," said I.

"Yes!" said Sammy. And there I would have left the matter, but it wouldn't leave me alone.

The next day we were at gun-drill again when one of our carronades displayed a particular trick of its species that made gunners like Sammy Bone so wary of them. It was a hot, airless day, with barely enough wind for steerage way and Lieutenant Seymour took advantage of this to practise shooting at a mark: a tub with a spar and a scrap of canvas lashed to it for a flag. This time he picked on the carronade crews, and with the long guns silent and their crews greeting our efforts with derisive cheers, each carronade fired in turn with the ship fifty yards from the target. This was hard, and not what carronades were good at. They were intended for rapid fire, blasting the enemy at a range too close to miss.

So we sweated and ached and missed and tried again. And the jeering from the gundeck grew louder and the carronades got hotter. Hot guns shoot harder than cold guns, and they recoil harder. Especially carronades do and they don't recoil like normal guns, which roll back on their trucks. Instead there's an upper carriage to which the barrel is fixed, and this runs back along an oak slide that's fastened to the deck by a pivot so the whole thing can be trained from side to side. As with long guns, the recoil is checked by heavy ropes, the breeching tackles.

On that day, thanks to Mr Seymour's constant firing, the carronades were now far too hot to touch, and the recoil was frighteningly violent. Perhaps he should have stopped the drill, I don't know. I'm not the expert that he was. But what happened was sudden and shocking.

"BOOM!" Number two fired and jerked viciously backwards. The tackles parted like cotton and 1500 pounds of smouldering iron smashed free of the slide and slammed monstrously down on the deck. Matthew O'Flaherty, with the trigger-line still in his fist, was right in the way. When a gardener kills a slug, he puts it on a big stone and smacks another stone down on top. O'Flaherty's arms and legs were still there, but the rest of him looked like what's left between the stones, except there was more of it. The slimy innards of his body sizzled and fried under the hot gun.

There was a silence and everyone on the fo'c'sle gaped in disbelief. Then men were shouting and running along the gangways from the quarterdeck: the Captain, the Lieutenants, and others. For a minute all was confusion: a ship's boy retched in horror, blood ran round the ruined gun and the colour drained from Lieutenant Seymour's face. He stood stunned and gaping as the Captain shook him by the shoulders.

"Fortunes of war!" says the Captain. "As much as if he were slain by the enemy. No blame attaches." But they were hard men who'd grown up with the sudden disasters of seafaring, so they didn't spend long in worrying. Soon they had one party hauling the gun clear by tackles rigged to the fore-stay, while another cleaned the deck with mops, water and sand, and the Surgeon's mates came with buckets to collect something for the Chaplain to say a service over. Finally, Lieutenant Seymour checked the tackles of every gun in the ship and fired a round from each with his own hand.

And that was the end of Matthew O'Flaherty. His

goods were auctioned off by the first Lieutenant and his "body" went over the side with due ceremony. But one of his possessions came to me. At dinner time, as I was sitting with my mates, I felt a touch on my shoulder. I looked round and there was Kate Booth. She looked tiny and pale close to, and quite young. Younger than me, I'd have thought. But she stared me boldly in the eye.

"Jacob Fletcher?" says she.

"Yes," says I.

"I want to talk to you," says she. "Come and find me in the hold tonight." Then she walked off. Everyone followed her with their eyes and then turned to look at me, nudging each other and licking their lips.

"Huh!" says Sammy, shovelling salt pork into his mouth with his knife. "You're the one then. It had to be you or Mason, so I'm not surprised."

"What?" says I. Sammy chewed hard and swallowed.

"One woman, 250 men . . . she'll need a protector with the Irishman gone, and she's picked you. You'll find she's got a little nest in the hold, aft of the main magazine." Briefly he stopped eating and stared at me wistfully. "Stripe me!" says he. "Wish I was you."

That night while my mates were in their hammocks I crept off and went on an expedition to the fore-hold.

There was little light and the place was full of the noises of the ship's timbers, groaning and wheezing as she rolled through the night towards France. Down here, below the water-line, was a dark, lumpy world of casks and barrels crammed in tight over the ballast, with the stink of the bilge and the squeaking rats for company. The ship's boys slept down here as well, in such wretched corners as they could find. A few well-aimed kicks soon got rid of them and then I was alone in the dark in as private a place as there could be inside one of King George's frigates.

With an intense and growing excitement, I saw what I was after: an oblong shape that glowed in the dark. Against the hull, hidden among the bulk of the ship's stores, was a little cabin made of canvas and scraps of timber. It was some eight feet long by five feet wide and the yellow light of a lantern dimly threw up the shadow of a figure within.

The figure moved and an end of the canvas tent twitched open. Kate Booth was frowning at me in the gloom. A frosty welcome, but the sight of her sent a shock running through me like the electricity up a telegraph wire.

"Hmm," says she, "it's you. Come in." So in I scrambled and sat down. There was not much to see inside, only the bare canvas, an old lantern and a few bundles. A piece of an old sail was folded up to make a softer floor to the little space over the assorted objects beneath. "What's that?" said she, pointing at a bundle I had brought with me. It was a bottle of grog and some food: biscuit, cheese and salt pork. Well, you have to make an occasion of these things, don't you? And I'd not seen her sit down to eat at supper time, so I thought she might be hungry. I undid the bundle.

I was right, too. She was hungry. She took what I'd brought and set to without a word. But the strange thing was the way she ate: neat as could be, like a lady of quality, with back straight and knees folded beneath her. She even produced a little silver knife to cut the cheese with, and a bit of cloth to wipe her mouth.

I stared at her in wonderment, enjoying the thrill of being here with her, alone in this secret place. She was wearing a man's shirt and breeches cut to her size and I was fascinated by her great dark eyes and short hair that left the nape of her neck all smooth and naked. Neither of us spoke until she had finished eating.

"I was hungry," says she, stone-faced. "Give me that." She pointed at the bottle of grog. I passed it over and she pulled the cork and poured some into a little cup. I watched her white throat pulse as she drank. "Ah!" says she. She wiped her mouth, folded her scrap of linen, and looked me over like a master taking on a new hand. The coldness of it irritated me. This wasn't what I'd come for at all.

"Well?" says I. "What do you want from me?"

"Listen, Jacob Fletcher," says she, "I did not choose this life, but I stayed with Matthew O'Flaherty because I liked him. And now he's gone. But I am not to be had by every drunken beast who takes the fancy."

Her hand darted down and came up with something

that gleamed iron and brass in the lantern light. It was a pocket pistol, short and heavy in the barrel. She aimed it squarely at my head. "Do you understand?"

"Yes," says I. I took the point. She looked perfectly capable of pulling the trigger.

"Now," says she, "you're young but you look like a man. Can you be my man?"

"Yes."

"Then how shall you do it?"

"I'll wring the neck of any other man who comes near you. I can do that."

"I know," says she, "that's why I chose you. And now here's my hand on it." She put down the pistol and offered me her hand. I was none too pleased with this. Polly Grimshaw had gone at it whole hearted. She giggled and sighed and made you feel ninety feet tall.

So what was this solemn little elf doing, with her long looks and handshakes like a Lancashire merchant closing a deal on wool? I was half decided to leave her to her misery and go back to my mates where at least I was among smiling faces.

And then I changed my mind. With the pistol gone she looked so tiny and forlorn and I thought of her dead lover, mashed before her eyes, and I thought of being one lonely woman among hundreds of men. A mixture of pity and tenderness welled up from inside me and instead of clasping her hand, I took it gently in both of mine and bent my head to kiss it. She hadn't expected that, and as I looked up I saw her face soften for the first time. She looked sad and happy at the same time.

"And now I must be your woman," says she, and my bowsprit stood like a marine on parade as she pulled her shirt out of her trousers and wriggled it over her head. Then she stood up, unbuckled her belt and threw off the trousers as well. She was slender and muscled like an athlete, and her white skin shone in the light, with small breasts that stood out like figureheads.

I sighed and reached out for her.

"No," says she, "you're too big. You must do as I say." And damn me if she didn't insist! Her style wasn't the mad frolics I'd enjoyed with Polly Grimshaw but a sort of slow, oriental progression that nearly murdered me with impatience. For one thing she had me strip off and lay back so she could climb aboard in her own time. (That's what you get for weighing sixteen stones, women have made me do that all my life.) But, by George, once she was in the saddle and had clapped on her hold she had tricks to play with her inside muscles that made me burst like a mortar-shell! After that, we talked a bit, drank some more grog and went back for another round.

Later, when we were lying quietly together, a thought came to me.

"If you hadn't chosen me," says I, "who would it have been . . . Billy Mason?" She sneered.

"That ugly pug? Never! Not with a King's Officer waiting his chance."

"What?" says I. "I didn't think officers . . . that is I didn't think . . . " She finished it for me.

"You didn't think officers went with common doxies?" She laughed a laugh that wasn't funny. "Well, this one would have — if I'd let him! He was creeping round me before Matthew was cold!" I was puzzled.

"Then why didn't you go to him?" says I. "Who is he?"

"He's the one half the girls in Portsmouth won't go near, not at any price. He cut up one of my friends with a horsewhip. And he's supposed to have actually killed a girl once, and it was all hushed up with money. He's dangerous, though you'd never know it to look at him."

"Who is he?" said I. "Tell me!"

"Your First Lieutenant, Mr Williams."

"What?" says I. "Mr Williams?"

"Yes, the pretty one."

"No! He's the finest man in the ship."

"Is he now?" she said, cynically. "Then would you like to know what your 'finest man' does with girls? He likes to . . . " But she looked at me for a moment and changed her mind. "No," says she, "you're a kind man. You don't want to hear that." And she fell silent.

I was still wrestling with disbelief when the second wave of amazement hit me, as I realised what this meant. I knew my enemy at last, and I wanted badly to tell Sammy. So first I told Kate she'd mess with me and my mates from now on — and God have mercy on any man who offered her the slightest insult! Then I left her for the moment in her little tent and went back to the lower deck.

But Sammy refused to be woken and I had to wait until morning when I went up and down the deck with the Bosun and his other mates, bawling and yelling and helping lazy sailors out of their hammocks to meet the new day.

And a grand game for a lad that is too! The trick of it is to catch them before they know it. A quick upward heave of the shoulder, and you can have them turned out of their hammocks and on their way to the deck five feet below before they're even awake. So in all the busy routine of the early morning, stowing away hammocks in the bulwark rails and swabbing the decks, I never spoke to Sammy, but in the event I didn't need to for I soon came face to face with Lieutenant Williams.

At first, I still couldn't believe what was in my mind. The mere look of him banished all thoughts that anything bad could exist in such a body. A born leader with the devil's own charm. It's hard to believe ill of a handsome face. He greeted me as always, friendly yet permitting of no familiarity, easily keeping the distance between officer and seaman. Or at least he tried to, but something was changed.

I saw it as he looked at me: a downward flick of the eyes and a second's faltering of the smile. Such a thing had never happened before, and it was there and gone in an instant. But I saw it all right, a spark of fear struck from him by the shock of the moment, for I'd changed as well. I was glaring steadily back and thinking, "Right, you swine, let's see what you can do now I'm ready!"

So it really was Lieutenant Williams. I knew from that moment. Yet it was the most staggering thing. He was a black-hearted, murdering swine, and by all accounts a perverted creature. But he was also the best officer in the ship, admired by everyone and loved by the lower deck: hadn't Norris given up the chance of home and family so as not to disappoint him? But if it was him, then *why* was it him?

When I did talk it over with Sammy, he shook his head.

"Don't ask me," says he. "What worries me, lad, is that if you saw it in his face, then he'll have seen it in yours. He's warned, and God knows what he'll do now!"

Chapter 24

What Lieutenant Williams *did* do came as a surprise. It was underhand and clever and I suppose it was typical of him to identify my weakest point so precisely and to know exactly how to exploit it. It was also fast. He made his move that very night, after I'd first looked him in the eye and seen what he was.

I was busy below decks with the Bosun's records. My pretence of selling off a cable had returned to haunt me. I'd only mentioned it as part of my plan to get off the ship, but now the idea was tormenting me. Never mind all this seafaring nonsense. That unsold cable was a matter of business. It was a challenge to the part of me that I took a pride in. I'd just managed to square everything nicely when Sammy appeared. He was obviously worried but wouldn't say what was wrong and led me off to a quiet corner of the lower deck, where Johnny

Basford was crouched against the hull, hugging his knees, with the big tears rolling down his cheeks. As we knelt beside him, he recognised me and turned his face away.

"None o' that!" says Sammy sharply, and pulled him round to face me. Dimly visible in the great space all around, the off-duty watch were swaying in their hammocks as the ship rolled, and we spoke in whispers. "Now then," says Sammy, "you just say you're sorry to Jacob like I told you, and he won't mind a bit." Sammy turned to me, "Your friend's been at him. He told Johnny he'd . . . "

"He said he'd flog I, he did, and I never done nuffin!" says Johnny miserably. "He *made* I tell him . . . "

"'Tain't Johnny's fault," says Sammy, "he can't bear a flogging, everyone knows that. That bugger cornered him and got it all out of him."

Sammy sighed and looked at me. "Jacob, I'm sorry, mate, but Johnny was listening when we was ashore. I should've been more careful. He heard everything and now he's told Williams. He's told him all about you doing away with that Bosun on the *Bullfrog*."

"An' he said . . . he said . . . " Johnny sputtered and mumbled, searching his store of words, "he said he gonna send a writing ashore. He gonna put it in his sea-chest, so whatever happens it'll go to them ashore . . . to his brother and his ma. So's they'll know what you done . . . And he laughed at I, he did . . . I'm sorry, Jacob."

Then, with his tale complete, he blew his nose into

his fingers and wiped them on his breeches, greatly encouraged by his confession. He grinned happily.

Sammy put an arm round his shoulders and looked to me for agreement.

"Johnny can't help it," says he. "'Tain't his fault." At that moment, I could cheerfully have hanged Johnny from the main-yard and watched him choke. But it wouldn't have helped. So I made the best of it and forced a smile.

"All right Johnny," says I. "You couldn't help it." After all, we were only a few days from the certainty of action against the French. However brilliantly Captain Bollington planned the affair, and however lucky we proved to be, some of us were sure to be killed. Williams might be dead before *Phiandra* returned to Portsmouth. So might I, and the ship might be wrecked or burned or captured. I was coming to share some of the fatalistic attitudes of my mates. One day at a time would do.

Then, on the evening of 11th July, the look-outs sighted the French coast and a stream of orders from our noble First Lieutenant sent the hands rushing across the decks and swarming up the shrouds to shorten sail. I joined the Bosun and the other mates in repeating orders on my silver whistle, a trick I was still working hard to perfect. The trouble was, it felt such a straw in my hand, too small by half. But I stumped along beside Mr Shaw and cursed like King Neptune himself.

"Haul away there, you idle sods! Get up them shrouds

you slovenly buggers! Damn your eyes for a set of bloody farmers! . . . etc, etc, etc." Oh yes. That's what the King's Service had done for Jacob Fletcher of Pendennis's Counting House, and destined for respectable trade. If only Dr Woods could have seen me at that moment, me and the Bosun, in our glazed round hats, with our tarred pigtails and silver whistles. Him lashing out with his cane and me roaring like a bull. I never used a cane though; nor a starter. Not then or ever, for the memory of what Dixon did to me. Mind you, if I've kicked one backside then I've kicked a thousand in the encouragement of sailors to their duty. I doubt they'd have been happy without it.

As dusk fell that night, we crept up to the particular part of the French coast that Captain Bollington had chosen. His plan was to take out a prize from under the noses of the French in one of their safest anchorages: the Passage D'Aron. He knew the area intimately since his father had been British Charjay Daffaires (and if that ain't how the Frogs spell it, I don't give a damn) at the nearby town of Beauchart during the years between the Peace of Aix-la-Chapelle in 1748 and the resumption of our natural state of war with France in 1756. So the young Harry Bollington had spent long hours in small boats in and around the estuary of the river Aron and the Lance archipelago at its mouth.

I have made a map to show how things lay, and you will see that the Passage D'Aron is a triangular area of coastal water bounded on the west by the islands of the Lance and on the east by tall cliffs. The Lance, with its rocks and sand-banks, is impassable to all but small boats. It sticks out about ten miles, north-west into the sea from Cape St Denis on the south bank of the river Aron. Two miles upriver is the important market town and seaport of Beauchart.

In peacetime there was a busy coastal trade between Beauchart and the Gironde estuary, and Bordeaux which was less than thirty miles north, up the coast. The mouth of the Aron and the narrow seaway southwards, the Beauchart Straits, were protected by no less than five forts with over a hundred heavy guns between them. In wartime, the southern end of the Passage D'Aron was a death trap to the enemies of France.

Consequently, any French Merchant Master who got his ship inside the welcoming mouth of the Passage D'Aron thought himself entirely safe from the interests of those English and their damned Navy. And it was precisely to destroy this happy belief that Captain Bollington brought *Phiandra* and *Ladybird* slowly up towards the westerly, seaward side of Les Aiguilles to lay to for the night. He chose an anchorage just off one of the islands from where, come the morning, we should be hidden from sight to those inside the Passage and from look-outs on the French forts less than eight miles away.

What we were about to attempt was extremely

dangerous. It would be like a French cruiser trying to take a prize out from Chatham or Portsmouth and I suspect the sheer devilment of it appealed to Captain Bollington as much as the profit. Not only was there every chance of our being pulverised by the massed guns of the forts, but at that time, so early in the war, there was still a steady flow of French warships in and out of their major ports. So we might run into a powerful enemy squadron. All in all, most British Captains would have left Passage D'Aron alone.

In the early morning of the 12th July, which was a Friday, *Ladybird* was ordered to hoist French colours and sail up and around the long sand-bank at the end of Les Aiguilles to take a look into the Passage D'Aron to see what shipping might be present. We shouldn't want to go charging in on the morrow like Rollocking Bill the Pirate, only to find the Passage full of Line-o'-battle ships.

Ladybird was gone all day and aboard *Phiandra* we were occupied with preparations for our expedition. It was to be a regular cutting-out raid led by the Captain himself and including over ninety men. Two boats would take part: the launch and the barge, and the hands couldn't have been happier if they'd been about to go ashore on holiday. Nobody thought of any other subject than prize money.

By four bells in the first watch, as darkness was falling, Ladybird was sighted coming round Les Aiguilles under easy sail. In half an hour she was close alongside. We were under orders that there should be no hailing or loud noise to alert the enemy, so Bollington was rowed across the short distance between the two ships, to report.

He was a nice lad, not much older than me, and he was grinning all over his face as he came over the rail. The word ran round the ship like lightning that the game was afoot. We didn't have long to wait for the full details, for the Captain mustered the officers in *Phiandra's* great cabin for a conference and after that the individual groups of marines and seamen got their orders from their own officers. In my case, as I was to go in the launch, I stood with the rest before the Captain who was to command it. There were about sixty of us, so it was a large enough audience.

"Now lads," says the Captain, "Lieutenant Bollington tells me that the Passage is full of merchantmen but there's no warships. It's dark now and they will have anchored for the night rather than run the risk of rocks and shoals on the way up to Beauchart. There's powerful tides in the Passage, so unless there's a strong wind blowing straight out to sea, any of them who are outward bound will stay anchored until the tide runs out at half past six tomorrow. Now . . . I intend that well before then, we shall be alongside our prizes . . . " A delighted murmur ran through the men at this wonderful word and the Captain smiled.

"Yes, my boys," says he, "prizes! I shall command

the launch with Lieutenant Clark and Mr Percival-Clive, and Lieutenant Seymour shall take the barge with Mr Wilkins. We must be alongside the French at dawn, so it's up-hammocks, breakfast done, and boats manned an hour before first light. I want to be pulling through the Lance islands and well into the Passage as the sun rises. Then we shall lay on our oars and pick our prizes as the light comes. And while we attend to the French, Mr Williams shall bring *Phiandra* and *Ladybird* round to the mouth of the Passage, to meet us as we come out on the tide. If there's a fair wind, then well and good, but we'll have the tide come what may and if the worst comes to the worst, we shall tow our prizes out with the boats. Every seaman shall have a pistol and five rounds beside his cutlass, and the marines shall bear muskets as usual. But mark me well . . . there must be no use of firearms except in the utmost peril. We shall operate beneath powerful shore batteries and the longer they remain ignorant of us, the better. As a further precaution, the marines shall wear seamen's jackets and hats. We may as well run in under the Union Jack as show those lobster-coats!"

And after that, Captain Bollington carefully allotted groups of us to individual tasks about the French ships we were to take: some to cut the cable, some to shake out the foresail, the marines to secure prisoners, and so on. It was as thoroughly well planned as ever such a thing could be and I was most impressed with Harry

Bollington's grasp of detail. I thought that should ever I establish a substantial business, then there would be a place in it for such a man. For his part he had noticed my own talents, though not those I set much store by. To my surprise, he sought me out personally.

"Fletcher!" says he. "In case I may be occupied with other matters, you shall stay by me and note the actions of the enemy immediately to my front." In short I was appointed his personal bodyguard.

For some reason, this irritated me. I felt like a servant and said so later to Sammy Bone. What Sammy said about this I shall not bother to record, for it would burn the printed page to ashes. But his drift was that if there wasn't a promotion in this for me somewhere, then I was more stupid even than I looked, if that were possible.

Soon after, *Phiandra* and *Ladybird* fell silent, as all hands, barring look-outs, were ordered to their hammocks to rest until the unknown perils of the day ahead. But my day was not yet over. Before I could get to my hammock, Bosun Shaw came to me with a most unexpected order.

"Fletcher!" says he. "At the double now, Mr Williams wants a word on the quarterdeck."

"About what?" says I, suddenly nervous.

"Bleedin' get along there and you'll find out, my lad!" says he. "Go on now. Get along!" God knows what this meant and I didn't know what to do. Williams had ignored me for the last few days as if nothing had happened. But I couldn't keep an officer waiting so I went up on deck. No lights were showing but there was a bit of moon about. A marine sentry stopped me at the companionway leading to the quarterdeck, but Williams's voice called from the darkness.

"Let him pass!" says he. "Over here, Fletcher." I looked around nervously. It was dark, but not that dark, and there was a sentry at the other companionway as well as the look-outs in the tops. So there were witnesses if need be. What the hell could he be playing at? There was no chance here for secret murder. All the same, I was wound up tight. What should I do if he went for me? Would he have a knife? Or a pistol?

"Mr Williams?" says I, edging closer to the dark figure with its gleaming buttons and white stockings. He was completely at his ease, leaning against the mizzen mast with his hands deep in the pockets of his coat. I stopped well clear of him, wondering what might be in his pockets. He noticed my hesitation and I saw the flash of his teeth as he grinned.

"Don't be afraid, Fletcher," says he quietly so nobody else should hear. "I mean you no harm . . . see?" And out came the hands — empty, palms upward, fingers spread. "I want to talk to you, that's all."

"About what . . . sir?" says I, still keeping a good distance between us. I looked around again. The two sentries were close enough to see what we were doing and even as he spoke, Lieutenant Seymour came on deck and began to pace up and down, lost in thought. That reassured me. With another officer on deck there was no chance of his getting away with an attack on me. Mr Seymour would see it for sure.

As I realised that, and saw that he was unarmed, I lost my fear. In fact, as I looked at him more closely and saw the mocking smile on his face, and I remembered what he'd done, and what he'd tried to do, and especially as I realised how much the bigger man I was . . . a slow anger grew instead. If I'd thrashed Billy Mason, I could thrash this one.

"Fletcher," says he, "there are certain facts that I should like to acquaint you of. First, it was entirely by my actions that you were brought to this ship. Even your friends at Pendennis's, Ibbotson and Bradley, were bribed to tell Lieutenant Spencer, of the Polmouth Press, how and where you might be captured with the least trouble. You may have wondered why you were pressed and they were not. Well, now you know."

He paused to let me digest that and near as damn it got my fist in his face that very second. I was boiling with rage.

"Now," says he, "it is my most devout hope that you will be killed in action tomorrow. Or at least that you might be blinded and crippled. However, should you survive, I have taken action to ensure that you will be arrested the instant you set foot on British soil. I am in touch with powerful interests ashore that will bring you to trial for the murder of Bosun Dixon of His Majesty's brig *Bullfrog*. I shall have you hanged for this crime. Do you understand?"

I understood all right. It was an uncanny moment. After all the months of wondering what was happening and piecing things together, here it all was in plain English. And this man, who'd always behaved as a perfect gentleman, was pouring out venom like a serpent. The anger grew within me. Why should I suffer this? Why should I be dragged into this mad world of ships and fighting? Then a thought came to me.

"Why are you doing this?" says I. "What am I to you?" He stretched back comfortably against the mast.

"I am doing all this, Fletcher, for excellent reasons that would interest you most extremely and which I am therefore going to keep secret from you. I know everything about you, Fletcher. I know who you are and what you are . . . and I'm not going to tell you."

"You back-stabbing bastard!" says I. He laughed at that.

"Yes and no, Fletcher," says he. "It is true that I have twice tried to stab you. And I've played you lots more little tricks as well. Why d'you think I kept you out of the Purser's service when first you came aboard? Did you think it was to do you a good turn? I did it to set the Purser against you. And didn't it just work? Did you enjoy boiled rat for dinner? And it was I who set Mason on you. All it took was a little word in his ear."

He was getting excited now and his tongue ran away

with him. "And what an utter fool you've been, Fletcher. When I think of you crawling after me to secure that loose gun with that stupid look in your eyes and me planning to shove you under the bloody thing all the while! Why do you think I laughed when I looked at you? And who do you think tripped you when we were dancing round it? Isn't it just a pity the wrong man got his leg broke? By Christ I wish it'd been you, you . . . "

He was spitting out words in fury. There was froth on his lips and he was shaking. For the first time I could actually *see* the evil side of him.

Then he took a grip of himself . . . and paused . . . and the calm smile was back again.

"Hmm," says he. "Nevertheless, Fletcher, you are wrong in one important respect. It is you who is the bastard. You were conceived in filth and dropped in a dung heap. It's the truth, believe me. I've documents to prove it. You are no more than a dirty whoreson."

That was it. I pulled back my fist to smash his loathsome face to pulp . . . and then, thank God, I saw the delight in his eyes and I realised what he was at. I was a split second from an act of mutiny that would hang me far quicker than any legal process ashore. It was a trap. The witnesses on the quarterdeck would be his, not mine. My legs wobbled with the shock of it, it had been that close.

But I wasn't so green as I had been and I took hold fast.

"Aye aye, sir!" says I, in a loud voice for all to hear. "Very grateful to you for that, sir," and I turned round and left him before anything else could happen. Perhaps that surprised him, I don't know, but he didn't call after me and I simply went back to the lower deck and got into my hammock. And there I lay for hours trying to sleep. Strangely enough I felt safe there. Sammy's hammock was on one side of me and Kate's was on the other. And I was enough of a seaman for the constant sounds and movement of the ship to be comforting. Finally I fell asleep wondering what would happen on the morrow.

Chapter 25

I write concerning the dreadful disaster which has befallen my employers Mr Richard Lucey and his son Mr Edward. Alas, I must tell you that Mr Richard is dead and Mr Edward's life is in the hands of the doctors.

(Letter of 22nd July 1793 to Mr Nathan Pendennis at Polmouth from Mr A. Day, Chief Clerk to Lucey and Lucey of Lonborough.)

*

Late on Friday evening, 19th July, Victor Coignwood made his way along Market Street, a narrow, ancient street of half-timbered houses crammed one against the other. It was dark and nobody was about. He was heading for number thirty-nine, the offices of Lucey and Lucey. The Luceys lived at number thirty-seven, next door, and he didn't want to be seen, so he was wrapped in a large cloak with a hat to match, and he came from the direction which avoided passing their house.

Victor was in a high state of excitement. His heart pounded with anticipation as he thought of what he was about to do. Even for Victor there were still some experiences yet to be sampled. And besides, he was happy. Things were going well. Pendennis and Edward Lucey had been dealt with, and since the return of Victor and his mother to Coignwood Hall (always regrettable when London beckoned, but necessary), they'd found a local lawyer who'd take their case.

The man was a clod, and could never win against the Luceys, but after his fashion he was fighting the 1775 Will and seeking provenance for the earlier Will which named the Coignwoods as beneficiaries. At least this established the claim and kept Richard Lucey on his toes.

Meanwhile, the Coignwoods were informed of Lucey's actions by the spy that Victor had inserted into his office. More accurately, Victor had *made* a spy of someone already at number thirty-nine. By one of life's happy chances, a junior clerk in the Luceys' office, one Andrew Potter, shared the same appetites as Victor. This had introduced Potter into a discreet circle of friends through whom the two had met. Seizing his chance, Victor had devoted special attention to Potter, to recruit him to the

Coignwood cause. At first, Potter balked, but he saw reason when Victor explained what would happen to his employment should Mr Lucey learn of his recreational activities.

So now there was not a letter, document or memorandum that passed across Richard Lucey's desk, that was not read by Lady Sarah and Victor (and Victor was at the peak of favour compared with the wretched Alexander who, to judge from his last letter, was still trying to get his knife in the right place). Victor smiled to himself. He'd never seen his mother laugh so much as when he'd showed her Pendennis's letter to Richard Lucey, confessing to his seduction!

However, despite all these good things, the Clod would surely fail in competition with Richard Lucey, and Alexander might fail with the Brat. So Lady Sarah had decided to be done with peering into letters and waiting while others made the running. She had decided on direct action and given Victor his orders. At this, Victor had gone paper-white and tried to find alternatives. But he could never defy her for long. Also, the more she explained what he must do, the more fascinated he became with the thought of doing it. With these happy thoughts in his mind, Victor knocked gently on the door of number thirty-nine. He glanced at the Luceys' house and all was quiet. Soon, through one of the windows of number thirty-nine, he could see a light approaching. There came a sliding of bolts and the door opened. Potter stood there with a candle. He was nervous.

"Mr Coignwood!" he said. "Come in, quickly!"

Victor stepped inside and Potter made haste to lock the door.

"Good evening, Andrew," said Victor, and his heart thudded so hard that he felt the Luceys must hear it through the party wall.

"Quick, follow me!" said Potter, and led Victor through the outer office and into a small room at the back. He shut a door behind them and relaxed. He grinned, pleased with himself.

"There," he said, "you are in, Mr Coignwood. And nobody can see us. We are quite safe."

"Well done, Andrew," said Victor. "And have you told the Luceys you're here?"

"Yes, Mr Coignwood, just as you said. I told them I'm working late." Potter laughed. "They think I'm no end of a diligent fellow! If only they knew . . . "

"Good," said Victor. "And has anything changed? Have you any further news?" His mother had insisted he should ask that first.

"No, Mr Coignwood. Mr Edward still refuses to take part in the Fletcher work and he hasn't told his father what happened in London, though I think the old man has guessed." He smirked and lifted his eyebrows in an arch expression. "Well!" he said. "We all know your dear mother, don't we?"

"Yes," said Victor. He saw that his dear mother was right. Potter was already impertinent and might soon become dangerous.

"Now," said Victor, with his most winning smile. "My dear Andrew, I have a surprise for you."

"Have you?" said Potter.

"Oh indeed!" said Victor. "But first you must close your eyes."

"Wait," said Potter, "I'll just put down the candle."

"Yes," said Victor, "now stand there, and put your hands to your sides."

"Yes," said Potter.

"Now, eyes *tight* shut, and lift your chin a little."

"Ah," said Potter, as something brushed gently against his throat, "it tickles."

"Does it?" said Victor, and thrust upwards, driving a needlepoint, razor-edged blade through Potter's larynx, through the roof of his mouth, and into his brain.

Potter fell backwards, with the steel embedded inside his skull. He pawed at it and his heels drummed the floor as he jerked from side to side and his breath whistled impotently through his mangled neck.

Victor watched with bulging eyes as Potter died. When it was over, Victor sniggered nervously, and when his hands stopped shaking, he took the weapon and jerked it free. He wiped it on Potter's coat and slid the three feet of gleaming steel back into his walking stick.

For a few seconds Victor stood admiring his handiwork. He wished that his mother had been there to see it. Nobody could have done it better, not even Alexander. But he had work to do. It must look as if Potter had fallen asleep and caused the fire.

There were papers everywhere so it was easy to build a great pile of them on Potter's body. He piled more to either side, making sure some were nicely crumpled to let the air in. Then he took a light from the candle and applied it in several places. He backed away as flame and smoke filled the room with amazing speed. He stayed a while to see what a man looked like as he burned, but soon it grew too hot and Victor knew it was time to leave. Already the light of the fire would be plainly visible to anyone on the other side of the street.

Victor sauntered to the front door. He drew the bolts and pulled at the handle. But the door wouldn't move! A tinge of fright ran up his spine. Christ! There was a lock! Potter had locked it. Where was the key? Victor looked at the back room, and felt the heat of it. The furniture and fittings were well ablaze and the old dry timbers of the room were smoking. If Potter had the key then it was lost.

Victor tugged at the door again, then ran round the outer office throwing open desks and cupboards in a vain search for a key. He found one, a tiny thing intended for a cash-box, and in his panic he jammed it uselessly into the massive iron lock on the door.

"God damn!" he cried, and hurled the key away. He looked for another way out. He took a chair and smashed one of the windows, but the Luceys kept valuables on the premises and the windows were armed with inch-thick iron bars on the outside. Immediately there came a roar from the back room as the fire felt the draught of the opened window and the main timbers went up in flame. A shower of sparks burst forth, and one scorched the back of Victor's hand. It broke his nerve, and he shrieked in fear of being burned alive. He hammered on the door and called for his mother. He screamed and screamed, and tried to break through the heavy oak planks with his fists.

Then, wonderfully, someone was turning the lock from outside and swinging the door inward. Two men stumbled in, right into Victor's arms. It was the Luceys, come to investigate. For a few seconds the three glared at one another in hatred, and Victor knew he was found out. It would be impossible to say who was most shocked at their meeting.

But Victor recovered first. He drew his sword-stick and shoved it through Richard Lucey. Lucey groaned and grabbed at Victor.

"Father!" cried Edward and leapt forward, but the older man was hanging on to Victor and got in Edward's way. Victor jerked out his blade and slashed at Edward's eyes while shoving the old man off. Richard Lucey sank on his office doorstep as Victor steadied himself, and deliberately thrust at the blinded man before him. Edward Lucey fell beside his father as Victor slammed the door on them and ran for his life, leaving three victims to the fire.

Chapter 26

On the morning of Saturday 13th July, dawn came just
after five o'clock and found two boat-loads of us rowing
through the Lance archipelago in the dim light. It was
an uneasy experience, that brief pull through the islands,
for it was more dark than light and we could see no
more than a few boat-lengths ahead and the seas foamed
and broke all around us on the grim black islands of the
Lance. The narrow channel we were passing through
could not have been more than twenty yards wide and
the islands rose up sheer, like teeth. It was just like the
fjords of Norway only shorter and more broken and
there was a deal of white water over glossy rocks that
barely broke surface.

The rowlocks were muffled with rags to silence the
clanking of the oars, but the regular splashing of the
blades was thrown back by the echoing walls in an eerie,

wet sound. Heaven only knows how Captain Bollington knew his way through, but he got himself up into the very bows of the launch which was leading, and gave his orders to the coxswain by hand signals. I have often wondered if he wasn't simply taking a chance on distant memories and his own skill in conning us around the hazards as they came into view. We were not going fast enough for the boats to be stove in, should they come upon a hidden rock, but the swirls and eddies around some of the rocks looked capable of oversetting us should we fall into their grip, so there was danger enough in all truth, and the whole party was silent with the thought of it.

But Captain Bollington did it . . . he *did* it, and soon we were sliding away from the Lance and into the anchorage. Into the Passage D'Aron. And one thing was sure. Nothing bigger than a ship's boat had any chance of running through the Lance as we had done. The only way out for us with our prizes would be down the Passage to the open sea.

Once clear of rocks and islands, we could see the dim outlines of ships anchored all up and down the Passage. Excitement began to mount in the boats as, according to plan, we lay upon our oars to consider the next move. With the bows of the boats pointing across the Passage towards the shore, some three miles ahead, we sat silently in our bobbing craft as the light grew stronger and the officers conferred on what was the best to take, from that which was on offer. At least we were supposed to be quiet but there were whispers and nudges and the oarsmen edged round on their thwarts for a look over their shoulders at what was going on.

Captain Bollington was now back in the stern sheets and I was sat facing him. He was conversing in a low voice with Lieutenant Seymour and pointing out first one ship, then another. By now it was about half past six and the sky above was light. Though with the sun still hidden by the cliffs to the east, we were still in shadow in the Passage D'Aron. But we could see upwards of fifty merchantmen at anchor, the bulk of them deeper in the anchorage than ourselves, nestling under the protection of the batteries around the mouth of the Aron.

And that gave us pause. The sight of all those fat geese ready for the plucking was one thing, but there was also the realisation that we were very much in an enclosed place and totally separated from our swift and powerful ship. We had cut through the Lance about half way down its length, and behind us the islands stretched up and down like a giant's fence while ahead the shore reared up into cliffs that ran for endless miles away to the north. And to the south, the cliffs funnelled in to meet the Lance at the narrow Straights of Beauchart and the Aron. Most chastening of all was the sight of the French batteries themselves, quietly sleeping as the dawn touched them.

The ninety of us in our two boats were like the old moggie creeping forward to take Bonzo's food from under his mouth in Mrs Wheeler's back yard.

Not a happy thought at that moment, for we could see the forts quite clearly now: the thick, low walls and the neat rows of black embrasures for the guns. The ancient St Denis castle was also visible, but it was too far away for its guns to reach us. But two of the forts, given their ideal situation, with big guns fifty feet above the water, would be able to drop shot all about our ears the minute they found out what we were doing.

But the game was one of secrecy and speed so the batteries should not be able to interfere. The tide would be on the ebb in half an hour's time and if we did our work well enough, we should be beyond range of the French guns, before they knew we were there. There was even a breath of wind blowing out to sea that should help us on our way once we had a prize to take out. Meanwhile, the Captain had made his decision.

"There's your prize, Mr Seymour," says the Captain, pointing, then, "Silence!" in a savage hiss, as a growl of anticipation ran through the eagerly awaiting men. "I'll have no talking unless any of you can do it in French! Remember, we're Frenchmen until the minute we're actually climbing aboard of 'em." The noise died away, Captain Bollington exchanged a few more words with Lieutenant Seymour, and then the boats were under way as our oarsmen pulled with a will.

Looking over my shoulder, I could see which ships we were after, a pair of big three-masted vessels, about three hundred tons apiece. As far as I could tell, the Captain had just chosen the two most seawardly ships to give us the least distance to carry them off, but he might have considered factors beyond my inexperienced view. In any case, it took us no more than ten minutes to come upon our victim.

Captain Bollington waved to the barge as we slowed and it went gliding past towards her target. By now I could even make out the name on the stern of our ship: *Bonne Femme Yvette* she was called, and she was waking up, as were most of the other vessels anchored there.

Up and down the Passage, there arose a gentle chorus of noise that told the assembled vessels were stirring: muttering voices, squealing blocks and the clattering of pots and pans for breakfast. All these pleasant morning sounds drifted clearly over the quiet waters. Everything was still. There was not a sign of the French Navy and it all seemed so easy. I thought, surely *some* of the Frogs must have kept look-outs aloft for all that they were supposed to be safe here. For now there was plenty enough light for all the world to see our two busy boats. But nobody took the least notice of us, and I could see the wisdom of getting our marines out of their scarlet tunics. Anyone could see that they were soldiers, sat there in rows with their cross-belts and muskets between their knees. But in their dark blue jackets it was a mystery as to just whose men they were. And as for our officers, it would have taken an uncommonly sharp eye and a taste for uniform to tell the British from the French Service coat until such time as you could actually examine the buttons and lace.

Then, as we bumped alongside *Bonne Femme Yvette*, I nearly jumped out of my skin as someone aboard the ship yelled out a challenge. There was one look-out awake, after all, and he was asking some sort of question.

"Steady lads!" says Captain Bollington, and yelled back something in fluent French as a row of heads popped over the quarter of the ship and peered down at us, round eyed. One was a fat, bald-headed little man who turned out to be the Master. Captain Bollington concentrated on him. I've neither the gift, nor the slightest inclination to understand foreigners' languages, so God knows what Captain Bollington was saying. But, by George, it was good!

"Pollywog-pollywog-pollywog!" says the Captain, firmly.

"Pollywog?" says Froggie, and up went his eyebrows in amazement.

"Pollywog!" says the Captain, sharply, and for all the world like some sort of official, he produced a paper from his pocket and waved it for the Frenchman to see. It was a letter from Mrs Bollington. I saw it, but the Frog was too far away and he peered down trying to make sense of it.

"Ah," says he, finally, "pollywog," and gave that strange shrug of the shoulders with the corners of the mouth turned down, that the French use to express emotions of puzzlement. But he stopped his questions and one of his men dropped us a line to make fast by. And then, that miserable little worm, Midshipman Percival-Clive, shoved in his pennyworth. He was in charge of the oarsmen and suddenly remembered his duties. Loud and clear, in the King's own English, he screeched out.

"Ship oars now, you men, and smartly with it!"

Up in the ship they heard this and a torrent of French poured upon us, but it was too late. *Bonne Femme Yvette* rolled as sixty men went swarming aboard by the main chains. I stuck close to the Captain as I'd been told and in an instant we were facing the French shipmaster and a couple of his men on the quarterdeck while the rest of our party ran swiftly to all parts of the ship, to secure her as planned. It was done well and silently. The loudest noise we made was the rumble of marine boots down the companionways as they went below to rout out the French crew.

There was no possibility of their resisting. We outnumbered them three to one, and we were armed and ready while they were not. But Captain Frog was high up on his dignity and starting to make trouble. I think it was his ship and his own property that was being took from him. He'd been roused from sleep by our arrival and stood before us bare legged in his shirt, but he gibbered and gabbled and had the gall to shake his fist at Captain Bollington. The Captain snapped at him in French, giving him his orders and no mistake, but the man would not be told and started to shout. Captain Bollington turned to me.

"Silence him!" says he, so I tapped Froggie on the arm to catch his attention.

"Mossoo?" says I, polite as could be, and he looked me up and down as if I'd farted in church. So I flattened the little bastard with my fist. (Served him right, too. Foreigners should give respect to a British man-o-war's-man. Especially Frogs should.) After that, things went smoothly.

It could not have been more than ten minutes after we first came over the rail that Mr Percival-Clive was reporting to the Captain.

"All's well, sir. Cable's cut, topsails set, and the prisoners secured on the forecastle."

"Excellent!" says the Captain, and looked about him. Indeed, everything looked as it should be, with our men at the wheel and in the rigging, and sails unfurled above.

"The tide should be on the ebb soon and we've some wind to take us out. We should be joining *Phiandra* within a couple of hours . . . Now then, Mr Percival-Clive, why don't you see if you can turn out the Captain's papers, so we can see what cargo's aboard."

And in that moment, our plans ran foul of the unexpected. Perhaps Captain Bollington had been over-ambitious to seek two prizes. Perhaps he should have kept the whole enterprise under his own hand to employ his French-speaking skills to the utmost, for suddenly we were all reminded of Lieutenant Seymour and the barge.

Bang! The silence of the Passage D'Aron was broken by the roar of a ship's gun. The echoes rocked back from the cliffs and the gulls rose screaming into the air. The desperate cries of men and a volley of musketry rose to join them.

Aboard *Bonne Femme Yvette* we rushed to the stern-rail to look back up the Passage to the sounds of action. Half a mile away, the barge was locked in action with a French merchantman. Pop-bang! More muskets went off, then a bigger puff of smoke shot from the rail of the ship, and, Bang! There came the sound of another gun. Then another and another just the same. Far beyond our aid, the little black figures of our shipmates threw up their arms and died, and the thin cries of the wounded came to us over the water. The barge drifted out from the ship with her oars crossed and tangled. Less than half were moving. Bang! Another gun went off and an oar jumped and splintered as the charge struck home.

"Hell and damnation!" says Captain Bollington, hammering the rail with his fists. "Damn! Damn! Damn! Look there Percival-Clive. D'ye see? There's a line of swivels down the rail of that ship and they're firing them off into our lads!" One Frenchman at least had taken his precautions before bedding down for the night, and kept her guns primed and loaded. Once an enemy was spotted, it was the easiest thing in the world to set them off. One man with a match could do it.

Five two-pounder swivel-guns was all they had for a broadside, but they were stuffed with pistol-balls, and to a boat crammed with men, each blast was devastating.

"Lieutenant Clerk!" cries the Captain. "Take a boat's crew and half your marines, and give what aid you can to Lieutenant Seymour. Tow them clear if need be . . . Make haste!"

The marine Lieutenant was away on the instant, shouting orders as he ran. His party tumbled over the side into the launch and took up the oars. The marines pulled double-banked with the tars and the boat sped away with Mr Clerk urging on his men.

"Heave!" says he. "Put your bloody backs into it!" But as the launch rowed to rescue our comrades, the gunfire and shouting had well and truly awakened the other ships in the anchorage. It was full daylight and a cacophony of noise came from each vessel. Shouts rang out, men leaped into the rigging to see what was going on and, worst of all, signal guns fired and hoists of flags shot up to the mastheads of some of the ships.

"Damnation!" says the Captain, again, and glared at the French signals. "Fletcher! Get me that Frenchie you knocked down. I must know what those flags mean." I turned and ran for the fo'c'sle where our marines had

the French crew sat on the deck, under guard. As I ran
I heard from the direction of our launch a further clatter
of muskets as our men opened fire on the defiant
merchantman. Then: bang! One of the swivels barked
again. But I was pushing through our marines and seizing
the French Master.

"Up!" says I, hauling him by the collar of his shirt.
If looks could kill he'd have dropped me on the spot
and he cursed me viciously. But I'd no time for his
nonsense so I fetched him a clout to shut him up,
scragged him off his feet and hauled him to the quarterdeck. As we joined Captain Bollington he was in a
passion of anxiety for our boats, staring back over the
rail with Mr Percival-Clive for company.

"Come on there! Come *on* lads!" says he. I saw the
launch towing the barge and pulling slowly towards us.
A steady crack of muskets came from the launch as our
marksmen kept the enemy from manning the swivels
again. Soon this ceased and the two boats came safe out
of range.

Captain Bollington spun round and turned his attention on the little Frenchman. He glared into the man's
eyes and pointed at the hoist of flags hanging from the
mainmast of a nearby ship. He poured out a stream of
words, obviously asking a question. I needed no French
to understand what he was after. The Frogs had a pre-ar-
ranged danger signal to warn their batteries that intruders
were present and Captain Bollington wanted an expla-

nation of this. But the French Captain had some pluck, and faced him like a man, drawing himself erect with folded arms.

"*Non!*" says he. Just the single word.

Captain Bollington stormed and roared, but the Frenchman only held his head all the higher and repeated, "*Non!*"

I don't know what Captain Bollington might have done to him if this had continued, but suddenly the questions became irrelevant. From less than a mile away, down at the narrows of the Passage, there came the faint sound of a bugle and a roll of drums. The sound came from one of the menacing forts on the cliff-top. We all turned to look, and very soon there came a great ball of white smoke from one of the embrasures, followed by the reverberating boom of a gun. It was unshotted and fired as a warning. As well as the sound there came a fluttering of signal flags from a flagpole set over the fort. Ominously, the other forts began to wake up, and more bugles and drums sounded out.

Captain Bollington snapped out his telescope and looked up at the flags.

"Damned if I know what that means," says he. Then he tried the little Frenchman once more, and this time the man actually smiled. He pointed at the nearest fort and rattled off something at Captain Bollington, with obvious satisfaction.

"Bah!" says the Captain. "Send him for'ard again.

He'll tell us nothing." He turned to Percival-Clive. "You, boy! See if you can turn out a signal-locker and copy what these others are showing." He indicated the other French ships, now every one with a string of signals run up. "Copy them flag by flag, d'ye hear? And I'll have every sail set. The sooner we're out of here the better!"

So we did as he bid. Percival-Clive copied the French identification signal and tried to convince the gunners up in the forts, against the evidence of their own eyes, that we were not a prize crew, while the seamen set every inch of canvas that *Bonne Femme Yvette* could carry.

It was a race. On the one hand, there was the feeble wind, barely twitching our sails, and there was the ebbing tide that was slowly sweeping us beyond the reach of the batteries. On the other hand, there was the matter of how long it would take some French officer to decide to open fire on us, given that the anchorage was laid out before him like a pond full of toy ships, and ours was the only one trying to get out. Already we were far enough from the other ships to give the gunners a clear field of fire.

Another element in the race was the progress of our boats. Aboard *Bonne Femme Yvette* we were hanging over the side urging on our mates. With sails barely drawing, we had no more speed than the tide was giving equally to us and the boats together. So, even towing the barge, the launch was overhauling us fast. In fact, Lieutenant

Seymour and those of his men still capable, had manned the oars and were trying to help. But otherwise, the scene in the barge was grim, with dead and wounded swilling around in the bilge water under the thwarts.

Then a cheer went up as they bumped alongside. The barge's crew had been badly mauled. Of thirty-five men who'd set out fit and well, nine were dead, and fifteen badly injured. Lieutenant Seymour was among the lucky few who were unmarked. We had no time to be gentle so the dead were left where they'd fallen and the wounded heaved into *Bonne Femme Yvette* like bundles of rag. They lay in the waist twitching and moaning. Midshipman Wilkins was whitefaced and shuddering with his arm laid open from wrist to shoulder and blood spraying in all directions. He was in need of the Surgeon's needle and thread to close the wound properly but all he got was a length of line twisted round his upper arm to stop the flow. I did that. Surgeon Jones had shown all hands how to set a tourniquet and I probably saved the lad's life by doing it but the poor little devil screeched fearfully as I tightened the cord.

As I stood up from my doctoring, I was reminded of our danger by the sight of Percival-Clive running up a hoist of signals. I hoped he had made a good guess in picking the flags but it was wasted effort. Our actions, in full view of the forts, told their own tale. Finally, at about seven in the morning, in easy range of the nearest fort, there came a deep roll of thunder as five huge guns bellowed in rapid succession. Compared to this, the gunfire heard earlier was but the crackling of wood on a bonfire. A bank of smoke temporarily hid the fort as their first salvo came shrieking down upon us.

Chapter 27

Chop! Chop! Chop! Up went the columns of water hundreds of yards ahead of us. Some of our men gave an ironic cheer at this poor shooting, and thought we were safe, but Captain Bollington disagreed. He was on *Bonne Femme Yvette*'s quarterdeck with his officers, and now that all his men were gathered into the ship, he'd calmed down and was steadily contemplating the fort that was firing on us.

"Mr Percival-Clive," says he, "you may remove your signal and run up British colours. There's no point in further attempts at deception." He turned to Lieutenant Seymour, and pointed at the fort. "Now those are *real* guns!" says he, with enthusiasm. "Sixty-eight-pounders I should think. That's what they kept up there when I was a lad." He indicated the disturbed water where the shot had come down. "Of course, that was just ranging. They'll do better presently." He smiled at his gunnery expert. "Now, Mr Seymour, let's see how quickly French gunners might work a battery of sixty-eight-pounders." And he took out his pocket watch to time them. Lieutenant Seymour copied him and the pair of them stood there talking gunnery, as merry as could be, or pretending to be.

And the Captain was right. Within a few minutes they fired their second salvo. Again there came the terrible roar of shot in flight, then water spouts were leaping up in a cluster, a hundred yards ahead and somewhat on our larboard beam. Then the pause while they reloaded, and I imagined the gun-captains staring over their sights and barking orders to their men.

"Please God, don't let there be a Sammy Bone among them!" I thought. And the worst of it was that there was absolutely nothing we could do to hit back while they took their target practice.

Up in that fort were men in perfect security, not threatened by any danger, and provided with heavy guns on a steady platform. Unless they were profoundly incompetent, their fire must be far more accurate and deadly than any gunfire from a moving ship. And all we could do was wait for the tide to drift us clear. Without a decent wind, the ship didn't have even sufficient way on her to give effect to the rudder and she progressed crabwise, with her starboard quarter slewed round to the fore. Boom! Boom! Boom-boom! And the third salvo dropped into the waters of the Passage D'Aron close enough for us to hear the hiss and splash of the upthrown water as it spattered back on to the waves. They were getting closer.

A sixty-eight-pound shot, French measure, is a great iron ball nearly eight inches in diameter. Such a missile, coming from a gun sitting fifty feet above the sea, would smash right through *Bonne Femme Yvette* with a downward angle, tearing a ragged hole through her bottom on its way out. A few such hits would undoubtedly sink her. Even one alone might do it.

"Should we not take the ship in tow, sir, with the launch?" says Lieutenant Seymour. "We'd be away all the faster."

Captain Bollington shook his head. "I seriously doubt it'd be worth the effort, Mr Seymour," says he. "Go ahead, if you wish, to keep the men busy, but the thing reduces to a matter of arithmetic. I time the fort at six minutes to reload and aim — a poor performance, don't you think?"

"Indeed, sir," says Mr Seymour, "they're delivering controlled salvoes to increase the chance of a hit, which is very proper of 'em even if it's slower. But they are slow! I can only think they've neglected their drill. I venture to think I could improve their speed, given the training for 'em for a week or two."

"I'm sure you could, Mr Seymour! However, to pass beyond their effective range, we must move at least a mile down-channel. Now, the tide here runs at three knots per hour. That will carry us a mile within twenty minutes and towing would not much improve that." He waved his watch at the fort. "Our friends must hit us with their next three salvoes or they've lost the game. And if their accuracy is equal to their speed of fire, then my estimation is that they're not good enough to do it in three."

"Quite so, sir," says Lieutenant Seymour, "though if I might make so bold, that is strictly according to calculation and makes no allowance for a lucky shot."

"Precisely!" says the Captain. "Then let us see what French gunners can do in reality." And he and Seymour stood together, hands clasped behind their backs, calmly facing the battery. Lieutenant Clerk joined them. They were fellow members of a caste. Officers born and bred, all three, who'd known no other life. They'd been trained to look the enemy's guns in the eye and that's what they did. Percival-Clive copied them, learning as they had learned, though his knees were knocking furiously. Mind you, they all ducked as the next salvo roared overhead, missing us by inches . . . WHOOOOOSH! The five big round-shot dropped so close that water from the splashes came aboard and soaked the quarterdeck.

Six minutes later, by the Captain's watch, we were hit. *Bonne Femme Yvette* shuddered as a shot tore into the fo'c'sle by the larboard rail, right at the feet of one of the marines. He dropped stone dead on the deck, without a mark on his body, killed by the wind of the hurtling ball. His mates clustered round him, gawping in horror.

"Mr Percival-Clive!" cries the Captain. "See if we're hurt below, and take any men you need for the pumps or to plug the hole. At the double!" The lad dashed off, yelling at the seamen on the fo'c'sle to follow him. In his excitement he seemed unable to open the hatch in the fo'c'sle bulkhead, and he seized an axe from one of the men and laid into the woodwork with a rain of blows.

"What is that boy doing?" says the Captain. "That hatch ain't barred, is it?"

"Don't think so, sir," says Lieutenant Seymour, and the Captain sighed deeply.

"It sticks, sir," says Lieutenant Clerk, "it just needs a sharp pull, that's all."

"Just look at him!" says the Captain, as young Percy, yelling wildly, sent splinters flying in all directions. "God knows I've tried with that young gentleman, but I despair of him, I really do! What frightens me is that his fami-ly'll give him command of a ship before long. Mark my words, gentlemen, he'll drown more British seamen than ever the French will."

As he spoke, Percy burrowed through the remains of the hatch and vanished below decks. But he was back in seconds, scuttling along with his gangly limbs working like a manic spider. His eyes were as round as cannon-balls.

"It's gone straight through, sir," says he, his boy's voice

cracking with excitement. "Through the deck and out the hull. There's a great big hole."

"Damn your eyes, boy!" says the Captain. "Give a proper report. Is she taking water or not?"

"No sir, it's all right, sir. The hole's a foot above the waterline."

"Is it now?" roars the Captain. "Then so soon as we're on a larboard tack . . . THE BLOODY THING'LL BE UNDER WATER! It'll come in like the Thames under London Bridge! Do you know nothing? Find the carpenter's tools and get it plugged. Move yourself, you slovenly puppy!"

And having damned the Mid up and down, Captain Bollington resumed his contemplation of the fort. He was all the better for the chance to curse someone in that tense moment. Personally, I was shrivelling with fear. Like the French privateersmen I'd seen drowning alongside *Phiandra*, I couldn't swim, and I was wondering how long I'd last in the Passage D'Aron without a ship. As far as I could tell, the Frog gunners had got our range nicely. Within a few minutes they would drop four or five shot on to our deck and *Bonne Femme Yvette* would go down like a paving slab. Then the luck that Mr Seymour had mentioned took a hand. A south-easterly wind got up that filled our sails and set the rigging creaking.

"She's answering the helm, sir!" cries the quartermaster. "Very good," says the Captain, "steer for the open sea and keep the centre of the channel."

Under sail, *Bonne Femme Yvette* made four or five knots which, together with the tide, soon took us beyond reach of the fort. They fired again once or twice, but their shot came nowhere near us.

Soon after that, with the Passage D'Aron yawning wider and wider, we all cheered with relief as the foretop hailed the deck. "Sail-ho! *Phiandra* in sight off the Aiguilles point!" Lieutenant Williams was under orders to hold *Phiandra* and *Ladybird* on the seaward side of the Aiguilles sand-bank to be out of sight of French shipping in the Passage. But he was to enter to meet any ship coming out under British colours. As we saw *Phiandra* her look-outs saw us and she made sail on the instant and steered to converge with our course, with *Ladybird* following astern.

By half past eight, our cutting-out expedition was complete, with *Bonne Femme Yvette* hove to alongside the two British ships a few miles off the mouth of the Passage D'Aron. A busy traffic of boats followed as our boarding party and their wounded were returned to *Phiandra* and a prize crew under Mr Webb was put aboard the merchantman. Finally, the little bald-headed French Captain and his crew were set free to row ashore in their longboat. The sea was calm and a few hours' hard labour at the oars would see them in Beauchart. But that Captain was not a bit grateful and he stood up in the stern sheets and cursed us to the last as his men bent to the oars.

Then, as the three ships filled their sails and headed

out to sea, still in close company, we began to think what fine fellows we were. After all, we'd brought out a ship from one of the best-protected anchorages the French possessed, and if we'd lost men killed and wounded, well that was the price that had to be paid in war. Besides, *Bonne Femme Yvette* was a fine ship and proved to be laden with brandy, wine and cheeses. An expensive cargo that would add greatly to her value before an Admiralty Prize Court. We thought we had carried off the thing splendidly and escaped the risks of the operation.

I found Sammy and Kate on *Phiandra*'s gundeck with the rest of my mates. Sammy was dancing about with the others singing and clapping their hands to keep time.

"Shall we be rich, Sammy?" cries Johnny Basford.

"God bless you, lad," says Sammy. "Spanish dollars and a bottle of rum for all hands!" And he danced round the shot garlands.

"Yo-ho, Sammy!" says Norris. "Here's Jacob." Sammy turned and grinned at me.

"Now then, Mr Counting House," says he, nodding at our prize, "what d'you think of the King's Navy *now?*"

"Depends what she's worth, Sammy," says I happily. "What do you think?" He gave *Bonne Femme Yvette* a careful eye. "Well," says he, "depends what the Prize Court thinks. It could be two and a half, maybe three thousand pounds for the ship, and for the cargo . . . "

"Will it be Spanish dollars?" says Johnny, and we all laughed.

And then the whole affair turned on its head. In my opinion, for all his talents and seamanship, and his passion for gunnery, Harry Bollington was a fool to take us into the Passage D'Aron. Not only was it a major enemy seaport, but (if you look at my map) you will see that the out-jutting Cape St Pierre, less than five miles to the North, was likely to hide any ships coming southbound down the coast. And with most of France to the North, that's where their ships must come from. So it's not surprising that Captain Bollington got the fright that he deserved, but it was hard luck on the rest of us, particularly myself.

"Sail-ho!" cries a voice from aloft. "Enemy on the starboard beam!" The joy went out of *Phiandra* like the air from a pricked bladder and there was a thunder of feet across the planks as every man rushed to see what our fate was. There was a great and dreadful sound, between a gasp and a moan from two hundred men. A couple of miles astern, and off to starboard, two big ships were emerging from Cape St Pierre and cracking on sail even as we looked. The French Tricolour was straining at their mastheads.

"Damn!" says Sammy. "Forty-gun ships. Either one is a match for a thirty-two like us." And we watched in silent horror as the two big frigates bore down upon us.

"Can't we out-run 'em?" says I.

"Never a chance, lad," says he. "Not under Captain Bollington. He'd not run from a line of first-rates. And he won't strike, neither." Sammy turned to me and held out his hand. "Give us your hand, lad," says he. He was deadly serious and I went cold all over. "You're like a son to me, Jacob. You know that, don't you?"

"Yes," says I. It was nice to know, but I wish he hadn't said it, because it meant that in the considered opinion of this veteran, expert seaman, we were all going to die.

God, but it was awful! There was no escape, no way out, nowhere to run. I was bottled up again. Worse than the *Bullfrog*, worse than facing Mason. I don't know who I hated the most: Captain Bollington for getting his ship into this trap, or Williams for getting me personally into it. What the hell was I doing there?

Johnny had been studying this exchange in some alarm.

"But we shall beat 'em though, shan't we?" says he. Sammy forced a laugh.

"Course we shall!" says he. "We're British tars, ain't we? And they're just a load of Johnny Crapauds! Nothing to worry about at all."

All over the ship men were muttering to each other while the enemy plunged towards us with deadly intent. They were making the ancient, traditional agreement.

"If I get killed you can have my goods, and if you get it then I can have your'n, right?"

Then Captain Bollington stirred himself. He gave what the world calls a display of leadership. That is to say, he cursed us to our guns and damned us for sons of bitches to be standing idle in the face of the French. We were in easy hailing distance of our two companions, so he took up his speaking-trumpet and gave them their marching orders as well.

"Mr Webb!" he cries. "I've no time to take you off so you must stand clear and make your own way home if you must."

"Aye aye, sir!" says Mr Webb, from *Bonne Femme Yvette*, the disappointment plain in his voice. He was sorry to miss the fight, though you'd hardly credit it. I'd have given anything to change places with him.

"Mr Bollington!" cries the Captain, turning to *Ladybird*, "Take station astern of me at once, and exert yourself to the utmost. I shall engage the enemy as he comes down, and endeavour to destroy him. Do what you may but do not try to attack alone!"

"Aye aye, sir!" cries Lieutenant Bollington, and *Ladybird* fell off astern even as he spoke.

Having disposed of the rest of his little fleet, Captain Bollington turned to us.

"Men!" says he, in a big bold voice. "There's no way home for us than past that squadron!" He indicated the approaching French warships. It was so quiet as the men strained to catch his words that we could hear Mr Webb and Lieutenant Bollington yelling at *their* men. And faintly, we could even hear the rolling of drums aboard the Frogs as they beat to quarters.

"But I say this," cries the Captain, "we're Britons all,

and the best damn gunnery ship in the King's Navy. And I tell you now there shall be no hauling down of our colours while I live!" The intensity of his feelings drove home the words and he smashed his fist on the quarterdeck rail as he roared out the words.

And the men lapped it up. Sammy, Norris and all the others, and all the officers too. Lieutenant Williams (the bastard) seemed alive with joy and threw his hat in the air as he called out at the top of his voice.

"Three cheers for the Captain! Hip-hip-hip . . . "

"HURRAH!" came the thunderous bark from every man aboard.

"Hip-hip-hip . . . "

"Hurrah!"

"Hip-hip-hip . . . "

"HURRAH!"

And I cheered too, in the excitement of the moment. You who read this will understand that I never wanted to be in such a position, but the only real friends I'd ever known were going into battle, and they weren't going without me.

"God bless you, men," says Captain Bollington, deeply moved, and he raised his hat to us all. "And now, Mr Williams, bring her about and take me across the bows of that ship!" He pointed at the leading Frenchman. "And Mr Seymour . . . "

"Sir?" says Lieutenant Seymour from the gundeck.

"The battle is yours, Mr Seymour. I ask you to make

best use of your aimed fire. We cannot stand a battering match against such odds!"

"Aye aye, sir!" cries Seymour, as a volley of orders from Lieutenant Williams sent the sail-trimmers jumping as *Phiandra* was laid upon the starboard tack to meet our foe. Also, as was usual in those days, we shortened sail to go into action under topsails alone.

The wind had come round to the east and we were steering roughly north-easterly so as to converge with the leading Frog. The intention was to give him the benefit of the larboard battery as we went past. As the enemy approached we could see that in addition to their republican tricolours they were flying great white banners with black lettering upon them:

LIBERTÉ

EGALITÉ

FRATERNITÉ

That's what they said and much good may it do 'em. (Damn the bloody Frogs. Do you wonder I can't stand 'em? Them and their bloody revolution?) Seeing this, the Captain ordered the Union Flag to all three mastheads and a huge white ensign at the spanker gaff astern. And reserve colours were secured in the shrouds ready to be broken out should the others be shot away. Sammy was right. Harry Bollington would sink or burn before striking to the French. And that, my lads, is a singular thing to ponder on as you go into action against overwhelming odds.

My station at general quarters was upon the fo'c'sle where the Bosun commanded the four carronade twenty-four-pounders mounted there. The long bronze bow-chasers were left under their covers for a close action such as this must be. A full crew for these carronades was but six men and I was Captain of number one pair. In fact my crew had one odd member, being five men and one woman, Kate Booth. From the time of my promotion and winning of her, she had stuck close by me. And this included her joining my gun-crew. Dressed in her seaman's rig, she ran cartridges from the magazine just as she had for her Irishman before me.

I looked at her and noticed she seemed unafraid so I attempted a smile and said something to show I wasn't either.

"Shan't be long now, Kate."

But in fact, with only a light wind blowing, we had a while to wait with little to do. Like every other gun aboard, our carronades were ready loaded, but since a close action was intended, we passed the time before action by ramming down a round of canister on top of the round-shot: 400 musket-balls lovingly sewn into a canvas sack by the Gunner's mates. As well as the great guns on the fo'c'sle, there were a dozen marines under Sergeant Arnold. These were there with their muskets as sharp-shooters. Overall command was Bosun Shaw's but should he fall, then I would be in charge.

Mr Seymour thought of one other thing to do while we waited, and that was to train all our guns as far forward as could be. He came briefly to the fo'c'sle to give his orders to the Bosun.

"Haul 'em round, Mr Shaw," says the Lieutenant. "We shall take the first of 'em no more than a point off the bow, so the further forward we train, the better our chance of firing first." He was in his very element, I suppose. Everything that he had trained us for was about to be tested.

I threw my weight on the "monkey-tail" lever that stuck out at the inboard end of our carronade and shoved the gun round unaided. The great mass of oak and iron moved easily on its rollers. On the gundeck the larboard battery was similarly training forward. Mr Seymour's voice rose above the squeals and groans of his guns.

"Steady fire, lads, and double-shotted," says he. "In your own time as your own gun bears. We shall take the first at a steep angle and your point of aim is between his first and second gun-ports. That way we shall sweep his decks on the diagonal. But wait till you're sure, and never mind if they fire first!"

I looked at those around me, the other men at my gun, stripped to the waist as I was, and with a cloth bound round the brow for the sweat.

Kate looked up at me, pale as death, as always, and with no expression that I could read. The Bosun was staring at the Frogs, pulling his lip and scratching his chin. He was muttering and shifting his weight from one foot to the other.

"Here it comes. Here it comes," says he.

I peered at the enemy. They were no more than half a mile off, coming on under topsails. One fine big frigate was in the lead and his fellow close astern. With our speed and theirs combined, I would guess we were closing at about five knots. But the wind was dropping and we were all moving slowly. *Ladybird* was in our wake and *Bonne Femme Yvette* making slowly out to sea. It could not be long now before someone found the range and started the slaughter.

Then a pair of white clouds burst from the bows of the leading Frenchman, with twin spurts of flame and a heavy thud-thud followed by the awful, familiar howl of approaching shot. I was under fire again.

Chapter 28

Having spared his unfortunate father a hideous death by fire, the NOBLE MR LUCEY, blinded, burned and wounded as he was, proceeded to arouse the street to the danger, and on the arrival of the PHOENIX COMPANY'S FIRE BRIGADE added his strength to the manning of their pump until the bleeding of his many wounds cast him down, a hero in the forefront of the battle.

(From a special edition of the
Clarion of the North, 20ᵗʰ July 1793.)

*

Two men sat in a private room at the *Royal Oak*, Lonborough. It was a beautiful day outside and summer birdsong came merrily through the open windows from the rose garden. But inside, the room was cold with a broken friendship. Nathan Pendennis struggled for something to say that would melt the frost.

"The newspapers have made a hero of you," he said. "Have you seen the reports?"

"No," said Edward Lucey, "I've been these last ten days in bed, here at the *Oak*, as you know."

"Ah," said Pendennis, feeling as if he'd somehow deserted Lucey in the face of danger. He looked at the sickly face, heavily bandaged over the right eye, and felt embarrassed. Edward Lucey had lost his father and his home, and almost lost his sight. For a week after the fire his life had hung on a thread and only in the last few days had the doctors known that he would survive. Today, 30th July, was Lucey's first day out of bed. Pendennis actually blushed as he remembered how they'd parted in London; his own high tone of disapproval and then his own stupid folly in doing the self-same thing that had brought down that disapproval on Edward Lucey's head.

"I came as soon as I could, Edward," he said, as if in mitigation. "Your Chief Clerk's letter reached me in Polmouth on the 26th and I came at once." He smiled weakly. "Three nights on the road again."

"Yes," said Lucey.

Pendennis fumbled in a leather satchel and offered some newspaper cuttings to Lucey.

"Look, Edward," he said, "see what they've said of you. These came with your Chief Clerk's letter. My wife and daughters wept over them. They think you a very Sir Galahad."

But Lucey turned his face away.

"No," he said, "it's my fault. I brought this on my father. Now he's dead, and half Market Street is burned to the ground."

"But you brought him from the fire," said Pendennis. "He was still alive when you brought him out. He died a Christian death with friends around him."

"Yet it is still my fault," insisted Lucey. "I have done wrong."

"No more than I," said Pendennis, and both men hung their heads. Each was smarting under a wholly unaccustomed burden of guilt. And each was grieving for the tragic loss of his innocent, unquestioning sense of moral superiority over the common herd.

"Edward," said Pendennis, at length, "whatever we have done, whatever has passed between us, we must act together in this. In the name of your father's memory, I offer you my hand. We cannot allow the Coignwoods to succeed."

For a moment Edward Lucey didn't move. Then he nodded and took Pendennis's hand. They looked each other in the eye. Each forgave the other, which was relatively easy, and each forgave himself, which was extremely hard. At once the sunshine came into the room and the two men could speak more easily.

"Was anything saved from the fire?" asked Pendennis.

"Nothing," said Lucey, "the destruction was complete."

Pendennis nodded gloomily.

"No doubt that was the Coignwoods' aim in starting the fire," he said, "to hinder us in the Fletcher campaign. Well, at least we have my copy of the Will! But what of this young man, Potter? Your Clerk said you have suspicions."

"Yes," said Lucey, "all our people were strictly enjoined never to admit the Coignwoods, and the outer door was locked. Yet Victor gained entry. Perhaps Potter betrayed us? Who knows? All that was found of him was bones."

"Yes," said Pendennis. "Now, Edward, I have something to say to you. Please hear me out before you make a reply." Lucey nodded and Pendennis continued, "Edward, I have seen the ruins of your father's offices. A legal practice of forty years lies in ashes." He looked enquiringly at Lucey, "Were the premises insured?"

"Yes," said Lucey.

"Well and good," said Pendennis. "And yet the practice itself is stopped, and you must wonder what your future may be." Lucey shrugged. "In that case, I propose that you leave your Chief Clerk to salvage what he may of the practice, while you return with me to Polmouth. The climate is healthful for your convalescence, and I have need of talent in my business, and . . ."

"No sir!" said Lucey. "I have an obligation to . . . "

"Please," said Pendennis, "allow me to finish. There's

more." He sighed and shuffled in his seat. "Edward, I've five daughters who live for nothing but new gowns and going to balls. But they think you a hero, and as far as I'm concerned, you can have any one of 'em you choose. I've no son, Edward. D'you see what I'm offering?"

Lucey did see, and was not such a damned fool in the face of a golden opportunity as to let his pride stand in the way. He smiled and the matter was settled between them.

"Now," said Pendennis, "to business. Who else knows about Victor Coignwood?"

"Only Mr Day, our Chief Clerk," said Lucey. "I told him on the night of the fire. He knows everything of the Fletcher business." Lucey paused and added, "And Day knows how to hold his tongue."

They looked at each other and shared unspoken thoughts and all the bounce went out of Nathan Pendennis.

"Mr Pendennis," said Lucey, "this cannot go on. We are both afraid of what the woman can say about us, but we cannot be blocked by it." Pendennis sighed and looked at his boots. The optimism of a few seconds ago had died horribly and the muscles of his stomach turned in knots at the thought of facing ridicule from all those whose respect he was used to enjoying. And this in the very year that he'd finally got himself elected Lord Mayor! It was a tremendous fence to jump and Pendennis faltered.

"Is there no other way?" he mumbled. "I'd hoped things might be arranged quietly."

"How?" asked Lucey. "What other way *is* there than through the courts? Victor Coignwood must answer to the Law."

"But could we win in the courts?" said Pendennis. "It would be your word against his. And *she* will swear that he was with her on the night of the fire. Only imagine the effect of that woman on any man that sits on a jury! They'd believe her if she said Victor was in the moon that night! She can have no fear of the Law, else they'd have fled, and they're still living at Coignwood Hall."

"Yet we must do what is right," said Lucey. "We must try. And as for our own reputations, we must hope that enough of our past credit will survive to enable us to ride out the storm."

"But my wife," groaned Pendennis, "my wife will . . ." He lapsed into silence. The thought was too ghastly for words.

So Pendennis and Lucey argued the matter to and fro. Eventually, and with many forebodings, they resolved to do their duty at whatever cost to themselves.

It is very much to their credit that they reached this decision *before* rather than *after* the entry into the room of a Mr Taylor, bookseller of 38 Market Street.

"Beggin' your pardons, gennelmen," said the landlord, as he opened the door, "but Mr Taylor here, he wouldn't take no refusal, but must see you at once."

"Mr Lucey!" cried the bookseller, rushing forward to clasp Lucey's hand as if it were royal. "Only your warning saved my house and the lives of my family! We saw everything Mr Lucey! First my wife saw the glow of the fire and then we looked out together. I'd have come before, but the shock brought her to bed with the child, a month before her time, and I feared to leave her side."

Pendennis and Lucey stared at Mr Taylor, not grasping the meaning of his words.

"Victor Coignwood!" he explained. "We saw him emerge from your house that night. We saw the blade shining in his hand. I am come to offer my wife and myself as witnesses in your behalf."

"At last!" cried Pendennis, jumping to his feet, "We have the advantage of 'em!" He turned to Mr Taylor. "Sir," he cried, "you and I shall go at once to the Magistrate's to obtain a warrant for the arrest of Victor Coignwood on a charge of arson and murder, and for his mother as an accessory to these crimes!"

Chapter 29

"Down lads!" cries Mr Shaw, the instant the Frenchman's bow-chasers fired. "Everyone down!" So we all laid flat on the deck except for him. He had to keep an eye on the enemy's progress to judge the moment when we should fire. The Bosun muttered some more and squinted at the Frog under his upraised hand.

"Come on, then . . . come on . . . come on!" says he, and I realised he was not urging on the French but impatient for the range to close so we could begin. Nothing happened for an age, then I heard "thud-thud" again. Then the rushing of shot and the most appalling crash as a shot thundered into the fo'c'sle bulwark just ahead of us. Big splinters, the length of a man, came whirling through the air, end over end. A terrific thump sounded nearby.

"Christ!" I thought. "Missed us." And in that moment

Bosun Shaw tumbled on to his back, not a foot from me, jerking in all his limbs and the clothes torn off him. I lifted my head and gasped at the terrible wound that had laid open his head and breast down to the shattered bone. Blood pumped out and he no longer had the look of a human being. Even as I looked he rattled out his last breath and died. He was still within seconds.

"Over the side with him!" says a voice. It was Kate Booth.

"What?" says I.

"Over the side," says she. ""Tis the way of it in action."

"Aye!" says one of my gunners. "Poor sod's gone now. Nothing to be done than heave him over." They looked at me as their leader so I got up and took the remains of Bosun Shaw, who'd been so pleased with my book-keeping, and who'd thought his fortune made, and rolled him dripping and half-naked over the rail. Then, being stood up with all the rest laid down, some twenty marines and seamen together, I realised that the command of the fo'c'sle was mine. I gulped at the responsibility but there was no avoiding it, so I looked at the enemy to see how close they were.

They were close. A hundred yards or less. I could even see the busy efforts of the men at their bow-chasers. I was amazed to see them working their guns on the non-recoil principle, lashed permanently in the run-out position so that one of the crew must swarm along the barrel to ply rammer and sponge with his legs dangling over the waves.

But they were still too far off for carronade fire. I wanted to be inside fifty yards for that. We edged closer. Then . . . BOOM! BOOM-BOOM! BOOM! In a ragged volley our maindeck battery opened fire. Not a fancy drill-broadside to impress the ladies but steady, aimed fire as each gun-captain saw his target. The noise was staggering as the whole row of guns blasted out fire and shot. But there's nothing so wonderfully uplifting as the fire of your own guns and the fo'c'sle crew leapt to their feet as one man and burst into spontaneous cheering.

With my own eyes I saw the mighty blow fall upon the leading Frenchman. Dust and splinters burst up as our shot tore through her sides and scoured her decks, smashing guns and men together. Lieutenant Seymour must have been delighted. At his point of aim, a gaping hole yawned through the ruin where her second and third ports had been. Screams echoed across the water and the dull roar of exploding cartridges came from within the hull.

It was as perfect an opening broadside as could be imagined and must have done dreadful harm to that ship. Meanwhile their gunners hadn't fired and ours were already ramming home their second rounds. But my turn was coming.

"Man the gun!" says I, and took up the lanyard where it lay coiled round the head of the breech-screw. I stared over the sights and tried to judge the moment as Sammy had taught me. I wanted to put my fire right into the great hole blown by our guns. Slowly the Frog came on and his bowsprit lunged into my line of fire. Pop! Pop! Pop! came the small arms from their fighting tops. And Crack! Crack! Bang! as Sergeant Arnold's men returned it. Then the gilded bulk of the enemy's figurehead swayed into my sights and I took up the slack on the trigger-line. As the gap in her hull came under my gun I saw the darting living figures.

BOOM! I fired and the target vanished in our smoke. The carronade drove back up its slide and we fell upon it to reload. Kate thrust a cartridge to our loader and I made ready to prick it and prime the lock. Such is the handiness of carronades that I fired again before our maindeck gave their second broadside. With the two ships inching past each other, bow to stern, the ripple of concussions ran from end to end of our ship as each gun, now trained square on the beam, bore on the wretched Frenchman. We were about thirty yards apart and our guns double-shotted, each throwing a pair of round-shot sewn together in a canvas bag for quicker loading. Six hundred and forty-eight pounds of hurtling iron, and too close to miss.

The Frenchman fired too. Lacking the skill to train on the bow, her gunners had waited with their guns on the beam and they fired as they slid past. More than half their guns were silent, thanks to the mauling we'd given them, but shot came aboard us none the less. Then she was running past and I heaved round my gun to deliver a raking shot into her stern.

The load was double canister: 800 musket-balls and I sent it straight down her gundeck, through the stern windows. I saw the window — panes, frames, glass and paint — smash into a shower of twinkling shards. I saw her name too, *Thermidor*, picked out in gold leaf among ornately carved laurel wreaths done in oak. And I saw *Ladybird* run past her, in our wake, and pour in her small broadside, adding insult to injury.

Phiandra's two broadsides effectively ruined *Thermidor* as a fighting ship. I would guess about five minutes of intense action achieved that and we saw no more of her thereafter. She ran downwind to tend her wounded and fight her fires, and left her consort to do battle alone. But now we were cutting their line, passing astern of *Thermidor* and about to run across the bows of our second enemy. Things were looking distinctly better. We faced one opponent with ourselves and *Ladybird* barely touched. We also had the chance of another raking broadside, if anything more damaging than the one we had given *Thermidor*. If we were quick, our starboard battery could fire straight into the bows of the second ship.

"Starboard gun!" says I to my gun-crew and saw Sergeant Arnold yelling at his marines to bring them to the starboard bulwark. He was a good officer, calm and deliberate under fire and in complete control of his men.

So across the deck we went. And from below, I heard the main-deck guns being made ready. Also I saw two of our larboard eighteen-pounders thrown over in a jumble of gear with dead men beneath them. We weren't entirely as untouched as I'd thought. Then . . . Thud-thud! And it was the same story again as the second Frog's bow-chasers fired. The shot roared through our rigging and a splintering crash came from above. Men jerked up their heads to see the damage. A flutter of torn canvas and cord marked the spot. Our main topmast was chopped to a stump and the men in the top were struggling to clear away the hanging end with its useless sail and spar. Axes flashed and men shouted.

"Never mind that!" cries Lieutenant Seymour, from the gundeck. "Mind your guns. She's coming into range."

I looked at the second Frenchman, another frigate, every bit as fine and large as the first. With the wind slacking, she was barely creeping towards us. *Taureus*, her name was. But, if anything, we were closing too fast. We would pass across her bows too soon and with the range too great for accurate fire. Even as I thought this, Captain Bollington's voice rang out.

"Back the fore topsail and take some of the way off her!" Men leapt to obey and our speed slowed just sufficient to bring us to the right place at the right time. I bent over my gun again, to take a sight. We were all set to rake them by the bow. But we never did.

"Damn their eyes!" says Kate Booth. "Look, they're

coming about!" Sure enough, *Taureus* was slowly coming before the wind to direct her broadside upon us. Her Captain knew enough of his trade to avoid the threat of being raked, and was manoeuvring for a broadside-to-broadside slogging match. It was a sound move for him to make. He had the bigger ship with thicker sides to resist shot. He had twenty main battery guns to our sixteen. And he had eighteen-pounders, French measure, which threw a ball of nearly twenty English pounds.

But he was just a shade late and once again *Phiandra* shook to the detonation of her guns. The gunners marked their aim and fired double-shotted at an enemy still barely a quarter turned. My carronade could do nothing. I was still out of range and, in any case, I was blinded by the choking clouds of powder-smoke lit orange by the flaring guns. I looked back and caught a glimpse of our main-deck guns, bounding like live things in the midst of their half-naked crews with all the tools of their trade: rammers, buckets, tackles and shot-racks. On the quarterdeck, Captain Bollington was alive with delight and yelling encouragement to his men.

I turned back to my gun and searched for a target but there was nothing to see for the smoke. And then, in an instant, something happened that no human eye ever witnessed before the age of gunpowder. Fifty yards away, a bank of flame leapt from *Taureus* as she let off her broadside in a simultaneous roar. Instinctively I ducked as the shot found us, and as I did, my eyes swept across the backs of Kate and my gunners to see the most hideous thing. A few paces off was a file of marines, ready with their muskets. Faster than thought, a round-shot passed through them with a deep, swift VOOM! Seemingly without cause, three men exploded before me in a hideous smackety-smack like the slapping of some monster fish on a slab. Blood and flesh sprayed everywhere and the deck ran slimy with it. A man's torso, limp and severed, rolled against my foot with the lungs and pipes trailing out behind. The face drained its living colour and stared up at me, waxy yellow. It was Sergeant Arnold. Automatically, I seized the thing and hurled it over the side. And the ghastly part that lingers in my memory was the lack of weight in that gutted piece of a man that seemed whole to me because I'd known him.

The other marines were badly shocked by this but they copied me and cleared the fo'c'sle of the scattered pieces of their comrades. I saw the value of the practice in that instant. No good came from looking at such things. I realised that the marines were looking to me for orders. Their corporal was dead too.

"You!" says I, to the nearest redcoat.

"Aye aye, sir!" says he, without thinking.

"Take hold of your men," says I, "you're rated corporal and in charge."

"Aye aye, sir!" and he actually saluted me with his

musket before setting to, yelling to the others and pointing out targets through the smoke.

The murk had cleared enough for *Taureus* to be visible. There were shot-holes in her hull and damage to her sails but no sign of the devastation we had wrought aboard *Thermidor*. She was fighting mad with her teeth intact. Meanwhile, my own gun was in range and I fired again. And so did our main-deck. *Phiandra* was enveloped in smoke and so we all worked blinded. You've no idea just how much smoke pours out from a battery of guns. One or two broadsides covers a whole ship in a gritty white fog-bank.

In the midst of our reloading came a tremendous roaring of guns as *Taureus* fired. To my horror, a crackling and rending of timber came from over my head, then a mad chaos of screams and something rumbled down upon me and smashed me to the deck. Something massive and irresistibly heavy. It laid me flat, grinding my nose into the planks. The smell of canvas and tarred rope was all about me and something pressed cruelly into my back. It was hard even to breathe and a weaker man would have been smothered. But I'm not weak. I'm extremely strong and by heaving mightily I was able to get free of the wreckage of the foremast, which lay with its yards, shrouds and sails in horrible ruin all across the fo'c'sle.

I staggered to my feet and looked around me. Everything was shockingly changed. Twenty feet above the deck, the broken stump of the mast jutted out like a shattered limb where the enemy's shot had severed it. Worse still, the useless sails hung over the starboard rail trailing into the sea and obscuring a good quarter of our starboard battery. The gunners dared not fire for fear of setting wreckage and ship ablaze together.

I must have been dazed for I staggered about aimlessly until I heard a voice.

"Fletcher!" it cried. "This way, man!" and there was Williams and a dozen men hacking their way with axes into the crazy jumble on the fo'c'sle.

"The shrouds!" says he. "Cut the bloody shrouds!" I looked about and realised what he was at. The damage was indescribable. The neatly-ordered fo'c'sle was a jungle of fallen sailcloth, heaving spars and splintered timber which shifted and grumbled with each roll of the ship. Williams and his men had come up the larboard gangway and were trying to get at the larboard shrouds which were still unbroken and were binding the wreckage to the ship. These must be cut for us to have any chance of survival.

They couldn't get at the shrouds but I thought I could, and I pushed and scrambled across the wreckage. The shrouds were under fearful strain, pulled taught as bowstrings by the hanging mast, and canted crazily across the deck, almost parallel to it.

As I came within reach, I hauled out my cutlass and fell upon the thick, tarred lines with all my might. A cutlass was a poor tool for the work and a heavy axe would have been better, but I laid on like a mad thing and the lines parted, one after another, with terrific snaps. The last line of all went without my even touching it. At once the mass of wreckage heaved like an earthquake and sent me spinning over as it scraped and groaned its way over the starboard bulwark. It took the hammock nettings and all their contents with it, and ripped out like cottons the few strands of rigging still holding the mast. Finally the forestay itself parted with a twang like the devil's banjo and vanished over the side.

That cleared the fo'c'sle and opened the way for Williams and his men. They pressed forward and completed the job of heaving useless wreckage overside as the foremast fell slowly astern of the ship. Williams himself nearly ran into me in his haste to come forward.

"Good man, Fletcher!" says he, panting, "I trust you're not hurt?" And this from the man who'd wished me blinded and crippled last night! Don't ask me why he said it, but I'm sure he meant it. The heat of the moment, I suppose.

"No, sir," says I, "I'm not hurt," and I looked down at myself to see if this might be true.

"Good," says he. "Then you must bring your gun into action at once. The main deck is free to fire and we must have every gun served." But I saw the remains of the fo'c'sle. It was swept bare. Even the belfry and the cook's chimney were gone and, of course, the towering mast with its sails was no more.

"Christ!" says I. "How shall we manage?"

"Belay that!" says he. "We've the mizzen topsail drawing and the main deck's intact. Man your gun!"

"Aye aye, sir!" says I, and looked for my gunners. They were gone. Kate and all the others. There were only ugly stains on the deck left by our dead. Williams followed my eyes and called three men to join me at the carronade.

"Fall to it!" says he, and dashed off along the gangway to the quarterdeck followed by the rest of his men. I stared across the water. *Taureus* was really close. Twenty yards away and blazing gunfire up and down her length.

"You!" says I, bawling over the din, and pointing to the nimblest-looking of my new gunners. "You're powder-man. Down to the magazine at the double. I'll have a one-third charge to throw off splinters." He was off like a hare as I gave the others their duties.

"You . . . You're loader! You . . . you're sponger! Fire double-shotted 'til I say otherwise."

Soon the squat gun was pouring out its forty-eight pounds of iron at every discharge. It was pure heavy work at range too close to miss. Everything reduced to a race of smoking bores and spurting firelocks in a continuous roar of cannon, in a bank of smoke, with death whistling past our ears. On either side, spars and wreckage thundered down like rain. It was a hammer-and-tongs contest to decide who could stand it the longer:

them with their bigger ship and heavier guns, or us with our faster firing.

Then Kate Booth was beside me, shouting into my deafened ear.

"Jacob! Jacob!" says she. "They're hauling off!" I was so dazed and exhausted that I hadn't noticed. Through the smoke, I saw *Taureus* drawing away as her fire slackened. She was trailing her mainmast over the side and her sails were in tatters. But she still had more canvas aloft than *Phiandra* and I wondered if she was simply pulling ahead of us. Then a thought struck me.

"Kate!" says I. "I thought you were gone."

"Well, I ain't," says she. "I was thrown into the waist with the others, that's all. And you're to cease firing at once, Captain's orders. He's going to make repairs. Look! They've all stopped, see? You're to give a hand with repairs . . . "

She was right. We weren't firing and were drifting away from *Taureus*. Both ships were so badly damaged aloft that they could hardly make way. Captain Bollington and the unknown French Captain must have decided at about the same moment that repairs to the rigging were in order.

On both ships men abandoned the guns and set to with spars and rope and tackles, and brought up new sails from the lockers. I helped rig a jury foremast. Fifty men were needed for this monstrously heavy work, manhandling a spare main-yard and raising it to be lashed vertically to the stump of the old mast. Then new shrouds and stays were rigged, and a yard hung in place to support a sail with its tacks and sheets. Everyone aboard, from the lowest ship's boy to the Captain himself, joined in the work. It was another race, equally deadly, equally urgent. For these weren't just running repairs. Whichever ship, *Phiandra* or *Taureus*, completed the work first would bear down upon the other while she was still unable to manoeuvre, lay under her stern, and pound her into a wreck. The battle was by no means over. It was only now becoming serious.

Chapter 30

Fortunately for us, the worst did not happen. The Frenchman did not catch us without steerage. By the time she resumed the fight, we had sails set on all three masts and were ready for them. I suppose that was another sign of the superiority of British seamanship, as *Phiandra* had been a damn sight more damaged aloft than they had. But all credit to the Frogs, she came on like a good 'un, with drums rolling, bugles calling, and the hands cheering at their guns.

Standing waiting at my gun with Kate and the gunners round me, I got new orders. Mr Midshipman Percival-Clive came pounding up the gangway from the quarterdeck, waving a cutlass wildly in excitement.

"Mind that, sir," says I, taking hold of his sword-arm before he did someone a mischief.

"Captain's orders!" says he, and pointed at the enemy.

"He will lay us alongside of her!" He took a deep breath and spoke, his words coming out in a rush. "The Captain says to take up small arms, every man. He plans to bring her round by the head to engage the starboard battery which has less guns unseated than the larboard. We're to give 'em double shot and canister from every gun as we lay alongside." He blinked at me, awaiting some response.

"Aye aye, sir!" says I. "But why the small arms?"

"Oh," says he, recalling his lines like an actor, "cutlass and pistols for all hands." He pointed at the Frog again. "The Captain is resolved to conclude the battle hand-to-hand. We shall go across in two divisions, Mr Williams shall lead the larboard watch from the fo'c'sle and the Captain shall lead the starboards from the quarterdeck. Carry on, Mr Fletcher!" says he and ran off.

It was only as he went that I saw we could not obey his orders. Our starboard carronades were dismounted. It must have happened when the foremast went.

"Damn," says I. "Down to the gundeck, lads. We'll lend a hand there." So off I went with my band of followers. The first time in my life that I led men forward in action. This was an event, even if there were only four of them and one a Portsmouth doxy.

On the gundeck there was furious activity. Three things were going on at the same time. Lieutenant Haslam and the Mids were dishing out small arms to all those who hadn't already got them, the sail-trimmers were racing to their duty as we came about, and Lieutenant Seymour was dividing up the surviving gunners to man as many as could be of the starboard guns. He was standing with his back to me, leaning on Percival-Clive in a puzzling fashion.

"Mr Seymour, sir!" says I, pushing forward. "I've four men here and no gun to serve on the fo'c'sle. Where shall . . . " And my heart jumped in my breast. As the Lieutenant turned to face me I saw that his left arm was off at the elbow and ended in a mass of bloody rags that had been clapped on for bandages. He was grey as death and Percy was holding him up.

"Fletcher . . . Fletcher . . . " says he, straining to think. He looked along the gundeck. Of the sixteen starboard guns, all but four were serviceable. "There!" says he. "Number six has no crew. Take your men there . . . "

So off we went across the wreckage and splinters and smashed gear.

"Jacob!" cries a voice, and there was Sammy Bone grinning at me from number eight. "Are you all right lad?" I couldn't see Nimmo or Thomas but Norris, Johnny and the others were there. "Didn't we give it to that first bugger though, eh? An' two broadsides was all it took!" I nodded at *Taureus*.

"We're going to board that one, Sammy," says I.

"Aye!" says he, and pointed at number six. "Best serve your gun while you can. She ain't loaded."

It wasn't either. God knows how he'd time to notice

such a thing, in the heat of action, but that was Sammy Bone. So we loaded double round-shot and a bag of bullets on top and waited for the fun to start again.

Lieutenant Seymour just had time to come round with a final word. The poor devil was barely conscious and staggered like a drunken man. He addressed every gun-captain by name.

"Good man, Fletcher," says he faintly, swaying on his feet. "One round all together then over the side we go!" And off he went, clinging to Poxy Percy. The youth looked as bad as he did, near rigid with terror.

As far as I could see, the Frog Captain had the same idea as we did and the two ships came slowly together to finish the business one way or the other. At pistol-shot range, *Taureus* ripped off her broadside in a simultaneous roar. But we fired as each gun-captain thought best.

At least, that was our intention, for the Frogs aimed squarely into our gundeck and at too close a range to miss. The impact was terrible. Men went down left and right about me. They went down smashed and split and shrieking. Timbers shattered with murderous cracks and shot scoured along the deck throwing over guns and carriages like toys. One of my gunners suddenly shot back past my arm and his bare foot kicked me as he passed. God knows what had hit him or where he came to rest. I jolted with shock and jerked my lanyard, wasting my fire without thought of aim.

Then came a thunder of feet and a pandemonium of voices with men elbowing each other aside. Above it all came Lieutenant Seymour's voice, still with enough strength to make it carry.

"Away boarders!" says he. "Larbo'lins to the forecastle, Starbo'lins to the quarterdeck!"

"Boarders . . . boarders . . . " I thought. "Come on Kate . . . Sammy!" And I searched out these two and dragged them behind me as I pushed through the stream of men. Together we struggled across the wreck of Lieutenant Seymour's beautiful gundeck, over men and pieces of men and spars and rope and spent shot still hot from the gun. Then up the ladders to the fo'c'sle, to join the men of the larboard watch.

"Fletcher!" booms a voice in my ear. It was the Captain with his coat thrown off and a cutlass in his hand. He nodded at me in satisfaction and reached out to thump my shoulder. "Now then, Mr Champion Cudgeller, you shall stand beside me when the time comes!" He was actually smiling. Sammy was right as usual, he *was* a mad bugger. He actually enjoyed fighting, buying special guns with his own money and paying for powder and all the rest of it. Over the years I've met others like him, and a fine, bold set of fellows they are too. Just the sort to let loose on anyone who gets in England's way — Frogs, Dagoes, Hottentots, whatever — if only you could leave 'em to it and not get involved. "Shoulder to shoulder, eh Fletcher?" says he.

"Aye aye, sir!" says I. What else could I say?

"Good man!" says he, and turns to the men gathered all around him. "See there!" he cries, jabbing his cutlass at the quarterdeck carronades. "We take our time from those guns. The Frenchie's coming down to board but he's heeled over with his decks laid open and he'll get double canister into his boarding party as he comes alongside. Then every man after me!" This raised the expected cheer from the men and then he made them all lay flat behind the bulwarks to be out of sight of the French small-arms men. I made sure that Kate was out of the way. She wouldn't go below but I told her I'd brain her if she tried to go with the boarders.

And then . . . well . . . in for a penny in for a pound, I went and stood beside the Captain. He expected it and I hadn't the strength of will not to.

"See, Fletcher," says he, "look how she comes, they're massing on the fo'c'sle just as we are." He laughed and waved his cutlass in the air. And coming they were. With her gundeck silent, the Frenchman had brought up his crew to carry the day by boarding. There were drummers and seamen, and there were officers leaping about with their hats on the ends of their swords. I looked back at our quarterdeck and saw the snouts of three carronade twenty-four pounders training on the enemy's fo'c'sle. Six bags of shot, and 2,400 musket balls.

At less than twenty yards, *Taureus* gave us her quarter-deck guns. Five brass nines threw their shot across the brief gap. One ball burst through the fo'c'sle bulwark and killed three men. Badly aimed, the others whizzed overhead or hammered uselessly into the empty gundeck. But a great cheer rose from their boarding party, now only yards away. She was coming to strike us a glancing blow, fo'c'sle to fo'c'sle. I saw faces, weapons, even buttons on their coats. Many were soldiers with muskets and they were crammed densely together and yelling wildly. They didn't look a bit like frogs, or crapauds or anything less than men.

Finally, at such a range that I could have spat across the gap, our three carronades fired directly into the French boarders. I have never seen such a sight as the result. Men struck by small shot are not thrown down as they are by a cannonball. Rather they crumple as their legs go weak beneath them. Thus, some hundred men suddenly swayed back all together, like corn in the wind, and fell down upon their deck. Then the two ships rumbled together with a jarring crash as the mass of *Taureus*'s bowsprig and fore-rigging towered across our fo'c'sle. The impact hurled me over and laid the Captain on the deck beside me. I leaped up and hauled him to his feet.

"Grapnels away! Lively now!" says he, and the men told off to secure the ships sent their grappling tackles curving away. Clunk! Thunk! Clunk! The heavy hooks took hold and our men hauled on the lines. The wind and the rolling waters ground the vessels together so first we rose over their bulwarks and then they were high above ours. But Captain Bollington didn't hesitate an instant.

"With me, lads!" says he, and he was off like a greyhound, leaping into the Frenchman's fore-shrouds and down on to his fo'c'sle. I went with him and the hands poured across in a wave, screeching and roaring, half-naked and filthy, ripping and slashing like mad dogs. Talk about your wild Turks or American Indians! You should have seen a British boarding party of my young day. Most of the time they were screwed down so hard by Naval discipline that the chance to pay someone off for it, hand-to-hand with the cutlass, was like a holiday to them. I've seen it. I know.

For a moment, though, even this was checked as we scrambled over the remains of the French boarders. A horrid mass of bleeding bodies piled in a heap and some with life still in them. But we shoved through and raced up their larboard gangway between the rail with its tight-packed hammocks and their boats stacked over spars in the waist. A spatter of musketry came down from their tops and a dense body of men formed on their quarterdeck, led by an officer in a plumed hat. These men hurled themselves at us with a roar.

Half way between the fo'c'sle and the quarterdeck we clashed. The gangway was no more than eight feet wide and in that narrow space, some two hundred men jammed together in deadly combat. Carried forward by a howling mass of our men, I was in the front rank with Captain Bollington on one side of me and a couple of his "excused fighting" Sicilians on the other.

The impact as we met drove the breath from my body and for some seconds I was packed too close to move, let alone to fight. The officer with the hat was struggling to bring up a small-sword to stab me. He yelled something, spraying me with spittle, and I could smell the sweat on him. I couldn't do a thing. My arms were held somewhere and I cringed in every muscle with anticipation of the blade. Then I hauled my right arm free and raised my cutlass in the air. Jammed nose-to-nose I could strike with neither edge nor point so I beat the iron hilt down on his head, again and again in my terror. The hat collapsed and the man went limp but he couldn't fall with bodies all round him so I shoved him aside. Then a pistol came and put its muzzle under my nose. I punched it away with my cutlass hilt and sliced the blade down the hand that held it, like carving roast beef. Bang! The ball went nowhere and a voice screamed.

Then the press eased and the fight proper commenced. A soldier in a grey coat lunged at me with a bayonet and I cut at his head. Clunk! The cutlass jarred on his musket-barrel as he swept up the weapon to save himself and clouted me viciously in the ear with the brass butt-plate. The blow left me sick and dizzy and

I staggered back as he moved on, jabbing down at an officer who'd tripped over and was on his back, gasping like a landed fish. It was Captain Bollington. The Frog missed once and the Captain slashed at the bayonet with his sword, but the fellow stamped down, pinning the Captain's arm, and drew back for a thrust that would nail Harry Bollington like an entomologist's moth. I leapt forward, stumbled, made a bodge of my sword-stroke, lost my footing and cannoned into the Frog. Somehow I kept upright and grabbed him. Instinctively, I locked hands and squeezed with all my might. I felt ribs crackling and soft things bursting within him. He rattled in his throat like a hanged man and I dropped him dead on the deck.

After that I got more room to move and did what came naturally, which was to grab my cutlass and slash with all my might at anything French, as fast as ever I could: left-right-left! Over and over again.

(If ever you have to fight with a cutlass you should try to do the same. It'll keep the bastards off you for a bit and there's even the chance you might hit one of 'em. Shout as loud as you can, it doesn't matter what, and just keep going. It works as long as your strength lasts. Fortunately it actually helps to be terrified 'cos that makes you work all the faster and harder. But above all, don't start prancing about, trying to fence. That's certain death.)

There were more of them than there were of us, and

sheer weight of numbers was driving us back towards the fo'c'sle, when a roar of British cheering came from behind them. At almost the same instant, our starboard watch reached *Taureus*'s quarterdeck and Lieutenant Bollington and his "Ladybirds" came over the rail. Heads turned in horror as the French found themselves attacked from the rear.

Williams was in the front of the fight, chopping men like a meat-grinder. His speed was uncanny and he was every bit as deadly at the real thing as he was at practice. That finished it. Taken from two sides at once, *Taureus*'s crew caved in. Some ran below and had to be chased out of dark corners but most dropped their weapons and threw up their hands. An instant later, Captain Bollington was accepting the Frog officers' swords on the quarterdeck and Percival-Clive was hauling down a Tricolour to replace it with British colours. (What a handy lad with flags he had become.)

So there we stood, panting with the sheer physical effort of it, and glaring at one another, we in triumph and them in dismay. And what a butcher's yard it was! No one can say they gave up easily. They'd lost at least thirty, killed and wounded by our boarders, not to mention those mown down by our carronades.

But with the battle over we had more to do than ever. *Phiandra* and *Ladybird* rolled helpless against *Taureus*'s sides, with hardly more than their ship's boys aboard. There were nearly 200 prisoners glaring in sullen hatred at the bayonets of our marines, and the wind was rising. Captain Bollington gathered his officers on *Taurous's* quarterdeck for an instant conference. This included me, as sole-surviving Bosun's mate — Acting Bosun in fact.

"Gentlemen," says he, "well done! I rejoice to see you. My only sorrow is for those who are lost." We looked round to see which familiar faces were gone: Lieutenant Bollington, Lieutenant Haslam, Mr Shaw, Sergeant Arnold, and Lieutenant Seymour (though he was alive and nursing his mutilated arm aboard *Phiandra*). I was sorry to see that Williams was intact and unscratched. I caught his eye and he smiled at me as if nothing had ever passed between us. The Captain continued.

"We must leave this place at once, for the French must have observed a battle so close to their shores and we shan't be left alone for long. So! We have prizes to man, and prisoners to deal with, even though we have lost men. We must make shift! I shall place the prisoners in *Ladybird* and let them take her. We cannot guard so many and bring the other vessels home to England. As to command, *I* shall stay with *Phiandra* and Mr Golding shall take *Taureus*."

He paused and looked at Williams, whose face had fallen like a dropped round-shot. "She should be yours, Mr Williams, as First Lieutenant. But you must take the merchantman. She's holed beneath the water-line and I need your seamanship to keep her afloat. Even more, I need your leadership to keep the men from what she's carrying. She has thirty tons of brandy aboard and I doubt any other of my officers could keep the men sober. You may take Percival-Clive as second in command and a dozen others. Take any you chose." Williams nodded and looked thoughtful.

"Thank you, sir," says he, "I'll need less than that, and I won't take Mr Percival-Clive . . . "

"Won't you, though?" says the Captain, irritated.

"Forgive me, sir," says Williams quickly, "what I meant was . . . "

"Damn you, sir!" says the Captain. "Do as you're bid! I've no time to argue. You need another officer and you'll take him!" And that was that.

Then, tired as we all were, we had to pitch into the heavy work of redistributing men and gear among the four ships.

A dozen things went on at once. The dead went over the side in cascades, the wounded went to the Surgeon, and the prisoners were herded into *Ladybird*, even as her crew were handing out their belongings to move across to *Phiandra*. The Frogs were delighted to be escaping imprisonment, perhaps for years, in England.

Or rather, the *men* were pleased. I think the officers would have preferred to be made prisoners. They were all worried about what their precious revolutionary masters in Paris would make of their defeat: *Phiandra*'s 250 men with thirty-two broadside guns had beaten

Thermidor and *Taureus* with 600 men and eighty guns between them.

As for me, I was glad to be alive and unwounded and to see that Sammy, Norris and Johnny were, too, even though Thomas, Jem and Nimmo had all been killed. Also, I saw Kate Booth on *Phiandra*'s fo'c'sle. She waved to me, though without much enthusiasm. Then I got a shock when Captain Bollington turned his attention to me.

"You must be Bosun, Mr Fletcher," says he. "Take the starboard watch and secure anything parted or sprung aloft!" That meant command of half of our seamen in the vital task of repairing *Taureus*'s masts, sails and rigging. Much to my surprise, I found I could do it. I'd taken no real interest in these things, but my months aboard ship had taught me more than I realised. The intricacies of lifts and halliards, tacks and sheets, were a mystery no more. Like anything else, once you know it, it's obvious.

I even set Sammy and Norris to work, and they jumped to it as if I were a real Bosun. And in the middle of this, up comes Williams all bright and cheerful.

"Fletcher!" says he. "I'm taking you aboard *Bonne Femme Yvette* as Bosun. Gather your belongings at once like the good fellow you are." I didn't know what to think. He was just the way he used to be. Had something changed?

"Aye aye, sir!" says I.

"Good!" says he. "I've picked you and six others." He paused and watched my reaction. He was waiting for me to speak.

"Which others, sir?" says I, and he exploded his mine.

"Some friends of yours, Fletcher. Billy Mason and his mates. We'll make a tight little company, don't you think?"

Chapter 31

Percival-Clive was my lifeline. Without him I was dead meat. I realised that as soon as I got aboard *Bonne Femme Yvette*. I came over the rail with my hammock and a bundle of belongings and there was Billy Mason waiting for me with Barker and another of his chums. The others were below and I heard thumping and hammering as they worked to strengthen the repairs to the hole knocked in the ship's side by the Frog fort. Mason swaggered up to me, full of bravado.

"Look'ee here, lads!" says he. "Just look what we've got for a Bosun!" His mates sniggered. I wasn't standing for that. I clenched my fist to knock him down and show him what was what. I didn't give a Chinaman's fart for Mason. Compared with what I'd faced in the last few hours, he was nothing. But he saw the movement and skipped back.

"Don't you fuckin' try it, my cocky!" says he, and reached for the pistols stuck in his belt. That gave me a jolt. I knew he hated me and I was ready to fight him. In fact I expected to. But he wasn't looking for a *fight*, he was threatening *murder*! His mates gathered round to watch. I was at a loss. I had no pistols. Should I use my cutlass? Should I leap at him before he could draw? Or simply back off and let him win? I didn't know what to do. Then I got help from an unexpected quarter.

"Mr Fletcher?" calls Williams, from the quarterdeck. "You may secure small arms from the hands. There's a locker in the Master's cabin. Bring me the keys when you're done. Lively now!"

Mason and the others looked at Williams and handed over their weapons. It was too easy. Seconds before, they'd been threatening outright mutiny, and now they were obeying like lambs. Were they *his* men, in his plot, whatever it was? I didn't know. Meanwhile, the boat that had brought me the short distance to *Bonne Femme Yvette* was gone and the frigates were filling their sails. I was on my own.

Then I saw Percival-Clive, with his index finger busy up his left nostril, peering across at the Frogs as they tried to get *Ladybird* under way. The wind was a dead muzzler for them, and in an unfamiliar ship, over-crammed with men, they were making a hash of it. Angry shouts drifted across. Percival-Clive laughed as she missed stays and hung in the eye of the wind, with her mainsail flapping. In that moment I saw why Williams hadn't wanted him aboard and why I couldn't just be shot like a dog.

Poxy Percy was the very last of *Phiandra*'s crew that I'd have chosen as an ally. But as long as he was there, Williams had to avoid anything outright illegal. Or, at least, he had to unless he was prepared to kill young Percy into the bargain. And I didn't think Williams'd do that to the nephew of the First Sea Lord and the Prime Minister. I hoped not, anyway.

So I made the best of it. I gathered in pistols and cutlasses, not forgetting the working party in the bows, and locked them in the Frog Master's cabin. I thought of hiding some pistols away for myself but Barker was sneaking about, keeping an eye on me. Then I found myself a cabin to put my things in. The crew live under the fo'c'sle in a merchantman but I wasn't slinging my hammock beside Mason and his pals. I didn't want to wake up with a cut throat.

When I came on deck again we were kept busy making sail. Captain Bollington was signalling for *Taureus* and *Bonne Femme Yvette* to follow in line astern of *Phiandra*. But with our small crew we were slow and clumsy and we fell behind the other ships even though they were jury-rigged. This wretched performance brought a sharp signal from *Phiandra*, telling us to keep better station. At this, and much to my surprise, Percival-Clive ventured an opinion.

"Please sir, Mr Williams," says he, "wouldn't she ride better with the fore staysail set?"

"Ah!" says Williams, smiling. "So you'd have her a little more down by the head, would you?" The Mid nodded eagerly. "A common error," says Williams. "She's too full in the bow for that, but I appreciate your suggestion none the less. It shows that you are attending to your duties."

Percy beamed stupidly at these kind words. But Williams was talking nonsense! *Bonne Femme Yvette was* badly trimmed. The fore staysail would have eased her passage and given her another knot or two and enabled us to keep up with *Phiandra* and *Taureus*. And if a relative novice like me could see it, then Williams certainly could. So why was he sailing her like a pig? Obviously he wanted us alone on the ocean.

For the rest of the day I kept as near to Percival-Clive as I could and wondered what would happen next. Mason and his collection of pimps and pick-pockets sneered at me and muttered among themselves, but did nothing, and Williams went through the motions of command. He divided us into watches, and appointed a cook to feed us from the ship's stores. Then it got dark and the fun started.

Williams was easily the best quartermaster among us and he had the wheel himself. He stood swaying with the motion in the dim light of the binnacle. We'd eased down sail for the night, leaving enough canvas aloft to give steerage way, and Mason and his mates were dark figures lounging about the waist, occasionally peering expectantly towards Williams.

There was enough moonlight to see beyond our bows and some way across the waves. The horizon pitched and rolled and the stars turned above our heads. I stood beside the Lieutenant with Percy dropping on his feet with tiredness. I was dreading the moment when he should fall asleep.

"Mr Percival-Clive!" says Williams, in a kindly voice. "I think you'd be all the better for a night's rest. You may go below."

"Aye aye, sir!" says the Mid gratefully, and promptly disappeared down the nearest hatchway. The hands stirred in anticipation and my heart started to hammer against my ribs. This could be the moment. I looked about for something to fight with. The ship had a few small guns and beside the nearest one was a handspike: an oaken lever five feet long with a steel tip. I couldn't win against seven, but I could mangle one or two of them with that — starting with Williams. Then I jumped as he spoke to me.

"Mr Fletcher!" says he. "I'd be grateful if you'd keep an eye on that shot-hole. I don't want water coming aboard us in the dark. I'll send one of the hands to relieve you presently."

What was this? He was separating me from him and the others. Why should he do that? Would it be better or worse for me to obey! I didn't know, but to refuse an order would be an instant spark in the powder-keg. So I took one of the lanterns hanging on the quarterdeck rail and went forward. Nobody tried to stop me.

The shot-hole was in the hold, under the main deck, under the fo'c'sle. But I ducked into the fo'c'sle and stayed there with the light hidden, peering back along the deck through the hatchway in the fo'c'sle bulkhead. I considered barring the hatch to stop them creeping in on me but, thanks to young Percy, the hatch was no more. There was another hatch inside, in the deck. It led to the companionway to the deck below. That one still had its cover intact. Perhaps I could secure that and leave them only one way in. Then I heard voices from the stern.

I looked through the bulkhead hatchway. There was a big windlass immediately aft of the fo'c'sle, then a boat secured in the waist, and the towering mainmast aft of that. So I couldn't see clearly what was happening at the wheel, but I could hear Williams's voice speaking softly to the hands. I couldn't quite make out what he was saying.

Suddenly a figure flitted past and feet padded over my head as a man ran forward across the fo'c'sle. It was Barker. He was silhouetted against the sky and you couldn't mistake him, long and thin as he was. I stuck my head out and listened intently. He was moving about in the bow and nobody was with him. He was using the heads. I crept out and on to the fo'c'sle and caught him just as he came back fastening his belt. He nearly jumped out of his skin when he saw me looming up on him.

"Gawdamighty!" says he.

"What are you doing?" says I, and stood in his way as he tried to pass me. He was nervous and wouldn't meet my eye.

"Took short. I was took short, that's all," says he. As he fumbled to hitch his belt buckle, something rapped against my leg. He had a cutlass! But I'd locked the arms away myself and given Williams the key . . . We reacted together. He tried to cry out and I drove my fist into his belly so he couldn't. The breath went out of him in a wheeze and he went limp. I grabbed him and whipped him off his feet like a dead worm. I scragged him by the neck and the seat of his breeches and hauled him into the fo'c'sle. He was half-stunned with the blow and by the time he'd got his breath I'd bound him hand and foot with hammock lashings.

I took the cutlass and hung it from my belt.

"Barker!" says I, shaking him by the hair.

"Leggo!" says he, weakly. "We'll soon see you off, you bugger! Mason'll soddin' kill you."

"You bastard!" says I, and slammed his head against the deck two or three times.

"Oh! Oh! Oh! Stobbit!" says he.

"Shut up!" says I and squeezed him by the throat. I held it for a while and then let him have a few breaths.

I was angry enough to kill him, but I needed to know what was happening.

"What are they doing?" says I. "Williams and the others? Tell me." He shook his head so I nipped his windpipe again. He struggled furiously, but I sat on his chest and held him choking till his lips were black and his eyes were popping. I only let go when his struggles were dying away. He choked and rattled, deep in his throat. Not quite dead but very nearly. He gulped in air and looked up at me in terror.

"Ready for some more, Barker?" says I, clutching his throat. "No! No!" says he. "Alright, I'll tell you . . . They're going to kill you. But it wasn't me. It wasn't my idea."

"Why?" says I, and shook him.

"Mr Williams," says he, "he says you bin trying to kill him for months. He says you went for him with a knife when you was ashore that time. He says you're a right bugger and we'll all get fifty guineas a man for . . . for . . . doin' it."

"What about Percival-Clive? What happens to him?"

"Mr Williams'll tell him you was lost overside."

"When are they coming?"

"Dunno. Mr Williams says we're to wait a bit 'til the Mid's properly asleep, and maybe you are too."

"Where are they?"

"They're all with Williams, by the wheel."

"How are they armed?"

"Williams's got his pistols an' he give us cutlasses. He says it's to be done quiet."

He never knew how close to death he was that minute. I was shaking with anger and one twitch of my thumbs would have snapped his scrawny neck. But I thought he'd do for a hostage and gagged him with his shirt instead.

"Listen, Barker," says I. "I'll be gone a minute or two, but if you make a noise, any noise at all, I'll run right back here." I drew the cutlass and jabbed the point under his chin, just breaking the skin, "And then, never mind what happens to me, I swear to God I'll kill you before anyone can stop me. Understand?"

He nodded and I darted off down the companionway to the dark, rolling lower deck and hurried aft, between tight-packed bundles of cargo to the cabin doors in the stern. Right aft there was a sort of narrow corridor, with doors on either side leading to a series of tiny cabins. The Master's cabin was at the stern, running right across the ship. And there was the arms locker, stuffed with firearms but too stout to break into without alerting Williams and the others. Here, I was directly below them and I could hear muffled voices and the sounds of movement from above. If they caught me here, I was lost. I was after Percival-Clive, but I didn't know which cabin he was in and I had to search and hope that nobody else was down here. Without the Mid I couldn't even fight back without the fear that they'd all swear together that *I* was the guilty one.

But young Percy was snoring loudly and I found him fast enough, asleep in the Master's cot. I clapped my hand over his mouth as I shook him awake.

"Sir! Mr Percival-Clive!" says I. "We're in deadly danger . . . Mutiny!" That of all words was the one to rouse a sea officer, however young he was, and I saw his eyes widen. I let him go and he sat up and swung his feet to the deck.

"Where's Mr Williams?" says he. "Is he . . . "

"No, sir," says I, ducking that one for the moment. "But you must come at once." I dragged him away.

"Wait!" says he.

"No!" says I, urgently.

"But my pistols," says he, "should not I bring them?"

"Yes!" says I, blessing the day he was born. "But hurry!"

He had his sea chest with him and I had to wait, fretting anxiously, while he fumbled for the key, threw open the chest, and rummaged inside.

"Here they are!" says he loudly, and pulled out a shiny wooden case. "My Mamma gave them to me when . . ."

"Shh!" says I. I grabbed him and hustled him aft. Once in the fo'c'sle, I searched for something to fasten down the hatchway to the lower deck, so the only way in would be the bulkhead hatch leading aft.

The fo'c'sle was a low, cramped place; no more than

five and a half feet of headroom, with the round bulk of the foremast running down through the middle of it, and the bowsprit coming in at an angle from the bows to bed against a massive beam. There wasn't much in there, some hammocks and bundles left by the French crew, but nothing heavy or bulky enough to secure the hatch. But I found a large seaman's knife which gave me an idea.

I dragged Barker to the hatch and laid him across it.

"Here!" says I to Percy, offering him the knife. "Sit by him, please, sir. With two of you on the hatch they won't be able to open it from below. And if he tries to move or cry out . . . then kill him!" He peered at Barker's bound figure in amazement but he didn't move so I shoved him in place, and stuck the knife in his hand. Damn! I'd started badly; Percy was wondering which man was the mutineer, me or Barker. I tore off the gag.

"Tell Mr Percival-Clive what's going on," says I. Barker licked his lips and his eyes flickered from me to the Mid. Confessing to me was one thing, but the same words to an officer could mean the noose.

"T'weren't me," says he.

"Tell him!" says I, taking a firm grip of his throat.

"Barkie?" cries a loud voice from outside. It was Mason. "Where are you, mate? Ain't you done yet?" I jammed the rags back into Barker's mouth and bound them hard in place.

"Not a sound!" says I in his ear, and turned to Percy. "Are the pistols loaded?"

"Don't know," says he, the useless lubber. He didn't even know!

"Best let me, sir," says I, grabbing his case. "It's the mutineers."

"Where's Mr Williams?" says the Mid, getting frightened. "Barkie?" cries Mason again. "You alright there?"

I tore open the case and snatched out the pistols from their green baize nest. They were top-class weapons, of Navy calibre and complete with powder, shot, flints, bullet mould, the lot. Must have cost Percy's darling Mama a tidy sum from one of the London makers, but I shook everything out of the case and loaded with service cartridges for speed, as the footsteps approached. I felt as if I had five thumbs on each hand.

"Barkie?" says another voice, then four or five of 'em were calling out. They were all there, just outside the fo'c'sle. We could see their dark figures against the sky, but they couldn't see us in the gloom inside.

"Fletcher, you bastard," calls Mason. "What you done to Barker? You just let him out, d'ye hear."

"Ungh-ungh-ungh!" says Barker.

"That you, Barkie?"

"UNGH! UNGH! UNGH!"

"I'll kill you, Fletcher!" screams Mason and rushed the hatchway with drawn cutlass and his five mates behind him.

Bang! And the flash of the discharge lit the fo'c'sle like a lightning bolt as I shot Mason squarely in the chest at three feet range. The one-ounce ball hit him like a brick and he collapsed with the man behind stumbling over him in the rush.

Bang! Flash! And the next man through the hatch howled and dropped his cutlass. I hauled out mine and drove the point right through the man sprawled over Mason. He shrieked horribly and the fight turned in that instant, with the late Billy Mason's messmates fighting each other to get out and away from the fo'c'sle. For the moment, I was master of the field.

Chapter 32

There was always something about the Brat that disturbed me, though I never knew precisely what. But now that he is grown so big, and fights like a bear, I know what it is, and the thing has put a fear into my heart.

(From a letter of 13th July from Alexander
Coignwood aboard *Bonne Femme Yvette*
to Lady Sarah Coignwood.)

*

In the dark of the night, with a lamp swaying over his head, Alexander Coignwood sat alone in the Master's cabin of *Bonne Femme Yvette*. He'd given the wheel to one of his men, chancing that the lubber would do no irremediable harm, and told Mason and the rest to do *nothing* until he returned. Normally, he'd never have doubted that they'd obey plain orders, but since he'd explained what they were going to do aboard this ship, they'd begun to take liberties and he couldn't trust them out of his sight. Despite the tale he'd told them, they knew that something wasn't right. He'd read it in their eyes. So he must make haste and get back on deck.

Alexander was writing a letter. He intended to write it, seal it, and put it in his sea-chest so that later he could burn it. But should things go wrong, he knew that the chest and its contents would be returned to his family. It would then be up to his mother and Victor to take revenge on Fletcher. He made sure to put in every detail that the moron Basford had told him about the murder of Bosun Dixon.

His pen flew over the paper as he recorded these simple matters of fact. Then it stopped and Alexander bit his lip. Never in his entire life had he kept a secret from her. She was the one fixed point in his warped and furious life. He'd had many companions but no friends. He'd had many lovers but loved none of them. *She* was the only one he had ever wanted, and he worshipped her with every atom of his being. So his pen moved again, and he told her the thing that he'd kept even from himself. He told her of the fear that had grown within him like the maggot in an apple. He was afraid of the Brat.

Fletcher had grown monstrous big and strong. He'd pounded Billy Mason into unconsciousness. He'd crushed a man to death with his bare hands, Alexander had seen that with his own eyes in the fight for *Taureus*. But that wasn't why Alexander was afraid. His skill at arms would overcome brute strength. Sword-to-sword or pistol-to-pistol, he would win. The fear was deeper. Always there had been something about Fletcher that had disturbed Alexander and now he recognised it for what it was.

Jacob Fletcher was the living image of their father, Sir Henry Coignwood, but not the sad old man that Alexander remembered. Fletcher was Henry Coignwood come back in the flower of his youth. The likeness was so shocking that Alexander shivered with the thought of it. At a visceral level of superstition Alexander feared that Fletcher was the dead, returned for vengeance. He knew this was impossible but he could not expel it from his mind (after all, Alexander Coignwood's was not a normal mind). Yes! That was it! He made himself write the words, and with the writing of them, some of the fear faded away. The worst fears are those we dare not name.

He finished the letter and sealed it, and put it into his chest. As he closed the lid there came the sound of gunshots from the direction of the fo'c'sle where he'd sent Fletcher. He cursed Mason and his insubordinate rabble, and rushed out of the cabin and up the companionway to the quarterdeck, as fast as he could go.

Chapter 33

"Oh Christ! Oh Christ!" groans the man I'd struck. He wasn't dead; the point had gone in at the buttock and down the length of his thigh. He was bleeding heavily.

"Mr Mason?" cries another voice, from right aft. It was Williams himself. "Mr Mason? Report at once, d'you hear? What's happening?"

He was anxious, even frightened. And that was very good. In all this mysterious struggle between him and me, *he* had always arranged everything. *He* had contrived and planned and I hadn't even known what game I was playing. Now, for the first time, I was a step ahead.

"Is that you, Mr Williams, sir?" says I, as steady as I could manage. There was a silence. The swine was at a loss. I prodded a bit more. "Beg to report no water coming aboard and all's well in the fo'c'sle."

"Mason! Where are you!" cries Williams, at the top of his voice.

"He's dead!" says I, with immense satisfaction. "And I've got two prisoners and I've shot one other. You'll have to do your own dirty work next time, Williams."

"Then don't feel too secure, Fletcher," says the voice coming from the dark, invisible stern. "You're still outnumbered four to one! I shall await daylight and then, indeed, I shall come for you myself. In the meanwhile, my men and I shall sleep by turns, but you are alone, so you'd better stay awake all night, hadn't you? Or you might not wake up."

But I wasn't alone. I had Percy, for what he was worth. I sat down where I could keep an eye on the deck and loaded the pistols. The Mid looked at me. He'd not the least idea what was happening.

"Is not that Mr Williams?" says he.

"Yes," says I.

"Then should not we join him to fight the mutineers?"

"He's *leading* the bloody mutineers. He's mad."

"Mad?"

"Yes." I tried to explain but I don't know how much he understood. He was quite obtusely stupid. Johnny Basford would have caught on faster and he was better company. Fortunately Percy was one of those with so little of his own imagination that he believed the last thing he'd been told irrespective of what was in his mind before. So I managed to convince him (for the moment) that it was death for him to go outside. So he sat still, goggling at me, as I made what preparations I could: I shoved Mason's body across the bottom of the hatchway to trip anyone trying to run in, and I put Barker back across the hatch, from which he'd wriggled clear. Then I started to bind the wounded man but he was so weak with bleeding that he was no possible threat, so I left him be and shoved him in a corner so he shouldn't make the deck too slippery.

I thought of sharing watches with Percy but we had nothing to keep time by. And, moreover, I was afraid that if he saw me asleep he'd run off to Williams after all. So in the end I just tried to keep awake. But I couldn't do it. I'd spent too much sweat and fury that day, what with fighting my own shipmates as well as the enemy. I was asleep seconds after I'd wedged myself upright with the fixed determination to keep guard. I was out for hours until shouting and screaming on deck woke me up.

*

It was full daylight and men were yelling at one another. Percy was awake too and peering round the side of the hatchway, looking at what was going on outside. I joined him and saw three men scrambling up the mainmast shrouds. Another was trying to climb, but got ten feet up and crashed back to the deck. He got to his feet as best he could and stood doubled over in pain, looking aft. He clutched at a bloodstained wound in his belly. This must be the man I'd shot last night.

"No! No!" says he, raising his arms in terror, as something flickered in the light. He cried out and fell on his back, and there, standing over him with a bloodstained cutlass, was Williams. He looked up and yelled at the three men sat in the maintop.

"It was Mason's fault!" says he in a passion. "Mason should've followed my orders and not gone charging in like a mad bull!"

"'Tain't no use," says one of the others, equally determined, "you said it'd be easy. You said the bugger didn't have no arms. But he did. And he done for Mason and Barkie. So we ain't gonna do it again!"

"You damned poxy bastards!" screams Williams. "Look about you! If you won't obey orders, we'll all drown. The wheel's lashed for the moment, but the ship won't sail itself!" Even as he spoke, *Bonne Femme Yvette* lurched and her canvas flapped. "See?" says he. "She's falling off the wind! She'll be taking the seas broadside on in no time."

"You pitch your weapons over the side an' we'll come down!" says the seaman.

"Damn you!" says Williams. "Don't try to set conditions with me! I'm done arguing and you'll do as you're bid or else!"

There was a shriek as he twisted the tip of his cutlass in the fallen man's leg.

"This man's still alive, d'ye see? Now either you mutinous lubbers come down at once and follow me, or I shall start with him! You have a count of three: one . . . two . . . three . . ."

"What you doin'?" says the other voice.

"Will you obey orders?" says Williams.

"No!"

"So . . ." says Williams, and deliberately leaned forward on his cutlass.

There was a long gasp from the man on the swordpoint and a furious chorus of shouts from above.

"See!" says I softly, to Percival Clive. "He's mad! I told you he was mad." Percy frowned.

"But are not those the mutineers?" The light hadn't dawned. But Williams was in plain view, only thirty feet away. Quietly I drew one of Percy's pistols from my belt and took careful aim.

"What are you doing?" says Percy.

"Oh shut up!" says I, losing patience with him. I held my breath, took my best aim and squeezed the trigger.

Bang! And he staggered. The filthy swine staggered!

"Got you!" says I, in profound relief. But I hadn't. He was only jumping with surprise. I'd missed. With frightful agility he whipped out a pistol and snapped off a shot as he dived behind the boat in the waist. He was taken unawares with a split second to aim but I felt the whizz of his bullet as it sped through my hair. He'd have killed me for sure with a deliberate shot such as I'd had.

"Morning, Fletcher!" says he, from behind his barricade. "Did I hit you? I do hope so."

"Come and find out!" says I.

"And give you another chance to shoot me?" says he. "Who's the back-stabber now, eh? Why don't you come out? Then we can settle the matter like gentlemen."

"Go to hell!" says I. It was an impasse. Neither of us was going to emerge to give the other a clear shot. But young Percy was still puzzled.

"Why should not we go to him, Fletcher?" says he, tugging at my elbow. "Mr Williams cannot mean you harm. I cannot understand why we delay?"

"Cos he's bloody mad!" says I. "Don't you understand?"

"Who's that with you, Fletcher?" says Williams. "Would it be Mr Percival-Clive?" And before I could stop him, Percy had darted out of the hatch and was standing on the windlass waving his arms.

"I am here, sir! It is I," says he, swaying to keep his footing. The ship rolled heavily as the wind took her and spray crashed over the weather beam. I dared not go after him; I could see the briefest corner of Williams's face and the gleam of a pistol-barrel peeping out from behind the boat. He could hit a mouse in the eye at that range.

"Were you there all the time?" asks Williams.

"Aye aye, sir!" says Percy brightly.

"And have you seen all that has happened?"

"Oh yes indeed, sir!"

"What a pity," says Williams. "And you with every imaginable advantage to further your career." Three things happened at once. I dived at Percy, the ship wallowed horribly, and Williams fired.

Percy dropped like a sack of dead eels between the windlass and the fo'c'sle bulkhead. I shoved him sprawling into the fo'c'sle and crawled in behind him, keeping low, out of Williams's sight.

I got my back to the bulkhead and pulled Percy's body alongside of me, raising his head in the crook of my arm. He'd been hit smack in the middle of his suety face and there was blood everywhere. The ball had split his lower lip, knocked out some teeth and torn a hole in his cheek on its way out. But he opened his eyes and blinked at me in pain. He'd taken a terrific knock and was half-stunned, but he was alive. The movement of the ship had thrown off Williams's aim. And better yet, he'd learned an important lesson.

"Fletcher!" says he, in amazement, spluttering blood and tooth fragments. "D'you know, I think Mr Williams has gone mad! He tried to kill me!"

"Thank God!" says I, and clutched him as the ship rolled deeply and we slid into a corner with our two bound prisoners and a jumble of loose gear on top of us.

"Fletcher!" cries Williams. "This cannot go on or we shall lose the ship. We must have a truce to make her safe. I swear I shall offer you no harm. We are equals now, Fletcher, we have each done murder!" I didn't trust him, not for a second, the cunning swine, but he gave me an idea.

"Here," says I, stuffing the loaded pistol into Percy's hand. I shoved Barker and the other man out of the way and hauled open the hatch to the lower deck. "He thinks he's killed you! Quickly now! Down here, along the lower deck and up out of the quarterdeck hatch behind him. I'll keep him talking so you can surprise him. Shoot the bastard then get out of the way. Kill him if you can but I'll rush him anyway, the instant you fire. Can you do that?"

"Yes," says he, but his eyes glazed over and the pistol was slipping from his hand. "It hurts," says he. "Why must I go to sea, Papa? I don't want to . . . " and he slumped back muttering to himself.

"Damn!" I thought, and I sheathed the cutlass, took the pistol and screwed up my courage. I'd like to say that I was fed up hiding and wanted to face Williams at last. But it wasn't that. A fight between him and me could only end one way. He was vastly my superior, both as a swordsman and a marksman, and my strength wouldn't save me from that. No, it had to be *now*, before he could reload. But which way? I decided the main deck would be quicker and scrambled out and over the windlass as fast as I could go.

Bonne Femme Yvette was beam on to the wind by now,

and rolling her lee rail under, so it was hard to keep upright let alone charge the batteries like the Light Brigade. I staggered aft, bouncing off the boat, grabbing its gunwale and hauling myself along it, and round the stern. And there he was. There he was! Blue coat, shiny buttons, white face, black hair, crouching with rammer and cartridge, caught and glaring at me with an empty pistol up-ended in his hand. Caught and close enough to touch.

His mouth fell open, I raised my pistol and hauled on the trigger. Bang! But something had flown at my eyes. I flinched and the shot went wide. Thump! A glancing blow on my face; too light to harm, but it saved Williams. He'd spun the useless pistol at me the instant I appeared. By George but he was fast! He was dancing to his feet and slashing at me with a blade. I jerked back and the cut sunk into the side of the boat. Then out with my cutlass and on guard, with the deck bouncing like a see-saw.

Clash! Scrape! Clang! I blocked three blows and gave ground fast. Then I nearly had him! He slipped back as the ship heaved, windmilling his arms to keep balance, and off guard for an instant. I rushed in slashing with all my might. But it was useless. He turned the blows so cleverly that he never even felt them. It was like cutting at a glass pyramid. My blows just slid off his guard. I laid on all the harder and he laughed at me.

But it wasn't true laughter. It was hysterical and mad.

You'd have thought he was frightened if he hadn't fought so bloody well. He flicked his wrist this way and that, meeting my strength with consummate skill. God knows how long it went on but he made no attempt to strike back. He just let me wear myself out. Finally, he turned to the attack.

"Goodbye, Fletcher!" says he and lunged like a fencing master. Again the ship saved me. On level ground he'd have spitted me, but we both staggered as the deck dropped away beneath us. He laughed again, wildly, "Shall I *never* get it quite right?" says he. "You really have led me the most tedious dance, my dear brother."

"What did you call me?" says I, amazed even in my fear and exhaustion.

"Brother," says he, "you're my bastard half-brother. You stand between me and a fortune." And he came on again. I did my best but found my cutlass suddenly twisted away from my body, leaving me open to a thrust. His eyes widened with joy to deliver the death-blow . . . Then there was a bang behind me and his sword-arm twitched and there was a hole in his coat over the forearm. His face twisted in pain and he tried to take the cutlass in his left hand. The right hand wouldn't move and he was trying to unwrap its fingers from the hilt when my point crunched through his breastbone and a foot out behind his back. I jerked the blade free and stood back as he howled in pain and slid to the deck. But he hauled himself upright in an instant, and sat there awkwardly with his legs splayed apart and his one good arm braced against the deck.

"No! No! No!" says he, and grabbed at his cutlass. But I kicked it away or he'd have come after me on his knees. So he damned and moaned in impotent fury and tried again and again to get up. And he glared at me in diabolical hatred the whole while. He was fuller of life than any man I've ever met and he struggled to live, with a fierce power of will. But even he couldn't hang on with his heart pumping blood straight out through his chest, and he was dead in under a minute. He went quick but he didn't go easy.

And there he was at my feet, his waxy yellow face slopping this way and that as the ship rolled. The creature that mutilated my life and turned me into what I am.

I noticed Percival-Clive was standing beside me, trying to say something, but his face was swollen and his words were painful mumbles. Then he showed me the smoking pistol and I understood. He'd woken up and used some initiative for once.

"Thank you," says I. He mumbled again and pointed to the sails. We weren't saved yet by a long way. *Bonne Femme Yvette* was only waiting a strong gust of wind and she'd be over on her beam ends. There was a lot to do if we were to save the ship.

Chapter 34

I was deadly tired but there was no possibility of rest.

"We must get her before the wind at once . . . Sir,"
says I, remembering who was supposed to outrank whom.
"And we need more hands urgently. If you would release
Barker, I'll deal with these lubbers." I pointed at the three
faces peering down from the maintop. They'd followed
everything in amazement.

"Ahoy, maintop!" says I, but they were already moving,
climbing down the swaying shrouds.

"Tweren't us, Mr Fletcher!" calls one of them. "It was
all Mason and Barker. But we was frightened of that
Williams. He weren't no proper officer, not at all." They
were bobbing their heads and knuckling their foreheads
frantically. It was almost comical to see how hard they
were trying to please. And they never gave me a second's
trouble. They leapt like monkeys to my every command.

So we pitched in and slackened off the few sails she was carrying, so as to lessen the chance of her being blown right over. Then we set the fore staysail to try to lever her bow round so she'd have the wind astern of her. Luckily for us, the weather stayed moderate. Had it been any rougher we'd never have done it with only four men fit to work. Barker could hardly stand, after hours bound hand and foot, Percy was in too much pain with his wound, and the man I'd run through the thigh had died in the night.

Once she was before the wind, everything was easier. The ghastly rolling ceased and her motion steadied. So we braced her yards round, one at a time as best we could, and got her under way. One of my "crew" said he'd been a quartermaster in a previous commission, so I set him to the wheel to hold her on what I hoped was the course for England.

And every decision was mine, I might add. I was amazed how much I'd learned, which was just as well for I was in sole command of the most complex of all of man's machines: a fully rigged ship at sea. Mr Midshipman Percival-Clive was no help at all. I knew as much as he did on matters of straightforward seamanship, so I didn't need him to get the ship on an even keel and sailing easily. But, as regards where in God's name should we steer on the great desert of ocean, as regards the setting of our course, which should have been his particular responsibility as an officer, he was totally useless.

I grant he was wounded, but he was ignorant with it. I'd seen him with the other Mids, with sextants and charts, under instruction from Mr Golding. Some of them could find the ship's position and plot a course, near as well as the Sailing Master himself. But when I asked Percy if he could do the like, he just picked his nose and looked away. So I did what I could on my own. I found the French Captain's charts and made what sense I could of his log (precious little, seeing as it was in French). I looked at the brief log that Williams had kept, and I made some calculations of speed, wind and distance run and estimated the compass bearing we must follow to reach Portsmouth.

In the event, a day's sailing brought us in sight of *Phiandra* and *Taureus* labouring along, battered and leaking, and we overhauled them steadily.

With no British signal flags aboard I couldn't warn Captain Bollington that we needed assistance so I simply sailed past *Taureus* and came within hailing distance of *Phiandra*. Lines of curious faces peered at us from each ship and I could see the anxious expression on Captain Bollington's face as he examined *Bonne Femme Yvette* from end to end.

"Ahoy, there!" says he. "Where is Mr Williams?"

"Lost, sir!" says I.

"Report to me at once!" says he. "I'll send a boat."

Within ten minutes I was aboard *Phiandra* with a circle of curious faces all around me. Sammy, Norris and Kate were asking questions but I was hustled off to the quarterdeck at once. On the way, Percy collapsed and was carried off to the Surgeon, so I was able to make my case to the Captain alone. Better still, I persuaded him to see me in his cabin and not on the open deck for all to hear.

"Fletcher!" says he, with a smile. He seemed damn pleased to see me. "What's happened?"

"Mutiny!" says I, lowering my voice to utter the plague word, the one subject of all others that no Captain would have discussed in the hearing of his crew. It did the trick.

"What?" says he in alarm, glancing round the deck. "Come below at once!" So I followed him to the Great cabin and made my report. I was too tired to be clever and I had no contrived tale to tell so I told him the truth. With Percy to back me up I couldn't see why I shouldn't. I told him the whole story from the time I was pressed, leaving out only the death of Bosun Dixon of *Bullfrog*. I was talking the best part of an hour and he listened sympathetically. In fact, to my great relief and even greater surprise, I could see that he was on my side from the first moment. He was nodding in agreement with whatever I said, and frowning at Williams's iniquities almost before I could get the words out. He was believing me!

When I'd done, he was silent a while then shook his head.

"I suppose Bone and the others will corroborate your

account of what happened ashore at Portsmouth, when there was an attempt on your life?" says he.

"Yes, sir," says I, "Bone still has the button he pulled from Williams's coat."

"And this Booth woman would repeat her accusations against Mr Williams's character?"

"Yes, sir. I think so."

"Hmm," says he. "You may not be aware of it, Fletcher, but certain . . . ah . . . stories have circulated about Mr Williams for a number of years. I had my doubts of taking him into this ship." Then he fell silent for a long while and stared into space. Finally, he cleared his throat and spoke.

"Fletcher!" says he. "If you'd come to me with such a tale a week ago I shouldn't have believed you. But two things have happened since then. First, I owe you my life! In the battle for *Taureus* you stood between me and a French bayonet." The mists cleared. *That* was why he was on my side. I'd actually forgotten; so much had happened in between. He smiled warmly. "Because of that I am for ever in your debt. Second, in three days or so I shall take this squadron into Portsmouth where I have every expectation of being most warmly received. I shall drop anchor at Spithead with two French prizes, one of them a ship more powerful than my own and I have certificates attesting to my destruction of a second powerful ship. I shall let nothing interfere with that event. I'll have no spoiling of my triumph with dragging dead

men's names through courts of enquiry. And I'll have
no feuds with Williams's family. They're not without
influence, and if I know 'em they'll fight like the devil."
He paused to see how I'd take this. "I admit you to this
confidence, Fletcher, because you have power to stir up
this matter if you choose. And I'll not have it stirred.
Do you understand?"

"Aye aye, sir," says I, wondering where this was leading.

"Then I have a proposition to put to you, and an
offer. My proposition is that Mr Billy Mason broke into
the spirits aboard *Bonne Femme Yvette* and, while drunk,
led a mutiny. Mr Williams fell in action against the mutineers and Mr Percival-Clive, though badly wounded,
courageously rallied the loyal hands and restored discipline. All the mutineers were killed in the fight and Mr
Percival-Clive brought the ship out to join my squadron."
He looked at me forcibly and tapped the arm of his
chair in emphasis. "This story will cause the least possible
disturbance since it reflects credit on everyone who
matters. More important, it will readily be accepted by
Percival-Clive's family, whose opinion is the most important of all."

"Will *he* accept it, sir?" says I. The Captain sighed.

"It is in his interest to accept it," says he, "and in any
case, his stupidity is so fathomless that he believes
everything he is ever told! You may rely on me to put
it to him. Now, as to the offer, I cannot give you the
credit you deserve in this matter, but any other thing I

can do to advance your career is yours for the asking. For instance, I could arrange for you to re-enter this ship as a first-class, gentleman volunteer . . . as a Midshipman."

"Sir," says I, "you are most generous. It is a handsome offer and I am truly grateful . . . but I don't want a career at sea. And I've learned that I have a family ashore that I knew nothing of. So I ask for only two things. First, let me leave the ship a free man at Portsmouth . . . " He was obviously disappointed at that.

"If that's what you want, Fletcher," says he.

"Thank you, sir," says I. "The other thing is delicate and concerns Williams. I must know who I am and why he did all these things. There may be papers in his cabin or his sea-chest. I should like to look at them."

"Hmm . . . " says he, "I suppose I am obliged in any case to parcel up the Lieutenant's effects, so I promise that you may examine any papers that I find." He tapped his foot, shifted in his chair and looked at me. "So you don't want a career at sea, eh?"

"No, sir," says I.

"Do you realise the risk you took in heading out to sea in *Bonne Femme Yvette*? Four hands and no navigator in a three-hundred ton vessel out of sight of land? You could have been blown out into the Atlantic! You could have miscalculated! How'd you know what sail to carry? How'd you set your course?"

"I did what I could, sir. Calculations come easily to me."

"Damn it!" says he. "Can't you see it, man? You're a natural born seaman! What do you *mean* you don't want a career afloat?" I didn't know what to say. I was tired and confused and simply wanted to fall into a hammock. "Bah!" says he. "You look more dead than alive. Go and get some sleep. If you've any wit at all you'll realise you've made a discovery about yourself."

I suppose he was right. But it was nothing like the discovery I made the next day. Captain Bollington was almost respectful when I saw him again. He'd been through Williams's things and he'd obviously read some of the letters he'd found. His whole manner towards me had changed as he presented me with a thick sheaf of papers. Some of the most important ones are on the next pages, and you might like to look at them yourselves:

I Henry Jacob Coignwood of Coignwood Hall in the County of Staffordshire, do declare before Almighty God that I am of sound mind and that this is my last will and testament.

Herewith I do bequeath:

To my wife, Sarah, Lady Coignwood, £100 per annum for life, and her personal jewels, together with an expression of satisfaction that I shall not see her again in this life, and a prayer that by God's Grace I may not meet her in the next.

To her sons Alexander and Victor, £50 each per annum, for life.

These aforementioned bequests are granted on the strict

condition that Sarah, Alexander and Victor Coignwood do immediately remove themselves from Coignwood Hall and never return there again.

To the Reverend Doctor Charles Woods, of Polmouth in Cornwall, £1,000 and my grateful thanks.

To my faithful and honest butler, Mr Henry Porter, £1,000 and my humble apologies for a wrong that I did him. For this I beg his pardon and the forgiveness of the Merciful Deity.

To the Society for the Advancement of Philosophical Investigations into the Manufacture of Pottery, £500 and the use of the Library at Coignwood Hall for their quarterly meetings, in perpetuity.

To my housekeeper Mrs Mary Maddon, £30 per annum for life, and to each of my other servants at my various establishments, £10 per annum for life.

To Jacob Fletcher of Polmouth in Cornwall, whom I acknowledge as my beloved son, all my other monies, properties, effects, funds or interests of whatsoever kind absolutely, to fall to him upon his twenty-fifth birthday.

In particular, this shall include:

£73,000 in gold, together with such interest as shall have accrued, held to my account at Nathan and Levi's Bank, off the Strand, London.

All shares, funds, monies or investments held under my name by other institutions.

Coignwood Hall and the 6,450 acres of Coignwood Park, with stables, livestock and tenancies.

The Coignwood Pottery Manufactory in the County of Staffordshire, and all profits deriving therefrom.

My other estates in Cornwall, Suffolk, and Ireland. My houses and other properties in London, Bristol, Bath, Hull, Dublin and Edinburgh.

I hereby name as my executor Mr Richard Lucey, Solicitor of 39 Market St, Lonborough, and invest in him full power to administer my affairs on behalf of my son Jacob until he shall reach his twenty-fifth birthday.

Signed this day 20th November 1775

Henry Coignwood.

Witnessed by

R. Lucey.

A. Day.

*

Coignwood Hall,

20th November 1775

To Mr Jacob Fletcher.

My Son,

If my plans have been followed you must now be twenty-five years old and I must be dead.

You are now one of the richest men in England, much good may it do you. I know to my cost that wealth don't make a man happy. But it do make him his own master and it puts choices into his hands. As to those choices, I'll not give you no advice, for look at the ruin I've made of things. All I ever was good at, or wanted to do, was to make money through trade. I hope that you may make some good out of my money and that you may forgive me for the way you was raised as an orphan alone.

I cannot know what kind of man you are nor what you know of me. I saw you but the once, as an infant, and it shall be my eternal sorrow that I knew you not, year by year, as you grew. But I had to put you away for your own safety, for it be a right family of rascals you was born into.

As to them, you have two step-brothers, Alexander and Victor, who are a choice pair of serpents that I can't believe are mine. Both of them despise me. The one 'cos he's an officer and thinks himself a Gentleman and the other 'cos he's a vile pervert and thinks he's a lady! Pray God I am a cuckold and some villain fathered them on me.

Keep your back to the wall and your fists up when you meet them. They'll do away with you if they can. Alexander will for sure.

Their mother is Lady Sarah Coignwood. And she is the proof that beauty don't guarantee happiness neither. I married late and, like an old fool, I bought myself the loveliest creature I could find. Many's the long year I've had to regret marrying that woman, but what man could resist her? I says that in my own behalf. As a young girl she was so lovely that men were struck, fixed to the spot, gaping at her as she passed. Even women loved her and nobody could refuse her whatever she wanted.

Her family had not three ha'pence to rub together, but thought themselves better than me, 'cos I was in trade and them in the Sea Service. She was young when I married her, though they told me sixteen. But she was grown beyond her years and soon exhausted me, and looked elsewhere for her pleasures. And she's vicious with it. As bad as her sons, so watch her, too. The three of them are an evil trinity but she's the one that drives them on and rewards them in filthy ways I cannot bring myself to set down on paper.

All this I bore for many years before I met your mother. Her name was Mary Fletcher and a gentler creature there never was. And she became my dear companion. Thus you was born outside of wedlock and many will give you the cruel name that attaches to that condition. But I says this to you. You was conceived and born in love, and your parents held you in their arms together and were united in their joy. Had Mary lived, I should have claimed you both and damned the world. But she didn't.

Should you wonder what I looked like, you will find my portrait by Mr Reynolds in the Library at Coignwood Hall. I ask you to cast an eye over it, since it's only for you I had it done. It's a good likeness.

Your father,
Henry Coignwood.

Chapter 35

Those who went to arrest LADY SARAH and her son were:
Mr Forster the magistrate, his constable, his coachman, three
others and Mr Pendennis, a respectable merchant of Cornwall.
This party believed itself sufficient to the task, but events
proved that a regiment of dragoons would not have been exces-
sive force.

(From the *Clarion of the North* of 31ˢᵗ July 1793.)

*

To his great annoyance, Pendennis had difficulty in
persuading Mr Forster, the magistrate, to issue a warrant
for the arrest of the Coignwoods. Forster knew Lady
Sarah, and Pendennis recognised all the symptoms of
the man's fascination with her.

"Dammit, sir!" cried Pendennis. "Have you not heard

what Mr Taylor has said? D'you not believe him? D'you not believe me? I'm a magistrate myself, dammit!"

"Not in Lonborough, sir!" replied Forster with maddening complacency. Longford and his wife had dined at Coignwood Hall. He had, himself, led Lady Sarah into dinner and been duly dazzled by her. It was asking a lot for him to overturn, in an instant, his respect for the leading family in the town.

But Pendennis would not be denied, and battered away like a siege gun until finally he turned Forster's opinion.

"I must confess, Mr Pendennis," said Forster eventually, "that there are certain rumours, current among the vulgar, that Lady Sarah is not all that she seems. Of course I pay no attention . . . "

"Believe them, sir!" cried Pendennis, snatching at this advantage. Forster frowned heavily and looked up from his table at Pendennis and Taylor. He dropped his voice.

"I had even heard," he said, "that . . . "

"Yes?" said Pendennis.

"That Mr Victor was . . . was . . . less than a man."

"Bah!" said Taylor. "Everybody knows *that*! One look at him tells you it." Forster coughed to cover his confusion. "And we saw him that night," insisted Taylor, "my wife and I saw him. Who could mistake that painted fop?" Forster sighed and reached for his pen.

"I see that I cannot refuse you, gentlemen," he said. "I shall prepare the papers and we shall go together to the Hall."

"Wait, sir," said Pendennis, "I know the Coignwoods! No move should be made against them other than by a band of sturdy men. They are dangerous."

An hour later, Mr Forster's carriage was brought to his door and he and Pendennis set out, followed by the parish constable and his three brothers. These four were armed with heavy staves. In addition, Forster's coachman had his blunderbuss. Taylor was intensely curious and wanted to go too, but Pendennis said that he was too important a witness to be put at risk, and Taylor was sent home to his wife. He grumbled that he was being set aside, but Pendennis's wise precaution undoubtedly saved his life.

Later, as the carriage reached the Hall and passed through the great gates and along the drive, the party saw that the house was shuttered and the grounds were unkept.

"Mr Pendennis," said Forster, with a sigh. "I'm sorry you should see Coignwood Hall like this. It is the foremost estate in the county, and everything was just so when Sir Henry was alive. He kept a full house of servants."

But when they reached the door, not a servant was to be seen and they had to hammer to rouse a response. At length, with much grinding of bolts, the doors were opened and a grubby little maid stood peering out from the gloom within.

"Where is Porter?" said Forster. "Mr Porter the Butler, and the other servants?"

"They's all gone," said the girl. "Missus couldn't pay. There's only me." She made no sign of admitting them, so Forster pushed open the door.

"Stand aside, girl," he said. "I've business with your mistress. Take me to her at once!" And he thrust open the door and led the way in with a clatter of boots on the chequered tiles of the hall. The girl was terrified and promptly burst into tears, hiding her face in her apron. "None of that!" said Forster. "'Tis no use! Take us to your mistress or it'll be the worse for you."

And then, like an actress in a drama, the lady herself appeared. She swept down the broad staircase from the upper floor and smiled at them as if they were guests.

"Mr Forster!" she cried. "What a pleasure! And is that my old friend Mr Pendennis?" Pendennis felt his knees go weak. "Good day to you, sir!" she said, smiling with her faerie eyes boring into Pendennis's brain. "I do *so* well remember our last meeting. Do not you?" Pendennis was totally thrown aback and mumbled something to his boots.

Lady Sarah surveyed them like a queen.

"How may I help you, gentlemen?" she said.

She'd chosen her ground well. Just far enough up the stairs to give her the advantage of height, but close enough for every man to get a good look. Pendennis saw his companions gaping, and pulling off their hats and knuckling their foreheads. And that fool Forster swept her a bow, with the stern resolve melting off his face like snow in the sunshine.

Pendennis's heart sank. Even within himself, there awakened desires for the woman, and hot memories of the enchanted moments on that sofa. But he thought of the foul murder of Richard Lucey, and he gathered up his courage.

"I'll tell you how you may help," he said. "We are here, Lady Sarah, with a warrant for your son's arrest on a charge of murder! We have witnesses to prove his involvement!" She said nothing, but fell back in terror, as if she'd been struck, and collapsed in the most graceful way imaginable. Pendennis was sure it was play-acting, but it worked like a charm.

The others were like Ulysses's crew in the fable, turned to swine by the sorceress Circe. They rushed forward to her aid, elbowing one another aside for the privilege of lifting her up. They got her into the withdrawing room and propped her up with cushions in an armchair and Forster sent the servant for hartshorn and sherry wine to revive her. The constable was fanning her with his hat, his brothers were busy opening windows for the fresh air, and Forster was on his knees patting her hand. Only the coachman seemed unmoved. He was fingering the brass barrel of his gun and staring fixedly at Lady Sarah. A thought came to Pendennis.

"You, there!" he said to the coachman. "Go at once

to the back of the house, lest Mr Victor try to escape that way." The coachman turned as if to reply.

"What a woman!" says he, with a lustful look in his eye. "I'd give all I own . . . "

"Enough, sir!" said Pendennis. "He may escape at any moment!"

"Gentlemen!" said a loud, clear voice from the doorway. "You will all be so good as to stand exactly where you are. I shall kill the first man who moves."

And there was Victor Coignwood, in a striped suit with gilded buttons and his hair worked into a riot of curls. His smooth, pretty face was like a girl's, but in each hand he held a large double-barrelled pistol.

Instantly, Lady Sarah made the most remarkable recovery from her faint and slipped out to stand beside her son, while Forster's men huddled together for support. The magistrate himself stepped forward.

"Now then, Mr Victor," he said, "it won't do, sir. We're seven to your one."

"Have a care, sir!" said the lady. "You are in peril."

"You'll never master so many," said Forster.

"Show them!" she said to her son. "Pick any one you wish." "You, sir!" said Victor, aiming at Forster's heart. Forster clenched his fists and held his head high.

"You dare not!" said he. "I am the Law. If you fire on me you fire on your King!"

"And why not?" said Victor. "Isn't King George going to hang me?"

"No!" says Lady Sarah. "He's right. They'd turn the country over to find us. One of the others will do just as well." Victor smiled.

"Would any of your witnesses be here, Mr Pendennis?" he asked.

"No," said Pendennis.

"How lucky for them," said Victor, and changed his aim, "*You* then!" he said, and fired. Smoke and fizzling powder grains shot past Pendennis, and every man flinched. Then the coachman was falling, shot through the body and mortally wounded. His gun clattered to the floor.

"You swine!" cried Forster and started forward. But Victor fired again. This time, the constable roared in pain as a bullet broke the bone of his leg. His brothers seized him and held him up. Victor's eyes glittered with spite as he dropped the empty pistol and drew another from the waistband of his breeches.

"Who shall be next?" said he. "There's plenty for all." Forster, Pendennis and the rest were checked.

"Now, Mr Pendennis," said Victor, with the same wicked smile. "I presume it is you who would swear evidence against me?" He took aim, and death stared Pendennis in the face. In that dire moment, strangely enough, he thought of his dragon of a wife.

"Not he!" cried Forster. "Three others saw you at your devil's work."

"Ah!" said Victor. "Then there would be little point,

would there?" And Pendennis was left trembling and faint, but alive.

Lady Sarah took up the fallen blunderbuss, and she and Victor herded their prisoners down to the cellars and there locked them up with Sir Henry's port and claret, and with the maid for company.

A few minutes later there came the distant sound of gunshots, then all was silent. With nobody to hear their shouts, and an iron-bound door to deal with, an hour passed before Forster's men could break their way out. There were no tools in the cellar and the best they could do was to attack the door with a cask, swung as a battering ram. At least there was plenty of refreshment to hand.

When at last they escaped, they found that the Coignwoods had effectively prevented any pursuit. Forster's horses had been shot, and when Pendennis and Forster went to the stables, they found that a light travelling-coach was gone and with it two horses, but every other horse had been lamed in the most brutal and disgusting fashion.

Someone had gone from stall to stall with a hedging bill and deeply slashed a leg of each animal. They found the blood-stained instrument laid aside in the straw. Forster, who loved horses, stood and wept at the sight.

"Despicable!" he gasped. "Even Brutus! Look!" And Pendennis saw the whimpering wreck of a splendid chestnut stallion. "Brutus!" cried Longford. "Sir Henry's pride and joy! Bought for a thousand guineas! I ask you, Pendennis, how could an Englishman do such a thing?"

Pendennis felt sick. Every animal would have to be destroyed. He left Forster sobbing and cursing in the stable and went to see what else could be done.

He made sure the constable was as comfortable as could be contrived, and sent the youngest of the three brothers to walk to Lonborough for help. Even at best it would be hours before anything further could be done to apprehend the Coignwoods. A pity, but with the Coignwoods running from the Law, Pendennis saw that things were not so bad after all. *He* was alive, *Edward Lucey* was alive. And, best of all, Lady Sarah's evil tongue was silenced. She and her son would be too busy escaping the gallows to bother Nathan Pendennis. For the first time in weeks, he began to hope that his reputation might be saved.

Now he and Edward would proceed unhindered to prove the 1775 Will. Then, so soon as Fletcher's ship came into port, they would secure his release and they would break the wonderful news to him. Pendennis mused over the fact that young Fletcher was entirely ignorant of the great struggle that had been fought on his behalf. He turned his mind to the fascinating matter as to how he might advise Fletcher to invest his money.

Chapter 36

So I knew everything. I knew it to the degree where I was bloated with knowledge. All my questions were answered and I saw, from his side, the game that had been played with me by my half-brother, Lieutenant Alexander Coignwood (or Williams, as he called himself). I saw myself through his eyes and learned to my wonderment that he had been afraid of me at the last. And I learned that I had a stepmother and another half-brother ashore who sounded like characters from a story-book in their wickedness.

As to my newly discovered father, I knew not what to think. Any harm he'd done me was long ago and I could imagine the forces that had worked upon him. I didn't doubt for a minute that Alexander would have killed me as a child, given the chance. Furthermore I now knew where my gifts for business enterprise came from. And I didn't need to visit Coignwood Hall to know what Henry Coignwood had looked like. According to Alexander, I had only to find a mirror.

But the two things that chased each other round and round in my brain were the fact of the vast wealth that I was heir to as Jacob Fletcher, and the fact that there were still two men, Oakes and Pegg, who, according to Norris, had seen me kill Dixon and could therefore get me hanged as Jacob Fletcher.

"If you ask me, I don't see no problem!" says Sammy Bone when I told him. I told him everything, for I valued his opinions like no other. "You daft bugger!" says he. "Get yourself some lawyers, and brass it out. Say it was self defence. Say anything you bloody well like! You don't suppose nobody gets hung who's got that sort of money, do you? You go back and fight for what's yours. Me and the lads always knew you was meant for more than a common tar."

"I don't know, Sammy," says I.

"What's the matter with you?" says Sammy, irritated. "Look at you! You're beat before you've started to fight. I'm telling you, lad, they'll never hang a man who's got that much money. It just ain't the way of the world."

"Damn the bloody money," says I.

"Huh!" says he. "That's easy to say for them as has it! 'Tis different for the rest of us."

Indeed it was. The money had already set me apart. The word had gone round the ship and everyone knew that Jacob Fletcher was heir to an enormous fortune. And it changed the way they treated me. It surprised me at the time for I was young and I didn't know that wealth means position and influence and power. They were all thinking what I might do *for* them if they played their cards right . . . or *to* them if they didn't!

Even the Captain was wary. He would catch my eye and nod at me, as if he and I shared a secret. And everyone else treated me with a sort of exaggerated politeness. Even Norris did, though he was embarrassed by it and he made the effort to be a messmate as before. It didn't quite work though. No doubt it was my fault, for I was in a deep state of uncertainty at the time.

The only exceptions to this were Sammy, who treated me exactly the same as ever, Johnny Basford who didn't understand, and Kate Booth. Kate I could not understand at all, particularly as she'd finally taken quite a fancy to me and had even begun to smile a bit. So I'd assumed that when I went ashore I'd take her with me and look after her. But when I told her that, she wouldn't have it! She said that now I'd got money I wouldn't want a ruined woman, and nothing that I could say would shift her. All in all, an odd piece of behaviour for a lady in her line of business. But then, a blind man could see that there was more to her than the average lady of the town, so I suppose she had her reasons. We both of us shed some tears when we parted, though.

And there was one other who was totally unimpressed

with my wealth: Mr Midshipman Percival-Clive. Once the Surgeon had stitched his face, Percy made a fast recovery and came to thank me. He'd been bred up among money and power. He'd wallowed and frolicked in it, which means he'd never even noticed it, and genuinely thought nothing of it. He treated me the same as before except that he looked a bit sheepish.

"Fletcher," says he. "I should like to thank you for your assistance in quelling the mutiny."

"Aye aye, sir!" says I.

"Hmm," says he, still looking as if he'd peed his breeches. "Mason led the mutiny . . . and I restored discipline, didn't I?" I understood. Captain Bollington had spoken to him.

"Aye aye, sir," says I, "you restored discipline, sir. And a most creditable piece of work for a young gentleman, if I might say so."

"And Mr Williams was killed by the mutineers?"

"Quite so, sir." He smiled and relaxed. He believed it already. A few more repetitions and he'd forget there'd ever been another version.

Three days later, Harry Bollington brought *Phiandra*, *Taureus* and *Bonne Femme Yvette* safe home to Portsmouth and duly received a triumph like a Roman General. The Channel Fleet was there as we came in, anchored in long lines at Spithead, three miles out from Portsmouth Point. There were over ten frigates and a host of lesser craft as well as the flagship *Queen Charlotte* bearing Admiral of the White, Richard Lord Howe. There were two more huge three-deckers, *Royal George* and *Royal Sovereign* and lines and lines of seventy-fours and sixty-fours. It was a city afloat.

Without doubt it was the supreme moment of Harry Bollington's life to bring before such an audience an enemy man-o-war taken in action. It was such a moment as sea officers sighed and died for. And here it was, not a tale in a story book, not a dream, but hard reality.

The shot-battered state of the two warships told their own tale as did the Union Flag flying over French colours from *Taureus*. Compared to this, the other honours that were heaped upon Harry Bollington were as nothing. He stood on his quarterdeck in full dress, with his surviving officers around him, and received the thundering acclamation of the Fleet. Each ship manned her yards as we ran past and the Captain raised his hat in salute to their wildly cheering crews. Our musicians thumped out every tune they knew and the bands of a dozen other ships joined in. It was an intoxicating moment and I saw the tears of pride streaming down Harry Bollington's cheeks.

It is worth pointing out that this was July of 1793, well before any of the great victories of the war. There had even been some defeats. The fear was abroad that French revolutionary zeal might overcome British seamanship. In that case they'd sooner or later come ashore at Dover with their enormous armies. And that would mean the extinction of our nation. So when the Fleet cheered us, they were cheering with mighty relief, and from the heart, at a bang-up victory in the grand old style. It showed God was an Englishman after all and was still damning the Frogs. At least, He was damning them at sea where it mattered.

Finally, we hove to alongside *Queen Charlotte* as a perfect swarm of boats put out towards us. It seemed as if every officer in the Fleet was trying to come aboard and our three ships were ringed with thrashing oars and bumping boats. In the midst of this, Captain Bollington went across to report to the Admiral, the swarthy-faced, gruff old Lord Howe. By all accounts "Black Dick", as the tars called him, received our Captain like a darling son and port wine flowed like water. Then *Phiandra* and *Taureus* were ordered to proceed around Spit Sound and into Portsmouth harbour to be docked for repairs.

By nightfall, *Phiandra* was in the hands of the dockyard people and her present commission was at an end.

Between them, *Thermidor* and *Taureus* had inflicted enough damage to put her out of action for many months. Her permanent cadre of officers: Master, Bosun, Gunner and Carpenter, would stay aboard and the rest of us, from Captain to ship's boy, would be posted to other ships. There was far too great a demand for men for two hundred prime seamen to stand idle. *Phiandra* would sail again as soon as she was ready, but with a different Captain and crew.

But I would be gone before that could happen. I'd made my mind up over the last couple of days and I went to speak to Captain Bollington that very night to redeem the favour he'd promised me. Once, I could never have dreamed of simply arranging to speak to him in his cabin, but now it was easy. He even offered me a chair and a glass of wine.

"Will you not reconsider?" says he. "It would be my pleasure to advance you in the Service."

"Thank you, sir, but no," says I.

"I understand," says he. This time he accepted it more readily. "I suppose you have your responsibilities ashore to occupy you."

"Yes, sir," says I.

"Then what may I do to assist you?"

"Sir, I shall need a certificate of honourable discharge to enable me to pass through the dockyard without being pressed again." He smiled.

"Certainly. I shall have my Clerk prepare one immediately." "Then, as I am due my pay, and as I might expect to receive prize money in due course . . . "

"Of course, of course," says he, leaping in to relieve me of any awkwardness. "I should be happy, personally, to advance you a sum to cover your immediate expenses." He licked his lips, balanced one consideration against another and plumped for generosity.

"Would one hundred pounds be sufficient?"

"You are most generous, sir, but twenty would be

adequate and you could easily recover that from what's due to me."

"Oh," says he, "as you wish, of course."

He was as good as his word and I had the money and his certificate within the hour. Then I had to say goodbye to Sammy and my mates. This was much, much harder than I had expected because I knew that they valued me only for myself and not for any hope of gain. They'd shown that a thousand times over.

Sammy said the same thing the Captain had said.

"I suppose you've got your responsibilities ashore to take care of now, lad."

"No," says I. "I don't want any of it."

"What?" says Sammy. "You're not still frightened of trouble over Dixon, are you?"

"No, it's not that," says I. "Not entirely. Though I'm not as sure as you are that they *can't* hang me. So I don't intend to give 'em the chance. But that's not it. The thing is that all I've ever wanted was to make my own way in trade. You all know I can do that."

"Aye!" says Norris. "You got more grog and baccy than the Purser!" And they all laughed.

"I want to make my *own* way," says I, "and I can do it. I don't want someone else's money. I want my own. So I'm going ashore, and I'm changing my name and I'm going into business on my own account."

"And good luck to you mate!" says Sammy.

"Aye!" said the others.

Last of all I said goodbye to Kate. I tried once more to change her mind, but she refused, even as she kissed me. If I'd had any sense I'd have snatched up the poor little thing and took her with me, whether she wanted or no. She didn't exist far as the Navy was concerned, so nobody would've stopped me. But I didn't. And by God didn't I just live to regret it?

And that was the end of my time aboard *Phiandra*. As I climbed over the side, I felt that my heart would break. But I went anyway. Young men do these things. They think they're going to live for ever.

Chapter 37

Hail noble Bollington,
Bold England's champion!
Conq'ror at Sea!
Bless'd be thy Victory,
O'er Foreign Tyranny,
God's Blessings fall upon,
Great Bollington!

(First verse of a song, to the tune of "God Save the
King", composed and sung by the boys of
the Ludgate Orphans' Charity School at the Lord
Mayor's Banquet given at the Mansion House,
on 17th August 1793 for Sir Harry Bollington. There
were another twenty-three verses.)

*

"Lady Margaret!" cried Patience Bollington.

"Lady Patience!" cried Margaret Percival-Clive, and the two ladies flew to each other's arms like the old friends that they were. Servants ducked and bobbed as the ladies proceeded in triumph up the marble stairs and through the Palladian portico which dignified the entrance to the London house of Sir Reginald Percival-Clive, the sugar millionaire.

Both ladies were in the upper reaches of ecstasy. Lady Patience Bollington was ecstatic because an hour ago she'd seen her husband knighted by the King, and had then sat at Sir Harry's side while their open carriage was drawn round the city by sailors from *Phiandra*, to the deafening adulation of the London mob. And Lady Margaret was ecstatic because she was hostess to Lady Patience and Sir Harry Bollington (the lion of the hour), and every other society hostess in London was tortured with envy.

Meanwhile the lion himself was giving a guinea a man to each of the dozen *Phiandras* who'd been trusted to accompany him to London and were now in charge of his carriage. This money would enable them to get properly drunk in celebration. His friend Sir Reginald Percival-Clive instantly called for his purse and added a guinea a man from his own pocket. At this, the tars gave three cheers and headed for the grog shops at a wild run with the carriage swaying dangerously behind.

Sir Harry was somewhat dazed. He watched the

carriage disappear with a flushed, silly smile on his face.

"Grand fellows!" he said, with emotion.

"More power to their elbow, say I!" agreed Sir Reginald, and grabbed Sir Harry's arm as he staggered on his way into the house.

"Make sail!" bawled Sir Harry. "Get her under way and she'll not roll so!" And he laughed loudly at his own joke.

Already that day, Sir Harry had met the King, the Prime Minister, the First Lord of the Admiralty, and a string of lesser dignitaries, and the Lord Mayor's banquet was yet to come, later in the afternoon. He was drunk, not only from the port wine that he'd been offered but from the honours that were being showered upon him.

Sir Reginald smiled indulgently and led Sir Harry into the withdrawing room and ordered tea, judging that his friend had taken enough wine for the present. Sir Harry sat down with his head swimming and a grin on his face. He nudged Sir Reginald and they nodded benignly at the familiar spectacle of their wives buried deep in conversation.

Lady Margaret Percival-Clive, sister to the Prime Minister and the First Lord, and whose intelligence upon Naval matters vastly exceeded that of mere Sea Officers, was ticking off points on her fingers.

"So dear Sir Harry shall be given *Taureus* which shall be taken into the service and renamed as *Sandromedes* and shall mount carronades in place of her brass nines. Mr Webb, the Master's mate shall be promoted Lieutenant. The senior Marine Lieutenant shall be promoted Captain, and best of all, " she broke off and looked at the gentlemen, "dear Sir Harry!" she cried, "Now *do* pay attention, for if you're quick you might be the first with the good news. You must write to him at once!"

"To whom?" said Sir Harry.

"To poor Seymour. Lieutenant Seymour is to be given *Phiandra* and made post. He shall be a Captain. By all accounts his recovery proceeds well, and the good news will speed him on his way to health."

"'Tis only a pity that Lieutenant Williams was not spared," said Sir Reginald.

"Indeed," said Sir Harry, and began to examine the star and sash of the Bath that hung across his chest.

"I read your report in the Gazette," said Sir Reginald, "and I believe that Williams died a warrior's death. Mutineers are no less perfidious enemies of England than are the French themselves. God save the brave memory of Lieutenant Alexander Williams, say I!"

"Hmm," agreed Sir Harry, playing with the sash to observe how the sunlight moved over the silk.

"But one thing above all others gave me cause for delight when I read your report," said Sir Reginald. "Can you guess what that was, my dear friend?"

"Ah . . . no," said Sir Harry.

"My boy Cuthbert!" said Sir Reginald, with the pride

shining in his moist eyes. "Now that he is revealed for what he is, I may confess that there were times when even I doubted him."

"Hmm," said Sir Harry, and his interest in his sash and star became intense.

"There were times," said Sir Reginald, "when I feared that my boy was, in some way, less quick of mind than others are."

"Ah," said Sir Harry.

"But now Cuthbert is revealed in his true light!" said Sir Reginald. "My son is a tiger in a fight and a leader of men!"

Sir Harry groaned inwardly at what might be coming, and his worst fears were realised.

"And so, my dear Sir Harry, for our friendship's sake, I beg that you will take Cuthbert with you into your new ship."

For friendship's sake there was only one answer that could be given, and Sir Harry gave it with as good a grace as he could. Sir Reginald put his friend's peculiar expression down to tiredness and to the wine that he'd drunk, and Sir Harry consoled himself with the hope that, with any luck, Cuthbert might fall overboard and drown.

Epilogue

I lasted two weeks ashore. I called myself Jacob Bone and went to London. I took lodgings with a stay-maker in Brazenose Street and started to deal in tobacco. The business flourished but the plan failed.

I was too strange and too different and had SAILOR written all over me in letters a foot high: tanned face, rolling gait, and a peculiar way of speech. I just wasn't a landsman any longer. What's more, I'd grown an inch or two and put on some weight. I was even bigger than I'd been aboard *Phiandra*, and there was no chance of my trying to hide in a crowd.

So I was bound to attract the attentions of the Press who were vigorously working the Port of London at that time. I couldn't use Captain Bollington's certificate because that was in the name of Jacob Fletcher, and I wanted that name to die, so I had to keep my eyes open and make sure that I saw them before they saw me.

That got me off several times but finally a group of them caught me in an alley. They were only doing their duty, and I'd no wish to hurt them so I knocked a couple of them down, entirely without malice, and warned the rest off. But they wouldn't have it, and ran off for the pistols and cutlasses they'd left at their Rondy, while one of them sneaked after me to find out where I lived.

He was a careful, crafty fellow and I didn't notice him until I was back at my lodgings and heard him asking questions of my landlord. Unfortunately, that roused my temper and I heaved the gangsman out through a front downstairs window without troubling to open the window first. The result was that the landlord told me to pay for the damage and pack my bags. I suppose you can't blame him.

So I bowed to the inevitable and did the only thing that would save me from the press-gang. I signed on as second mate aboard a West Indiaman, anchored in the Pool of London, and I bought a share in the cargo.

I'd got plenty of money for this because by that time, I'd turned my twenty pounds into nearly a hundred. Oh, yes! I could make money all right. It was God's own truth that I didn't want someone else's. I had a natural, instinctive nose for business and if only I'd been left alone, I'd have made my fortune in the snuff and tobacco trade. But I wasn't left alone, as you've seen.

In that case, I decided to combine my skills. If fate was insisting that I be a seaman, then I would be one at a profit. Into the bargain, the Master of the Indiaman said he'd instruct me in navigation, so I could eventually become a Master Mariner in my own right if that's what I wanted. Despite what I'd said to Captain Bollington so very recently, I realised that that is what I *did* want. I might not have wanted it with any great enthusiasm, but it was the only road open to me at the time.

So I went to sea again. But this time I went of my own free will, or as the Navy would have put it, "volunteerly".

ENDEAVOURINK

Endeavour Ink is an imprint of Endeavour Press.

If you enjoyed *Fletcher's Fortune* check out
Endeavour Press's eBooks here:
www.endeavourpress.com

For weekly updates on our free and discounted eBooks sign up
to our newsletter:
www.endeavourpress.com

Follow us on Twitter:
@EndeavourPress